2012 NIAN QUANGUO SHUOSHI YANJIUSHENG RUXUE TONGYI KAOSHI
YINGYU KAOSHI DAGANG PEITAO QIANGHUA ZHIDAO

2012年
全国硕士研究生入学统一考试
英语考试大纲配套强化指导

● 全国硕士研究生入学统一考试辅导用书编委会
● 主　审　吴耀武　墨东博　付　博
● 参编人员　蒋　华　李秀敏　吴本文　牛锦儒
李　伟　陆汉艳　孔令香　毛利锋
方会岩　李彩春　刘　娟

高等教育出版社·北京
HIGHER EDUCATION PRESS　BEIJING

图书在版编目(CIP)数据

2012年全国硕士研究生入学统一考试英语考试大纲配套强化指导/全国硕士研究生入学统一考试辅导用书编委会编.—北京：高等教育出版社，2011.8

ISBN 978-7-04-033108-0

Ⅰ.①2… Ⅱ.①全… Ⅲ.①英语-研究生-入学考试-自学参考资料 Ⅳ.①H31

中国版本图书馆CIP数据核字(2011)第154714号

策划编辑 刘 佳　责任编辑 李 民　封面设计 王凌波　版式设计 马敬茹
责任校对 刘 莉　责任印制 张福涛

出版发行 高等教育出版社
社　　址 北京市西城区德外大街4号
邮政编码 100120
印　　刷 北京市白帆印务有限公司
开　　本 787mm×1092mm 1/16
印　　张 14.5
字　　数 380千字
购书热线 010-58581118

咨询电话 400-810-0598
网　　址 http://www.hep.edu.cn
http://www.hep.com.cn
网上订购 http://www.landraco.com
http://www.landraco.com.cn
版　　次 2011年8月第1版
印　　次 2011年8月第1次印刷
定　　价 30.00元

本书如有缺页、倒页、脱页等质量问题，请到所购图书销售部门联系调换
版权所有 侵权必究
物 料 号 33108-00

前　言

《全国硕士研究生入学统一考试大纲》(以下简称《考纲》)明确规定了硕士研究生入学考试各科目的考查目标、考试形式、考试内容和考试要求,是考试命题和考生备考的唯一依据。为了帮助考生准确理解、深度掌握《考纲》,更好地发挥《考纲》对考生备考的指导作用,万学海文名师团队组织精干力量编写了"2012年全国硕士研究生入学统一考试大纲配套强化指导系列图书"(以下简称"系列图书"),包括英语、数学和思想政治理论三科。本系列图书是目前考研市场上一套高质量的《考纲》配套指导用书。

作为《考纲》的配套强化指导用书,本系列书的配套作用、强化作用、指导作用集中体现在以下三个方面:

一、编者团队的权威性和专业性

本书由曾任教育部考试中心研究生入学考试阅卷组组长、命题组组长的专家和研究生入学考试测试与辅导专家张锐博士共同担任主审,知名高校专家学者和考研行业各学科辅导名师担任主编,其中部分成员曾经参与过《考纲》的修订与审核工作。编写组成员的权威性和专业性,确保了"系列图书"的权威性、专业性、指导性和高品质。

二、内容编排与《考纲》严密配套,并对《考纲》要求和考查内容进行强化指导

"系列图书"以《考纲》为纲,根据编写组成员多年的命题、阅卷和考研测试、辅导经验,结合历年考研英语、数学和思想政治理论试题的命题规律、命题趋势和内在逻辑悉心编撰而成。

针对《考纲》规定的考查目标与形式,"系列图书"对各项目标进行逐项分解、逐级细化和深度解读,使考生更加明确考查目标、考试形式等潜在、必需的能力要求。

针对《考纲》规定的各科考查内容,"系列图书"按章、节、知识点内在逻辑配以清晰的学科逻辑体系图,构建起完整、系统的知识体系,并对《考纲》考点、历年考查重点、难点和高频考点通过理论解析、例题实证、命题角度分析等多维度多形式进行深度分析,强化考生对大纲考查内容的理解和掌握。

三、极具针对性,实用价值突出

"系列图书"不仅能够指导考研学生更加有效的使用《考纲》,从而显著提高考生学习效率和应试能力,同时也对研究生入学考试各学科考研辅导教师以及相关学术研究人员和自学者等都具有较高的参考和使用价值。

本书编写组

2011年8月

目　录

第3部分 试题分析 94

附录 161

第1部分 《考纲》基本信息详解指导

1.1 考试性质详解

全国硕士研究生入学统一考试英语(一)考试是为我国高等学校和科研机构招收硕士研究生(非英语专业)而设置的常模参照性水平考试。一方面,研究生入学英语考试的目的是考查非英语专业的考生是否具备在研究生阶段继续学习和研究所需的英语语言知识和语言应用的能力。因而,它是一种水平考试。另一方面,研究生入学考试是具有选拔功能的考试,其作用就是有助于高等学校和科研机构择优选拔。每个考生的成绩都要与其他考生的成绩作比较,根据考试成绩的总分以及单科最低成绩,并根据各个专业的招收计划,从高到低,择优录取。所以,研究生入学考试又是具有选拔功能的常模参照性考试。

尽管大多数考生都通过了CET四、六级考试,但也要清楚地认识到,CET四、六级考试只是综合能力测试,而全国硕士研究生入学统一考试英语考试主要是为了选拔高层次人才。所以,考生只有从英语能力的各个方面加以提高,才能在激烈的竞争中立于不败之地。

1.1.1 关键点之一:考试内容

全国硕士研究生入学统一考试英语(一)考试(以下简称"考研英语")是英语语言知识和运用能力的综合测试。其中,英语语言知识包括语法知识和词汇。但是,《考纲》中并未列出对语法知识的具体要求,其目的是鼓励考生强化自身的语言技能,力求在交际中能更准确、自如地运用语法知识。

针对这个特点,广大考生一方面需要加强自身对语法知识的运用能力,摆脱英语学习死抠语法规则的习惯;另一方面,需要仔细研究考研英语真题,总结归纳考研英语的各类题型在语法知识方面的体现形式和要求,做到在备考过程中有的放矢,有针对性地弥补自身在相关方面的缺陷。例如,在阅读理解A节,对考生语法知识的要求基本体现为对各类长难句的理解能力;而阅读理解C节对语法的考查则相对细致,既要求考生能够理解画线部分的长难句,又要求考生能够掌握英汉之间的互译原则,准确地进行英汉语言之间的转化;写作部分对考生的语法知识的要求不仅是再认,而是能够再现,考生需要写出语法正确、结构完整的句子。总而言之,考研英语对语法知识的考查不能只是单纯地理解为"鼓励考生用听、说、读、写的实践代替单纯的语法知识学习",进而忽视掌握相关语法知识的必要性。

关于词汇部分,《考纲》规定"考生应能掌握5 500左右的词汇以及相关词组",但并未列出这些单词及词组的汉语释义。这意味着考生备考的难度及任务量都增大了,也体现出考研英语的考查角度更为灵活。换句话说,单词的考查也有和考查语法方面类似的趋势,考生需要仔细研究真题中单词的考查情况,对《考纲》列举出来的单词进行仔细的划分,对于不同分类的单词采取不同程度的记忆方式。例如,对于考频非常高的基础词汇,考生需要全面掌握它的词义、用法、近义词和形近词,更重要的是,这类词汇基本上是写作词汇,要求考生能够准确地再现;而对于核心词汇,基本上属于四级以上词汇,考生对这类词汇的掌握就不需要做到准确的再现;至于超纲词汇,考生不需特别地进行记忆,而是需要掌握相关构词法和锻炼由已知推未知的能力,能在具体的语篇中猜测出这些生词的含义。

考查的另外一个方面就是语言的运用能力,具体体现在考研英语试卷上就是英语知识运用、传统阅读理解、新题型、翻译和写作五种题型的解题能力。本书的第2部分将对这点进行详解。

1.1.2 关键点之二:评价标准

评价标准是要求非英语专业优秀本科毕业生所能达到的及格或及格以上水平。考研英语试卷分为主观和客观两种题型,评价标准具体到这两类题型又各有侧重。客观题型要求"考生应能读懂选自各类书籍和报刊的不同类型的文字材料(生词量不超过所读材料总词汇量的3%),还应能读懂与本人学习或工作有关的文献、技术说明和产品介绍等"。主观题型要求"考生应能写不同类型的应用文,包括私人和公务信函、备忘录、摘要、报告等,以及一般描述性、叙述性、说明性和议论性的文章"。

明确考试的评价目标不仅有利于命题工作的展开,使命题工作有章可循,还有利于考生了解考试要求,为应考做好准备。考生可从以上的评价目标了解到:英语考试不仅是单词的记忆、语法的使用,涉及更多的是运用层面的问题。要想学好英语,不但要有一定的词汇量,更重要的是要学会如何使用这些词汇来表达自己的思想。英语考试不再是单纯地考查考生对知识点的记忆能力,而是考生运用语言知识的能力。打个比方,要想在考研英语这个没有硝烟的"战场"上取胜,不仅要有兵(词汇、语法结构知识),还要会用兵、懂得用兵之道(综合运用技能)。

1.2 历年《考纲》发展变化及对考生能力要求的变化

自2001年起,命题者对20世纪90年代一直沿用的考研英语试题进行了重大调整。调整的总方向是,淡化了对单纯语法知识的考查,逐渐转向对考生阅读、写作等综合能力的考查,对考生的英语水平的要求也提出了更高的要求,首次在试卷中加入了20分的听力测试,以强调交际性功能。这也是试题最大的一个变化特点。

经过三年对考研英语命题形式、考查要求和测试目标的探索,命题者在2005年又对考研英语试题进行了大变革,这次大变革的影响深远,表现在:(1) 词汇难度加大,词汇量从5 300左右增加到5 500左右,同时取消了汉语释义。这种考查方式从常规考查单词的横向联系转至对单词的纵向延伸的考查。(2) 试卷中取消了听力部分,将听力考试放到复试当中进行。(3) 阅读理解部分增加了填充式阅读题型,现在称之为新题型。(4) 写作部分分值增加。作文部分首次增加了10分的应用文写作。作文的比重在整个考研英语试题中再次得到了提升。

1.3 考试能力如何提高

1.3.1 对考生能力要求的变化

考研英语一直处于不断完善发展的过程中。总体来说,对考生英语能力的要求越来越全面。

首先,表现在基础知识方面。表现最突出的是进入21世纪后,考研英语试卷删除了语法和单词的考查题型,并明确在《考纲》里提出灵活考查考生语法知识运用能力的目标;2005年的《考纲》中调整删除了单词的汉语释义,增加了考查的词汇量,使得单词考查的深度和广度都有了极大的改变。

其次,表现在试卷结构方面。进入21世纪以后,考研英语试卷发生的另外一个变化就是题型更为全面,题型的分值比重安排更为合理。作为全国最高水平的选拔性考试,考研英语在经过2005年的重大调整后,更加明确了考试的选拔目标,对考生的阅读能力和写作能力的考查更为全面。

1.3.2 基础能力提高

首先,量身制定复习计划。

做任何事情都要有计划,考研英语复习更是如此。对于英语基础阶段词汇,考生不需要大量做题,只需要大量阅读,考生应该把复习内容量化,比如每天完成一个单元单词(30~50 页为一单元)的学习。语法的学习比较枯燥,所以要在练习中找到自己的语法盲点,不断巩固相关语法知识。

其次,采取科学合理的复习方法。

《考纲》上要求考生掌握5 500 个词汇以及相关词组,但要达到真正掌握的程度需要从以下几方面入手:

(1) 发音:很多考生在背单词时并不注重其读音。其实,多读单词并不是在浪费时间,而是有助于记忆的,并且在熟读之后会形成一定的条件反射。

(2) 词形:词形包括单词的拼写及其各种词性的变化。例如,"distribution"是名词形式,"distribute"是其动词形式,而"distributive"是其形容词形式。以此类推,需掌握名词的复数形式,动词的各种时态,以及形容词与副词的比较级和最高级形式。

(3) 词义的巧记:词义需全面掌握。当一个单词的释义超出三个时,后面的释义往往是要考的内容。这也是在做阅读理解和翻译的过程中出现了自认为很熟悉的单词,但依然很难完全理解的原因所在。

(4) 用法:学单词,背单词,最终的目的是要会用单词。但对这个环节的疏忽或抵触情绪导致一些考生在单词上所花费的时间和精力付之东流。在这里要掌握词的固定搭配,并记住随之出现的例句。这个过程就是培养语感的过程,可使单词的记忆更加牢固,也利于考生完成英语知识运用、阅读理解以及写作各个部分的考试。

对于语法,要多练习,应在句子中学习语法。

考生可把做题过程中的错题整理成集,并要条理化。因为,语法不仅涉及规则的词语句法的变化,很多词句的特殊用法也需要花费时间和精力去熟记。

词汇、语法复习目标是:掌握《考纲》要求的词汇及短语,全面复习语法,争取语法无盲点。如果词汇掌握不好,对英语考试来说是非常不利的。英语考试中,谁知道的词汇多谁就占优势。有些考生单词都认识,但是句子、文章还是读不懂,原因就是语法没有掌握的,而且翻译题主要考查的就是词汇、语法和语言组织能力。由此可见,词汇和语法是英语复习中的基础。

最后,及时复习。

复习是容易被很多考生遗忘的一个环节。殊不知,每读完一篇文章,里面的"得"与"失"都是考生成长过程中难能可贵的"养分"。所以,必须及时地、反复地复习,不断来摄取这些"养料",直到考试前的最后一周。切忌采用"题海"战术,因为4 000 道题做一遍的效果绝对比不上1 000 道题做四遍的效果。与其博览群书,不如精读一本。

1.3.3 应试能力提高

为提高应试能力,考生应该进行模拟试题或者真题的实战演练。在这个过程中,注意答卷时间的分配,重视考场心态的调整。无论自己的模拟考试成绩如何,都要保持良好的心态。得了高分,不要洋洋自得,毕竟真实的考场上压力和环境与平时不太一样;得了低分,也别灰心丧气,要认真总结经验教训,况且一般模拟题都要难于真题。

此外,考生还需要特别注意以下几点。

(1) 对真题答题规范进行研究。因为考试题量大、时间紧,很多人都感觉时间不够用。按照规范,需要写的不要落掉,不需要写的绝不多写。这样的话,一方面可以节省时间,另一方面可以规范做题的思路。只有平时养成良好的习惯,考试的时候才能做到心中有数,不至于惊慌失措。

(2) 要做好总结与归纳,自己不扎实的题及出过错误的题,都要全部记录下来。在这个阶段不应该有盲点了,要做好整体的梳理、总结和归纳。也要注意强化记忆,调整心态,保持状态,积极应考。

(3) 考生需要对考研英语试卷的各类题型有一个客观准确的认识,做到知己知彼百战百胜,这点非常重要。考研试卷中的英语知识运用主要考查三点:词汇、语法、篇章。阅读理解A节主要考查英语词汇、短语、句型等习惯表达方式,尤其是出现在篇章中的语言知识和语言技能的掌握情况。另一个方面,它也包含了对英语国家和世界其他国家的政治、经济、文化、历史、社会等背景以及科技发展动态、热门话题乃至西方人的思维、交流方式等非语言性知识和学习能力方面的考查。因此,本部分是一个综合性很强的能力测试试题。阅读理解B节主要考查考生对连贯性、一致性、逻辑性等语篇、语段整体性特征以及文章结构的理解,即要求考生在理解全文的基础上把握文章的整体和微观结构。考生既要理解和掌握文章总体结构和写作思路,又要理清上下文之间的逻辑关系。阅读理解C节在考查考生对文章深层次理解的同时,还要求考生掌握并运用最基本的英译汉技巧。写作A节考查考生进行一般性应用文写作、运用英语书面语言表达日常交际实际需要的能力。英语应用文指在日常工作和生活中应用的文体,其类型多样,包括信函、备忘录、摘要、报告、通知等。写作B节规定考生应根据题目以及写作提纲或规定的情景、图表、图画等写出大约200个词的短文。

第2部分 《考纲》考查重点强化指导

考研英语所考查的主要能力有两个方面:英语语言知识和语言技能。就语言知识而言,《考纲》强调考生应该能够熟练地掌握和运用语法知识和5 500个《考纲》词汇,而词汇和语法作为英语考查的基础知识,是通过对各种题型的考查得以体现的,体现词汇和语法最基础的题型是英语知识应用。就语言技能而言,《考纲》突出了阅读和写作两个技能的重要性。关于阅读,强调"考生应能读懂选自各类书籍和报刊的不同类型的文字材料(生词量不超过所读材料总词汇量的3%),还应能读懂与本人学习或工作有关的文献资料、技术说明和产品介绍等";另外,《考纲》给出了对于所读材料学生应具备的八条阅读语言技能,这八条技能的考查是通过英语知识运用以及阅读理解两个客观题型来实现的。考生的主观写作技能的考查则通过应用文和短文写作来实现,《考纲》强调考生"应能写不同类型的应用文,包括私人和公务信函、备忘录、摘要、报告等,以及一般描述性、叙述性、说明性或议论性的文章(实际就是应用文和图画作文)"。考生应掌握的语言知识和技能贯穿在各个题型中,具体体现如表2-1:

表2-1 考生应掌握的语言知识和技能

评价目标	词汇	语法	阅读8种能力考查	写作要求
英语知识运用	√	√	√	
阅读理解A节	√	√	√	
阅读理解B节(新题型)	√	√	√	
阅读理解C节(翻译)	√	√	√	
写作	√	√	√	√

2.1 基础知识复习指导

通常来讲,语法和词汇都是考研英语的基础知识。但《考纲》对语法知识没有专门列出具体的考查要求和内容,其目的是鼓励考生用听、说、读、写的实践代替单纯的语法知识学习,以求考生在交际中能更准确、自如地运用语法知识。一般情况下,考研英语所考查的语法知识,大部分属于考生在上大学前所掌握的语法内容,复习时只需在其原有基础上深入理解和加强运用即可,所以在此不对语法知识进行独立讲解。

而词汇部分,由于加入了考研必备的新词汇,且有很多熟词生义的考查难点等存在形式,所以在此进行独立讲解。

2.1.1 《考纲》词汇评价目标详解

《考纲》对词汇的评价目标是"考生应能熟练掌握5 500左右的词汇以及相关词组。除掌握词汇的基本含义外,考生还应掌握词汇之间的词义关系,如同义词、近义词、反义词等;掌握词汇之间的搭配关系,如动词与介词、形容词与介词、形容词与名词等;掌握词汇生成的基本知识,如词源、词根、词缀等"。

1. 掌握词汇的基本含义

【理论解释】

词汇的基本含义是指针对含有多个释义的词汇中构意能力最强的(至少能构成三个或三个以上)一组互相独立的含义。即一个词对应的若干个含义,虽然各不相同,但它们之间是密切相关的,都是由词汇的基本含义在不同的语境中引申出来的。

因此,要求考生在强化记忆考研单词的第一步就是要将词汇的基本含义进行有效地甄别并熟练掌握。因为,第一,考研试题中常出现的词汇,其释义多为该词的基本含义;第二,只有熟练掌握词的基本含义才能达到在不同的语境下进行词汇释义的全面记忆,进而才能理解考研英语文章所表达的准确含义。

【举例说明】

下面以单词“capital”为例说明词汇的基本含义,如图2-1所示。

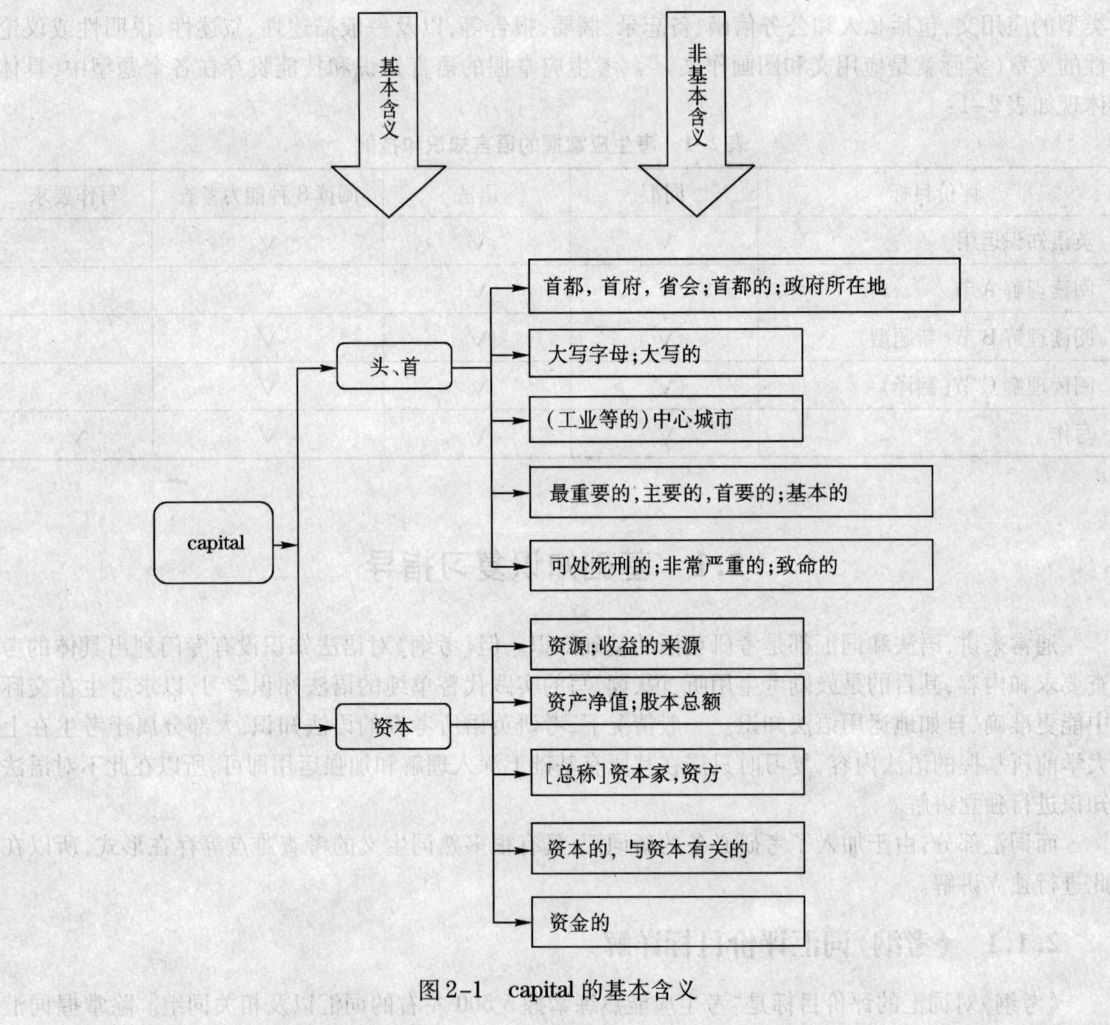

图2-1 capital的基本含义

例如:

① When the United States built its industrial infrastructure, it didn't have the *capital* to do so.（2001 年考题 Text 2）

此处“capital”意为“资本”。

② The details may be unknowable, but the independence of standard-setters, essential to the proper functioning of *capital* markets, is being compromised.（2010 年考题 Text 4）

此处“capital”意为“资本”。

③ The railroad industry as a whole, despite its brightening fortunes, still does not earn enough to cover the cost of the *capital* it must invest to keep up with its surging traffic.（2003 年考题 Text 3）

此处“capital”意为“资方”。

④ In the last half of the nineteenth century “*capital*” and “labour” were enlarging and perfecting their rival organizations on modern lines. Many an old firm was replaced by a limited liability company with a bureaucracy of salaried managers.（《考纲》样题）

此处“capital”意为“资本家、资方”。

2. 掌握词汇之间的词义关系（如同义词、近义词、反义词等）

【理论解释】

单个词的词义有基本意义和指示意义之分，而词语之间则有不同的词汇关系之分。词语之间的词汇关系主要包括：同义关系、反义关系和上下义关系。

同义关系：意义十分接近的、通常可以在句中互换的两个词就是同义词，它们之间的关系就是同义关系。比如：produce-yield 和 fancy-reverie，surrounding 和 environment 等。

反义关系：词义相反的词叫反义词，它们之间的关系就是反义关系。比如：old 和 young，big 和 small 等。

这些词义关系在考研英语的考查主要以以下几种方式反映在各个题型中：① 填空题型中常考近义词或同义词辨析；② 阅读理解 A 部分中常考同义词替换、反义词推理；③ 写作题型中的同义词替换。

【举例说明】

（1）英语知识应用中常考近义词或同义词辨析。例如：

Analysts do agree on another matter: that the number of the homeless is 8 .（2006 年考题第 8 题）

8. [A] inflating [B] expanding [C] increasing [D] extending

例题分析：以上几个选项中的单词为近义词，解答本题时考生要能够辨别近义词之间的不同，以下是这几个单词的具体含义。

“inflate”指在体积、价格和程度等方面的膨胀；“expand” 指范围、程度、体积和尺寸等方面的扩大或增加；“increase”指数量、强度和大小等方面的扩大或增加；“extend”指时间或空间的延长，也可指影响和使用范围等的扩大。

（2）阅读理解 A 节中常考同义词替换、反义词推理。

① 历年阅读理解 A 节正确选项与原文之间词汇的同义替换。例如：

Bankers have been blaming themselves for their troubles in public. Behind the scenes, they have been taking aim at someone else: the accounting standard-setters. Their rules, moan the banks, have forced them to report enormous losses, and it's just not fair. These rules say they must value some assets at the price a third party would pay, not the price managers and regulators would like them to fetch.（2010年考题第36题）

36. Bankers complained that they were forced to ________.

[A] follow unfavorable asset evaluation rules

[B] collect payments from third parties

[C] cooperate with the price managers

[D] reevaluate some of their assets.

例题分析：本题正确答案[A]选项和原文中有三组同义词和同义词组，为解答本题提供了线索，这几个同义词分别为："complain"="moan"，"not fair"="unfavorable"，"value some assets"="asset evaluation"。所以，本题属于同义词替换。

② 历年阅读理解A节词义推断题中的同义词替换和反义词推理。例如：

What might account for this strange phenomenon? Here are a few guesses：a) certain astrological signs confer superior soccer skills；b) winter-born babies tend to have higher oxygen capacity，which increases soccer stamina；c) soccer-mad parents are more likely to conceive children in springtime，at the annual peak of soccer mania；d) none of the above.（2007年考题Text 1）

The word "mania"（Paragraph 2）most probably means ________.

[A] fun　[B] craze　[C] hysteria　[D] excitement

例题分析：本题要求考生猜测"mania"的词义，选项中"craze"和题干中"mania"为同义词。

（3）写作题型中的同义词替换。

在考研英语写作中，为了避免词汇的重复以及实现词汇的多变，常常要用到同义词替换，例如：

① important：essential，significant，vital，crucial

② difficult：hard，tricky，complicated，complex，intricate

③ good：marvelous，fabulous，gorgeous，spectacular，outstanding

④ bad：awful，terrible，dreadful，defective，faulty

⑤ beautiful：charming，charismatic，attractive，gorgeous，pretty

3. 掌握词汇之间的搭配关系（如动词与介词、形容词与介词、形容词与名词等）

【理论解释】

掌握词汇之间的搭配关系，首先要求考生不仅要将单词作为一个独立的语言要素进行记忆——记住它的发音、拼写和中文释义，还要学会如何将这些语言要素按照搭配选词的基本原则有效地搭配起来，形成能表达更为复杂、精确含义的词组。

其次，"单独词汇量对了解文章中的词汇含义只起47%的作用，而单独词汇辨认也只占阅读速度的28%的比例"（引自孙兴文，1998）。所以，不掌握词的有限组合而只单纯记忆词的"意义"，对于提高阅读理解的准确度和速度都是不够的。

考研英语中对于词汇之间搭配关系的考查方法有：① 英语知识运用中的固定搭配；② 写作中的用词准确；③ 提高阅读的准确度和速度。

【举例说明】

（1）英语知识运用中的固定搭配。

① 动词与介词搭配。例如：

Roman Catholicism had been the state religion and the only one allowed by the Spanish crown. While most leaders sought to maintain Catholicism __13__ the official religion of the new states, some sought to end the exclusion of other faiths. (2007 年考题第 13 题)

13. [A] as [B] for [C] under [D] against

例题分析:正确答案为选项[A]。"as"可用在"动词+宾语"结构后引导宾补,意为"作为,当做"。它用在文中和动词"maintain"搭配表示"继续将天主教作为新兴国家的国教"。

② 形容词与介词搭配。例如:

The brain finds it best to keep smell receptors __19__ for unfamiliar and emergency signals such as the smell of smoke, which might indicate the danger of fire. (2005 年考题第 19 题)

19. [A] available [B] reliable [C] identifiable [D] suitable

例题分析:正确答案为[A]。其中选项[A]available 表示"可得到的,可用的";选项[B]reliable 意思为"可信赖的,可靠的";选项[C]"identifiable"表示"可识别的";选项[D]suitable 意思是"适合的"。四个选项中只有选项[A]和选项[D]能和介词"for"搭配,再结合文意,只能选[A]。题目的意思是:大脑发现,最好让气味感受器可随时用于接受不熟悉的、危急的信号,比如那些可能引发火灾的烟味。

(2) 写作中的用词准确。

考研英语写作要求考生能够做到用词准确,因此考生需熟练掌握词汇之间的搭配关系,如常见的形容词和名词的搭配:

① 常和"attention"搭配的形容词:"(pay) close attention"(密切的),"(pay) full attention"(充分的),"(pay) further attention"(进一步的)。

② 常和"attitude"搭配的形容词:"optimistic"(乐观的),"pessimistic"(悲观的),"sympathetic"(同情的),"open-minded"(开明的)。

③ 常和"audience"搭配的形容词:"attentive"(专心的),"cynical"(爱讥讽的),"enchanted"(着了迷的),"frenzied"(疯狂的),"hostile"(不友好的),"listless"(无精打采的),"unresponsive"(没有反应的)。

4. 掌握词汇生成的基本知识(如词源、词根、词缀等)

【理论解释】

构词法是组成单词的一种方法,它有清晰严谨的结构形式,而且有规律可循。利用构词法记忆单词,可以加速记忆、举一反三,简化难词记忆并有效提高推测词义的能力。学生掌握了一定的词源、词根、词缀的知识不仅能迅速扩大词汇量,并且能够利用词根或词缀猜测单词的含义。

词根词缀法是把一个单词分解为前缀、词根、后缀三部分,以帮助记忆。如"permission"一词中,"miss"是词根,"per"是前缀,"ion"是后缀。"per"=全部,"miss"=发射,"ion"是一个名词后缀,两个词缀和词根共同构成了"permission"一词,表示"允许"。由此可见,词根、前缀、后缀是构成单词的三个元素、三个"构件"。词根是主要元素,前缀、后缀是次要元素。由上述例子可以看出,一个英语单词并不是一些毫无意义的孤立的字母的随意排列,而是由一些含有具体意义的词根词缀所构成的有意义的整体。因此,要记忆一个单词,就不能按照一个个字母排列顺序去记,而应按照词根、词缀的意义去记。

【举例说明】

(1)《考纲》重点前缀及后缀。

常用的前缀和后缀见本书附录 1。

(2) 构词法在真题中的应用。例如:

In spite of "endless talk of difference," American society is an amazing machine for homogenizing people.（2006年考题第21题）

21. The word "homogenizing" most probably means ______.

[A] identifying [B] associating [C] assimilating [D] monopolizing

例题分析：可以利用词根词缀知识来判断"homogenizing"一词的含义，其中前缀"homo"表示"同一"，词根"gene"是"产生"的意思，"ize"是个表示"使动"的动词后缀，而"ing"是表示动名词的后缀，因此可以推测出该词的基本含义为"使……产生一致"，而选项中"assimilating"的词义和"homogenize"最为接近，意思是"同化"，因此可以判断正确选项为[C]。

2.1.2 《考纲》词汇考查目标强化指导

《考纲》中要求考生掌握5 500左右的词汇以及相关词组，并要求掌握词汇之间的词义关系及词汇生成的基本知识，但在实际学习中，需要把词汇分成不同的级别并采用不同的记忆原则和记忆方法，考研英语词汇可以分为基础词汇、核心词汇、常备词组及超纲词汇。

1.《考纲》基础词汇

【理论解释】

使用《考纲》中的2 000左右的英语单词，基本上就可以解释所有其他单词的含义。这些词汇称之为基础词汇（见附录2）。大部分基础词汇是考生在初中、高中就学习过的常用词汇。

【简要分析】

对《考纲》规定词汇考查范围进行匹配搜索、核对，可以看出，《考纲》词汇中有2 000左右的单词属于近、现代英语的基础词汇范围。同时，自1999年至2011年13年的考试真题中，通过对比统计可以看出，这些基础词汇的出现频率均高于10次。

【价值分析】

（1）基础词汇作为直接出题的考点情况：第一，全面考查词汇的含义，常会出现词汇熟词僻义的考核；第二，基础词汇的搭配关系；第三，基础词汇的词义关系题。

（2）基础词汇作为间接出题的考点情况：第一，在阅读理解B节选择搭配题型中的上段与下段之间关键词的复现，是基础词汇的重要功能之一；第二，对于每篇阅读文章中3%的超纲词汇，文章中会出现使用基础词汇对超纲词进行注释或多种形式的解释说明；第三，写作题型中要求会使用基础词汇表达中高难度词汇的含义。

【举例说明】

This group generally do well in IQ test, scoring 12-15 points above the __10__ value of 100, and have contributed disproportionately to the intellectual and cultural life of the West, as the careers of their elites, including several world-renowned scientists, affirm. They also suffer more often than most people from a number of nasty genetic diseases, such as breast cancer.（2008年考题第10题）

10. [A] normal [B] common [C] mean [D] total

例题分析：本题空格处填入的形容词修饰名词"value"，表示"……值"。[C]选项"mean"有"平均"的含义，代入文中意思是"100分的平均值"，符合文章的意思和常识。

【学习指导】

对于基础词汇，采用一般性快速记忆即可。考生在学习基础词汇时应注意以下事项：

第一，熟练掌握基础词汇的常考生僻释义。关于基础词汇，虽然考生比较熟悉，但也最容易忽视。建议考生应该将基础词汇常考的生僻释义通过历年真题归纳出释义列表。对于其他基础词汇，记忆时也要注意其释义的全面性。

第二,基础词汇搭配关系。基础词汇的词性和词义都是比较灵活的,只有将它放在具体的语境和搭配关系中,才能把握其准确的含义和用法。建议考生将基础词汇的记忆重点放在记忆其典型例句和常用搭配上。

第三,中、高难度词汇的基础词汇英文释义。基础词汇的功能之一是解释说明其他词汇。因此,考生在阅读和写作时,如遇到无法理解和无法表达复杂含义的词汇,可以通过其英文释义的准确理解和转换来表达其复杂含义。建议考生常备英英词典,对于考研英语核心词汇的英文注解要特别注意。在平时的阅读和写作练习中,要注意培养词汇间的转换表达能力。

2. 核心词(必备词汇)

【理论解释】

核心词汇(见附录3)是指《考纲》中除去基础词汇外,历年真题中经常出现的词汇。这些词汇的总和构成了考研英语的核心词汇,统计结果显示:该类词汇在历年真题中出现的频率大于等于两次。

【简要分析】

通过对《考纲》规定词汇范围进行匹配搜索、核对发现:《考纲》词汇中有约3 000个单词属于近、现代英语的核心词汇范围。同时,自1999年至2011年13年的考试真题中,统计结果显示这些核心词汇的出现频率为2~10次。

【价值分析】

核心词汇作为出题的考点情况:第一,文章核心句、转折句、因果关系和主题句等多种重要信息处常常出现核心词汇;第二,核心词汇的词义考查题。

【举例说明】

It identifies the undertreatment of pain and the aggressive use of "ineffectual and forced medical procedures that may prolong and even dishonor the period of dying" as the twin problems of end-of-life care. (2002年考题第39题)

Which of the following best defines the word "aggressive"?

39. [A] Bold [B] Harmful [C] Careless [D] Desperate

例题分析:该题考的是核心词"aggressive"的词义推理,该词所在上下文谈到临终护理的两大问题,即"对病痛处理不力以及对无效和强制的医疗程序的使用,可能会延长死亡期,甚至让病人死得不体面"。"aggressive"用于褒义时,意为"强有力的,坚持己见的",用于贬义时,意为"攻击性的、不顾后果的"。根据上下文意思可知,句中"aggressive"应取其贬义,"bold"用于贬义时意思为"大胆的、冒失的",含义和"aggressive"最为接近。

【学习指导】

第一,掌握核心词汇的基本含义。核心词汇相比基础词汇来说,其词义、词性相对固定,搭配关系也相对较少。对于这部分核心词汇,建议考生着重记忆词汇的基本含义与拼写方式,最终能够快速、准确地将二者对应起来并进行有效识别。

第二,掌握核心词汇的构词方法。在记忆核心词汇时,可采用多种记忆方式强化记忆,比如构词法、联想法等高效率的记忆方法。还可通过学习词根、词缀知识,识别其他构词法生成的词。

3. 常备词组

【理论解释】

词组(短语)是指由两个以上的词语组合而成的语法单位。要区分词组的类型要注意掌握三点:① 词性;② 词与词之间所构成的关系;③ 词的位置。

【简要分析】

常备词组(见附录4)来源有两大部分:一是真题阅读理解中考过的词组;二是每年《考纲》针对完形填空解析部分所归纳的词组。

【价值分析】

常备词组的考查方式多种多样,以上所述的词汇考查方式都可以是词组的考查方式。但出题频率最高的是完形填空的词组搭配题。

【举例说明】

2010 年考题中的词组搭配题:

Instead, the studies ended __2__ giving their name to the "Hawthorne effect"...

2. [A] at [B] up [C] with [D] off

__7__ someting was changed, productivity rose.

7. [A] as far as [B] for fear that [C] in case that [D] so long as

After several decades, the same data were __11__ to econometric analysis.

11. [A] compared [B] shown [C] subjected [D] conveyed

Hawthorne experiments have another surprise store. __12__ the descriptions on record...

12. [A] Contrary to [B] Consistent with [C] Parallel with [D] Pealliar to

__15__, lighting was always changed on a Sunday .

15. [A] In contrast [B] For example [C] In consequence [D] As usual

上述例题分析及答案参见本书第3部分2010年研究生入学统一考试英语试题。

【学习指导】

(1) 联想记忆。

有些短语可以根据意思或者用法,举一反三。例如,"be associated with""与……有关(系)","associate ... with""由……联想到……","把……联系起来"。这两个词组都涉及甲事物与乙事物之间的联系,曾在考研英语真题中多次出现。像这种重点词组适合用联想记忆法进行区分。

(2) 阅读记忆。

通过阅读英语文章、小说等记忆词汇和短语。阅读材料最好是选择由比较权威的教师根据《考纲》内容编写的阅读书,这样难度较好把握。

4. 部分超纲词汇

【理论解释】

所谓超纲词汇(见附录5),是指超出《考纲》附录所列出的单词及词组范围的词汇。《考纲》自2006年起删除了词汇表中的中文释义,这就意味着以后考试中出现《考纲》中所列单词的所有释义都不算作超纲词汇。

【简要分析】

《考纲》明确要求每年的超纲词汇控制在3%左右。主要包括以下三种情况:① 文章中学科核心概念或专有名词;②《考纲》词汇的变形或组合;③ 构词法生成词。

【价值分析】

超纲词汇作为出题的考点有:第一,阅读理解A部分常出现的词义推理题;第二,阅读理解部分中文章主题句或段落中心句中出现超纲词汇,并且该词为句子核心词汇,题目中涉及文章主旨题和段落中心题,其实就是考查考生的词汇推测能力;第三,翻译题型中部分核心词汇的翻译也会涉及超纲词汇,这就要求考生能够对其做出正确的推理。

【举例说明】

As a result, the modern world is increasingly populated by intelligent gizmos whose presence we barely notice but whose universal existence has removed much human labor. Our factories hum to the rhythm of robot assembly arms. Our banking is done at automated teller terminals that thank us with mechanical politeness for the transaction. Our subway trains are controlled by tireless robot-drivers. And thanks to the continual miniaturization of electronics and micro-mechanics, there are already robot systems that can perform some kinds of brain and bone surgery with submillimeter accuracy—far greater precision than highly skilled physicians can achieve with their hands alone.(2002 年考题第 27 题)

27. The word "gizmos" most probably means ________.

[A] programs [B] experts [C] devices [D] creatures

例题分析:本题是一个词义猜测题,而"gizmo"是一个超纲词汇,需要通过上下文来猜测词义,由文章可以得知"gizmo"的特点是:普遍存在和节省劳动力。下文提到的"工厂的组装臂"、"银行的自动柜员机"、"驾驶地铁的机器人司机"、"医院做手术的机器人系统"都是对"gizmo"的举例说明。由此可推断出"gizmo"指的是"机器、设备",因此正确答案为选项[C]。

【学习指导】

《考纲》要求考生必须掌握推测词义的能力,那么考生在平时的学习中应着重从以下几方面进行培养:

第一,通过上下文的逻辑关系推测词义。这就要求考生对于文章中句内和句间的各种逻辑关系非常清晰,熟练掌握各种逻辑关系的标志词,如因果关系、转折关系、递进关系、并列关系等标志词。

第二,利用前后缀及词根解构词汇。考生应掌握大纲附表中的常用前后缀及构词法中最常用的词根。这样不仅能够有效拆分、理解一些构成词的大致含义,还能够辅助记忆大纲中的核心词汇。

第三,扩充背景知识。在复习备考阶段,要通过英语文章的精度训练,了解各学科的基本概念、基本实验手段和学科前沿问题,这是作为一名合格研究生候选人的必要条件。同时,充足的背景知识也可以帮助考生快速、准确地理解超纲词汇的大致含义。

2.2 英语知识运用

2.2.1 《考纲》基本信息详解

该部分不仅考查考生对不同语境中规范的语言要素(包括词汇、表达方式和结构)的掌握程度,还考查考生对语段特征(如连贯性和一致性)的辨识能力等。该部分考试共 20 小题,每小题 0.5 分,共 10 分。

在一篇 240 ~ 280 词的文章中留出 20 个空白,要求考生从每题所给出的 4 个选项中选出最佳答案,使补全后的文章意思通顺、前后连贯、结构完整。该部分考试要求考生在答题卡 1 上作答。

2.2.2 《考纲》考查目标强化指导

1. 测试要点

为了从总体上把握考研英语的命题趋势,明确命题者的意图和考查要点,我们对历年真题中的英语知识运用部分进行了系统研究,细致分析了从 1992 年到 2011 年(20 年)的英语知识运用文章,共计20篇,310道题目,1 240个选项。经分析,考查知识点为370个,知识点分布如图2-2所示。

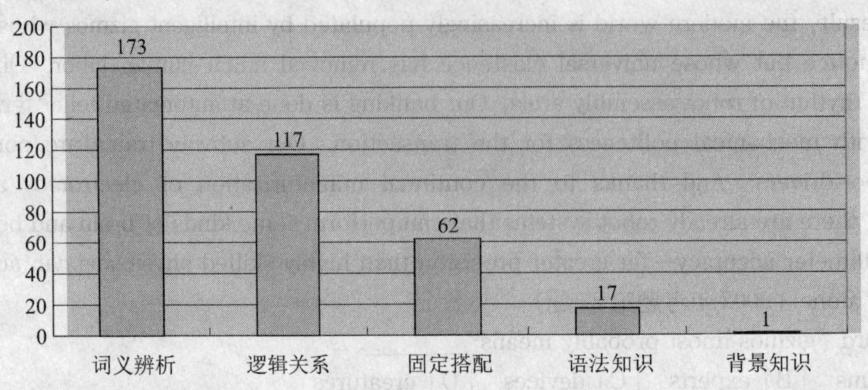

图2-2 英语知识运用知识点考查分布

(1) 词义辨析。英语知识运用部分的词义辨析题,主要考查名词、动词、形容词以及副词的形近、义近词辨析。解答这类题目时,不仅要考虑文章的中心主线,还要考虑各词本身的功能或特点。比如,动词辨析题就要考虑到动词的及物或不及物,以及动词的主语或宾语对其产生的限制。

(2) 逻辑关系。除词义辨析外,英语知识运用部分还考查逻辑的连贯性,即句与句之间的逻辑关系,归纳起来有六种:并列关系、递进关系、因果关系、对立关系、总分关系及条件关系。其最直接的体现是对连词的考查。

(3) 固定搭配。固定搭配考查频率不高,其特点在于技巧性不强,突破的关键在于考生平时的总结和积累,主要参考历年英语知识运用真题中出现过的相关固定搭配。

(4) 语法知识。英语知识运用部分测试的发展趋势为长句、难句越来越多,而其考查的特点又是填空内信息和填空外信息的有机互动。如果不具备扎实的语法功底,就无法理清句子结构,从而难以得出正确答案。由此可见,掌握相应的语法知识,不仅有助于解决直接考查语法的题目,也是解决其他题目的必要手段。

(5) 背景知识。虽然英语知识运用部分中直接考查背景知识的题目比重很小,但考生也不应忽视。比如,可以多阅读一些相关的社科类文章,进行有效的积累,以提高做题的速度和准确率,避免遇到不熟悉的话题不知所措,影响正常发挥的现象。

2. 考查目标一:词汇

【理论解释】

词汇是英语知识运用部分测试的重点和难点,大约占题目的60% ~70%,在《考纲》要求考生掌握的5 500个词汇及相关词组中,使用在完形填空中的大约有1 500 ~1 600个。这些词汇本身并不难,但词汇题的得分率普遍不高。原因之一在于,考生没有全面把握这些词的各种含义,或者没有准确把握其中近义词的细微差别。

【举例说明】

(1) 名词题的解题线索。

第一点,应根据文章中心判断名词。

英语知识运用部分文章中一般都有非常明确的中心主线。从理论上讲,正确的选项一定是与文章中心主线关联的。因此,看上去与文章中心主线无关的选项基本上可以排除。例如:

In a significant __2__ of legal controls over the press, Lord Irvine, the Lord Chancellor, will introduce a __3__ bill that will propose making payments to witnesses __4__ and will strictly control the amount of __5__ that can be given to a case __6__ a trial begins.(2001年考题第5题)

5. [A] publicity [B] penalty [C] popularity [D] peculiarity

例题分析:此题可以根据文章中心选词。本题所考查的名词作为“control”的宾语,同时还受到“that”定语从句的限制。根据文章的主题“政府要禁止媒体曝光案件内幕”,可以判断这三个选项[B]penalty“惩罚”、[C]popularity“流行”、[D]peculiarity“特征”与文章的主题无关,政府不可能去控制这些东西。政府要控制的是选项[A]publicity“公开度”。

第二点,名词作主语时,通过已知的谓语动词判断主谓搭配的一致性,或者通过已知的表语形容词判断主表搭配的一致性。例如:

When the work is well done, a __3__ of accident free operations is established where time lost due to injuries is kept at a minimum.(1999年考题第3题)

3. [A] regulation [B] climate [C] circumstance [D] requirement

例题分析:本句中的时间状语从句指出“当安全保障工作做得很好的时候”,后面讲述的内容应当是描述工作氛围的,而不是还要讲安全规则的制定。所给四个选项的意思分别是:[A]regulation“规定”;[B]climate 在本文中是“氛围,环境”;[C]circumstance 的复数形式指“环境,情势”;[D]reqirement“要求”。只有在理解文章的基础上,再比较所给选项在意义、用法上的细微差别,才能做出正确的选择。而且,在这个语境中,只有[B]climate 这个名词作主语与谓语“is established”搭配最合适。

第三点,名词做宾语时,通过已知的谓语动词判断动宾搭配的一致性。例如:

And they also need to give serious __1__ to how they can be best __2__ such changes.(2003年考题第1题)

1. [A] thought [B] idea [C] opinion [D] advice

例题分析:第1题要求填入一个名词,且要与前面的动词“give”搭配。选项[A]可以与其搭配构成“give thought to sth.”,意思是“认真考虑……”。选项[B]搭配“give sb. an idea (of)”意思是“使了解……的情况”,选项[C]搭配“give opinion to sb. (on sth.)”意思是“向某人提出对于某事的意见”,选项[D]搭配“give advice to”后面应接人,表示给某人一些建议,不符合文意。故正确选项为[A]。

第四点,名词被前置定语修饰时,通过前置定语与名词的修饰搭配关系判断名词。例如:

As time went by, computers became smaller and more powerful, and they became “personal” too, as well as __13__, with display becoming sharper and storage __14__ increasing.(2002年考题第14题)

14. [A] ability [B] capability [C] capacity [D] faculty

例题分析:四个选项均有“能力”的意思。此题关键是判断选项中哪个词能与前置定语“storage”搭配。从语义上看,“计算机也成了个人和团体机构的工具,是随着显示效果越来越清晰和存储……”。因此空格与“storage”搭配后应指计算机的存储能力,四个选项中只有“capacity”可以指“承受力”或“容纳力”,与“storage”形成固定搭配,指“存储能力”。

第五点,名词前后出现介词时,通过介词和名词的习惯搭配关系判断名词。但近几年英语知识运用常考查不同名词可以跟同一介词搭配时的词义辨析,这种情况下的正确答案就取决于文章想要表达的意思。例如:

For example, changes in the economy that __10__ to fewer job opportunities for youth and rising unemployment __11__ make gainful employment increasingly difficult to obtain. The resulting discontent may in __12__ lead more youths into criminal behavior.(2004年考题第12题)

12. [A] case [B] short [C] turn [D] essence

例题分析:空格要求填入的名词与“in”搭配后在句中做状语。文章所要表达的意思是:社会经济变化→青年失业或难找工作→青年的不满情绪→青年的犯罪。这是一个因果关系的链条。四个选项中只有“in turn”(反过来,转而)代入后能表达这一因果层次关系。而选项[A]、[B]与[D]同介词“in”搭配,分别表示:“免得,以防(万一)”、“简言之”、“在本质上”,均不符合文意。

第六点,名词后出现定语从句或同位语从句时,需要以后面的从句为线索。例如:

__11__ when homeless individuals manage to find a __12__ that will give them three meals a day and a place to sleep at night, a good number still spend the bulk of each day __13__ the street.(2006年考题第12题)

12. [A] lodging [B] shelter [C] dwelling [D] house

例题分析:题中所给的四个选项中[A] lodging 指“旅馆”,[B] selter 指“收容所”,[C] dwelling 指“住处”,[D] house 指“房子”。第12个空要求填一个名词,其后“that”引导的定语从句修饰这个名词,这时可以根据定语从句来判断该名词。该定语从句“that will give them three meals a day and a place to sleep at night”意为“提供一日三餐和住宿的地方”。由此可知,选项[B] shelter“收容所”为正确答案。

(2) 形容词题的解题线索。

第一点,形容词作表语时,通过主表搭配的一致性判断形容词。例如:

The speaker who does not have specific words in his working vocabulary may be __49__ to explain or describe in a __50__ that can be understood by his listeners(1994年考题第49题).

49. [A] obscure [B] difficult [C] impossible [D] unable

例题分析:本句的主干为“The speaker who... may be... to explain...”,其中“who”引导的定语从句修饰“the speaker”。因此,该选项要填入的是“the speaker”的表语,而选项中只有“unable”能与之相搭配,因此正确答案为[D]。

第二点,形容词修饰名词或名词性词组时,通过形容词和名词修饰搭配的合适性和褒贬意义的一致性判断形容词。例如:

A variety of small clubs can provide __10__ opportunities for leadership, as well as for practice in successful group dynamics.(2003年考题第10题)

10. [A] durable [B] excessive [C] surplus [D] multiple

例题分析:根据词语搭配和褒贬意义的一致性,所选的形容词应该与“opportunities for leadership”既可以构成修饰关系,又保持褒贬一致。而选项[D] multiple“多种多样的”符合这一要求。选项[B] excessive“过多的,额外的”和[C] surplus“过剩的,剩余的”与“opportunity for leadership”褒贬色彩不一致;选项[A] durable“持久的,耐久的”不可用于修饰“opportunity for leadership”。

第三点,形容词出现在概括性的总述句中时,通过分析总句后面的分句来判断形容词。例如:

If no surplus is available, a farmer cannot be __7__. He must either sell some of his property or seek extra funds in the form of loans.(2000年考题第7题)

7. [A] self-confident [B] self-sufficient [C] self-satisfied [D] self-restrained

例题分析：所给的四个选项[A]self-confident 表示“自信的”；[B]self-sufficient 表示“自给自足的”；[C]self-satisfied 表示“自我满足的”；[D]self-restrained 表示“自我克制的”。本句的条件句是“如果没有剩余”，那结果应该是“农民就不能自给自足”，所以选择[B]。从另外一个角度考虑，需要填出的形容词出现在总句中，可以通过分析总句后面的分句来进行选择，后面一句话的意思是：“他必须或者卖掉一些财产，或者通过贷款寻求资金”。那么农民必须要做这些事的目的是为了能够“自给自足”。

第四点，根据与主题相关原则和主旨导向或作者倾向一致原则判断形容词。例如：

Neither kind of sleep is at all well understood, but REM sleep is assumed to serve some restorative function of the brain. The purpose of non-REM sleep is even more __3__. (1995 年考题第 3 题)

3. [A] subtle [B] obvious [C] mysterious [D] doubtful

例题分析：本题要求从四个备选项中挑出一个修饰“non-REM sleep”的最佳形容词。本文总述句所表现的文章导向是两种睡眠都没有被很好地理解，后面的分述部分要服从这个导向，所以“non-REM sleep”作为两种睡眠的一种应该是不被理解，即[C] mysterious“神秘的”，与文章的主旨导向相一致。

(3) 动词题的解题线索。

第一点，动词作谓语时，通过主谓搭配的一致性判断动词。例如：

Specialists __8__ history and economics, have __9__ two things: that the period from 1650 to 1750 was __10__ by great poverty, and that industrialization certainly did not worsen and may have actually improved the conditions for the majority of the populace. (1998 年考题第 9 题)

9. [A] manifested [B] approved [C] shown [D] speculated

例题分析：这段中提到历史经济学家想要推翻第一段所陈述的观点，就必须提出事实来支持自己的观点。“manifest”指“表明、显示”，它的主语应该是某事或某物；“approve”指“批准、赞同”；“speculate”指“思索、推测”，是不及物动词，与“on/about”连用。从搭配和词义上看，以上三个词都不符合，故排除。而“show”可与句中的主语搭配和宾语搭配，故[C]为正确答案。

第二点，动词作谓语并且为及物动词时，通过动宾搭配的一致性判断动词。例如：

In a significant __2__ of legal controls over the press, Lord Irvine, the Lord Chancellor, will introduce a __3__ bill that will propose making payments to witnesses __4__ and will strictly control the amount of __5__ that can be given to a case __6__ a trial begins. (2001 年考题第 2 题)

2. [A] tightening [B] intensifying [C] focusing [D] fastening

例题分析：[A]tightening 表示“使更严格，使更有效”，与后面的“legal controls”搭配表示“将法律或法规加强或严格化”，符合题意。[B]Intensifying 表示“加强、加剧或使尖锐”；[C]focusing 表示“对准焦距，把（光线，注意力）集中于……”；[D]fastening 表示“扣紧，集中注意力于……”。这三个选项均不能与“controls”构成动宾搭配。

第三点，根据动词是及物还是不及物判断。例如：

Successful safety programs may __5__ greatly in the emphasis placed on certain aspects of the program. (1999 年考题第 5 题)

5. [A] alter [B] differ [C] shift [D] distinguish

例题分析：本题考查不及物动词的用法。[A]alter 表示“改变”；[B]differ 表示“使相异”，“differ in”表示“在某方面或某事上不同”；[C]shift 表示“改变，移动”；[D]distiguish 后面常跟

“from”或“between”，表示“从……中区别出来，不同”。比较四个选项的意义和用法，只有[B]differ这个不及物动词能与介词“in”搭配。

第四点，根据与动词构成习惯搭配的介词判断。例如：

The Lord Chancellor said introduction of the Human Rights Bill, which makes the European Convention on Human Rights legally binding in Britain, laid down that everybody was __15__ to privacy and that public figures could go to court to protect themselves and their families.（2001年考题第15题）

15. [A] authorized　[B] credited　[C] entitled　[D] qualified

例题分析：空格要求填入动词的过去分词，并能够与后面的介词“to”搭配，即“be+过去分词+to sth.”。选项[A]和[D]只能接动词不定式，即“be authorized to do sth.”和“be qualified to do sth.”，因此不符合文中的用法。选项[B]搭配“be credited to sth.”虽然在语法上可行，但在文中表达的意思是“把每个人归于隐私”显然不符合逻辑。符合题意的只有选项[C]固定搭配“be entitled to sth.”，它代入文中意为“每个人都享有隐私权”。

第五点，根据与主题相关原则或主旨导向一致原则判断动词。例如：

Estimates __6__ anywhere from 600,000 to 3 million. __7__ the figure may vary, analysts do agree on another matter: that the number of the homeless is __8__.（2006年考题第8题）

8. [A] inflating　[B] expanding　[C] increasing　[D] extending

例题分析：本题要求从四个备选项中挑出一个表示“the number of the homeless”状态的词。根据与主题相关原则，空格所填的句子应该是表示无家可归者数量的增加，而能表示数量增加的只有“increasing”，故选[C]。其他备选项[A]inflating表示“膨胀，鼓气，涨价”；[B]expanding表示“扩大，增加，增强”；[D]extending表示“扩充，延伸”。

（4）副词题的解题线索。

副词在英语中起修饰作用，所以可通过其被修饰成分判断副词。主要是从副词所表示的意义和程度以及褒贬性来判断是否与被修饰成分搭配一致。例如：

By 1830, the former Spanish and Portuguese colonies had become independent nations. The roughly 20 million inhabitants of these nations looked __2__ to the future.（2007年考题第2题）

2. [A] confusedly　[B] cheerfully　[C] worriedly　[D] hopefully

例题分析：空格处要求填入的副词修饰动词“looked to”，说明成为独立国家后这些原殖民地国家居民的心态。“Look to the future”表示“展望未来”。根据文章主旨，独立后的国家居民对于未来应该是“充满希望的”，故选[D] hopefully。本题考查副词的褒贬性。

【学习指导】

第一，准确掌握词汇含义和用法。

英语知识运用部分对词汇知识的考查重点体现在习惯用法和词汇辨析上。习惯用法是英语中某种固定的结构形态，不能随意改动。故考生平时应该多积累习惯用法。词汇辨析是英语知识运用考查的重点和难点，包括同义词、近义词及形近词的辨析。考生要做好这类题，需要掌握较大的词汇量和词语搭配、辨析，并具有在特定的语境中灵活运用的能力。同时，要求考生对词汇有深度的掌握，即不仅能认词，还要能分辨同义词、近义词及形近词的细微差别，掌握它们的含义、用法，会在不同语境中的使用。例如：

On the contrary, they can help students acquire a sense of commitment by planning for roles that are within their __20__ and their attention spans and by having clearly stated rules.（2003年考

题第20题）

20. [A] capabilities [B] responsibilities [C] proficiency [D] efficiency

例题分析：本题考查名词近义词辨析。空格所在部分是"that"引导的定语从句，修饰先行词"roles"，说明青少年策划的角色特点。四个选项中首先排除[C]proficiency和[D]efficiency，它们不能和"within"搭配，且与句意不符。选项[B]responsibilities是"commitment"的近义词，填入空中表示"在责任范围内的角色"不合句意。选项[A]capabilities代入文中意为"一些在学生能力范围和在其注意力持续时间之内的角色"，符合文意。

Boston Globe reporter Chris Reidy notes that the situation will improve only when there are __17__ programs that address the many needs of the homeless.（2006年考题第17题）

17. [A] complex [B] comprehensive [C] complementary [D] compensating

例题分析：本题考查形容词形近词辨析，空格处的形容词与"program"搭配，表示"……的规划"。下文"that"引导的定语从句说明了该规划的特点是：解决无家可归者的各种需求，所以空格处应填入[B]comprehensive，表示"全面的规划"。[A]complex强调复杂，[C]complementary强调互补，[D]compensating强调补偿，均不合文意。

第二，利用文章主题解题。

英语知识运用所选的文章一般综合性较强，并且主题明确单一，全文的信息与中心主题都息息相关，紧扣主题。根据这个外在特点，考生在解题时就要时刻把握"与文章主题相关原则"，即最佳选项理论上都应该与文章主题密切相关。通常文章的首句就是全文的主题句。因此，读英语知识运用部分文章的第一句话时，不仅要读懂其字面上的中文意思，而且要透过首句来预测文章的中心思想。同时，注意短文段落的划分以及各段的首句，因为各段的首句也是主题经常出现的地方。有时作者的遣词造句也能反映出文章的主题。例如：

Many theories concerning the causes of juvenile delinquency (crimes committed by young people) focus either on the individual or on society as the major contributing influence. Theories __1__ on the individual suggest that children engage in criminal behavior because they were not sufficiently penalized for previous misdeeds or that they have learned criminal behavior through interaction with others.（2004年考题第1题）

1. [A] acting [B] relying [C] centering [D] commenting

例题分析：首句是本段的主题句，讲述"有关青少年犯罪缘由的理论重点研究两个方面，即个人因素和社会因素"。由主题句推断出第二句应具体阐述关于个人因素的理论，"centering on"代入文中表示"以个人因素为中心的理论"，与文意吻合。"acting on"表示"对……起作用"，"relying on"表示"依靠，指望"，"commenting on"表示"表达意见，作出评论"，均不符合文意，故本题答案为选项[C]centering。

In a significant tightening of legal controls over the press, Lord Irvine, the Lord Chancellor, will introduce a __3__ bill that will propose making payments to witnesses illegal and will strictly control the amount of publicity that can be given to a case before a trial begins.（2001年考题第3题）

3. [A] sketch [B] rough [C] preliminary [D] draft

例题分析：这篇文章中出现了"ban"、"witnesses"、"cases"、"trial"等法律词汇，从作者的这些遣词上可以判断这篇文章的主题与法律有关。空格让填入一个词修饰后面的"bill"，四个备选项中只有[D]draft与"bill"形成固定搭配，表示法律专业术语"草案"。其他选项虽然都可以表示类似的"初步的，不完整的，简略的"的含义，但不与"bill"搭配。

第三,利用文章结构解题。

英语知识运用中所选文章在结构上常常采用总分对照的形式,这就为考生迅速从整体上掌握一篇英语知识运用文章提供了非常便利的条件。总分对照结构往往贯穿于英语知识运用文章,详细来说,一般可以应用于英语知识运用文章的三个层次中:

① 应用于整篇文章的结构:因为英语知识运用文章的篇幅限制,总述句往往处于文章的首句或首段,这样就使得英语知识运用文章通常显得"开门见山",即文章的首句或首段就是整篇文章的中心主线所在。

综观历年考研英语知识运用试题,其整篇文章结构基本上都采用了总分对照型。例如:2000 年考研英语的英语知识运用文章的首句是:"If a farmer wishes to succeed he must try to keep a wide gap between his consumption and his production."(假如一个农民想要成功的话,他必须在消费和生产之间保持一个大的差额)。

本文的整体结构是明显的总分对照结构,文章的首句就是总述句,直接概括出了整篇文章的中心主线。

② 应用于文章中的段落结构:段落也常常采用总分结构,此时的总述句是概括出本段的中心主线,即本段的核心主题。例如:1999 年考研英语知识运用文章的第二段。

"Successful safety programs may differ greatly in the emphasis placed on certain aspects of the program. Some place great emphasis on mechanical guarding. Others stress safe work practices by observing rules or regulations. Still others depend on an emotional appeal to the worker. But there are certain basic ideas that must be used in every program if maximum results are to be obtained."

③ 应用于段落中意群的结构:即使一个段落之中也会存在独立的意群,不管这个意群有多短小,由于其具有相对独立的意义,因此也可以采用总分对照的结构。例如:2000 年考研英语知识运用文章中的一个意群。

"If no surplus is available, a farmer cannot be self-sufficient. He must either sell some of his property or seek extra funds in the form of loans. Naturally he will try to borrow money at a low rate of interest but loans of this kind are not frequently obtainable."

该篇文章在这里进入一个新的意群(该文章在此之前都在讲述农夫假如有盈余会如何),这个意群也采用了经典的总分对照结构。分述中几个排比句的重点谓语动词实际上非常形象地支持了总述中"农夫没有 surplus,就不能 self-sufficient"这个意群的中心主题。例如:

Fruit flies who were taught to be smarter than the average fruit fly tended to live shorter lives. This suggests that dimmer bulbs burn longer, that there is a(n) __4__ in not being too terrifically bright. Intelligence, it turns out, is a high-priced option. (2009 年考题第 4 题)

4. [A] tendency　[B] advantage　[C] inclination　[D] priority

例题分析:解答本题的关键是从上下文已知信息中寻找解题线索。上文中指出"更聪明的果蝇寿命更短,不太亮的灯泡使用时间更长",下文提到"(获得)智力是一种代价高昂的选择"。由上下文可推知,不特别聪明是有益处的。因此,选项[B]advantage 代入空格符合题意。选项[A]tendency 与[C]inclination 都指"倾向,趋势",不符合文意。选项[D]Priority 强调"多个事物中最重要的或优先考虑的",而文中没有比较,也不强调"不特别聪明"的重要性,所以排除。

3. 考查目标二:语法

【理论解释】

近年来,英语知识运用部分单纯考查语法知识的题越来越少,但是考生也不应忽视语法知识的复习。因为,一方面这类题也偶有出现,另一方面语法知识也是解决其他题目所必不可少的。其中,常用来直接考查的语法知识点主要包括:定语从句、同位语从句、强调结构、倒装结构等。考生要做到熟知这些语法知识的基本概念、构成及具体用法等,并在此基础上加以灵活运用。

【举例说明】

定语从句考查举例:

Children are likely to have less supervision at home __15__ was common in the traditional family structure. (2004 年考题第 15 题)

15. [A] than [B] that [C] which [D] as

例题分析:本题直接考查了特殊关系代词"than"引导的定语从句。考研英语中对于"than"的考查非常多见,如考查"rather than"、"other than"等比较短语以及"more... than..."、"less... than..."等比较结构,其中在比较结构中的"than"引导的是比较状语从句,即"than"后面是完整的句子,作比较状语。而在本题中,可以发现,空格后是一个缺少了主语的不完整句,不可能是"than"引导的比较状语从句。经过分析,选项[B]、[C]、[D]都不符合句中要表达的比较意义,因此只有选项[A]最合适。之所以有好多考生不敢选这个选项,是因为不了解"than"也可以作为关系代词引导定语从句这个知识点。

强调结构考查举例:

As was discussed before, it was not __2__ the 19th century that the newspaper became the dominant pre-electronic medium... (2002 年考题第 2 题).

2. [A] after [B] by [C] during [D] until

例题分析:本题考查的是强调结构 it was...that...,本句中强调的时间状语"not until the 19th century",其中"not until..."意为"直到……才……"。另外,考生需知"it is not until...that..."常作为固定搭配一起出现。答案为[D]。

同位语从句考查举例:

Concerns were raised __19__ witnesses might be encouraged to exaggerate their stories in court to ensure guilty verdicts. (2001 年考题第 19 题)

19. [A] what [B] when [C] which [D] that

例题分析:本题考查的是同位语从句。空格前后都是完整的句子,选项中只有选项[B]、[D]可以考虑,因为选项[B]可以将空格的句子后变为状语从句,选项[D]可以将空格后的句子变为同位语从句。但是选项[B]代入后,出现了时态错误,故答案为选项[D]。实际上此处是"that"引导的同位语从句修饰抽象名词"concerns",对其进行了解释和补充说明。

倒装结构考查举例:

__5__ everyone agrees on the numbers of Americans who are homeless. Estimates __6__ anywhere from 600,000 to 3 million. __7__ the figure may vary, analysts do agree on another matter... (2006 年考题第 5 题).

5. [A] Generally [B] Almost [C] Hardly [D] Not

例题分析:解此题需要用到倒装结构知识。空格所在句的句意为"……每个人对无家可归人的数量达成了一致意见",后面两句话提供了解题的线索:"估计的数字从 60 万到 300 万不等""(关于无家可归人口的数量)分析家们可能众说纷纭,但是他们对另一问题取得了一致意见"。由此可知,空格中需要填入一个表示否定的单词,符合条件的只有选项[C]、[D],而"hardly"位于句首必须倒装,故排除[C]。"not"可以位于名词或代词之前进行部分否定,作用相当于一个形容词,如"not all the books are written in English"也是同样的道理,故答案为[D]。

They do not provide energy, __1__ do they construct or build any part of the body. (1996 年考题第 1 题)

1. [A] either [B] so [C] nor [D] never

例题分析:这道题也可以运用倒装结构的知识直接排除选项[A]和[B],因为空格所在句是个倒装形式,需要填入否定副词。因此,考生掌握必要的倒装结构知识是必须的。本题具体解题在此就不赘述。答案为[C]。

【学习指导】

对于此类题目,考生可以通过复习相关的语法知识进行准备。比如,讲定语从句离不开先行词和关系词,其中先行词可以由词、短语或句子充当,关系词包括关系代词(that、who、which 等)和关系副词(when、why、where 等)。此外,还要关注特殊的关系代词和关系副词,如 as、whereby、than 等引导的定语从句。对于名词性从句而言,考生重点关注的应是同位语从句,尤其是 that 引导的同位语从句。该从句常见于抽象名词之后,多是对抽象名词的解释和说明,其特点是 that 后面加完整的陈述句。倒装结构需要注意的是,否定副词或否定意义的介词短语等位于句首时构成倒装,解答完形填空时尤其需要注意这一点。强调结构注意其常用的构成形式。总之,虽然英语知识运用中单纯语法知识的考查频率在降低,但是英语知识运用文章结构和每个句子结构的分析都需要用到这些基本的语法知识,因此也不可掉以轻心。

4. 考查目标三:结构

【理论解释】

结构在英语知识运用部分测试中主要体现在逻辑关系的考查上,考生需要熟知各种常见的逻辑关系词。这些表达逻辑关系的词主要是连词、副词以及某些介词词组。可以分为以下几类:

表示转折/让步关系:but, however, nevertheless, whereas, although, despite, in spite of, still。

表示比较或对比关系:similarly, in the same way, likewise, whereas, in contrast to, rather than。

表示因果关系:because, since, now that, on account of, due to, on the ground of, accordingly, consequently, therefore, thus, hence。

表示并列关系:and, or。

表示举例与例证关系:for example, for instance, specially, such as, as follows。

表示强调关系:in fact, in particular, particularly, above all, undoubtedly, certainly。

表示顺承关系:in addition, furthermore, besides, likewise。

此外,逻辑关系不仅可以成为直接的考查对象,而且还可以利用这些逻辑关系寻找其他题目的解题线索。

【举例说明】

让步关系考查举例:

__7__ the figure may vary, analysts do agree on another matter: that the number of the homeless is... (2006 年考题第 7 题)

7. [A] Now that [B] Although [C] Provided [D] Except that

例题分析：根据选项可以得知本题是一道逻辑关系题，解此题需要判断空格所在句中主从句的逻辑关系。空格所在句的从句句意为"数字有可能不同"，主句句意为"分析家们对另一问题取得了一致意见"，由此可判断主从句之间是对立的逻辑关系，符合这一语义的只有让步关系的选项[B] Although。

In fact, __5__, we are extremely sensitive to smells, __6__ we do not generally realize it. (2005年考题第6题)

6. [A] even if [B] if only [C] only if [D] as if

例题分析：根据选项可以得知本题是一道逻辑关系题，解此题需要判断空格所在句中主从句的逻辑关系。经分析，两部分之间是让步关系，连接词应该是"虽然"或者"即使"。该句句意为"我们对气味还是极端敏感的，即使我们没有察觉到"。四个选项中只有[A] even if 表示让步。

因果关系考查举例：

Theories centering on the individual suggest that children engage in criminal behavior __2__ they were not sufficiently penalized for previous misdeeds or that they have learned criminal behavior through interaction with others. (2004年考题第2题)

2. [A] before [B] unless [C] until [D] because

例题分析：本句前一部分指出："儿童从事犯罪"，后一部分指出："他们没有为先前的错误行为受到足够的惩罚"。从上下文看，"没有受到足够的惩罚"是"儿童从事犯罪"的原因，因此两句话的逻辑关系是因果关系，在选项中只有"because"表示因果关系，因此[D]是正确答案。

可以利用这些逻辑关系寻找其他题目的解题线索，例如：

The communications revolution has influnced both work and leisure and how we think and feel both about place and time, but there have been __19__ view about its economic, political, social and cultural implications. (2002年考题第19题)

19. [A] competitive [B] controversial [C] distracting [D] irrational

例题分析：本题考查的是形容词辨析，但是逻辑连词"but"是本题的解题线索。上文说到"信息通信革命影响了我们的工作和休闲，同时也影响了我们对时空的看法和感受"，下文提到"关于通信革命的经济、政治、社会和文化意义，我们有……的看法"，逻辑关系词"but"表达前后文的转折对立关系。由此可见，"我们认可了通信革命在某些方面的影响，但其对政治、经济方面的影响，我们的观点并未统一"，因此答案为[B] contraversial。

【学习指导】

一方面，对于直接考查逻辑关系词的题目，考生应该首先掌握逻辑关系词所表达的含义，尤其是那些表达多种逻辑关系的词。比如，as 可以引导让步状语从句、原因状语从句、方式状语从句、时间状语从句等。另外，那些表达常见逻辑关系的较陌生的连词、副词或介词短语，考生也应该予以关注。比如，常见的表示因果关系的词主要是 because、as 等，但除此之外 on account of、due to、on the ground of、accordingly、consequently、therefore、thus、hence 等也可以表示因果关系。

另一方面，掌握了这些逻辑关系词后，考生应学会灵活运用这些逻辑关系词去解决其他题目。比如："Although he didn't get the first place in the speech contest, he felt ____"。根据"although"所表达的对立逻辑语义，可知后面应该和前面形成相反的意向，若选项中有"happy"和"worried"，据此逻辑关系，就可以排除后者了。

2.3 传统型阅读(阅读理解A节)

2.3.1 《考纲》基本信息详解

本部分要求考生根据提供的4篇文章的内容(总长度约为1 600词),从每题所给出的四个选项中选出最佳答案。

该部分主要考查对英语词汇、短语、句型等习惯表达方式,尤其是对出现在篇章中的语言知识和语言技能的掌握情况。从另一个方面说,它也包含了对英语国家和世界其他国家的政治、经济、文化、历史、社会等背景以及科技发展动态、热门话题乃至西方人的思维、交流方式等非语言性知识和学习能力方面的考查。因此,本部分是一个综合性很强的能力测试试题。

2.3.2 《考纲》考查目标强化指导

考生应能读懂选自各类书籍和报刊的不同类型的文字材料(生词量不超过所读材料总词汇量的3%),还应能读懂与本人学习或工作相关的文献资料、技术说明和产品介绍等。对所读材料,考生应能:① 理解主旨要义;② 理解文中的具体信息;③ 理解文中的概念性含义;④ 进行有关的判断、推理和引申;⑤ 根据上下文推测生词的含义;⑥ 理解文章的总体结构以及上下文之间的关系;⑦ 理解作者的意图、观点或态度;⑧ 区分论点和论据。

1. 考查目标一:理解主旨要义

【理论解释】

考研阅读理解部分测试的第一个考查目标就是要求考生理解文章的主旨要义,顾名思义,就是要求考生清楚一篇文章是围绕什么中心展开的,或者文章的写作目的;另外,除了清楚文章中心,还应包括段落中心。

阅读理解部分测试涉及的具体题型有几类,命题人对考生该能力的考查最直接体现在主旨大意题上,平均每年考查数量是2~3道,其难度不高,属于必得分点。但是,考生千万不要因此而放松这种能力的锻炼。因为,理解主旨要义更重要的意义在于,把握了文章的主旨大意,考生才能进行有效阅读,才能准确地区分论点论据,不至于淹没到大量的细枝末节中。此外,每篇阅读理解文章题目的确定都是围绕文章的主旨要义的,近90%的题目都间接考查到了理解主旨要义。因为英语阅读考查的核心是考查考生对所阅读文章的理解能力,而这一点是通过对文章中心的理解加以体现的,所以主旨题之外的其他题型也是对文章中心的一个侧面说明。

【举例说明】

(1) 主旨大意题。例如:

Why do so many Americans distrust what they read in their newspapers? The American Society of Newspaper Editors is trying to answer this painful question. The organization is deep into a long self-analysis known as the journalism credibility project.

Sad to say, this project has turned out to be mostly low-level findings about factual errors and spelling and grammar mistakes, combined with lots of head-scratching puzzlement about what in the world those readers really want.

But the sources of distrust go way deeper. Most journalists learn to see the world through a set of standard templates (patterns) into which they plug each day's events. In other words, there is a conventional story line in the newsroom culture that provides a backbone and a ready-made narrative structure for otherwise confusing news.

There exists a social and cultural disconnect between journalists and their readers, which helps explain why the "standard templates" of the newsroom seem alien to many readers. In a recent survey, questionnaires were sent to reporters in five middle-size cities around the country, plus one large metropolitan area. Then residents in these communities were phoned at random and asked the same questions.

Replies show that compared with other Americans, journalists are more likely to live in upscale neighborhoods, have maids, own Mercedeses, and trade stocks, and they're less likely to go to church, do volunteer work, or put down roots in a community.

Reporters tend to be part of a broadly defined social and cultural elite, so their work tends to reflect the conventional values of this elite. The astonishing distrust of the news media isn't rooted in inaccuracy or poor reportorial skills but in the daily clash of world views between reporters and their readers.

This is an explosive situation for any industry, particularly a declining one. Here is a troubled business that keeps hiring employees whose attitudes vastly annoy the customers. Then it sponsors lots of symposiums and a credibility project dedicated to wondering why customers are annoyed and fleeing in large numbers. But it never seems to get around to noticing the cultural and class biases that so many former buyers are complaining about. If it did, it would open up its diversity program, now focused narrowly on race and gender, and look for reporters who differ broadly by outlook, values, education, and class. (2001 年考题第 29 题)

29. What is the text mainly about?

[A] Needs of the readers all over the world

[B] Causes of the public disappointment about newspapers

[C] Origins of the declining newspaper industry

[D] Aims of a journalism credibility project

例题分析:这是一道标准的主旨大意题,提问方式也非常的典型——文章主要是关于什么的? 既然是对文章中心的提问,那么题目的答案必须是包含文章的中心观点句或是文章的中心词。本文的中心句是在文章首段提出,而且是以问句这种识别起来相当明显的方式提出。所以该文的中心句是"Why do so many Americans distrust what they read in their newspapers?"(为什么如此多的美国人不信任他们在报纸上读到的消息?)既然确定这句话是文章的主旨要义,那么,很容易确定选项[B]"Causes of the public disappointment about newspapers"(公众对报纸失望的原因)是正确答案。所以这道题日的解答有两个关键点:第一,准确辨认此题是否是主旨大意题;第二,准确判断文章的主旨要义。

(2) 以中心为解题导向的考题。例如:

In spite of "endless talk of difference," American society is an amazing machine for <u>homogenizing</u> people. There is "the democratizing uniformity of dress and discourse, and the casualness and absence of deference" characteristic of popular culture. People are absorbed into "a culture of consumption" launched by the 19th-century department stores that offered "vast arrays of goods in an elegant atmosphere. Instead of intimate shops catering to a knowledgeable elite," these were stores "anyone could enter, regardless of class or background. This turned shopping into a public and democratic act." The mass media, advertising and sports are other forces for homogenization.

Immigrants are quickly fitting into this common culture, which may not be altogether elevating but is hardly poisonous. Writing for the National Immigration Forum, Gregory Rodriguez reports that today's immigration is neither at unprecedented levels nor resistant to assimilation. In 1998 immigrants were 9.8 percent of population; in 1900, 13.6 percent. In the 10 years prior to 1990, 3.1 immigrants arrived for every 1,000 residents; in the 10 years prior to 1890, 9.2 for every 1,000. Now, consider three indices of assimilation — language, home ownership and intermarriage.

The 1990 Census revealed that "a majority of immigrants from each of the fifteen most common countries of origin spoke English 'well' or 'very well' after ten years of residence." The children of immigrants tend to be bilingual and proficient in English. "By the third generation, the original language is lost in the majority of immigrant families." Hence the description of America as a "graveyard" for languages. By 1996 foreign-born immigrants who had arrived before 1970 had a home ownership rate of 75.6 percent, higher than the 69.8 percent rate among native-born Americans.

Foreign-born Asians and Hispanics "have higher rates of intermarriage than do U.S.-born whites and blacks." By the third generation, one third of Hispanic women are married to non-Hispanics, and 41 percent of Asian-American women are married to non-Asians.

Rodriguez notes that children in remote villages around the world are fans of superstars like Arnold Schwarzenegger and Garth Brooks, yet "some Americans fear that immigrant living within the United States remain somehow immune to the nation's assimilative power."

Are there divisive issues and pockets of seething anger in America? Indeed. It is big enough to have a bit of everything. But particularly when viewed against America's turbulent past, today's social indices hardly suggest a dark and deteriorating social environment.（2006 年考题第21 题至第25 题）

21. The word "homogenizing" (Paragraph 1) most probably means ____.

[A] identifying [B] associating [C] assimilating [D] monopolizing

22. According to the author, the department stores of the 19th century ____.

[A] played a role in the spread of popular culture

[B] became intimate shops for common consumers

[C] satisfied the needs of a knowledgeable elite

[D] owed its emergence to the culture of consumption

23. The text suggests that immigrants now in the U.S. ____.

[A] are resistant to homogenization

[B] exert a great influence on American culture

[C] are hardly a threat to the common culture

[D] constitute the majority of the population

24. Why are Arnold Schwarzenegger and Garth Brooks mentioned in Paragraph 5?

[A] To prove their popularity around the world.

[B] To reveal the public's fear of immigrants.

[C] To give examples of successful immigrants.

[D] To show the powerful influence of American culture.

25. In the author's opinion, the absorption of immigrants into American society is ____.

[A] rewarding [B] successful [C] fruitless [D] harmful

例题分析:考生需要把握住文章的中心的意义不仅仅是做对几道主旨大意题,更重要的作用是为文章其他题目的解答提供一条内在的基准线。因为,几乎所有题目的正确答案都是与这个中心一致的。现以2006年的这篇考题为例进行具体的说明。首先可以确定一下文章的中心句——首段首句"In spite of 'endless talk of difference,' American society is an amazing machine for homogenizing people."通过这句话能够判断出,这篇文章主要围绕美国社会对移民的同化展开,而且通过"amazing"这个词的使用,可以判断出作者对美国社会的移民同化持一种积极肯定态度。该文章5道题目的答案分别是:21题为[C];22题为[A];23题为[C];24题为[D];25题为[B]。当把这5个正确选项:"assimilating";"played a role in the spread of popular culture";"are hardly a threat to the common culture";"To show the powerful influence of American culture";"successful"串到一起的时候,不难发现在这5个选项中,带有的感情色彩的选项和文章的基调是一致的,而且每个选项的内容和文章的中心词"同化"密切相关,都是对文章中心句的展开论述。由此,可以反推,在确定答案的时候,文章的这条中心线是一个重要线索,与中心无关的,以及与中心句体现的情感态度相悖的,基本上不是正确答案。这就是文章中心在解题时的导向作用。

【学习指导】

(1) 如何确定文章主旨要义。

考研阅读文章主旨要义的确定方法相对固定。其具体应对方法如下:

① 关注文章各段首句,尤其是第一段首句。这一点充分体现了西方人的思维习惯对语言的影响,西方人属于直线式思维模式,习惯于开门见山的表达自己的观点,然后通过各种论述方法论证自己的观点。因此通常情况下,文章首段首句就是文章的中心句,各段首句是段落中心句。例如:

Why do so many Americans distrust what they read in their newspapers? The American Society of Newspaper Editors is trying to answer this painful question. The organization is deep into a long self-analysis known as the journalism credibility project...(2001年考题Text 3)

In recent years, railroads have been combining with each other, merging into super systems, causing heightened concerns about monopoly. As recently as 1995, the top four railroads accounted for under 70 percent of the total ton-miles moved by rails. Next year, after a series of mergers is completed, just four railroads will control well over 90 percent of all the freight moved by major rail carriers...(2003年考题Text 3)

Americans no longer expect public figures, whether in speech or in writing, to command the English language with skill and gift. Nor do they aspire to such command themselves. In his latest book, *Doing Our Own Thing: The Degradation of Language and Music and Why We Should, Like, Care*, John McWhorter, a linguist and controversialist of mixed liberal and conservative views, sees the triumph of 1960s counter-culture as responsible for the decline of formal English...(2005年考题Text 4)

② 关注文章首段末句或是第二段首句。这类文章一个显著的特点是,作者先说明一个现象或讲述一个事件;在该段末,作者针对这个现象提出相应的观点。这类文章的首段有一个显著的特点,作

者在说明现象和讲述事件的时候通常使用描述性语言和记叙性语言；而在段末句或是第二段首句出现的文章论点通常是议论性语言。例如：

Wild Bill Donovan would have loved the Internet. The American spymaster who built the Office of Strategic Services in the World War Ⅱ and later laid the roots for the CIA was fascinated with information. Donovan believed in using whatever tools came to hand in the "great game" of espionage — spying as a "profession." These days the Net, which has already re-made such everyday pastimes as buying books and sending mail, is reshaping Donovan's vocation as well...(2003 年考题 Text 1)

When prehistoric man arrived in new parts of the world, something strange happened to the large animals. They suddenly became extinct. Smaller species survived. The large, slow-growing animals were easy game, and were quickly hunted to extinction. Now something similar could be happening in the oceans...(2006 年考题 Text 3)

If you were to examine the birth certificates of every soccer player in 2006's World Cup tournament, you would most likely find a noteworthy quirk: elite soccer players are more likely to have been born in the earlier months of the year than in the late months. If you then examined the European national youth teams that feed the World Cup and professional ranks, you would find this strange phenomenon to be ever more pronounced.

What might account for this strange phenomenon? Here are a few guesses: a) certain astrological signs confer superior soccer skills; b) winter born babies tend to have higher oxygen capacity, which increases soccer stamina; c) soccer-mad parents are more likely to conceive children in springtime, at the annual peak of soccer <u>mania</u>; d) none of the above...(2007 年考题 Text 1)

③ 关注文章首段或其他段落中表示转承、因果的句子。通常情况下，首段出现这样的句子，要么是中心句，要么与中心密切相关；而在文章其他段落出现这样的句子通常为段落主旨句。例如：

A great deal of attention is being paid today to the so-called digital divide —the division of the world into the info (information) rich and the info poor. And that divide does exist today. My wife and I lectured about this looming danger twenty years ago. What was less visible then, however, were the new, positive forces that work against the digital divide. There are reasons to be optimistic...(2001 年考题 Text 2)

Over the past century, all kinds of unfairness and discrimination have been condemned or made illegal. But one insidious form continues to thrive: alphabetism. This, for those as yet unaware of such a disadvantage, refers to discrimination against those whose surnames begin with a letter in the lower half of the alphabet...(2004 年考题 Text 2)

Many things make people think artists are weird. But the weirdest may be this: artists' only job is to explore emotions, and yet they choose to focus on the ones that feel bad...(2006 年考题 Text 4)

(2) 如何运用文章的主旨要义解题。

① 主旨大意题。

第一步：确认题目类型。主旨大意题的提问方式相对固定，基本上有三类："what is the best title for the text?"(文章最恰当的标题是什么)；"what's the passage..."(文章主要讨论了什么)；"The text intends to express the idea that..."(文章打算表达什么想法)。

第二步:判断文章中心句,主旨大意或是文章的中心词。正确答案是对文章中心句的同义替换。

第三步:代回原文,检测答案。主旨大意题的答案如同一个"帽子",尺寸正好符合文章,反之,如果所选标题范围太大或太小,会出现文章支撑不起"帽子"或是"帽子"太小,不能把整篇文章涵盖进去。例如:

It is said that in England death is pressing, in Canada inevitable and in California optional. Small wonder. Americans' life expectancy has nearly doubled over the past century. Failing hips can be replaced, clinical depression controlled, cataracts removed in a 30-minutes surgical procedure. Such advances offer the aging population a quality of life that was unimaginable when I entered medicine 50 years ago. But not even a great health-care system can cure death — and our failure to confront that reality now threatens this greatness of ours. (2003 年考题第 40 题)

40. The text intends to express the idea that ________

[A] medicine will further prolong people's lives.

[B] life beyond a certain limit is not worth living.

[C] death should be accepted as a fact of life.

[D] excessive demands increase the cost of health care.

例题分析:首先,透过题目的提问方式,可以确定这是一道主旨大意题;然后,通读文章首段,发现有一个转折句"But not even a great health-care system can cure death — and our failure to confront that reality now threatens this greatness of ours."(但是再伟大的医疗体系也不能治愈死亡,我们未能认识到这个现实正威胁着我们在医疗方面的伟大成就。)这句话暗含的意思是我们需要正确面对死亡。选项[C]正好是对这句话的同义替换。选项[A]只在第一段有相关表达;选项[B]内容只在第三段和第四段出现;而选项[D]未在原文出现,属于无中生有。

② 宏观指导其他类型题目的解答。

确定文章的主旨大意,也可以辅助解答其他类型的题目。第一,其他题目的正确答案必须和文章中心相关,同时这些答案的感情基调必须和文章中心体现的感情基调一致;第二,文章主旨大意和它所带有的感情基调是检验题目解答是否正确的有效手段。例如:

When it comes to the slowing economy, Ellen Spero isn't biting her nails just yet. But the 47-year-old manicurist isn't cutting, filing or polishing as many nails as she'd like to, either. Most of her clients spend $12 to $50 weekly, but last month two longtime customers suddenly stopped showing up. Spero blames the softening economy. "I'm a good economic indicator," she says. "I provide a service that people can do without when they're concerned about saving some dollars." So Spero is downscaling, shopping at middle-brow Dillard's department store near her suburban Cleveland home, instead of Neiman Marcus. "I don't know if other clients are going to abandon me, too." she says.

Even before Alan Greenspan's admission that America's red-hot economy is cooling, lots of working folks had already seen signs of the slowdown themselves. From car dealerships to Gap outlets, sales have been lagging for months as shoppers temper their spending. For retailers, who last year took in 24 percent of their revenue between Thanksgiving and Christmas, the cautious approach is coming at a crucial time. Already, experts say, holiday sales are off 7 percent from last year's pace. But don't sound any alarms just yet. Consumers seem only mildly concerned, not panicked, and many say they remain optimistic about the economy's long-term prospects, even as they do some modest belt-tightening...(2004年考题第31题至第32题)

31. By "Ellen Spero isn't biting her nails just yet" (Paragraph 1), the author means ______.

[A] Spero can hardly maintain her business

[B] Spero is too much engaged in her work

[C] Spero has grown out of her bad habit

[D] Spero is not in a desperate situation

32. How do the public feel about the current economic situation?

[A] Optimistic. [B] Confused. [C] Carefree. [D] Panicked.

例题分析：

对于31题，在通读全文之后，可以判断这篇文章的中心是"美国经济虽然出现了衰退，但是民众对经济的前景还是感到乐观"。分析四个选项，[B]、[C]选项属于就事论事，和文章谈论的经济话题无关；[A]、[D]选项中，[D]选项表达了和文章中心一样的感情色彩，而[A]选项的基调和文章中心相反。所以我们确定答案为[D]。

对于32题，在确定文章中心基调之后，该题的三个干扰选项基本上没有任何干扰性，很轻易地确定答案[A]。解题之后，把两个选项串在一起，"Spero is not in a desperate situation"和"Optimistic"的感情基调一致，都是乐观的基调。

2. 考查目标二：理解文中的具体信息

【理论解释】

阅读理解部分的试题中，大多数是针对段落的细节设计的，其目的是为了测试考生对组成段落的主体部分的理解。在每年的考试中，细节题的数量是最多的，大约占50%，其中涉及对文章中复杂句，以及列举、例证、引用、转折、因果关系等的处理，因此做好这类题至关重要。

另外，细节题的测试在另一方面也可以考查考生对段落结构的理解程度。哪些是辅助论点，哪些是主要脉络？只有对这些细节有一定的了解，才能更深入地领会文章。文章的细节并不是孤立的，它总要与其他事实前后呼应。一般来说，作者总会把同等性质的事实放在一起，并借助不同的衔接手段进行组合，从而达到说服读者或阐明观点的目的。其提问方式不外乎有以下几种：

The author provides following examples except...

According to the author, all of the following are true except (that)...

Which is among the best possible ways to...

Which of the following would NOT be an example...

Which of the following is the LEAST likely...

对于细节题，要从词义与语法(句法)着手。从这个角度来说，此类考题又可被细划分以下几个次范畴：

(1)因果标志语。

表因果关系的标志语可具体分为：

① 原因标志语。

because of, since, for, as, now that, seeing that, owing to, caused by, the main reason for...is

② 结果标志语。

hence, thus, so, therefore, consequently, as a consequence, accordingly, for that reason

(2) 结论标志语。

in general, generally speaking, in short, in a word, to be brief in all, in simple words

(3) 转折与对比标志语。

but, however, nevertheless, otherwise, dissimilarly, unlike, on the contrary, in contrast, in opposition to, on the opposite side

(4) 比较类型标记语。

similarly, likewise, in similar fashion, in similar way, in the same matter, just as

(5) 列举标志语。

one... another... still another, first... second... third

(6) 举例标志语。

for example, as an example, as an instance, take... as an example, let me cite... as a proof

【举例说明】

Specialization can be seen as a response to the problem of an increasing accumulation of scientific knowledge. By splitting up the subject matter into smaller units, one man could continue to handle the information and use it as the basis for further research. But specialization was only one of a series of related developments in science affecting the process of communication. Another was the growing professionalisation of scientific activity. (2001 年考题第 24 题)

24. The direct reason for specialization is ________.

[A] the development in communication

[B] the growth of professionalisation

[C] the expansion of scientific knowledge

[D] the splitting up of academic societies

例题分析:该题考查的是实行专业化的直接因素是什么,根据本文第一句即可找到答案,[C]选项为正确选项,其中"as a response to"表示的是因果关系。

类似的解题思路还可应用到以下两篇文章中:

What accounts for the great outburst of major inventions in early America—breakthroughs such as the telegraph, the steamboat and the weaving machine?

Among the many shaping factors, I would single out the country's excellent elementary schools; a labor force that welcomed the new technology; the practice of giving premiums to inventors; and above all the American genius for nonverbal, "spatial" thinking about things technological. (1996 年考题第 23 题)

23. According to the author, the great outburst of major inventions in early America was in a large part due to ________.

[A] elementary schools　　[B] enthusiastic workers

[C] the attractive premium system　　[D] a special way of thinking

The researchers studied the behaviour of female brown capuchin monkeys. They look cute. They are good-natured, cooperative creatures, and they share their food readily. Above all, like their female human counterparts, they tend to pay much closer attention to the value of "goods and services" than males. (2005 年考题第 23 题)

23. Female capuchin monkeys were chosen for the research most probably because they

are ________.

[A] more inclined to weigh what they get

[B] attentive to researchers' instructions

[C] nice in both appearance and temperament

[D] more generous than their male companions

例题分析:这两道题共同的特点就是题目中都有一个表示程度的限定词。第一道题中的限定词是"in a large part",第二道题中的限定词是"most probably"。这两个词语的出现本身就有一个暗示,说明选项中应该有不止一个原因,但是题目要求回答出其中最重要的一个因素。通过1996年考题第23题,可以发现定位句"I would single out the country's excellent elementary schools;a labor force that welcomed the new technology;the practice of giving premiums to inventors;and above all the American genius for nonverbal,'spatial' thinking about things technological"中含有四个并列成分,分别是"excellent elementary schools","a labor force","the practice of giving premiums to inventors"和"the American genius for nonverbal,'spatial' thinking about things technological"。上述四个内容在选项中都有出现,很多考生会因为先入为主的思维习惯选择[A]。但题干中的限定信息是要求找其中影响最大的一个因素,这就要比照四个因素哪个影响最大。原文中的第四点前出现了"above all",这个短语表示"最重要的是"。所以,此题应该选择[D]。

2005年考题第23题中也出现了同样的情况,题干中出现"most",选项中出现了列举。"They look cute. They are good-natured,cooperative creatures,and they share their food tardily. Above all,like their female human counterparts,they tend to pay much closer attention to the value of 'goods and services' than males".这些列举也分别被设计成了干扰项。但是其中强调的是"above all"后面的这个因素"like their female human counterparts,they tend to pay much closer attention to the value of 'goods and services' than males"。所以此题答案为[A]。

从上面的分析可以看出,阅读理解并不是简单的读懂文章就可以把题答对,还要能够审清题目,理解题目的要求。

【学习指导】

针对细节题,考生要注意分析句子和句子之间的关系,是因果、递进、转折关系,还是其他什么关系?尤其要注意文章的第一句和最后一句,以及每段的第一句和最后一句与其他句子的关系,要体会每句话在文章中的作用。在阅读过程中,要培养自己对文章主要讨论对象、关键词、作者和专家的观点,以及语气的把握。特别注意作者和专家的观点,专家和专家之间的观点是否相同或相反或互补,以及作者和专家的语气是赞成还是反对,是关注还是乐观等。如果是历年考题,还要仔细分析考点和正确、干扰选项的规律、特征。在此过程中,可把文章尽可能地多读几遍,甚至翻译一下,提高对文章中单词、短语、句型等的反应速度,阅读速度自然也就提高了。

此外,阅读的步骤也十分重要。许多考生拿到文章之后从头读起,读完再去一个一个选答案。这种方法十分传统,叫整体阅读法。其优点是可以有一种全局感或整体感。缺点是文章太长,读后细节记不住,再去找答案又费劲又容易出错,许多细节都混淆在一起了,得分经常不高。建议考生使用查找阅读法:读完第一段就做第一题。然后看第二个问题问的什么,带着这个问题去看第二段,然后是第三段、第四段,以此类推。(注意,有一种考题可能此方法不太适用,那就是:主旨性问题。)查找式阅读法虽然把文章看得支离破碎,但得分往往很高,因为刚看一段就去做一道题,对细节会把握得很准。

3. 考查目标三:理解文中概念性含义

【理论解释】

概念性含义主要指考生应把握词汇使用的准确性、形象性、多样性和感情色彩及语气角度,掌握复合词的使用,总结各类重要搭配,对各类重要词汇进行扩展,正确识别代词与抽象名词的指代,并记忆和运用可以在作文中使用的词汇。

(1) 准确性。英语初学者在词汇的使用上一般太宽太泛,欠缺准确性。比如想到走,只会用"walk"。其实表示"走"的词汇有很多,如"stroll"(漫步,闲逛);"stagger"(摇晃地走)。

(2) 形象性。母语是英语的人用词非常形象化,而考生一般用词就比较刻板。比如"上升",很多人只会用"increase",其实用"climb"这个简单的词就很形象。再如下文:

Diana's sudden death triggered a global outpouring of grief and boosted an already thriving "Diana Industry". Described in an editorial in the Daily Mirror tabloid as the "grief industry", interest in Diana has also spawned hundreds of "exclusive" biographies by people who claim to have been close to her.

trigger *n* (枪的)扳机; *v* 引发,引起,触发

spawn *n* (鱼等的)卵; *v* 产卵,催生,造成,使产生

(3) 多样性。词汇的多样性也是考查一个语言学习者词汇掌握是否丰富的重要方面。比如一篇关于汽车的文章,可以使用"car"、"motorcar"、"automobile"、"auto"、"vehicle"等词进行替换,如果都掌握了,就可以很容易判断文章的主题。还有一篇关于老年人的写作,一般人只会用"old people",如果使用了"the old"、"the elderly"、"the aged"、"the elderly population"、"senior citizens",显得就技高一筹。再如阅读理解中原文用"legislator",答案用"lawmaker"进行替换。这些例子都说明了词汇的多样性的重要。

(4) 复合词。现代英语中复合词的使用非常广泛,且很多词在字典上都不一定能查到,所以平时要注意多总结。比如"-free"这个词表示"没有,免除",可以组成很多复合词,"flood-free"为"没有洪水的","fat-free"为"没有脂肪的"。

【举例说明】

针对概念性含义题型,应把握以下两点:

第一,应根据出题顺序和行文顺序的一致性原则找到原文的大致位置,一般能定位到具体的段落,如第 N 段。第二,再根据题干关键词和(或)选项中的关键词找出在文中的对应句子,比如第 N 段第 N 句。这里的关键词定位,具体来说有 3 种情况:只要根据题干关键词或信息就可以在原文找到对应句子;只要根据每个选项的关键词或信息在原文中找到与之一一对应的句子;既要根据题干关键词或者信息定位,又要根据每个选项信息才能找到对应句子。

什么是"关键词"呢?关键词就是题干或者选项中的某个词或词组,它具有和原文中某个词或词组意思一致、相近或相反的特征,是可以帮助考生回到原文找到命题人隐藏答案的词或词组(起的是一个向导的作用)。这个关键词的寻找非常有价值,是考生能否找对答案的关键所在。例如:

Hunting for a job late last year, lawyer Gant Redmon stumbled across CareerBuilder, a job database on the Internet. He searched it with no success but was attracted by the site's "personal search agent". It's an interactive feature that lets visitors key in job criteria such as location, title, and salary, then E-mails them when a matching position is posted in the database. Redmon chose the keywords *legal*, *intellectual property*, *and Washington*, *D. C.* Three weeks later, he got his first notification of an opening. "I struck gold," says Redmon, who E-mailed his resume to the employer and won a position as in-house counsel for a company.

With thousands of career-related sites on the Internet, finding promising openings can be time-consuming and inefficient. Search agents reduce the need for repeated visits to the databases. But although a search agent worked for Redmon, career experts see drawbacks. Narrowing your criteria, for example, may work against you: "Every time you answer a question you eliminate a possibility." says one expert.

For any job search, you should start with a narrow concept — what you think you want to do — then broaden it. "None of these programs do that," says another expert. "There's no career counseling implicit in all of this." Instead, the best strategy is to use the agent as a kind of tip service to keep abreast of jobs in a particular database; when you get E-mail, consider it a reminder to check the database again. "I would not rely on agents for finding everything that is added to a database that might interest me," says the author of a job-searching guide.

Some sites design their agents to tempt job hunters to return. When CareerSite's agent sends out messages to those who have signed up for its service, for example, it includes only three potential jobs — those it considers the best matches. There may be more matches in the database; job hunters will have to visit the site again to find them — and they do. "On the day after we send our messages, we see a sharp increase in our traffic," says Seth Peets, vice president of marketing for CareerSite.

Even those who aren't hunting for jobs may find search agents worthwhile. Some use them to keep a close watch on the demand for their line of work or gather information on compensation to arm themselves when negotiating for a raise. Although happily employed, Redmon maintains his agent at CareerBuilder. "You always keep your eyes open," he says. Working with a personal search agent means having another set of eyes looking out for you.（2004 年考题第 21 题）

21. How did Redmon find his job?

[A] By searching openings in a job database.

[B] By posting a matching position in a database.

[C] By using a special service of a database.

[D] By E-mailing his resume to a database.

例题分析：考生既要根据题干关键词或者信息定位，又要根据每个选项信息才能找到对应句子。"Redmon 是怎么找到工作的？"利用行文顺序定位法则，本题是文章后的第一题，所以应该在文章靠前的段落寻找对应句子。可以定位在前一二段。然后，定位关键词。此题同时需要"题干和选项"的关键词定位。

题干的关键词是"find job"，与之对应的可以在第一段句首找到它的同义词"Hunting for a job"。这样一来，就知道应该在"Hunting for a job"的前后找对应句子了。再看各选项的对应句子，选项[A]的关键词是"job database"，根据它可以对应的句子是"He searched it（指代 job database）with no success..."由此可知，Redmon 并没有通过"a job database"取得成功（找到工作），所以错在"相互矛盾"；选项[B]的关键词是"posting a matching position"，对应的句子是"when a matching position is posted in the database"，可知"matching position"是被"别人"寄到资料库来的，不是 Redmon，所以[B]错在"张冠李戴"了；选项[D]的关键词是"E-mailing his resume"对应的

句子是"who(Redmon) E-mailed his resume to the employer..."，可知 Redmon 把简历寄给了雇主，不是资料库(a database)，所以[D]也错在"张冠李戴"；那么选项[C]为什么就是正确的呢？

先来分析一下第一段句子间的关系：第一段共六句话，其中第三句是解释第二句的"personal search agent"。第二句提到他被这个网址上的"个人搜索代理"所吸引。第三句是解释说明"personal search agent"的特征的。文章中对应的说明 Redmon 找到工作的句子是第五句"Three weeks later, he got his first notification of an opening"。那他又是怎么找到工作的呢？在这里就是一个很明显的例子。把这些"插入语句"(第三句和第四句)删掉不看，整个句群就变成了："He searched it with no success but was attracted by the site's 'personal search agent'. Three weeks later, he got his first notification of an opening."这样答案就非常明了了：他是通过"personal search agent"找到工作的，而选项[C]用"a special service of a database"替代了原文中的"personal search agent"，所以是正确答案。

【学习指导】

阅读的每道概念性含义题，其实都有原文出处。针对考点，对应题目和选项可以判断出关键词，在原文中定位考题源。首先，可以关注阿拉伯数字，阿拉伯数字的范围涉及的数据、年份、时间等；其次，可以关注一些特定名词，这些名词大都含有大写字母，比较好找，如人名、地名等；最后，可以用一些不常用的生僻单词予以定位。考生通过这样的方法可以快速找到出题点，然后结合出题点的上下文以及段落主题句，针对出题含义进行分析答题，这就节省了通读时在非有效信息上所耗费的时间。

此外，在概念性含义题型中，还可利用复现关系来解题。复现，是保证文章前后衔接而经常使用的一种写作手段，即作者在文章上下文不同的位置对同一个概念进行重复描述，从而使得同样的意思在文章不同的地方重复出现。复现关系，主要是指同义复现、近义复现、反义复现、平行结构复现、搭配复现等。

4. 考查目标四：进行有关的判断、推理和引申

【理论解释】

判断、推理和引申题型用来考查考生在现实生活中的阅读技能(快速、准确推导出所需信息的能力)，要求考生能够看懂题目提供的四个选项并在文中检索相关信息。这种题目比较耗费时间，在紧张的考试中，容易给考生带来心理压力，因此，面对此类题型时，考生首先要调整心理状态，细致冷静地返回到文章中，结合语境，运用逻辑思维去推导答案。这里请考生一定要记住：西方人习惯用从个别到一般的演绎思维模式，不同于中国人的从一般到个别的归纳思维方式。

面对判断原则的题目，考生必须先读懂题目所给的四个选项，记住它们的意思，返回原文去扫描，搜寻信息点，与题目不相关的句子、语段要很快掠过，相关信息语言区域则要求考生必须细致地对照原文中的信息，推导出相关结论。

引申即为词汇的内涵，与外延(字面意义)相对，是需要结合上下文(语境)来理解说话人或作者的真实想法。例如，当你对你的朋友说："咱们周末一起去吃饭吧！"而你的朋友回答道："我最近有考试。"那么在正常情况下，你就知道对方没时间和你度周末。可见语境是人们理解话语(discourse)的试金石。此外，引申也常常用隐喻的方式来表达。

【举例说明】

判断、推理和引申原则有以下两种题型：

(1)一正三误。要求考生找出四个选项中唯一正确的一个，检验答案时要注意这种题型最常采用的三种命题方式是：正话反说、反话正说和关键词替换。例如：

No company likes to be told it is contributing to the moral decline of nation. Is this what you intended to accomplish with your careers? Senator Robert Dole asked Time Warner executives last week. "You have sold your souls, but must you corrupt our nation and threaten our children as well?" At Time Warner, however, such questions are simply the latest manifestation of the soul-searching that has involved the company ever since the company was born in 1990. It's a self-examination that has, at various times, involved issues of responsibility, creative freedom and the corporate bottom line.

At the core of this debate is chairman Gerald Levin, 56, who took over for the late Steve Ross in 1992. On the financial front, Levin is under pressure to raise the stock price and reduce the company's mountainous debt, which will increase to $17.3 billion after two new cable deals close. He has promised to sell off some of the property and restructure the company, but investors are waiting impatiently.

The flap over rap is not making life any easier for him. Levin has consistently defended the company's rap music on the grounds of expression. In 1992, when Time Warner was under fire for releasing Ice-T's violent rap song *Cop Killer*, Levin described rap as a lawful expression of street culture, which deserves an outlet. "The test of any democratic society," he wrote in a *Wall Street Journal* column, "lies not in how well it can control expression but in whether it gives freedom of thought and expression the widest possible latitude, however disputable or irritating the results may sometimes be. We won't retreat in the face of any threats."

Levin would not comment on the debate last week, but there were signs that the chairman was backing off his hard-line stand, at least to some extent. During the discussion of rock singing verses at last month's stockholders' meeting, Levin asserted that "music is not the cause of society's ills" and even cited his son, a teacher in the Bronx, New York, who uses rap to communicate with students. But he talked as well about the "balanced struggle" between creative freedom and social responsibility, and he announced that the company would launch a drive to develop standards for distribution and labeling of potentially objectionable music.

The 15-member Time Warner board is generally supportive of Levin and his corporate strategy. But insiders say several of them have shown their concerns in this matter. "Some of us have known for many, many years that the freedoms under the First Amendment are not totally unlimited," says Luce. "I think it is perhaps the case that some people associated with the company have only recently come to realize this."(1997年考题第24题)

24. According to the passage, which of the following is TRUE?

[A] Luce is a spokesman of Time Warner.

[B] Gerald Levin is liable to compromise.

[C] Time Warner is united as one in the face of the debate.

[D] Steve Ross is no longer alive.

例题分析:一个标准的三误一正的推理引申题。答案为选项[D]。

(2)三正一误结构。要求考生判断哪一个选项与文章不符。检验答案时有两种方式:一是正确选项所给的信息在文中根本没有提到过,二是正确选项所给信息与文中其他内容相互冲突。例如:

With the start of BBC World Service Television, millions of viewers in Asia and America can now watch the Corporation's news coverage, as well as listening to it.

And of course in Britain listeners and viewers can tune in to two BBC television channels, five BBC national radio services and dozens of local radio stations. They are brought sport, comedy, drama, music, news and current affairs, education, religion, parliamentary coverage, children's programmes and films for an annual license fee of ₤83 per household.

It is a remarkable record, stretching back over 70 years—yet the BBC's future is now in doubt. The Corporation will survive as a publicly-funded broadcasting organization, at least for the time being, but its role, its size and its programmes are now the subject of a nation-wide debate in Britain.

The debate was launched by the Government, which invited anyone with an opinion of the BBC—including ordinary listeners and viewers—to say what was good or bad about the Corporation, and even whether they thought it was worth keeping. The reason for its inquiry is that the BBC's royal charter runs out in 1996 and it must decide whether to keep the organization as it is, or to make changes.

Defenders of the Corporation—of whom there are many—are fond of quoting the American slogan "If it ain't broke, don't fix it." The BBC "ain't broke", they say, by which they mean it is not broken (as distinct from the word 'broke', meaning having no money), so why bother to change it?

Yet the BBC will have to change, because the broadcasting world around it is changing. The commercial TV channels—ITV and Channel 4—were required by the Thatcher Government's Broadcasting Act to become more commercial, competing with each other for advertisers, and cutting costs and jobs. But it is the arrival of new satellite channels—funded partly by advertising and partly by viewers' subscriptions—which will bring about the biggest changes in the long term. (1996 年考题第 16 题)

16. In the passage, which of the following about the BBC is NOT mentioned as the key issue?

[A] Extension of its TV service to Far East.

[B] Programmes as the subject of a nation-wide debate.

[C] Potentials for further international co-operations.

[D] Its existence as a broadcasting organization.

例题分析:本题是三正一误结构,答案为选项[C]。

【学习指导】

从广义上讲,几乎所有的考题都是推理题,考题不会从字面意思告诉考生问题的答案,考研的试题追求的是对文章的深层理解及推理。所以,从这个意义上说,全部题目都属于该范畴。

从狭义上讲,该类题型指题干上有三个典型词:"infer","imply"和"conclusion"。例如:"What can you infer from the story?"或"What is the implied meaning of this sentence?""We can draw the conclusion from the passage that..."推理性问题在原文中没有现成的答案。答案是推想出来的,但不能凭空想象,必须以原文中某句话或某个词语为依据去合理推测,这样才能找到合适的答案。

逻辑推理关系解题方法及步骤如下:

(1)解题方法。

① 要做好推理判断题,要求考生能够充分理解阅读文章、分析语篇特征、寻找解题依据。考生应该在领会全文的基础上作出正确的推理和判断。

② 要理解文章的字面意思,弄清上下文的整体逻辑。在阅读过程中一定要留意那些似乎话中有话的间接表达句,它们往往采用说半句、打比喻、反过来讲的方式,留有让考生自己作结论或推理的余地。同时,还要留意含义深刻或结构复杂的句子。对作者表达的意思不能一下看透的内容,往往是命题点所在。

③ 要精读题干,充分了解题目要求考生进行推理和判断的内容,以免白费力气。

④ 仔细挖掘作者隐藏在文章中的一些重要含义,切勿用自己的主观判断来代替文章内容。

(2)解题步骤。

第一步:通读全文,尤其是首末段,迅速得知文章的主旨大意。

第二步:通读选项,在每个选项下边用笔标记该选项的大致中文意思,以做到心中有数,至少应该知道各选项的意思范围,以便在很短的时间里找到想找的选项。

第三步:迅速找到定位段落,重点关注定位段落的段落中心句和转折等逻辑关系后的内容。因为,推理引申题的答案一般是对文章或是段落中心句的同义替换。

第四步:在时间允许的情况下,明确该题已排除的选项的错误之处,进而确定所选答案是否正确。因为,考研阅读理解部分测试要求选的是最佳答案,考生最好是在全面衡量四个选项之后,再确定答案。

5. 考查目标五:根据上下文推测生词含义

【理论解释】

在英语学习中,学习者会遇到许多生词。这时,许多学习者会立即翻阅字典,查找词义。其实,这种做法是不科学的。这不但费时、费力,而且会影响阅读速度。事实上,阅读材料中的每个词与它前后的词语或句子甚至段落,有着互相制约的关系。考生可以利用语境(各种已知信息)推测、判断某些生词的词义。

【举例说明】

综上所述,利用各种已知信息推测、判断词义是一项重要的阅读技巧。在实践中,可以灵活运用,综合运用上面提到的几种猜测技巧,排除生词障碍,顺利理解文章的思想内容,以提高阅读速度。

考生应重点避免以下两种情况:第一,考生往往会随便猜一个选项,导致错误率很高;第二,落入命题专家的陷阱,不知不觉地丢分,主要原因是考生并没有掌握阅读词汇题的基本命题原则。在阅读部分的词汇题要考的并不是考生认不认识题中所考的单词,要考的是考生阅读中的推断能力。也就是说,题中所考单词的词义必定能根据上下文推断出来。所以,考生在遇到阅读中的词汇题时,一定要冷静,去上下文中细找,推断出词义后,可将词义代入原文中看是否通畅。例如:

Railroads justify rate discrimination against captive shippers on the grounds that in the long run it reduces everyone's cost. If railroads charged all customers the same average rate, they argue, shippers who have the option of switching to trucks or other forms of transportation would do so, leaving remaining customers to shoulder the cost of keeping up the line. It's a theory to which many economists subscribe, but in practice it often leaves railroads in the position of determining which companies will flourish and which will fail. "Do we really want railroads to be the arbiters of who wins and who loses in the marketplace?" asks Martin Bercovici, a Washington lawyer who frequently represents shippers. (2003年考题第34题)

34. The word "arbiters" most probably refers to those ________.

[A] who work as coordinators　　[B] who function as judges

[C] who supervise transactions　　[D] who determine the price

例题分析:该题的解题关键在于,是否知道“arbiters”后的介宾短语“of who wins and who loses in the marketplace”就是对该词的最准确定义。依据该介宾短语,不难得出“arbiters”是决定谁输谁赢的人,四个选项中只有选项[B]和这个意思最为接近。

For any job search, you should start with a narrow concept—what you think you want to do—then broaden it. “None of these programs do that,” says another expert. “There's no career counseling implicit in all of this.” Instead, the best strategy is to use the agent as a kind of <u>tip service</u> to keep abreast of jobs in a particular database; when you get E-mail, consider it a reminder to check the database again. “I would not rely on agents for finding everything that is added to a database that might interest me,” says the author of a job-searching guide. (2004 年考题第 23 题)

23. The expression “tip service” most probably means ________.

[A] advisory [B] compensation [C] interaction [D] reminder

例题分析:该题的解题关键在于充分利用分号。分号前面的短语“use the agent as a kind of tip service”和分号后的“consider it a reminder”属于并列关系,“it”和“the agent”都是指的文章中所说的搜索代理,自然就能找到“tip service”的同义词为“reminder”。所以该题答案为选项[D]。

【学习指导】

针对推测生词含义题型,可以从以下两个方面进行分析:

(1)利用内在逻辑关系。运用语言知识分析和判断相关信息之间存在的逻辑关系,然后根据逻辑关系推断生词词义或大致义域。

① 根据对比关系猜测词义。如果在一个句子或段落中,有对两个事物或现象进行对比性的描述,那么考生可以根据生词或难词的反义词猜测其词义。

例如:“Andrew is one of the most supercilious men I know. His brother, in contrast, is quite humble and modest.”句中“supercilious”对许多人来说可能是个生词,但是句中短语“in contrast”(相对照的,相对比的)可以提示“supercilious”和后面词组“humble and modest”(谦卑又谦虚)是对比关系。分析出这种关系后,便能猜出“supercilious”意为“目空一切的,傲慢的”。

表示对比关系的词汇和短语主要是 unlike, not, but, however, despite, in spite of, in contrast 和 while 引导的并列句等。例如:“A good supervisor can recognize instantly the adept workers from the unskilled ones.”该句中并未出现上面提到的表示对比关系的词或短语,但是通过上下文可以判断出句子前后是对比关系,即把熟练工人与非熟练工人区分开。这时也能够推断出生词“adept”的词义为“熟练的”。

② 根据比较关系猜测词义。同对比关系相反,比较关系表示意义上的相似关系。

例如:“Green loves to talk, and his brothers are similarly loquacious.”该句中副词“similarly”表明短语“loves to talk”与生词“loquacious”之间的比较关系。由此可以推断出“loquacious”词义为“健谈的”。表示比较关系的词和短语主要是 similarly, like, just as, also 等。

③ 根据因果关系猜测词义。在句子或段落中,若两个事物、现象之间构成因果关系,便可以根据这种逻辑关系推知生词词义。

例如:“Tom is considered an autocratic administrator because he makes decisions without seeking the opinions of others.”根据原因状语从句的内容,可以推断出生词“autocratic”为“独断专行的”。

又如:“There were so many demonstrators in the Red Square that he had to elbow his way through the crowd."此句为结果状语从句,根据从句的描书"许多示威者",便可推知"elbow"的词意为"挤,挤过"。

④ 根据同义词的替代关系猜测词义。在句子或段落中,可以利用熟悉的词语,根据语言环境推断生词词义。

例如:"Although he often had the opportunity, Mr. Tritt was never able to steal money from a customer. This would have endangered his position at the bank, and he did not want to jeopardize his future."句中作者为避免重复使用"endanger"一词,用其同义词"jeopardize"来替代它,由此推知其词义为"使……陷入危险,危及、危害"。

又如:"Doctors believe that smoking cigarettes is detrimental to your health. They also regard drinking as harmful."句中"detrimental"是个生词,但判断出"harmful"替代"detrimental"后,不难推断出其词义为"不利的,有害的"。

(2)外部相关因素。外部相关因素是指篇章(句子或段落)以外的其他知识。有时仅靠分析篇章内在逻辑关系无法猜出词义。这时,就需要运用生活经验和普通常识确定词义。

例如:"Husband:It's really cold out tonight. Wife: Sure it is. My hands are practically numb. How about lighting the furnace?"根据生活经验,天气寒冷时,手肯定是"冻僵的,冻得麻木的"。

又如:"The snake slithered through the grass."根据有关蛇的生活习性方面的知识,可以推断出"slither"词义为"爬行"。

在猜测词义过程中,除了使用上面提到的一些技巧,还可以依靠构词方面的知识,从生词本身猜测词义。

此外利用词缀亦不失为一种有效的手段。

① 根据前缀猜测词义。

例如:"He fell into a ditch and lay there, semiconscious, for a few minutes."根据词根"conscious"(清醒的,有意识的),结合前缀"semi"(半,部分的,不完全的),便可猜出"semiconscious"词义为"半清醒的,半昏迷的"。

又如:"I'm illiterate about such things."词根"literate"意为"有文化修养的,通晓的",前缀"il"表示否定,因此"illiterate"指"一窍不通,不知道的"。

② 根据后缀猜测词义。

例如:"Insecticide is applied where it is needed."后缀"cide"表示"杀者,杀灭剂",结合大家熟悉的词根"insect"(昆虫),不难猜出"insecticide"意为"杀虫剂"。

又如:"Then the vapor may change into droplets."后缀"let"表示"小的",词根"drop"指"滴,滴状物"。将两个意思结合起来,便可推断出"droplet"词义"小滴,微滴"。

③ 根据复合词的各部分猜测词义。

例如:"Growing economic problems were highlighted by a slowdown in oil output.""highlight"或许是一个生词,但是分析该词结构后,就能推测出其含义。它是由"high"(高的,强的)和"light"(光线)两部分组成,合在一起便是"以强光照射,使突出"的意思。

又如:"Bullfight is very popular in Spain.""Bull"(公牛)和"fight"(打,搏斗)结合在一起,指一种在西班牙颇为流行的体育运动——斗牛。

考生可参考本书词汇部分提供的词根词缀进行复习,以提高利用词根词缀猜测生词的能力。

6. 考查目标六:理解文章的总体结构及上下文之间的关系,以及区分论点和论据

【理论解释】

该目标旨在考查考生对文章逻辑关系的把握能力,考查考生对文章宏观的把握能力。这两种能力具体到题型中,会经常考到文章中某一句话,某一部分,某个例子的内涵。因此对大部分考生来说,在阅读文章的时候要注意分析句子和句子之间的关系。理清每句话之间的逻辑关系,把握住文章的总体结构之后,对考生阅读速度的提高也是意义非常重大的。

【举例说明】

It is said that in England death is pressing, in Canada inevitable and in California optional. Small wonder. Americans' life expectancy has nearly doubled over the past century. Failing hips can be replaced, clinical depression controlled, cataracts removed in a 30-minute surgical procedure. Such advances offer the aging population a quality of life that was unimaginable when I entered medicine 50 years ago. But not even a great health-care system can cure death—and our failure to confront that reality now threatens this greatness of ours. (2003 年考题第 36 题)

36. What is implied in the first sentence?

[A] Americans are better prepared for death than other people.

[B] Americans enjoy a higher life quality than ever before.

[C] Americans are overconfident of their medical technology.

[D] Americans take a vain pride in their long life expectancy.

例题分析:议论文和说明文都强调逻辑的严谨性,而转折和对比常常可以用来测试考生在这一方面的阅读理解能力。所以,考生要对文中的转折和对比关系高度重视,只要看到标明转折或对比的关系词,如“but”和“however”等,就应当立即在原文上进行标记。一般说来,转折后的内容多与上文表达的意思相反,而对比往往是强调其中的一方。这道题目也是同样的情况,题干问的是第一句话的含义,解题的重点在于把握住该段的转折之后的内容,转折之后讨论的是“再伟大的医疗技术也治愈不了死亡”。很明显,这个转折是对前文“美国人对自己医疗技术的过度自信”的不认同,该题答案确定为[C]。

Now the tide appears to be turning. As personal injury claims continue as before, some courts are beginning to side with defendants, especially in cases where a warning label probably wouldn't have changed anything. In May, Julie Nimmons, president of Schutt Sports in Illinois, successfully fought a lawsuit involving a football player who was paralyzed in a game while wearing a Schutt helmet. "We're really sorry he has become paralyzed, but helmets aren't designed to prevent those kinds of injuries," says Nimmons. The jury agreed that the nature of the game, not the helmet, was the reason for the athlete's injury. At the same time, the American Law Institute—a group of judges, lawyers, and academics whose recommendations carry substantial weight—issued new guidelines for tort law stating that companies need not warn customers of obvious dangers or bombard them with a lengthy list of possible ones. "Important information can get buried in a sea of trivialities," says a law professor at Cornell Law School who helped draft the new guidelines. If the moderate end of the legal community has its way, the information on products might actually be provided for the benefit of customers and not as protection against legal liability. (1999 年考题第 13 题)

13. The case of Schutt helmet demonstrated that ________.

[A] some injury claims were no longer supported by law

[B] helmets were not designed to prevent injuries

[C] product labels would eventually be discarded

[D] some sports games might lose popularity with athletes

例题分析:让事实说话往往是最有效的论证方式之一。命题专家在设置题目时往往也会针对文中的事例设问,考查考生对局部结构的理解。例证题1994年第一次出现在考研试卷上,共两道题,占4分。但在1995年至1998年间,没有出现过一道例证题,1999年再次出现,一样是两道题,占4分。之后,几乎每年的考题都有一至两道例证题。这就说明了考研命题的一大特点,命题规则总是不断重复的。考生们在应用例证原则解题时,还应注意常用的两种例证方式:一是先提出观点,后举例说明;二是先列举事例再作出结论。考生应当学会举一反三,不要被各种原则的变化形式所迷惑。具体到该题,该段文章的首句"Now the tide appears to be turning."是段落中心句,第二句"As personal injury claims continue as before, some courts are beginning to side with defendants, especially in cases where a warning label probably wouldn't have changed anything."是对第一句的具体阐释。所以,题目问"The case of Schutt helmet"的例子是为了说明什么,自然是为了论证文章的中心句。而选项[A]正好是文章该段落中心句的同义替换。

【学习指导】

第一,了解文章的总体结构及上下文之间的关系,以及区分论点和论据,应理清"文章思路",要求考生首先应对文章总体的思路和结构有一个大概的了解,先不要急于去读题目,而是应当将文章从头到尾看一遍,弄清楚文章的中心意思,这一遍阅读的目的并不是要立即找到答题所需要的信息点。在阅读的时候还要有主次之分,文章的第一段是文章的灵魂和核心,也应当是第一遍阅读的重点所在。考生要尽量将第一段的每一句话都理解透彻,因为掌握了第一段,就已经基本掌握了整篇文章的内容。至于其他段落可以加快速度,看得懂就看,看不懂就暂时跳过去,在不懂的地方做出记号,留待以后解决。

阅读理解的文章全部是议论文或说明文,这就决定了这些文章本身的叙述和展开方式,弄清楚这些文章的结构,即区分了论点和论据,自然在选择答案时就简单了许多。

第二,考生在宏观把握文章思路的同时,阅读其他段落时要注重了解句与句、段与段之间的关系,特别是文章中的转折关系,学会利用上下文进行必要的判断、推理和引申。只有掌握句段之间的关系,才能摸清作者深层思路上的逻辑关系。只有从句子与句子、段落与段落之间的过渡读出作者的整个思路及论证过程,才能作出正确的推理、判断或引申。

第三,熟悉西方"开门见山"演绎思维模式与中国人"层层剥笋"归纳式模式的区别。例如,阿迪达斯有句广告语:"Just do it."香港人最早直译为"想做就做",被很多青少年家长反对,认为有教唆孩子做坏事的感觉,后来改译为"该做就做",更符合东方人内敛的性格。又如,雀巢咖啡的英语广告词"It's the taste."与汉语"味道好极了"的区别,会更深地体会出文化的差异。所以,考生应在理解阅读题的时候,学会抓住英文作者的写作意图,更有利于对文章论点、论据的把握。

7. 考查目标七:理解作者的意图、观点和态度

【理论解释】

理解作者的意图、观点和态度,是要求考生把握作者写作某篇文章的目的,搞清作者论述的观点和态度。考研英语试卷对这一部分的考查主要表现为情感态度题。该题型常问作者对某事是什么态度:主观(subjective),还是客观(objective);肯定(positive),还是否定(negative);赞成,(approval)还是反对(opposition)等。解题的关键是要看作者在文中用了什么样的口气。若用褒义词,显然是赞成。若用贬义词,显然是反对。若客观陈述,则是中性的立场,不偏不倚。注意:作者态度常常在转折词后表明出来。所以,but 一词至关重要(还有类似的 yet, however, although, nevertheless 等)。

【举例说明】

In the last half of the nineteenth century, "capital" and "labour" were enlarging and perfecting their rival organizations on modern lines. Many an old firm was replaced by a limited liability company with a bureaucracy of salaried managers. The change met the technical requirements of the new age by engaging a large professional element and prevented the decline in efficiency that so commonly spoiled the fortunes of family firms in the second and third generation after the energetic founders. It was moreover a step away from individual initiative, towards collectivism and municipal and state-owned business. The railway companies, though still private business managed for the benefit of shareholders, were very unlike old family business. At the same time the great municipalities went into business to supply lighting, trams and other services to the taxpayers.

The growth of the limited liability company and municipal business had important consequences. Such large, impersonal manipulation of capital and industry greatly increased the numbers and importance of shareholders as a class, an element in national life representing irresponsible wealth detached from the land and the duties of the landowners; and almost equally detached from the responsible management of business. All through the nineteenth century, America, Africa, India, Australia and parts of Europe were being developed by British capital, and British shareholders were thus enriched by the world's movement towards?? industrialization. Towns like Bournemouth and Eastbourne sprang up to house large "comfortable" classes who had retired on their incomes, and who had no relation to the rest of the community except that of drawing dividends and occasionally attending a shareholders' meeting to dictate their orders to the management. On the other hand "shareholding" meant leisure and freedom which was used by many of the later Victorians for the highest purpose of a great civilization.

The "shareholders" as such had no knowledge of the lives, thoughts or needs of the workmen employed by the company in which they held shares, and their influence on the relations of capital and labour was not good. The paid manager acting for the company was in more direct relation with the men and their demands, but even he had seldom that familiar personal knowledge of the workmen which the employer had often had under the more patriarchal system of the old family business now passing away. Indeed the mere size of operations and the numbers of workmen involved rendered such personal relations impossible. Fortunately, however, the increasing power and organization of the trade unions, at least in all skilled trades, enabled the workmen to meet on equal terms the managers of the companies who employed them. The cruel discipline of the strike and lockout taught the two parties to respect each other's strength and understand the value of fair negotiation. (1996 年考题第 22 题)

22. The author is most critical of ________.

[A] family firm owners　　[B] landowners

[C] managers　　[D] shareholders

例题分析:在谈到"family firm owners"时,作者只是说:"通过雇用一大批专业人员,这一变化适应了新时代的技术要求,防止了效率的下降。而效率的下降通常是家族公司在精力充沛的创立者之后的第二三代破产的原因。"这是很客观的表述,在谈到"landowners"时说:"对资本与工业的如此大规模的非个人运作,大大增加了作为一个阶层的持股人的数量及地位的重要性。国民生活中这一现象的出现代表了不由个人负责的财富与土地及土地所有者的义务的分离,这也在同样程度上意味着与经营管理责任的分离。"也是很客观的表述,没有表明自己的态度。[C]选项在原文中有两处提及,但都是指带薪经理,对经理并没有进行任何批评性评论,因而也不符合题意。只有[D]选项对应原文中"The 'shareholders' as such had no knowledge of the lives, thoughts or needs of the workmen employed by the company in which he held shares, and his influence on the relations of capital and labour was not good.""像这样的'持股人'对所持股票公司雇用的工人的生活、思想和需求一无所知,他们对资本与劳工关系没有什么好的影响。"显然,作者对这种"持股人"持批判的态度,所以[D]是正确答案。

【学习指导】

这种题目对考生而言难度较大,迷惑性也较强,因为命题专家是针对整篇文章设问,考生很难找到具体对应的语言点,所以要把握整篇文章。例如,作者在谈一件事时是用反讽的口气,还是赞成的语气。此类题所给的答案选项一般是四个形容词,考生应在审题时就把握好这四个形容词所表达的意思,然后返回文章去寻找信息。特别提醒考生,要牢记所遇到的构成作者态度题选项中的每一个形容词。做题时,千万不要把自己的态度糅进文章中,同时要注意区分作者本人的态度与作者引用的观点态度。

理解作者的意图、观点和态度是近几年考试的热点题目,考生在做此类题时要把握这样的判断原则:既纵观全文、掌握主题思想,又要注意文章的措辞,把握文章的基调或主旨(tenor),还要分清文章的话语范围(field)及话语方式(mode)。

该题型常见的提问形式有:

① The tone of the passage can best be described as ____.

② The tone of the passage would be ____.

③ Which of the following best describes the tone of the passage ____.

④ What is the attitude of the author towards ____.

⑤ How does the writer feel about ____.

⑥ The writer is of the opinion that ____.

⑦ The author seems to be ____.

常用来表明情感和态度的词汇在考研中大致可分为三类:happy/unhappy; security/insecurity; satisfaction/dissatisfaction。它们作为标记语反映出作者对某个现象采取的姿态,并从情感的角度评价该现象。因此,考生既要将文章的中心思想作为前提,又要注意作者的措辞,尤其是作为修饰语的形容词。例如:

Yet there are limits to what a society can spend in this pursuit. As a physician, I know the most costly and dramatic measures may be ineffective and painful. I also know that people in Japan and Sweden, countries that spend far less on medical care, have achieved longer, healthier lives than we have. As a nation, we may be overfunding the quest for unlikely cures while underfunding research on humbler therapies that could improve people's lives. (2003 年考题第 39 题)

39. In contrast to the U.S., Japan and Sweden are funding their medical care ____.

[A] more flexibly [B] more extravagantly

[C] more cautiously [D] more reasonably

例题分析:作者用“limits”,“ineffective”,“painful”这些消极的词语暗示了美国医疗卫生系统的缺憾,通过把握这些词语,就能得出[D]为正确选项。

此外,人们对语言的理解是有一定差异的,如尼克松签订1972年公报时,对“一个中国”原则,他手下的修辞专家用了“acknowledge”而不用“recognize”。因为后者是正式的,表示发自内心的承认,而前者是一种模糊,对某种既成事实的有限度接受,但在中文里出现的就是我们理解的“承认”。

由此可见,考生在平时的单词理解中要结合不同的语境,不同的文章体裁,综合地认知寓意,才能透彻地理解作者的真正意图。

另外,判断作者情感态度除了关注作者的措辞,还要关注作者的举例角度和讲解角度,以此来判断作者的态度倾向。如果作者一直论述某事物积极向上的方面,其态度基本上是积极乐观的;如果作者举例论证某观点时,给的例子是正面的,那么同样可以判断作者的态度是积极乐观的;如果作者的论述有好有坏,举例有正面有反面,基本上可以判断作者的态度是客观的。例如:

It was 3 : 45 in the morning when the vote was finally taken. After six months of arguing and final 16 hours of hot parliamentary debates, Australia's Northern Territory became the first legal authority in the world to allow doctors to take the lives of incurably ill patients who wish to die. The measure passed by the convincing vote of 15 to 10. Almost immediately word flashed on the Internet and was picked up, half a world away, by John Hofsess, executive director of the Right to Die Society of Canada. He sent it on via the group's on-line service, Death NET. Says Hofsess: “We posted bulletins all day long, because of course this isn't just something that happened in Australia. It's world history.”

The full import may take a while to sink in. The NT Rights of the Terminally Ⅲ law has left physicians and citizens alike trying to deal with its moral and practical implications. Some have breathed sighs of relief, others, including churches, right to life groups and the Australian Medical Association, bitterly attacked the bill and the haste of its passage. But the tide is unlikely to turn back. In Australia — where an aging population, life extending technology and changing community attitudes have all played their part — other states are going to consider making a similar law to deal with euthanasia. In the US and Canada, where the right to die movement is gathering strength, observers are waiting for the dominoes to start falling.

Under the new Northern Territory law, an adult patient can request death — probably by a deadly injection or pill — to put an end to suffering. The patient must be diagnosed as terminally ill by two doctors. After a “cooling off” period of seven days, the patient can sign a certificate of request. After 48 hours the wish for death can be met. For Lloyd Nickson, a 54 year old Darwin resident suffering from lung cancer, the NT Rights of Terminally Ⅲ law means he can get on with living without the haunting fear of his suffering: a terrifying death from his breathing condition. “I'm not afraid of dying from a spiritual point of view, but what I was afraid of was how I'd go, because I've watched people die in the hospital fighting for oxygen and clawing at their masks,” he says. (1997年考题第14题)

14. The author's attitude towards euthanasia seems to be that of ________.

[A] opposition [B] suspicion [C] approval [D] indifference

例题分析:通过阅读该文,不难发现文章首段记述了安乐死法案通过以及当时在全球引起的反响,首段作者使用"it is world history"来表达他对该事件的态度,认为它意义重大。紧接着在第二段,作者先讨论世人对此态度不一,但是作者通过转折,指出这个潮流不太可能被逆转了。第三段,作者用一个肺癌病人为例,该病人认为安乐死法案的通过意味着自己可以平静地度过最后的时光,不用担心临死前要遭受的折磨。很明显,作者认为安乐死法案的通过是一件好事。那么文章就作者的态度来命题,答案肯定是"approval"。

2.4 新题型(阅读理解B节)

2.4.1 《考纲》基本信息详解

自2005年起,考纲首次增加了阅读理解新题型。2006年,大纲又在2005年的基础上将新题型调整为三种备选题型,每次考试从这三种备选题型中选择一种进行考查。三种备选题型分别为:

(1) 完形填句(段):本部分的内容是一篇总长度为500~600词的文章,其中有5段空白,文章后有6~7段文字。要求考生根据文章内容从这6~7段文字中选择5段分别放进文章中5个空白处。

(2) 排序题:在一篇长度为500~600词的文章中,各段落的原有顺序已被打乱。要求考生根据文章的内容和结构将所列段落(7~8个)重新排序,其中有1~3个段落在文章中的位置已给出。

(3) 小标题选择题或观点例证题:在一篇长度约500词的文章前或后有6~7段文字(概括句)或小标题。这些文字或标题分别是文章中某一部分的概括、阐述或举例。要求考生根据文章内容,从这6~7个选项中选出最恰当的5段文字或5个标题填入文章的空白处。

2.4.2 《考纲》考查目标强化指导

阅读理解B节试题主要考查考生对连贯性、一致性等语段性特征以及文章结构的理解,即要求考生在理解全文的基础上把握文章的整体和微观结构。考生既要理解和掌握文章总体结构和写作思路,又要弄清上下文之间的逻辑关系。

考查目标是:一致性、连贯性与篇章结构。

【理论解释】

(1)一致性:指全文围绕一个主题展开;每一个段落也只有一个主题。文章或段落的主题可能是显性的(有鲜明的主题句"topic sentence"),也可能是隐性的(主题隐含在细节的描述中),但文章或段落的展开却紧紧围绕着一个中心,并服务于这个中心,或陈述其原因,或叙述其结果,或罗列事实,或举例论证。这个主题或中心即文章或段落的主旨要义,因此理解了主旨要义就把握了新题型"一致性"这个考点,对于理解文章的总体结构以及单句之间的关系也非常关键。新题型三种题型都涉及对文章主旨要义的把握,其中最直接的考查在小标题选择题中。

(2)连贯性:在一篇文章里,语言的连贯性主要体现在段落与段落之间,段落内的句与句之间相互衔接清楚、自然、流畅、前后呼应,上句要能很自然地带出下句,后句与前句呼应,形成句句相连,句与句或段与段之间具有一定的内在联系或逻辑关系,同时文章或段落的论点与论据之间的关系必须清晰、合乎逻辑。

(3)篇章结构:对于一篇完整的英文说明文或者议论文来说,不论其形式看上去有多么复杂多样,但是每个作者都有自己的写作目的。为了达到写作目的,一般考研阅读的文章都是采取特定的篇章结构模式层层展开对文章主要内容的叙说,而一旦掌握这些篇章结构的特点,对理清文章脉络和把握主题很有帮助。

在做新题型时,尤其要善于把握文章的整体结构。通常而言,文章的结构有以下几种:

① 问题型:提出问题—分析问题—解决问题。

这类文章的基本模式是:文章通常以某种现象或话题开篇,该现象或话题可能涉及社会生活、文化教育等各个领域。接着,针对此现象或话题展开分析讨论,找出其存在或产生的根源从而得到解决问题的办法。

② 议论型:提出论点—列举论据—得出结论。

这类文章的基本模式是:在文章开始,作者列出自己的观点,接下来用所掌握的论据对此观点加以论证,最后得出结论。

③ 立论型(驳论型):提出观点—表示赞同(发表异议—驳斥观点—建立观点)—论证观点。

这类文章的基本模式是:在文章开始提出一种时下比较流行的观点或者现象,接着作者阐述自己对此现象或者观点的看法。在阐述自己看法的同时,作者会表明自己的态度,或赞成,或反对。如果作者持赞成态度,就直接对它加以论证;如果持反对态度的话,则还要提出自己的观点,并给出充分论据证明。

④ 因果型:结果(现象)—原因(成因)。

这类文章的基本模式是:文章大多以一种现象或者一种结果开篇,然后进一步探讨导致这种现象或结果的原因或成因。

【举例说明】

下面以具体的考题为例,从而形象的说明新题型的考查目标怎样体现在各种题型中:

(1) 一致性。一致性体现为一个中心思想统领整个段落的内容。也就是说,段落中所有的扩展句子都围绕一个主题内容展开,所有句子表达的内容是一致。因此,不论是新题型的哪一种备考题型,找出各句子与主题内容的联系,对解题都很重要。

① 一致性在小标题选择题中的应用。小标题选择题主要考查的是考生对文章各个段落的主旨要义的把握,即总结归纳段落大意的能力。该题型最鲜明地体现了对一致性的考查,需要考生选出最能概括段落主题或要点的标题,即一定要实现标题和段落主旨要义的一致性。

试题要求考生阅读一篇 500 词左右的文章,该文章由若干段落组成。选项是对各个段落主旨的概括,而且选项数量通常多于段落数量。考生在宏观理解各个段落的基础上,通过总结段落主旨大意,为其选出合适的选项,相当于为各个段落选出小标题。例如,2007 年考题的第 41 题和第 43 题。

A. Set a Good Example for Your Kids

B. Build Your Kids' Work Skills

C. Place Time Limits on Leisure Activities

D. Talk about the Future on a Regular Basis

E. Help Kids Develop Coping Strategies

F. Help Your Kids Figure Out Who They Are

G. Build Your Kids' Sense of Responsibility

41	

You can start this process when they are 11 or 12. Periodically review their emerging strengths and weaknesses with them and work together on any shortcomings, like difficulty in communicating well or collaborating. Also, identify the kinds of interests they keep coming back to, as these offer clues to the careers that will fit them best. (2007 年考题第 41 题)

例题分析:先要概括这一段落的主旨要义。本段没有明确的主题句,但是整个段落都是围绕父母应该帮助孩子了解其优缺点及兴趣这个主题展开的,确定了段落的主旨大意后,需要找出最能概括段落主题的选项,实现标题与段落主旨的一致。经过对各个选项作比较,[F]选项的内容是"帮助孩子了解自己",正好是本段内容的最好概括,因此为正确选项。

43	

Teachers are responsible for teaching kids how to learn; parents should be responsible for teaching them how to work. Assign responsibilities around the house and make sure homework deadlines are met. Encourage teenagers to take a part-time job. Kids need plenty of practice delaying gratification and deploying effective organizational skills, such as managing time and setting priorities. (2007 年考题第 43 题)

例题分析:本段的首句是段落的主题句,即"家长有责任教孩子如何工作"。段落其余部分围绕主题句展开,具体列举了各项工作内容。[B]选项内容是"培养孩子的工作技能",与段落主题句同义,实现了标题与段落主旨的一致,为正确选项。

② 一致性在完形填句(段)中的应用。从《考纲》和历年真题来看,完形填句(段)考查的文章以说明文和议论文为主。此类文章脉络清晰,层次分明,各段之间联系紧密,段中有过渡句以及表示不同逻辑关系的信号词等,这是考生正确答题的基础。做完形填句(段)题时,考生要注意把握空格中的句子与所在段落的一致性以及段落与整个篇章的一致性。例如:

Once you have a first draft on paper, you can delete material that is unrelated to your thesis and add material necessary to illustrate your points and make your paper convincing. The student who wrote "The A&P as a State of Mind" wisely dropped a paragraph that questioned whether Sammy displays chauvinistic attitudes toward women. ________.

[E] Although this is an interesting issue, it has nothing to do with the thesis, which explains how the setting influences Sammy's decision to quit his job. Instead of including that paragraph, she added one that described Lengel's crabbed response to the girls so that she could lead up to the A & P "policy" he enforces.

[F] In the final paragraph about the significance of the setting in "A&P" the student brings together the reasons Sammy quit his job by referring to his refusal to accept Lengel's store policies.

例题分析:本题的空格出现在段尾,本段的首句为段落的主旨句,指出在写作中要删去与主题无关的材料以及添加必要的材料使文章的论证更有说服力。在第二句就列出了具体的例子来验证作者的观点,即一个学生很明智地删除了怀疑 Sammy 有大男子主义倾向的段落。按照段落的一致性原则,接下来要填的内容必须要符合本段的主旨,而[E]和[F]选项都出现了很具体的线索:"The A & P"和"Sammy",通过对选项分析,可以看出[E]更好地体现一致性的原则,因为[E]选项开头处的"this"正好指代上文的"whether Sammy displays chauvinistic attitudes toward women";再者,[E]选项中的"has nothing to do with the thesis"和"add"分别与本段段首"is unrelated to your thesis"和"add material necessary"形成一一对应,用具体的例子验证了作者的观点。而[F]选项虽然提到了主题词,但只是说明对一个段落的写作,与本段主题不符。所以正确选项是[E]。

③ 一致性在观点例证题中的应用。这个题型的主要形式就是文章中给出五个论点,文章末尾有

六七个选项,其中五个是用来分别阐述这五个论点的,要求将选项与原文论点一一对应。这一题型主要考核的是论据与论点的一致性。需要说明的是,给出的选项并不一定都是具体的事例,也可能是对论点的进一步的阐释和说明。例如:

The main purpose of a resume is to convince an employer to grant you an interview. There are two kinds. One is the familiar "tombstone" that lists where you went to school and where you've worked in chronological order. The other is what I call the "functional" resume—descriptive, fun to read, unique to you and much more likely to land you an interview.

It's handy to have a "tombstone" for certain occasions. But prospective employers throw away most of those unrequested "tombstone" lists, preferring to interview the quick rather than the dead.

What follows are tips on writing a functional resume that will get read—a resume that makes you come alive and look interesting to employers.

41. Put yourself first:

In order to write a resume others will read with enthusiasm, you have to feel important about yourself.

[A] A woman who lost her job as a teacher's aide due to a cutback in government funding wrote: "Principal of elementary school cited me as the only teacher's aide she would rehire if government funds became available."

[B] One resume I received included the following: "invited by my superior to straighten out our organization's accounts receivable. Set up orderly repayment schedule, reconciled accounts weekly, and improved cash flow 100 per cent. Rewarded with raise and promotion." Notice how this woman focuses on results, specifies how she accomplished them, and mentions her reward—all in 34 words.

[C] For example, if you have a flair for saving, managing and investing money, you have money management skills.

[D] An acquaintance complained of being biased when losing an opportunity due to the statement "Ready to learn though not so well educated".

[E] One of my former colleagues, for example, wrote resumes in three different styles in order to find out which was more preferred. The result is, of course, the one that highlights skills and education background.

[F] A woman once told me about a cash flow crisis her employer had faced. She'd agreed to work without pay for three months until business improved. Her reward was her back pay plus a 20 percent bonus. I asked why that marvelous story wasn't in her resume. She answered, "It wasn't important." What she was really saying of course was "I'm not important."

例题分析:这是一篇关于如何写好个人简历的文章。在这篇文章中,作者给出了写简历的一些诀窍,每个诀窍都提炼出一个小标题,给出解释和举例。考生应该明确一点,这些小标题不一定等同于论点或段落总结句。小标题一般都较短,只看小标题不参考其解释,就会出现"只见树木,不见森林"的现象,很容易出现偏颇。因此,考生应该结合正文理解观点的含义,然后再结合小标题提炼出论点,最后再去和选项结合。

"Put yourself first",字面意思是"把自己置于第一位"。什么意思呢?下面的句子进行了解释,

“要想让自己的简历使人读起来富有激情,那么你首先要对自己有自信”。再看选项中哪个例子能进一步说明这一点呢?从选项中可以发现,有些例子是成功的例子,有些是不成功的例子。那么就有可能从正反两方面举例了,[F]项就是一个反例,从反面证明要认识到自己的重要性,所以该题应选[F]。作者通过例子说明,不要认为自己做过的事情不值一提,瞧不起自己的人又怎么会被别人重视呢?由此可见,[F]项以反面角度例证的方式实现了论点与论据的一致性。

④ 一致性在排序题中的应用。排序题要求考生将所给的一组段落排序,使其组成一篇条理清晰,内容连贯的文章。这就需要考生在阅读各段时把握它们的中心思想,并将各段的大意整合,注意各个段落应是合乎逻辑的展开对文章中心的推衍和阐述。例如:

[A] The first and more important is the consumer's growing preference for eating out: consumption of food and drink in places other than homes has risen from about 32 percent of total consumption in 1995 to 35 percent in 2000 and is expected to approach 38 percent by 2005. This development is boosting wholesale demand from the food service segment by 4 to 5 percent a year across Europe, compared with growth in retail demand of 1 to 2 percent. Meanwhile, as the recession is looming large, people are getting anxious. They tend to keep a tighter hold on their purse and consider eating at home a realistic alternative.

[E] Despite variations in detail, wholesale markets in the countries that have been closely examined—France, Germany, Italy, and Spain—are made out of the same building blocks. Demand comes mainly from two sources: independent mom-and-pop grocery stores, which, unlike large retail chains, are too small to buy straight from producers, and food service operators that cater to consumers when they don't eat at home. Such food service operators range from snack machines to large institutional catering ventures, but most of these businesses are known in the trade as “horeca”: hotels, restaurants, and cafes. Overall, Europe's wholesale market for food and drink is growing at the same sluggish pace as the retail market, but the figures, when added together, mask two opposing trends. (2010 年考题第 45 题)

例题分析:本题主要以一致性原则来分析[A]段为什么跟在[E]段之后。[E]段的尾句提到的“two opposing trends”,根据篇章展开的一致性原则,下文应该对这两种相反的趋势进行进一步的说明,而[A]选项的内容体现了这两种相反的趋势,即一方面消费者越来越趋向于外出就餐,而另一方面人们又开始看紧他们的钱包,并且认为在家吃饭是一种现实的选择。

(2) 连贯性。对连贯性的考查贯穿在新题型的三种备考题型中,尤其在完型完形填句(段)、排序题中体现的最为鲜明。下面以这两种题型为例,使考生明确在考试中怎样运用连贯性原则去解答题目。

① 连贯性在完形填句(段)中的应用。该题型在命题时有可能就一个段落中设置空缺句,也可能是在整个篇章中,将一个完整的段落设置为空缺段,不管是哪种考查形式,解答本题都要使已知信息和未知信息合乎逻辑,保持连贯性,要清楚地掌握文章发展的脉络、层次以及句子与句子之间、段落与段落之间的逻辑关系,注重文章各个段落和句子之间在内容上的衔接和连贯关系。例如:

Long before Man lived on the Earth, there were fishes, reptiles, birds, insects, and some mammals. Although some of these animals were ancestors of kinds living today, others are now extinct, that is, they have no descendants alive now. 1. ________. Very occasionally the rocks show impression of skin, so that, apart from color, we can build up a reasonably accurate picture of an animal that died millions of years ago. The kind of rock in which the remains are found tells us much about the nature of the original land, often of the plants that grew on it, and even of its climate.

2. ________. Nearly all of the fossils that we know were preserved in rocks formed by water action, and most of these are of animals that lived in or near water. Thus it follows that there must be many kinds of mammals, birds, and insects of which we know nothing.

3. ________. There were also crab-like creatures, whose bodies were covered with a horny substance. The body segments each had tow pairs of legs, one pair for walking on the sandy bottom, the other for swimming. The head was a kind of shield with a pair of compound eyes, often with thousands of lenses. They were usually an inch or tow long but some were 2 feet.

[A] The shellfish have a long history in the rock and many different kinds are known.

[B] Nevertheless, we know a great deal about many of them because their bones and shells have been preserved in the rocks as fossils, From them we can tell their size and shape, how they walked, the kind of food they ate.

[C] The first animals with true backbones were the fishes, first known in the rocks of 375 million years ago. About 300 million years ago the amphibians, the animals able to live both on land and in water, appeared. They were giant ,sometimes 8 feet long, and many of them lived in the swampy pools in which our coal seam ,or layer ,or formed . The amphibians gave rise to the reptiles and for nearly 150 million years these were the principal forms of life on land, in the sea, and in the air.

[D] The best index fossils tend to be marine creature . There animals evolved rapidly and spread over large over large areas of the world.

[E] The earliest animals whose remains have been found were all very simple kinds and lived in the sea. Later forma are more complex,and among these are the sea-lilies , relations of the starfishes,which had long arms and were attached by a long stalk to the sea bed ,or to rocks .

[F] When an animal dies, the body, its bones, or shell ,may often be carried away by streams into lakes or the sea and there get covered up by mud . If the animal lived in the sea its body would probably sink and be covered with mud. More and more mud would fall upon it until the bones or shell become embedded and preserved.

[G] Many factors can influence how fossils are preserved in rocks . Remains of an organism may be replaced by minerals, dissolved by an acidic solution to leave only their impression, or simply reduced to a more stable form.

例题分析:

第1题:解答本题,首先要看空格前的信息,作者告诉我们,早在人类出现以前地球上就有许多物种,现在有些物种的后代依然生存,而另外一些则没有留下后裔。在本题空格后,文章又说岩石上偶尔会留下数百万年前就死掉了的动物的精确印记。显然,空格处应该是关于岩石与灭绝的动物之间的关系,此外,空格处前面的“extinct”和“no descendant”均为否定意义的表达,而空格处的后面“accurate”和“much”则为肯定意义的表达;这意味着空格处的内容应该有一个逻辑上的转折,综上所述,只有[B]项符合要求,[B]项开头的“Nevertheless”表示转折,而且[B]项表达的内容起到了衔接上下文的作用,从而实现了句与句之间的连贯性。

第2题：依据语段的连贯性原则，空格处填入的信息应既能与第一段的内容有一定的连贯性，又能与第二段中的关键信息相关联。空格后主要在谈论化石的成因，“formed by water action”是关键信息，选项[F]与空格后的第一句紧密相连，选项[F]中涉及相关的“be carried away by streams into lakes or the sea...，get covered by mud”等，都是在讲靠水的作用形成化石，而选项[F]最后一句中的“preserved”一词在空格后第一句中重复出现，使前后两句之间紧密衔接。因此[F]项为正确答案。

第3题：空格后的第一句讲到还有像蟹一样的动物，其身体表面是一层角状物。本段随后的内容继续介绍了这类动物的外貌特征。根据空格后的“also”一词可知，要使填入的信息和空后内容保持紧密的连贯性，空白处也应讲到一种海洋生物，选项[E]中后面的一句提到“sea-lilies”这种海洋生物，与空格后正好衔接起来，实现了语意的连贯，故为答案。

② 连贯性在排序题中的应用。

在排序题中，既然是要求将打乱顺序的段落重新排序，从而组成一篇语意通顺，合乎逻辑的文章，那么，在做这种题时，就要使段与段之间保持连贯，尤其要注意段落的末句与下段首句之间的连贯性。当然，这种连贯性的实现必然要遵循一定的逻辑关系，这种逻辑关系可以用连词来明确表达，也可暗含在句与句之间。例如，2010年考题阅读理解B节：

[B] Retail sales of food and drink in Europe's largest markets are at a standstill, leaving European grocery retailers hungry for opportunities to grow. Most leading retailers have already tried e-commerce, with limited success, and expansion abroad. But almost all have ignored the big, profitable opportunity in their own backyard: the wholesale food and drink trade, which appears to be just the kind of market retailers need.

[F] For example, wholesale food and drink sales come to $ 268 billion in France, Germany, Italy, Spain, and the United Kingdom in 2000—more than 40 percent of retail sales. Moreover, average overall margins are higher in wholesale than in retail; wholesale demand from the food service sector is growing quickly as more Europeans eat out more often; and changes in the competitive dynamics of this fragmented industry are at last making it feasible for wholesalers to consolidate.

例题分析：本题主要以连贯性原则来分析[F]项为何应紧跟在[B]项之后。[B]项末句指出了本段的核心信息：“食品和饮料的批发行业正是零售商所需要的”。由此可见，此处只是笼统地提出了一种看法，依据篇章展开的逻辑，下文如要和上段在语意上保持连贯性，下文会就这一看法进行进一步的阐述，而[F]项以提示词“For example”举例说明批发业务给各国、各批发商带来的巨大利益，由此可见[F]项和[B]项是明显的观点与例证的语意关联，故[F]项应和[B]项衔接，从而保持语段间的连贯。

(3) 文章结构。不论是新题型的哪一种备考题型，考查时所选取的文章就主题的展开都会遵循一定的篇章结构模式。熟悉了这些结构模式，在做题时就可从整体上定位和预测各选项在文中的位置。对文章结构模式的考查，尤其在排序题中最为明显，下面着重以排序题为例，说明篇章结构怎样对解题起到帮助作用。

[A] "I just don't know how to motivate them to do a better job. We're in a budget crunch and I have absolutely no financial rewards at my disposal. In fact, we'll probably have to lay some people off in the near future. It's hard for me to make the job interesting and challenging because it isn't—it's boring, routine paperwork, and there isn't much you can do about it."

[B] "Finally, I can't say to them that their promotions will hinge on the excellence of their paperwork. First of all, they knew it's not true. If their performance is adequate, most are more likely to get promoted just by staying on the force a certain number of years than for some specific outstanding act. Second, they were trained to do the job they do out in the streets, not to fill out forms. All through their career it is the arrests and interventions that get noticed."

[C] "I've got a real problem with my officers. They come on the force as young, inexperienced men, and we send them out on the street, either in cars or on a beat. They seem to like the contact they have with the public, the action involved in crime prevention, and the apprehension of criminals. They also like helping people out at fires, accidents, and other emergencies."

[D] "Some people have suggested a number of things like using conviction records as a performance criterion. However, we know that's not fair—too many other things are involved. Bad paperwork increases the chance that you lose in court, but good paperwork doesn't necessarily mean you'll win. We tried setting up team competitions based on the excellence of the reports, but the guys caught on to that pretty quickly. No one was getting any type of reward for winning the competition, and they figured why should they labor when there was no payoff."

[E] "The problem occurs when they get back to the station. They hate to do the paperwork, and because they dislike it, the job is frequently put off or done inadequately. This lack of attention hurts us later on when we get to court. We need clear, factual reports. They must be highly detailed and unambiguous. As soon as one part of a report is shown to be inadequate or incorrect, the rest of the report is suspect. Poor reporting probably causes us to lose more cases than any other factor."

[F] "So I just don't know what to do. I've been groping in the dark in a number of years. And I hope that this seminar will shed some light on this problem of mine and help me out in my future work."

[G] A large metropolitan city government was putting on a number of seminars for administrators, managers and/or executives of various departments throughout the city. At one of these sessions the topic to be discussed was motivation—how we can get public servants motivated to do a good job. The difficulty of a police captain became the central focus of the discussion.

Order:

G→ 1. __ → 2. __ → 3. __ → 4. __ → 5. __ → F

例题分析:由文章的已知段落大致可得出文章的主旨是:"如何激励公务员干好工作,一个警长的困境成了大家讨论的焦点"。而且文章首段末句提到了"the difficulty of a police captain",由此表明本篇文章框架应是提出问题—分析问题—解决问题。按照文章的结构特点,在确定选项时,就应将提出问题的选项往前放,分析问题的选项放在中间,把提出解决办法或建议的选项往后放。[C]段首句明显是提出问题的表达,故可以把[C]项初步放在第1题,[D]项首句中的"Some people have suggested..."明显是提出建议的标志,故可初步把[D]项放在第5题。以此方法对选项进行大致定位后,在依据段落间的一致性和连贯性原则对段落进行复查和精确定位。这样在做题时,既省时又会提高答题的准确率(注:本题主要是分析运用篇章结构对选项进行大致定位的方法,因此不再对其他选项进行详解)。

【学习指导】

(1) 小标题选择题学习指导。

① 解题步骤。

第一步:先通读各个选项,从选项中推断出相关段落的大致内容。

第二步:细读所考段落,抓住每段主题句和核心词汇,正确答案常常是主题句的改写。

第三步:将从段落中提炼出的主题句和选项对比,选出答案。

② 解题技巧。

学会判断主题句或主题词,对解答好小标题很有帮助。主题句或主题词的判断方法:

第一,把握主题句。在阅读各个段落时,不要逐字逐句地分析阅读,以免浪费时间。正确的做法是先看首尾两句。因为主题句通常置于段落之首,这符合英语的语篇思维特征(先采用主题句开门见山地摆出问题,随之辅以细说)。当然,也有段落主题句设在段尾,相当于对上文的总结。因此,考生应该重点看第一句,看出首句与下文的关系,从而确定是否第一句就是段落的主旨句。如果首尾都得不出结论,再考虑阅读整个段落。找出段落大意之后,再与选项做比较,确定正确答案。

第二,对于主题句在段落中的情况,当段落中出现转折时,该句很可能是主题句。

第三,在一个段落或者一篇文章中,反复出现的信息往往都是主题,应予以重视。

第四,作者提出段落主题时,常常伴有文字提示,如"therefore","thus","but","however","in short"等。

(2) 完形填句(段)学习指导。

① 解题步骤。

第一步:通读文章首段,迅速得知文章的大意。

第二步:通读选项,在每个选项下标出该选项的大致意思,以便做题时能迅速找到所需选项。

第三步:根据各个空白处的所在位置,分析空白处的上下文,通过逻辑关系和语意内容分辨出各选项分别属于文章哪个部分,并尝试与空白处的上下文有机地衔接起来,选出正确答案。

第四步:将所选选项带入原文,通读全文,检测文章前后是否连贯,所选的选项是否和文章的主旨大意相吻合。

② 解题技巧。

第一,选项中出现时间、年代时,要注意与原文中时间、年代的前后对应关系。

第二,选项中出现代词时,该选项往往不能放在首句,要分辨出该代词所指代的内容:"it"可指代前面的单数名词或整个句子;"they"或"them"指代前面的复数名词;"one"指代前面的单数可数名词;"that"指代前面的不可数名词或句子;"this"指代前面的单数名词或句子。

第三,将选项与原文对比时,与原文重复或同义改写的词汇越多的往往就是正确选项。

第四,做完形填句(段)题时不必按顺序做,应先做简单的后做难的,注意寻找上下文中的关键信息。

(3) 排序题学习指导。

① 解题步骤。

第一步:通读文章首段,大致了解文章的主旨;如果首段没有确定,则应通过阅读各选项先确定首段。

第二步:迅速浏览各个选项,重点阅读各段首末句,概括出各个选项的大意,从而明确整个文章的大致内容,了解各个选项之间的内在逻辑关系。

第三步:根据各个段落的逻辑关系给选项排序。

第四步:把文章按所选的顺序带进文章,检查段落顺序是否合理。

② 解题技巧。

第一,文章结构解题法。因为阅读理解的文章全部是议论文或说明文,这就决定了这些文章本身的叙述和展开方式,弄清楚这些文章的结构,在选择答案时就简单了许多。

第二,逻辑关系解题法。逻辑关系主要有:并列递进关系、转折关系、因果关系、解释关系、例证关系、定义关系等。

并列递进关系标志词汇有:and, indeed, also, besides, similarly, like, accordingly, in the same way, meanwhile, furthermore, moreover 等。

转折关系标志词汇有:but, yet, although, however, on the contrary, on the other hand, instead 等。

因果关系标志词汇有:for, because, since, therefore 等。

解释关系标志词汇有:that is, that is to say, for example, such as, namely, in other words 等。

熟悉表示不同逻辑关系的词语后,考生就可以在掌握各段落大意的前提下,根据这些细节词语来推断彼此之间的关系,然后进行排序。

(4) 观点例证题学习指导。

① 解题步骤。

第一步:浏览全文,精读标题以及标题下解释性的文字。

第二步:阅读选项,画出每个选项中的关键词,并标注每个选项的大概意思,对备选的几个论据有个大致的把握。对于谈论相似内容的选项,需区别其相同处和不同处,应边读选项边将选项所给的论据逐一与标题相对照。

第三步:再次将选项与文中已选择的标题进行比较,检查二者是否一致。

② 解题技巧。

第一,观点例证题的目的在于考查考生的演绎能力,即给出论点,要求考生根据论点拓展,或是找出可以说明该论点的例子,或是找出进一步的阐释和论证。需要注意的是,要明确这些论据是从原文中抽出来的,论点和论据是一体的,要始终保持语段的一致性。

第二,论据是为论点服务的,所以论据不仅要和论点相关,而且还要可以说明论点。考试中会给出六七个备选答案,其中多余的选项往往与文中的小论点有关。对这种多余选项一定要提高警惕,这类选项和论点有点关系但并不能说明论点,考生要始终清醒地认识到:论点与论据只有相关性不行,还必须要能说明这个论点。

第三,既然选项是为论点提供论据的,那么其内容必定和文章给出的各个分论点存在逻辑关系,如并列关系、扩展关系、补充关系等。无论它们是哪种关系,必定有很多共同之处,而意思上的相近很容易带来同义词以及类似句型的运用。考生不妨从这里入手来解决问题。

2.5 翻译(阅读理解 C 节)

2.5.1 《考纲》基本信息详解

《考纲》对阅读理解 C 节的表述为:“主要考查考生准确理解概念或结构较复杂的英语文字材料

的能力。要求考生阅读一篇约400词的文章,并将其中5个画线部分(约150词)译成汉语,要求译文准确、通顺、完整。考生在答题卡2上作答。"该部分总分为10分。

英译汉翻译部分是考研英语试卷阅读理解的一部分,旨在测试考生根据上下文准确理解英语句子的能力。该部分五个画线需要翻译的句子难度较大,要么概念抽象,要么结构复杂,或者兼而有之,因此对考生理解英文句子的能力要求很高。与此同时,作为英译汉,还考查考生将英语句子准确转换成汉语的能力。因此,考生还需具备较好的汉语表达能力。

2.5.2 《考纲》考查目标强化指导

首先,考研英语翻译部分的五个画线句子每个2分,其采分点主要集中在词法和句法层面。词法层面的能力考查主要体现在:要求考生根据上下文推测词义,从多个词义中选出符合语境的恰当词义,并予以通顺、准确地表达;试题中一词多义现象普遍,很多时候还需要考生具备词义引申的能力;由于中英文差异的存在,词类转换技巧也经常考到。句法层面的能力考查主要体现在:要求考生理解英语特殊的表意方式和语序,理清句子的复杂结构,并准确翻译成符合汉语表达习惯的译文,此时考生需要掌握常用的翻译技巧,如定语从句的翻译技巧等。

其次,考研英语翻译部分的标准也不容忽视。俗话说,"没有规矩,不成方圆",《考纲》提出了六个字的翻译标准供考生参考,即"准确、通顺、完整"。"准确"就是翻译的句子要与英文原文意思对等,不能扭曲原文的意思;"通顺"就是翻译的译文要符合汉语表达习惯,表达要清晰、流畅;"完整"就是完整地传达原文的信息,不可漏译。

总之,翻译部分要求考生具备良好的英语基本功和汉语表达能力,并对中英文的差异有所了解。作为阅读理解的组成部分C节,《考纲》要求的八大阅读能力在此部分主要体现在推理引申以及上下文之间的联系上。下面通过具体的翻译技巧予以解析。

2.5.3 翻译高频考点精讲

1. 定语从句

【理论解释】

定语从句是英语学习的难点,也是考研英语翻译部分考查的重点。据统计,从2002年到2011年,考研英语试卷翻译部分对于纯粹的定语从句的考查就有30次之多。而且,考研英语翻译部分的画线句子从句嵌套现象严重,各种从句层出不穷。要理清这些长难句的层次,则需要快速鉴别出其中的各种从句。因此,了解定语从句的概念并准确将其识别是至关重要的。更为重要的是,中英文定语的位置存在一定差异,汉语中定语多前置,而英语中的定语包括前置定语和后置定语两种。考研英语翻译部分中后置定语居多(尤其是定语从句)。要翻译出符合汉语表达习惯的句子,就必然需要通过一定的翻译技巧进行语序的调整。因此,能够准确识别定语从句,并熟练运用定语从句的翻译技巧,是考生的必备素质之一。

【举例说明】

考研英语翻译部分中考查定语从句的两个典型例子如下:

Furthermore, humans have the ability to modify the environment in which they live, thus subjecting all other life forms to their own peculiar ideas and fancies. (2003年考题第41题)

Pearson has pieced together the work of hundreds of researchers around the world to produce a unique millennium technology calendar that gives the latest dates when we can expect hundreds of key breakthroughs and discoveries to take place. (2001年考题第43题)

例题分析:第一个例子包含一个定语从句“in which they live”,这个定语从句的特点是句子长度较短、信息量不大,比较好处理。而第二个例子中包含两个定语从句,分别由“that”和“when”引导,而“when”引导的定语从句修饰的是“that”定语从句中的宾语。如果把两个定语从句都翻译到所修饰的名词之前,其译文的繁琐程度是可想而知的。要想准确、完整、通顺的翻译好这个句子,就必须考虑如何处理这两个定语从句的语序。这就需要考生对定语从句的翻译技巧有所了解。

【学习指导】

常见的定语从句翻译方法有四种:前置法、后置法、融合法和状译法。考研英语翻译部分中应用最广泛的是前两种。

(1) 前置法。所谓前置法,是指把定语从句翻译在所修饰的先行词之前,一般用“的”字来连接定语从句和先行词。当定语从句长度较短,信息负载量不大,与所修饰的成分关系密切时,通常采取前置法。下面通过举例进行说明。

① All those who work hard should be encouraged.

② The point is that the players who score most are the ones who take most shots at the goal.

③ Only those who are not afraid of any difficulties have the chance of achieving outstanding results in their work.

例题分析:上面这三个句子包含四个定语从句,这些从句有一个共同点就是句子长度较短、信息含量不大,所以应首先考虑使用前置法。第一个句子的定语从句“who work hard”修饰“those”;第二个句子的定语从句“who score most”和“who take most shots at the goal”分别修饰“the players”和“the ones”;第三个句子的定语从句“who are not afraid of any difficulties”修饰“those”。找出了定语从句及其引导词之后,就可以采取前置法翻译了。以下是参考译文。

① 所有那些工作努力的人都应该受到鼓励。

② 问题在于得分最多者正是那些射门次数最多的球员。

③ 只有那些不怕任何困难的人才有可能在工作上取得卓越的成果。

(2) 后置法。所谓后置法,是指将定语从句独立翻译成句,放到所修饰的先行词之后。非限制性定语从句与先行词关系不是很密切,往往采用后置法。而在考研英语翻译部分中,有时画线句子所包含的定语从句虽是限制性的,但由于从句嵌套等原因,使得定语从句较复杂,这时如果直接将之翻译到所修饰的定语从句之前,就会显得臃肿不堪,读起来也与汉语的表达习惯相差很远。因此,只能另辟蹊径,采取后置法。具体操作方式是,通过重复先行词或者重复先行词的对应代词来引出定语从句的内容。下面通过具体的例子进行详细说明。

① One place where children soak up A-characteristics is school, which is, by its very nature, a highly competitive institution.

② They have been spurred in part by DNA evidence made available in 1998, which almost certainly proved Thomas Jefferson had fathered at least one child with his slave Sally Hemings.

③ Immigrants are quickly fitting into this common culture, which may not be altogether elevating but is hardly poisonous.

例题分析:这三个句子中出现了三个定语从句,这些从句本身较复杂,且作为非限制性定语从句,与各自先行词的关系也不密切,可以考虑采用后置法。第一个句子的定语从句“which is, by its very nature, a highly competitive institution”中包含一个插入语,较复杂,修饰先行词“school”;第二个句子的定语从句“which almost certainly proved Thomas Jefferson had fathered at least one child with his slave Sally Hemings”中介词短语较多,较复杂,修饰先行词“DNA evidence”;第三个句子的定语从句“which may not be altogether elevating but is hardly poisonous”中包含两个并列的谓语，较复杂。明晰了这些定语从句及其先行词后，就可以着手翻译了。以下是参考译文。

① 让孩子吸收A型性格的一个地方是学校。学校，就其本质而言，是个高度竞争的机构。

② 他们的兴趣部分源自1998年的DNA证据，它几乎肯定地证明了托马斯·杰斐逊曾与其奴隶萨利·赫明斯育有至少一个孩子。

③ 移民们正在快速融入大众文化，这种情况也许不能从总体上提升大众文化，但几乎没有什么害处。

(3) 融合法。所谓融合法，是指把主句和定语从句融合成一个简单句，将其中的定语从句译成单句中的谓语部分。由于限制性定语从句与主句的关系较紧密，所以，融合法多用于翻译限制性的定语从句，尤其是“there be”句型中的定语从句。此外，融合法也多见于主句过于简单，而定语从句较复杂，重心在定语从句的句子。下面举例说明。

① There is a girl who is waiting for you downstairs.

② We used a plane of which almost every part carried some indication of national identity.

③ We in America desperately need more people who believe that the person who commits a crime is the one responsible for it.

例题分析：这三个句子中出现了四个定语从句，其中第三个句子包括两个定语从句。第一个句子是“there be”句型，其定语从句是“who is waiting for you downstairs”。第二个句子的主干是“we used a plane”，从句是“of which almost every part carried some indication of national identity”。由此可见，本句主句很简单，从句较复杂，且重点信息都在从句里。第三个句子的主干是“We in America desperately need more people”，从句是“who believe that the person who commits a crime is the one responsible for it”，这个从句中嵌套了一个“that”引导的宾语从句和一个“who”引导的定语从句。因此，也具有主句简单、从句复杂的特点，且核心信息偏重于第一个“who”从句上。经过分析，这三个句子都符合融合法的特点，可以首先考虑采用融合法来翻译。下面是参考译文。

① 有个女孩在楼下等你。

② 我们驾驶的飞机几乎每一个部件都有某种国籍标志。

③ 在美国，我们迫切需要更多的人相信，一个人犯了罪应该为其罪行承担责任。

(4) 状译法。所谓状译法，是指把英文原句中的定语从句翻译成汉语译文中的状语从句。大家知道，英语是“形合”的语言，英语中的某些定语从句实际上与所修饰的成分之间关系并不密切，只是连接手段之一，是为了使句子更严谨，句式更多变。换言之，英语中的某些定语从句包含有状语从句的功能，与主句形成一种特定的逻辑关系，如原因、结果、目的、让步等逻辑关系。因此，在翻译的时候应该对这些逻辑关系敏感，善于从英语原文的字里行间发现这些逻辑语义关系，然后用准确的汉语表达出来。比如说，按照这种方法，可以把表示时间状语的定语从句翻译成主句的时间状语从句，把表示原因状语的定语从句翻译成主句的原因状语从句等。此种翻译方法多见于非限制性定语从句的翻译。例如：

① No one in the company likes their boss, who is stingy and bad-tempered.

② He insisted on buying another villa, which he had no use for.

③ This company, which wants to get their new product sold well in the market, is trying hard to perfect its packing and workmanship.

例题分析：这三个句子出现了三个定语从句。经分析发现，第一个定语从句“who is stingy and bad-tempered”与其主句之间存在一定的因果关系，此定语从句可以翻译成主句的原因状语从句；同样,第二个定语从句“which he had no use for”与主句之间存在一定的转折关系,此定语从句可以翻译成主句的让步状语从句;而第三个定语从句“which wants to get their new product sold well in the market”与主句之间存在一定的目的关系,此定语从句可以翻译成主句的目的状语从句。下面是参考译文。

① 公司里没有人喜欢他们的老板,因为他脾气不好,人又小气。

② 尽管他并没有这样的需要,但他坚持再买一栋别墅。

③ 为了使新产品在市场上畅销,这个公司正在全力改进产品的工艺和包装。

以上是定语从句常用的四种翻译方法,希望考生能够学以致用,融会贯通。最后再来分析本节开始【举例说明】部分提到的 2003 年考题第 41 题和 2001 年考题第 43 题,看它们符合哪种定语从句翻译方法的要求。

例题分析:第一个例句中的定语从句较短,信息量不大,符合定语从句的第一种翻译方法。因此它的“humans have the ability to modify the environment in which they live”部分就可以翻译成“人类有能力改造他们所居住的环境”,将定语从句“in which they live”前置了。而第二个例句中的“that”定语从句中还嵌套了一个“when”引导的定语从句,较复杂,因此“that”从句可采用后置法,独立翻译成句,而“when”从句可以采用前置法,翻译到所修饰的“dates”之前,即“它(独特的新技术千年历)列出了人们有望看到数百项重大突破和发现的最迟日期”。

2. 名词性从句

【理论解释】

名词性从句的考查在考研英语翻译部分中非常多见,经常出现名词性从句在画线句子中作主语、宾语、表语、同位语等,即大家熟知的主语从句、宾语从句、表语从句和同位语从句。名词性从句大多可以直接按照原文的顺序翻译成相应的汉语译文。因此,名词性从句在考研英语中不算难点,只要能将之辨认出来,就不需要太繁杂的翻译技巧去调整语序。但是,同位语从句的翻译则必须引起重视。同位语从句的主要作用是对所修饰的成分(往往是抽象名词)作进一步的解释说明。由于汉语中没有同位语从句这个成分,因此在翻译成汉语的时候,必然需要语序上的分析和调整。而且,同位语从句的考查在考研英语翻译部分中也是屡见不鲜。

【举例说明】

名词性从句考题举例:

He asserted, also, that his power to follow a long and purely abstract train of thought was very limited, for which reason he felt certain that ho never could have succeeded with mathematics. (2008 年考题第 47 题)

Being interested in the relationship of language and thought, Whorf developed the idea that the structure of language determines the structure of habitual thought in a society. (2004 年考题第 44 题)

But the idea that the journalist must understand the law more profoundly than an ordinary citizen rests on an understanding of the established conventions and special responsibilities of the news media. (2007 年考题第 48 题)

例题分析:这是考研英语翻译部分中对名词性从句考查的三个典型的例子,其中第一个例句中包含两个宾语从句,均由“that”引导,这两个宾语从句的位置和汉语中宾语的位置相吻合,所以不难处理。而后两个例句各包含一个“that”引导的同位语从句,前面已经提到汉语中没有这个成分,因此如何准确、通顺、完整地进行汉语翻译就需要一定的翻译技巧去进行语序等的调整了。

【学习指导】

关于名词性从句的翻译方法，需要考虑的还是中英文的差异问题。四种名词性从句中的主语从句、宾语从句和表语从句的位置分别与汉语中所对应的成分位置一致，所以翻译的时候基本上不用进行语序调整，直接按原文顺序翻译即可。而名词性从句中的同位语从句较特殊，在汉语中没有对应的成分，是英文特殊的表意方式和连接手段，所以同位语从句的语序调整就显得非常必要了。先看一下前三种从句的翻译例句：

① This is what we have long discussed about.

② Whether he decides to go or stay makes no difference.

③ She says that the length of military uniforms has not changed for some time.

例题分析：上面三个例句中均各包含一个名词性从句。第一个例句中是“what”引导的表语从句；第二个例句中是“whether”引导的主语从句；第三个例句中是“that”引导的宾语从句。这三个名词性从句都可直接按原文语序翻译，下面是参考译文。

① 这就是我们一直在讨论的问题。

② 不管他决定走还是留都没有关系。

③ 她说军队的制服长度已经很长时间没有改变了。

名词性同位语从句的翻译主要有以下三种方法：

第一，当同位语从句比较简单、短小的时候，可以翻译到所修饰的名词之前，相当于前置的修饰语。但并不一定非得使用定语的标志词“的”，有时可以通过增词来灵活处理。例如：

① The rumor that 2012 Doomsday is inevitable is unfounded.

② The fact that he is dead is kept secret.

③ Everyone knows the fact that the earth revolves the sun.

例题分析：上面这三个句子中“that”引导的同位语从句都是比较简单、短小的，可以翻译到所修饰成分之前。下面是参考译文。

① 2012世界末日不可避免的传闻是没有根据的。

② 他已死的事实被保密了。

③ 所有人都知道地球绕着太阳转这一事实。

第二，当同位语从句出现在主句之后时，一般通过增加“即”这样的词来翻译，或者用冒号直接引出同位语从句。这种情况下，同位语从句本身往往比较复杂。详细说来，可以将主句以逗号结尾，然后增加“即”来连接。或者只用冒号引出同位语从句。例如：

① We have reached the conclusion that practice is the criterion for testing truth.

② But this does not in any way alter the fact that they are now, from a practical point of view, irrational.

例题分析：上面这两个例子包含的同位语从句都位于主句之后，尤其是第二个例句较复杂些，故可以采用上述翻译方法。下面是参考译文。

① 我们已经得出结论：实践是检验真理的标准。

② 但这却丝毫改变不了这样一个事实，即从实用的观点来看，它们在今天仍是不合理的。

第三，当同位语从句位于主句的前半部分，本身又不是很短小的时候，往往采用先翻译同位语从句，再翻译主句的方法。在这种情况下，主句前要用个概括性的词概括一下前面的从句，起过渡的作用，常用的有“这种观点”、“这一理论”、“这一思想”、“这一发现”等。再来看前面【举例说明】部分给出的2007年考题第48题。

例题分析:这个句子包含“that”引导的同位语从句“that the journalist must understand the law more profoundly than an ordinary citizen”修饰“the idea”,此同位语从句位于主句的前半部分,且本身信息负载量较大,采用第一种方法翻译到“the idea”之前会使译文繁琐且不通顺,采用第二种方法则会使译文出现语序混乱。因此可以考虑第三种翻译方法。事实证明,第三种方法最适合这个例句的翻译。参看译文如下。

但是记者必须比普通公民对法律有更深刻的理解,这种观点是基于对新闻媒体既有惯例和特殊责任的理解。

以上分析了名词性从句,尤其是同位语从句的翻译方法。考生一定要注意实践运用。最后,再来分析【举例说明】部分给出的 2008 年考题第 47 题和 2004 年考题第 44 题。

例题分析:第一个例句中所包含的两个“that”引导的宾语从句,无需调整译文,直接按原先的语序翻译即可,即“他坚持认为自己进行长时间纯抽象思维的能力十分有限,由此他认定自己在数学方面不可能取得成就。”第二个例句中的同位语从句“that the structure of language determines the structure of habitual thought in a society”位于从句的后半部分,可以采用同位语从句的第二种翻译方法,整句话可以翻译为“沃夫对语言与思维的关系很感兴趣,逐渐形成了这样的观点:在一个社会中,语言的结构决定习惯思维的结构”。

3. 状语从句

【理论解释】

在考研英语翻译题中,状语从句是常考的知识点,考生需要重点关注的是状语从句的位置和逻辑关系辨别这两个方面。英文中状语从句的种类繁多,可以表示时间、地点、原因、结果、目的、条件、让步、方式、比较等。而且,英文的状语位置非常灵活,可以位于句首、句中或者句末。因此,考生需要首先判断状语从句的种类,即引导词所表达的逻辑关系,尤其是可以引导多种从句的引导词(如 that, as 等),以便翻译出引导词的意思(不同的引导词各有不同的意思,在翻译状语从句时,根据引导词的意思翻译即可)。然后,再将此状语从句置于合适的位置进行翻译。汉语中的状语多位于所修饰的谓语动词或者所修饰的句子之前。因此,翻译状语从句时,应以汉语表达习惯为主,尽量将状语从句翻译到所修饰的句子或谓语动词之前。

【举例说明】

And home appliances will also become so smart that controlling and operating them will result in the breakout of a new psychological disorder—kitchen rage. (2001 年考题第 45 题)

The behavioral sciences have been slow to change partly because the explanatory items often seem to be directly observed and partly because other kinds of explanations have been hard to find. (2002 年考题第 42 题)

例题分析:第一个例句是典型的主从复合句,其主句是“home appliances will also become so smart”。把握好这句话的关键在于抓住“so... that...”这个短语,它支撑了这个句子的构架。此处“that”引导的是结果状语从句,这个短语的意思是“如此……以至于……”。至于是否可以直接套入这个短语的意思来翻译,就看结果状语从句的位置是否符合汉语的表达习惯了。第二个例句除主句“The behavioral sciences have been slow to change”外,包含了两个由“and”连接的原因状语从句,即“partly because... and partly because...”,用于说明主句陈述内容的原因。翻译此句的关键点在于识别其中的并列原因状语,并翻译出符合汉语表达习惯的译文。

【学习指导】

英语状语从句的翻译,通常可以直接翻译。受汉英语言表达习惯的影响,在英译汉时,通常需要对状语从句的位置作适当调整。下面根据汉语表达习惯,来具体说明状语从句的翻译方法。

第一种:将状语从句翻译在所修饰的句子或谓语动词之前。例如:

When they analyzed these rocks, they found shocked quartz grains—slivers with a particular arrangement of micro cracks believed to represent the relic left by an extraterrestrial impact.

例题分析:本例句中包含一个"when"引导的时间状语从句,意思是"在……的时候"。由于此处时间状语从句的位置和汉语中的时间状语位置一致,即符合汉语表达习惯,可直接按照原先的顺序翻译。以下是参考译文。

在分析这些岩芯时,他们发现了冲击石英颗粒——带有特殊排列的微裂缝的薄片,科学家认为它们是外层空间来的物体与地球碰撞留下来的遗迹。

再如:

As long as a doctor prescribes a drug for a legitimate medical purpose, the doctor has done nothing illegal even if the patient uses the drug to hasten death. (2002 年考题 Text 4)

例题分析:本例句中包含"as long as"引导条件状语从句,意思为"只要",位于所修饰的句子之前。这和汉语中条件状语从句的位置是一致的,因此可以直接按照英文原文的顺序翻译。以下是参考译文。

只要医生开药是出于合理的医疗目的,那么即使病人因为服用该药而加速死亡,医生的行为也没有违法。

第二种:将状语从句翻译到所修饰的句子之后。以 2001 年考题第 45 题为例再作分析。

And home appliances will also become so smart that controlling and operating them will result in the breakout of a new psychological disorder——kitchen rage. (2001 年考题第 45 题)

例题分析:上面已经提到本句核心结构由"so... that..."构架,"that"引导的是结果状语从句,由于汉语中的结果状语从句也是位于所修饰的句子之后,因此可以直接按原文顺序,翻译到后面。以下是参考译文。

家用电器将会变得如此智能化,以至于控制和操作它们会引发一种新的心理疾病——厨房狂躁症。

再如:

I have excluded him because, while his accomplishments may contribute to the solution of moral problems, the has not been charged with the task of approaching any but the factual aspects of those problems. (2006 年考题第 48 题)

例题分析:这个例句中包含一个"because"引导的原因状语从句,且此原因状语从句中又嵌套了一个"while"原因状语从句。汉语习惯遵循先因后果的顺序,即先说主句,再说原因状语从句。其实,在大多数情况下,英译汉时,原因状语从句的翻译都应该遵循这一顺序。只是本句的原因状语篇幅过长,可以另辟蹊径,借"之所以……是因为……"这两个字来实现句子翻译的平衡和通顺。以下是参考译文。

我之所以将他排除在外,是因为:尽管他的成果可能会有助于解决道德问题,但他承担的任务只不过是研究这些问题的事实方面。

4. 被动语态

【理论解释】

英语中被动句式的形式较为简单,通常由助动词"be"或系动词的某一形式与动词的过去分词构成,二者结合在句中充当谓语;动作实施者一般不出现,如果出现的话,通常由"by"、"with"、"or"或

"through"等引出。

考研翻译的选材多是正式文体的科普、学术类文章。这类文章的特点之一就是被动句使用频率很高。而汉语中被动语态的使用远远少于在英语中的使用。这一差异的存在导致,在中英文转换过程中运用必要的被动语态翻译方法是非常重要的。多数情况下,英文中的被动语态句都能转换成汉语的主动表达,只有在强调被动意义时才使用被动句。翻译成汉语时应该灵活采用相应的翻译方法,以使译文符合汉语的表达习惯。

【举例说明】

考研翻译中被动语态的真题举例:

The behavioral sciences have been slow to change partly because the explanatory items often seem to be directly observed and partly because other kinds of explanations have been hard to find. (2002 年考题第 42 题)

But his primary task is not to think about the moral code, which governs his activity, any more than a businessman is expected to dedicate his energies to an exploration of rules of conduct in business. (2006 年考题第 49 题)

例题分析:这两个真题例句中分别包含了被动语态"be directly observed"和"is expected"。由于被动语态是考研英语翻译的重要考点之一,如果不作任何处理,直接简单翻译成"被"字句,不但有可能会导致译文不通顺,而且还会有扣分的危险。如果将例句的"be directly observed"和"is expected"直接翻译成"……(可以)直接被观察到"和"(商人)被期待……"则不太符合汉语表达习惯。因此,掌握必要的英文被动语态翻译方法是必要的。

【学习指导】

在英译汉中,通常将英文的被动语态句进行灵活的转换,以翻译出符合汉语表达习惯的译文。考研英语中有关被动语态的翻译方法一般有下面几种。

第一种,被动语态的动作发出者由"by"引出时,采用主宾颠倒的方式,即把"by"后的动作发出者作主语,将英文原句中的主语作宾语。例如:

① Effective measures should be taken by the government to solve the problem timely.

② During this transfer, traditional historical methods were augmented by additional methodologies designed to interpret the new forms of evidence in the historical study. (1999 年考题第 33 题)

例题分析:第一个例句中包含被动语态"should be taken",且有"by"引出动作的发出者,可以翻译为:"政府需要采取有效的措施来及时地解决这一问题"。第二个例句谓语部分使用了被动语态"were augmented by"。主语是"traditional historical methods",介词"by"引出施动者。因此,此处也可以将主宾颠倒,翻译为主动形式,即"新方法充实了传统的历史研究方法",整句话的参考译文为:"在这种转变中,历史学家研究历史时,那些解释新史料的新方法充实了传统的历史研究方法"。历年考题中出现过多次需要如此处理的被动语态,相对来说比较简单。

第二种,翻译成无主句,即将被动结构中的主语翻译为汉语的宾语。多为动作发出者一目了然或者不需要挖掘出动作发出者的情况。例如:

① Legal steps should be taken to reduce the high rates of traffic accident.

② Television is one of the means by which these feelings are created and conveyed—and perhaps never before has it served so much to connect different peoples and nations as in the recent events in Europe. (2005 年考题第 46 题)

例题分析:第一个例句中包含被动语态“should be taken”,此处可以转换成主动,翻译为“必须采取法律措施来降低交通事故的高发率”,这是符合汉语表达习惯的。第二个例句的定语从句“by which these feelings are created and conveyed”中,包含被动结构“are created and conveyed”。该被动结构的主语是“these feelings”。若按字面翻译,“通过电视这个手段,这些感受被引发和传递”,这显然不符合地道的汉语表达。动作“create and convey”和“these feelings”之间是逻辑上的动宾关系,因此可以翻译为“引发和传递这些感受”。将其与定语从句合并之后,即得到译文:“引发和传递这些感受的手段”。整句话的参考译文:“电视是产生和表达这些感受的手段之一——在欧洲近来发生的事件中,它把不同的民族和国家连在一起,其作用之大,前所未有”。

第三种,英语原文的主语在译文中仍作主语,即去掉“被”字,用主动的形式表达被动的意思。例如下题以及前面【举例说明】中提到的2002年考题第42题:

With the development of social economy, cultural traditions must be kept.

例题分析:前一个例句中包含被动语态“must be kept”,翻译成“文化传统必须被保持”很别扭,试着去掉“被”字,译文就成了“文化传统必须保留”,而这完全符合汉语表达习惯。2002年考题第42题的例句中包含被动语态“be directly observed”,字面意思为“直接被观察到”,显得较呆板,去掉“被”字后反而更符合汉语的表达:“解释的依据似乎可以直接观察到”。整句话的参考译文为:“行为科学之所以发展缓慢,部分原因是用来解释行为的依据似乎往往是直接观察到的,部分原因是其他的解释方式一直难以找到”。

第四种,译成汉语的被动句。汉语的被动句不只限于带有“被”字句。还有其他一些汉语特有的表达被动的手段,如“受”、“受到”、“遭到”、“让”、“给”、“把”、“挨”、“由”、“得到”、“加以”、“得以”、“为……所……”及“由……来……”等。例如:

① Over the years, tools and technology themselves as a source of fundamental innovation have largely been ignored by historians and philosophers of science. (1994年考题第73题)

② When that happens, it is not a mistake: it is mankind's instinct for moral reasoning in action, an instinct that should be encouraged rather than laughed at. (1997年考题第35题)

例题分析:第一个例句中包含被动语态“have been ignored”,并且出现了“by”引出动作发出者,只是此处若采取主宾颠倒的方式,将“by”后的动作发出者翻译成主语,则会出现这样的译文:“多年来历史学家和科学思想家们在很大程度上忽视了作为根本性创新源泉的工具和技术本身”,不是特别通顺;若采取翻译成被动句的方式,更符合汉语表达习惯:“工具和技术本身作为根本性创新的源泉,多年来在很大程度上被历史学家和科学思想忽视了”。第二个例句中这个句子中有两个被动语态:“should be encouraged”和“rather than laughed at”。按照汉语表达习惯,可以翻译为“得到鼓励、受到鼓励”,和“受到嘲笑、遭到嘲笑”。整句话的参考译文为:“这种反应并不错,这是人类用道德观念进行推理的本能在起作用。这种本能应得到鼓励,而不应遭到嘲笑”。

第五种,增加主语,即将英文被动句翻译成汉语的主动句,适当增添一些不确定的主语,如人们、有人、大家、我们等。这种翻译方法多用于“It+be+过去分词+that”这样的句型。再来分析前文举例说明提及的2006年考题第49题。

But his primary task is not to think about the moral code, which governs his activity, any more than a businessman is expected to dedicate his energies to an exploration of rules of conduct in business. (2006年考题第49题)

例题分析:此例句被动语态体现在“a businessman is expected to...”,此被动结构并未出现其主语,但翻译成“商人们被期待去……”不符合汉语表达习惯,可以通过增加主语“人们”来翻译。即

"但是他的首要任务并不是考虑支配自己行动的道德规范,就如同人们不能指望商人专注于行业规范一样"。

5. 代词指代

【理论解释】

为了避免名词或名词性成分的重复,英文中多用代词,而汉语多重复,故汉语中较少使用代词。这一差异的存在,就需要在英译汉的过程中加以适当的调整。具体说来,英文中的代词类别繁多,有人称代词、不定代词、指示代词、关系代词等;汉语中也有代词,但因为汉语多重复,且句子结构相对松散、句子相对较短小,不太注重形式,因而汉语里多用名词,使得语义更加清楚,用的代词相对少很多。这种语言和思维习惯上的差异会造成考生理解和翻译上的困难。在考研英语翻译题中,如果代词翻译不清楚会导致句义不完整或者意思不清晰的话,就一定要将此代词还原。因为从历年的考研翻译题来看,出题者的本意就是在于考查考生是否理解画线部分代词所指代的具体内容,所以一旦代词出现在主要成分的位置,往往要求考生通过还原其指代的内容来翻译。

【举例说明】

They are the possessions of the autonomous (self-governing) man of traditional theory, and they are essential to practices in which a person is held responsible for his conduct and given credit for his achievements. (2002 年考题第 44 题)

Actually, it isn't, because it assumes that there is an agreed account of human rights, which is something the world does not have. (1997 年考题第 31 题)

例题分析:第一个例子中出现了两个"they"和两个"his"(形容词性物主代词),根据其并列结构及句义可以判断这两个"they"指代的内容一致,且都是各自分句的主语,属于主要成分。如果不翻译出其指代的内容则会导致整句话的信息不完整,让人摸不着头脑,而这两个"his"属于句内指代,都是"a person"的形容词性物主代词,属于修饰成分,因此比较好处理。第二个例子出现了两个"it",都属于句中的主要成分,如果不还原其指代的具体内容的话,同样会导致意思不清,进而被扣分。

【学习指导】

代词指代也是考研翻译的考点之一。首先,不弄清代词(尤其是位于主要成分的代词)所指代的具体内容则不利于把握整个句子的意思。其次,不准确地翻译出代词所指代的对象,往往会导致扣分。

考生需要认识到,虽然有些代词指代对象出现在画线句子中,很容易予以还原,但绝大多数情况下,代词都需要返回上文寻找对应的名词、短语或句子。下面从两个方面加以简要解析。

首先,当代词出现在主要成分位置时,一定要联系上下文寻找指代内容。例如上文提及的 2002 年考题第 44 题。

例题分析:这个例句中的两个"his"都是本句中"a person"的形容词性物主代词,这一点毋庸置疑,翻译时只要符合汉语表达习惯,保证语句通顺即可。而这两个"they"分别是"and"连接的两个并列分句的主语,属于整句话的主要成分,因此有必要还原。而其指代的对象应该去上文寻找。前文提到"It will not solve our problem, however, until it replaces traditional prescientific views, and these are strongly entrenched. Freedom and dignity illustrate the difficulty...",其大体意思是:"然而,除非行为技术取代科学发展之前已形成的传统观念,否则它无法解决我们的问题,而这些传统观念已经根深蒂固。自由和尊严就能说明困难的程度"。由此可见,"they"指代的只能是"freedom and dignity"。因此,即使不还原其指代,也只能翻译为"它们",而不是"他们"。最保险的办法是将之还原,重复其指代的具体内容"自由和尊严"。整句话的参考译文就是"自由和尊严(它们)是传统理论定义的自主人所拥有的,是要求一个人对自己的行为负责并因其业绩而给予肯定的必不可少的前提”。类似需要还原指代的例子在考研翻译中还有很多,方法都是返回前文寻找指代对象,然后还原其具体指代内容。

其次,当代词出现在非主要成分位置时,如出现在插入语或者修饰成分等位置,一般不需要回原文找出指代的具体内容。例如:

Science moves forward, they say, not so much through the insights of great men of genius as because of more ordinary things like improved techniques and tools. (1994 年考题第 71 题)

例题分析:这个例句中的代词“they”出现在了插入语“they say”中,虽然“they”具有主语的功能,但在整句话中属于修饰成分。这句话的重点是考查“not so much... as...”这个比较结构。综上考虑,此处能还原指代更好,不还原指代也不会扣分。整句话的参考译文就是“他们说,科学之所以向前发展,与其说是源于天才伟人的真知灼见,不如说是源于改进了的技术和工具等更为普通的东西”。

下面再分析一下前文提及的 1997 年考题第 31 题。

此例句的两个“it”都出现在主要成分的位置,如若不还原则会导致语义不完整,因此需要到前文寻找线索。上文提到:“Do animals have rights? This is how the question is usually put. It sounds like a useful, ground clearing way to start”. 由此可判断,这里的“it”指代上文的“Do animals have rights?”或“the question”。而且画线句子中的“it isn't”是承接上文的省略,可以补充完整为:“It isn't a useful, ground clearing way to start.”因此,例句的前半部分可以翻译为:“实际上,这并不是一个有用的,有助于把问题搞清楚的问法,因为它认为人们对人权有着共同的认识……”另外,还可以把“Actually, it isn't”模糊处理成“事实并非如此”,然后别忘了把第二个“it”还原成“这种问法”,即“事实并非如此,因为这种问法认为人们对人权有着共同的认识……”

6. 比较结构

【理论解释】

比较结构是考研英语的重要考点,同时也是考研翻译的难点之一。由于比较结构是英语特有的表达方式,在汉语中没有对应的结构,所以,对于比较结构的理解和转换历来是考生的“软肋”。但只要抓住其精髓,理解其深层含义,就可以迎刃而解。

【举例说明】

比较结构的考题如上文提及的 1994 年考题第 71 题以及 2006 年考题第 49 题。

Science moves forward, they say, not so much through the insights of great men of genius as because of more ordinary things like improved techniques and tools. (1994 年考题第 71 题)

But his primary task is not to think about the moral code, which governs his activity, any more than a businessman is expected to dedicate his energies to an exploration of rules of conduct in business. (2006 年考题第 49 题)

例题分析:这两个例句中都包含比较结构,其中第一个例句的比较结构为“not so much ... as”;第二个例句的比较结构为“not any more ... than ...”。若对比较结构认识不清或掌握不透彻,则很难翻译出理想的译文。要想拿到这两个句子的理想分数,就必须认真学习比较结构的分类及深层含义。

【学习指导】

比较结构主要有两类,一类是“as”所表示的比较结构,另一类是“than”所表示的比较结构。

考研中“as”类的比较结构主要考查两个:“as... as...”和“not so much ... as...”。而对

"than"类的比较结构主要考查四个:"more... than..."、"less... than..."、"no more... than..."、"no less... than..."。比较结构必然有比较对象,为了更清楚地说明问题,下面把比较对象用A(前者)和B(后者)表示。

第一类:"as"的比较结构。

(1)比较结构"**as... as...**"

"A as... as B"表示"A像B一样……"或者"A和B一样……",而"... as A as B"则表示"既A也B"。具体说来,前一种是两个事物之间的比较,而后一种是一个事物两个方面的比较。下面是例句展示。

① She is as beautiful as Mary.

② Mary is as beautiful as intelligent.

例题分析:第一个例句符合"A as... as B"的结构,即表示A(she)和B(Mary)这两个事物之间的比较,因此套入结构后译文就是"她和玛丽一样漂亮";第二个例句符合"... as A as B"的结构,即表示Mary的外貌和智商这两个方面的比较:A(beautiful)和B(intelligent)。因此套入结构后,译文就是"玛丽既漂亮又聪明"。

(2)比较结构"**not so much... as ...**"

这个结构是"as... as..."的变体,实际上是其否定形式。"A not so much ... as B"表示"A不像B那么……"或者"A不如B那么……",而"not so much A as B"表示"与其说A不如说B"或者"是B,不是A"。例如:

① Li Yu is not so much interested in political power as his predecessors.

② Science moves forward, they say, not so much through the insights of great men of genius as because of more ordinary things like improved techniques and tools.

例题分析:第一个例句符合"A not so much ... as B"的结构,即A(Li Yu)和B(his predecessors)这两个事物的比较,由此可翻译为"李煜不像他的前任们那么对政治权术感兴趣",再调整成汉语表达习惯的句子就是"与他的前任们相比,李煜对政治权术没那么感兴趣";第二个例句符合not so much A as B的结构,即A(through the insights of great men of genius)和B(of more ordinary things like improved techniques and tools)这两个方面的比较,可以翻译为"科学之所以向前发展,与其说是源于天才伟人的真知灼见,不如说是源于像改进了的技术和工具等更为普通的东西"。

第二类,"**than**"的比较结构。

(1)比较结构"**more ... than...**"和"**less... than...**"。

这两个结构意思相反,在这里作为一组进行对照解析。"A more ... than B"表示"A比B更……",而"more A than B"表示"与其说B不如说A"或者"是A,不是B"。同样的,"A less ... than B"表示"A不如B……",而"less A than B"则表示"与其说A不如说B"或者"是B,不是A"。例如:

① China is larger than any country in Africa.

② A dictionary is more useful than interesting.

③ This dress is less beautiful than that one.

④ A dictionary is less interesting than useful.

例题分析:第一个例句符合"A more ... than B"的结构,即A(China)和B(any country in Africa)这两个事物的比较;第二个例句符合"more A than B"的结构,即同一个事物(a dictionary)的

A(useful)和B(interesting)这两个方面的比较;第三个例句符合"A less ... than B"的结构,即A(This dress)和B(that one)这两个事物的比较;第四个例句符合"less A than B"的结构,即同一个事物(a dictionary)的A(interesting)和B(useful)这两个方面的比较。根据这些结构所表示的含义,它们分别可以翻译成:"中国比非洲任何一个国家都大";"与其说字典有趣不如说它有用";"这件衣服不如那件好看";"与其说字典有趣不如说它有用"。

(2) 比较结构"**no more ... than...**"和"**no less... than...**"

这两个结构意思相反,在这里作为一组进行对照解析。"A no more ... than B"表示"A和B(一样)都不……",而"no more A than B"则表示"既不A也不B"。"A no less ... than B"表示"A和B(一样)都……",而"no less A than B"则表示"既A也B"。此外,"no more... than..."等同于"not any more... than...","no less... than..."等同于"not any more... than..."。例如:

① Mary is no more intelligent than Alice.

② Mary is no more intelligent than beautiful.

③ Mary is no less intelligent than Alice.

④ Mary is no less intelligent than beautiful.

例题分析:第一个例句是"A no more ... than B"的结构,即A(Mary)和B(Alice)这两个事物之间的比较;第二个例句是"no more A than B"的结构,即同一个事物(Mary)的A(intelligent)和B(beautiful)这两个方面的比较;第三个例句是"A no less... than B",即A(Mary)和B(Alice)这两个事物之间的比较;第四个例句是"no less A than B"的结构,即同一个事物(Mary)的A(intelligent)和B(beautiful)两个方面的比较。根据这些结构所表示的深层含义,它们分别可以翻译成:"玛丽和爱丽斯都不聪明";"玛丽既不聪明,也不漂亮";"玛丽和爱丽斯都聪明";"玛丽既聪明,又漂亮"。

以上是考研英语中常考的比较结构,考生的突破口就是抓住每个比较结构的深层含义,并在具体的例子中加以灵活转换。

下面再分析一下上文提及的2006年考题第49题。

例题分析:这个例子包含的是"than"类的比较结构"A not any more... than B",表示"A和B一样都不……",其中A为"his primary task is to think about the moral code",B为"a businessman is expected to dedicate his energies to an exploration of rules of conduct in business"。由此可见,译文应该为:"他的主要任务不是去思考支配其行为的道德准则,正如人们不应该期待商人致力于探索商业行为规范一样"。

7. 成分隔离

【理论解释】

考研英语中的成分隔离主要有两种:一种是成分插入,即所谓的插入语;另一种是顺序调整,即宾语后置。前者主要是指介词短语、分词短语、独立主格等置于主谓之间或主从之间,往往前后都加逗号。后者主要是指紧挨在动词之后的宾语后置到其他成分之后。其中,成分插入结构往往可以直接翻译,而宾语后置需要把宾语还原到原先的位置再进行翻译。总之,成分隔离结构翻译的关键是识别出隔离的具体内容。

【举例说明】

Thus, the anthropological concept of "culture," like the concept of "set" in mathematics, is an abstract concept which makes possible immense amounts of concrete research and understanding. (2003年考题第45题)

例题分析:本句包含了两个成分隔离现象。一个是在主句的插入语"like the concept of 'set' in

mathematics”,另一个是从句的宾语后置。主句中介词短语“like the concept of ‘set’ in mathematics”,将主句主语“the anthropological concept”与其谓语“is”分割开了。在“which”引导的定语从句中,动词“make”与其宾语“immense amounts of concrete research and understanding”被形容词“possible”分割开了。“immense amounts of concrete research and understanding”作“make”的宾语。因其结构稍长,故将补语“possible”置于宾语前。句子还原之后为:“which makes immense amouots of concrete research and understanding possible”。能否识别句子的分割现象,就成为解决翻译本例句的关键所在。

【学习指导】

在上面提到的成分隔离结构中,由于插入语通常都位于标志性的双逗之间,因而比较好辨别,在此就不再赘述;而宾语后置则需要花费一定的时间才能辨别,所以下面进行简单的解析。英文句子中之所以存在宾语后置的现象,是因为当动宾结构中的宾语过长或者过于复杂,且宾语后紧跟的补语或状语(多为介词短语)相对较短小或简单时,为了保持句子的平衡和可读性,往往将宾语后置到这些补语或状语之后,构成宾语后置。例如:

① I shall define him as an individual who has elected as his primary duty and pleasure in life the activity of thinking in Socratic way about moral problems. (2006 年考题第 46 题)

② On the other hand, he did not accept as well founded the charge made by some of his critics that, while he was a good observer, he had no power of reasoning. (2008 年考题第 48 题)

例题分析:第一个例句中的“elect”是及物动词,而出现在它后面的介词短语“as his primary duty and pleasure in life”,由此可判断发生了宾语后置。句中“elected”的真正宾语是这个介词短语后面的“the activity of thinking in Socratic way about moral problems”,由于里面的成分较复杂,故被后置了。判断出宾语后置后,就可以翻译了。参考译文为:“我把他(知识分子)定义为这样的人——他们把以苏格拉底的方式来思考道德问题作为自己人生的主要责任和乐趣”。

有了第一个例句的经验,第二个例句的宾语后置就好判断了。其中的“accept”也是及物动词,但是紧跟其后的并不是它的宾语,而是“as well founded”,由此也可判断本句中发生了宾语后置,即“accept”真正的宾语是“the charge”。这个宾语之所以后置,是因为它有一个过去分词短语“made by some of his critics”做后置定语,同时被一个“that”引导的同位语从句修饰,与此同时,这个“that”同位语从句中还嵌套了一个“while”引导的让步状语从句。这个宾语的复杂程度可见一斑。把这些成分归置好之后,就可以进入到翻译这一步骤了。参考译文为:“另一方面,某些人批评他虽然善于观察,却不具备推理能力,而他认为这种说法也是缺乏根据的”。

2.6 写 作

2.6.1 应用文写作指导

1.《考纲》基本信息详解

写作部分:A 节主要考查目标是要求考生运用英语撰写不同类型的应用文,包括私人和公务信函、备忘录、摘要、报告等。

A 节应用文写作部分的题型有两种,每次考试选择其中的一种形式。

备选题型包括:

(1) 考生根据所给情景写出约 100 词(标点符号不计算在内)的应用性短文,包括私人和公务信函、备忘录、报告等。

信函种类比较多,包括:道歉信、表扬信、投诉信、建议信、询问信等。备忘录是用于上级对下级或同级之间的半正式信函。报告是下级对上级的正式信函。常见的报告包括调查报告和工作总结。

(2) 要求考生所提供的汉语文章,用英语写出一篇80~100词的文章摘要。

摘要写作的具体出题形式一般是,给一篇1 500字左右的汉语文章,根据这篇文章写出一个80~100词的英文摘要。考生需要对整篇文章的内容做一个提炼,进而转化为精练的英文表达。

该部分考试要求考生在答题卡2上作答。共10分。

2.《考纲》考查目标强化指导

(1) 测试要点:信息点的覆盖,内容的组织,语言的准确性,格式,语域的恰当。

值得注意的是,对语法结构和词汇多样性的要求将根据具体试题做出调整。允许在写作中使用提示语中出现的关键词,但使用提示语中出现过的词组或句子将被扣分。就是说,文章中不可以出现提示语中出现的词组或句子,所以用到提示语中的词组或句子时,必须对其进行相应的改写。

① 信息点的覆盖。信息点的覆盖非常重要。写作时要认真读题,应把题目要求的信息点全部找到,进而完成写作任务。遗漏相关信息点会导致考生失分。

② 内容的组织。一般情况下,应用文内容组织非常的简单,一般写成三段。第一段是"介绍,写信目的";第二段"具体写作内容";第三段"表明期望"。

③ 语言的准确性。这涉及考生的语言基本功底。考研写作考查的核心内容就是语言表达,考生在平时的复习当中,需要积累相关词汇和句型的应用,逐步提高英文写作能力。

④ 格式。凡是应用文,一定是对格式有要求的。比如,书信类开头得有"Dear...",结尾得有"Yours..."或"Sincerely..."等。

⑤ 语域的恰当。所谓的"语域"指的是在恰当的氛围、恰当的时候说出合适的话。在写信的时候,一般情况下会涉及两种信件。一种叫私人信函,比如写给自己父母的家信,男女朋友间的书信。另外一种叫公务信函。私人信函里允许使用口语化的词汇,但在公务信函里不允许出现任何口语化的词汇或者非正式的表达。比如,写一封投诉信,这属于正式的公务信函,写信人跟收信人不认识,写信的时候要用正式的语言。

(2) 应用文分类讲解。

① 书信类应用文。

【文体说明】

书信是重要的交际工具,通常分为私人信函和公务信函两大类。公务信函一般谈论或处理重要事务,可能是推荐信、求职信、求学信、邀请信、询问信、投诉信等。除私人的信函外,其他信函都被称之为公务信函。

【举例说明】

下面2009年考试应用文写作范文。考生可以以此初步了解一下应用文写作的格式和内容。

Directions:

Restrictions on the use of plastic bags have not been so successful in some regions. "White pollution" is still going on.

Write a letter to the editor(s) of your local newspaper to

1) give your opinions briefly, and

2) make two or three suggestions.

You should write about 100 words on ANSWER SHEET 2.

Do not sign your own name at the end of the letter. Use “Li Ming” instead.

Do not write the address. (10 points)

范文如下:

Dear Editor,

I’m a sincere reader of your newspaper and I like your discussion of the social problems. Now I would like to give some opinions of myself about the “White Pollution”.

As we know, regulation was made to solve the problem in June 1st of 2008. The use of plastic bags was restricted in the supermarket and many other shops freely. At the beginning, it was carried on well, but now I found plastic bags were used in some small shops for free or with no pay.

I am writing to tell you that we should solve this problem soon with the help of your newspaper. You could make some investigators about it and write some reports of it, so as to appeal to all the people’s attentions of our society.

Sincerely,

Li Ming

范文解析:本文是2009年教育部公布的一篇9分应用文范文。根据题目要求,这篇小作文的内容要点应该包括三部分。第一,说明写这封信的意图:就“白色污染”问题给出自己的观点和看法;第二,具体说明“白色污染”问题:可以根据题目提示,对限塑令颁发的背景简要地做一个介绍,然后提出本地区或自己身边存在的对“限塑令”执行不力的现象;第三,阐明自己的观点、看法,给出两三条建议。该信第一段的内容很吻合题目的要求,首句为自我介绍,符合公务建议信的写作原则,即先肯定对方服务,再提建议;第二句点明写作目的。第二段改写了题目的提示部分:“Restrictions on the use of plastic bags have not been so successful in some regions. ‘White pollution’ is still going on.”介绍了背景,提出了问题。第三段满足了题目中的两个要求:给出具体观点,并提出两条建议。所以信息点覆盖十分全面。

首段首句自我介绍,使用了主系表结构和并列句;第二句在中心名词“opinion”之后使用了两个介词短语作后置定语。第二段共三句,四处使用了被动语态,其中第三句使用了代词“it”做主语,避免了重复。本段的精彩词汇有:“regulation was made”,“be restricted”,“for free”等。第三段共两句,首句使用了宾语从句和介词短语作状语,第二句使用了不定式作目的状语,本段的精彩词汇有:“inform,appeal to”,“attention”等。

这封信的语言读起来比较自然流畅,当然也存在个别的语法和用词错误。比如,第二段第二句点出了免费使用塑料袋的具体地点,但表达含混,“freely”既有“免费地”这层意思,也有“自由地”这层意思,句子应改为:“The use of plastic bags for free was restricted in the supermarket and many other shops.”第三句的时态出现错误,后半句不应该用过去时而应使用现在时,即“found”应改为“find”,“were”应改为“are”。第三段第二句中,“investigators”应改为“investigations”。这些错误不太影响理解,故可以接受。

文中有效运用了各种衔接手段,如:“now”,“as we know”,“at the beginning”,“but”,“so as to”等。逻辑组织也比较严密。

这封信格式正确,使用了正式的语言,讲话恰当得体,符合要求。

综上所述,该信很好地完成了试题规定的任务,对目标读者(即语言接受对象)完全产生了预期的效果。

【学习指导】

第一，对于书信格式，不同的应用文有不同的格式要求。总体说来，书信类写作格式大致相同。

英文书信通常由五个部分组成，包括信头及信内地址、称呼、正文、结束语和落款。在考研应用文写作中，只要求基本格式正确，所以把握称呼、正文和落款三个部分就可以。日期、地址等都不需要写。

称呼指写信人对收信人的称谓敬语。在第一行顶格写，后面加逗号。由于书信分为公务信函和私人信函，故称呼语也大致分为两种情况，如表2-2所示。

表2-2 称呼语的使用

书信的情况		称呼语
写给团体、组织或机构的负责人	给不认识的人	"Dear Sir or Madam",/"To Whom It May Concern",
	给认识的人	性别+姓："Dear Mr. Wang," 性别+职务："Dear Mr. /Ms. /President/Professor/Manager," 职务+姓名："Dear President (James) Wang,"
写给个人	认识，但关系不太亲密	同上
	熟人或亲属	直呼其名："Dear Mary",/"Dear John,"

正文是书信中最重要的内容，也是应用文的得分关键。英语书信写作有两种基本格式：缩进式和齐头式。缩进式是英国英语和传统英语中常见的写作格式，即每段第一行向后缩进4个字母，段与段之间不空行；称呼顶格写，正文缩进，落款位于中间偏右的位置。齐头式是在美国英语和现代英语，尤其是商务英语中常用的写作格式，即每段第一行顶格写，段与段之间空一行；称呼、正文、落款均顶格写。考研应用文写作建议考生采用缩进式格式。

落款包括结束语和署名两部分。结束语是表示礼节的套语，写在正文下面两三行处的右侧，从中间写起，第一个词的开头字母要大写，末尾用逗号。落款的表达法从严格意义上讲有多种。给机关团体或不认识的人可用："Yours truly"或"Truly yours"，"Yours faithfully"或"Faithfully yours"，"Yours sincerely"或"Sincerely yours"；给上级或长者可用："Yours respectfully"或"Respectfully yours"，"Yours obediently"或"Obediently yours"，"Yours gratefully"或"Gratefully yours"；"Yours sincerely"或"Sincerely yours"；给一般熟人或朋友可用："Yours"，或"Yours sincerely"。对于考生而言，有一种以不变应万变的表达法，即"Yours sincerely"，这种落款方式适用于各种关系，既可以是朋友，也可以是上下级，还可以是素不相识的人等。

写信人署名，要写在结束语下面一行处，要从结束语的中部写起。根据《考纲》，签名统一为"Li Ming"，千万不要写出自己的真实姓名。特别提示：考研书信类应用文不要求写日期。

第二，对于书信正文写作流程，考研应用文一般有三点提纲，即三个内容要点。因此，考生应严格按照《考纲》要求写成三句，每句表达一个提纲要点，顺序不要打乱，做到条理清晰，简明准确。下面介绍一种基本写法：

首段：1～2句，包括自我介绍和写作目的。私人信函不用自我介绍。自我介绍可以使用一句话，如"I am a freshman/sophomore/junior/senior/undergraduate/graduate from Shanghai Normal University."（我是上海师范大学一名大一/大二/大三/大四学生/本科生/研究生。）表明写作目的可以使用一句话，比如"I am writing the letter to offer my heartfelt thanks to your unselfish help."（我

写这封信的目的是真诚地感谢您无私的帮助。)

第二段:3 句,把每点提纲进行相应的改写,每点提纲写一句。

尾段:1 ~2 句,可以使用一句话表示感谢,比如"Words fail me when I want to show my sincere appreciation to your generous help."(我对您慷慨帮助的感谢难以言表。)还可以使用一句话表达期待回信,比如"I am looking forward to your favorable reply at your earliest convenience."(期待您在方便之时尽快给予我圆满的答复。)

第三,关于书信写作常用句型,在考研应用文书信写作当中,各类信函的开头和结尾段都有相对比较固定的句型可以套用。以下列出的是不同主题的信函常用的句型。

对于感谢信、致歉信、祝贺信、慰问信来说,这类信件主要是向对方表达感谢、歉意、祝贺、慰问等情感,开头直接表明写信目的。开头常用句型有:

I'm writing to	convey	my	sincere	thanks	to you for... 或
	express		hearty	gratitude	
	extend		heartfelt	appreciation	
				apology	
				congratulations	
				regret	

I'm writing to	thank you	for...
	apologize	
	congratulate you	
	comfort you	

结尾常用句型:

Once more, I will show my genuine gratitude/apology/congratulations/regret to you.

对于申请信和推荐信来说,申请信包括求职申请和求学申请,属于自荐;推荐信则属于推荐他人。正文一般都包括三部分:提出申请,介绍自己或被推荐人的情况,总结说明,期盼回复,表示感谢。

一般情况下,开头常用句型:

I'm writing to	apply for	the position advertised in...
I would like to		the vacancy that you have advertised in...
I hope to	express my interest in your recently advertised position for...	
	recommend sb. for...	

结尾常用句型:

Thank you for your consideration/ attention.

I look forward to your reply.

对于投诉信和建议信来说，二者目的都是为了解决问题。但前者重在反映并解释存在的问题，讲明自己希望对方做的事情；后者则重在提出建议及改进措施，语言上更加委婉和礼貌。开头常用句型：

I' m writing to	complain about...
	advise/ suggest/ recommend you do sth.

结尾常用语：

Please give this matter your immediate attention.

I am looking forward to an early reply.

Thank you for your attention.

② 通知。

【文体说明】

通知是告示类应用文的一种。具体来说，是上级、组织对成员布置工作、召开会议或传达事情等使用的一种应用文。平行单位之间互相协商讨论，也可以互发通知。通知有两种：一种通知对象较少，一般采用书信式，寄出或发送通知给有关人员，与书信写法相同；另一种通知对象较多，采用告示形式，张贴通知。此处指后者。通知一般使用第三人称，如果有称呼，则使用第二人称。

【举例说明】

2010年考题应用文题目如下：

Directions:

You are supposed to write for the Postgraduates' Association a notice to recruit volunteers for an international conference on globalization. The notice should include the basic qualification for applicants and the other information which you think is relevant.

You should write about 100 words on ANSWER SHEET 2.

Do not sign your own name at the end of the notice. Use "postgraduates' association" instead。(10 points)

范文如下：

Volunteers Needed

January 9, 2010

To improve student's ability and enrich extracurricular activities, the Postgraduates' Association is recruiting volunteers for an international conference on globalization to be held on April 10, 2010 in Beijing. To begin with, applicants should have Chinese nationality, strong professional spirit, cheerful personality and be aged under 35. In addition, candidates must have outstanding skills at English listening comprehension and the ability to speak Chinese and English fluently. Finally, students with relevant professional experience are preferred. Those graduate students who are interested in taking part in it may sign up with monitor of their classes before February 1, 2010.

Postgraduates' Association

范文解析：本文主体部分共六句。首句为全文总论，阐述了本次志愿者活动的目的、主办方、内容、时间、地点等告示的五大要素。选用了不定式短语放在句首做目的状语、介词短语做状语、不定式短语作后置定语等多种句型。具体看一下第一句:"To improve student's ability and enrich extracurricular activities, the Postgraduate Association is recruiting volunteers for an international conference on globalization to be held on April 10, 2010 in Beijing".(为提高同学们的能力并丰富课外活动,研究生会现为2010年4月10日在北京举办的有关全球化的国际会议招募志愿者。)本句里,不定式结构包含两个精彩词汇"enrich"和"extracurricular"。"enrich"的意思是"使……丰富","extracurricular"的意思是"课外的"。主句部分采用了进行时态,"to be held on April 10, 2010 in Beijing"动词不定式做后置定语修饰"conference"。这样一来,通过加入大量的修饰成分,句子就变得丰富起来了。

再来看第二到第四句。这三句紧扣提纲,分别说明了申请者的三点基本要求,第二句使用了平行结构,第三句使用了不定式短语做后置定语,第四句运用介词短语做后置定语。"To begin with, applicants should have Chinese nationality, strong professional spirit, cheerful personality and be aged under 35. In addition, candidates must have outstanding skills at English listening comprehension and the ability to speak Chinese and English fluently. Finally, students with relevant professional experience are preferred."(首先,应聘者必须具有中国国籍、较强的职业精神、开朗的性格,年龄在35岁之下。其次,申请人需要具备卓越的英文听力水平以及流利的中英文表达能力。最后具有相关职业的经验的学生优先考虑。)这三个句子通过三大关联词组"To begin with","In addition","Finally"来衔接,显得连贯而流畅。"strong professional spirit","cheerful personality"几个并置的词组,把申请者的基本条件完整地表述了出来。而"outstanding skills at English listening comprehension and the ability to speak Chinese and English fluently,"以及"students with relevant professional experience"均是简单的名词通过介词短语、动词不定式后置修饰,使句子变得丰富起来。这种增加修饰成分的方式是考生应该学到的。文章通过这种表达把题目中所要求的其他信息也写出来了。再看第五句。此句提供了报名的方式、时间及地点,运用了定语从句。其中"sign up with"是报名的意思。

全文语言精彩,结构严谨、论证充分,是一篇很优秀的文章。

【学习指导】

对于告示类应用文,考生要注意一下格式。标题放在首行正中央,要求点明所写告示的主旨,一般为词组性短语,基本结构是:名词+过去分词,如"Contributions Wanted"(征稿启事),"Child Lost"(寻子启事);现在分词+名词,如"Looking for a Spouse"(征偶启事),"Exchanging House"(换房启事);名词结构,如:"Invitation for Bids"(招聘启事),"Notice of a Decision"(决定通知)。

告示类应用文要写出时间,位置一般在标题的右下方。正文一般情况下写一至三段,五到七句话即可。另外,落款写在中间偏右的位置。

③ 摘要。

【文体说明】

摘要又称概要、内容提要。摘要是以提供文献内容梗概为目的,不加评论和补充解释,简明、确切的记述文献重要内容的短文。摘要应具有独立性和自明性,并且拥有与文献同等量的主要信息,即不阅读全文,就能获得必要的信息。

【举例说明】

2010年《考纲》应用文参考试题如下:

Directions:

Read the fdlowing Chinese text and write an abstract of it in 80 - 100 English words on

ANSWER SHEET 2. (10 points)

经济全球化的主要原因

20世纪50年代初以来,经济全球化获得迅猛发展。简单归纳,其原因主要包括以下几个方面:

全球化的技术基础。科技进步为全球化快速发展提供了物质基础和技术手段。科技革命是经济全球化发展的最根本的物质基础和动力,历史上历次科技革命都促进了社会生产力的飞跃发展,同时也促进了整个世界的融合。20世纪50年代以电子技术和信息技术等为主要标志的新的科技革命的兴起,使科技日益成为社会生产力发展的先导,成为影响生产力发展的至关重要的因素。科技知识在社会生产的各个领域中得到广泛传播和运用,劳动者的智能和技能得到进一步的开发,创造出越来越多的物质和精神财富,极大地促进了世界生产力的发展,生产社会化程度日益提高,国际分工日益深化,各国经济以此为基础紧密相连,世界经济进入一个全新的繁荣时期。同时,新科技革命使得科技成果积累的速度大大加快,新材料、新产品不断涌现,大量高技术产业不断产生,在世界范围内促进了产业结构的调整和转移,新的产业布局开始形成。以信息技术和产业为主导,以高新技术为基础的新兴产业部门也蓬勃兴起并迅速发展,快速取代了传统产业而逐渐成为经济的主导部门推进的重要动力源。

全球化的经济基础。市场经济体制的强势地位不断增强,跨国公司的突飞发展,国际经济组织的不断完善为经济全球化奠定了坚实的经济基础。

首先,市场经济体制成为世界各国发展经济的首选。20世纪80年代末至90年代初,世界形势发生了重大变化,东欧剧变,苏联解体,40多年的冷战格局最终结束。冷战结束后,国际形势总体上走向缓和。各国纷纷把发展经济列为首要目标,普遍扩大了对外开放,和平与发展成为当今时代的两大主题。前苏联和东欧国家先后走上了向市场经济过渡的轨道,改行自由市场经济,并积极致力于融入西方经济体系。中国在长期的实践中,也逐渐认识到计划经济的不足和弊端,自1978年起开始实行以市场为导向的、全面的经济改革,大力推行对外开放,努力实现同世界经济的接轨,目前已成为世界经济的重要组成部分。这一切都说明,市场经济体制已成为不同制度、不同发展层次国家的共同选择,市场经济已基本实现了全球化,经济全球化是以市场为基础的,没有市场经济就没有生产要素在国际间的自由流动,就谈不上经济全球化。

其次,力量不断壮大的跨国公司成为经济全球化的中坚力量。跨国公司是以本国作为基地,通过对外直接投资,在世界各地设立分支机构和子公司,从事国际化生产和经营的企业。跨国公司凭借其雄厚的经济实力和灵活的经营战略,以全球为工厂,以它所在的各个国家为车间,在全球范围内充分利用各地的优势组织生产和流通,通过自己广泛的经营活动,实现了商品和资本等生产要素在全球范围内的整合,促进了生产在国家间的水平分工和垂直分工,使之密切联系在一起,从而为经济全球化的发展打下了坚实的微观基础,并成为经济全球化的主要推动力量和主要载体。

最后,国际经济组织是经济全球化发展的组织保障。二战结束以后,生产力的不断提高,生产的国际化使得越来越多的商品、资本、劳动进入国际交流,各国的国际分工和相互依赖性不断增强。这种日益增强的经济联系要求突破原有的国家间的障碍,实现全球范围内的更高层次的经济合作,这就要求有超脱于国家之外的国际经济组织发挥重要作用。战后,国际经济日益明显,国际经济协作不断加强。在当今国际经济关系中,世行、世贸组织、国际货币基金组织等世界性经济组织的调节作用越来越大,而且还表现出进一步增强的趋势。世贸组织(WTO)所制定的关于贸易、投资等方面的制度和规则,成为规范全球经济运行,创造自由公平竞争环境的统一制度和规则。作为世界金融领域的重要国际组织,即国际货币基金组织(IMF)和世界银行(WB)也在国际金融全球化进程中扮演了重要的角色。这些国际经济组织的成立使得国际贸易和国际金融运行有了统一的规则，对成员国的经贸活动和经济行为起着协调和规范作用。这些都为经济全球化的发展起着制度保障作用。

范文如下：

Fundamental Causes of Economic Globalization

Economic globalization has been progressing rapidly since the beginning of the 1950s. Several factors have contributed to such development. Firstly, advancements in science and technology have offered a technical foundation by providing the material basis and the technical means. Meanwhile, a solid economic foundation for such a globalization has been laid by the market economy which is prevailing over the world. Other factors include the pillaring and propelling role of multinationals in micro-economic operations, the ever-growing coordinating and controlling power and function exercised by such international economic organizations as WTO, IMF and WB in the international trade and finance.

范文解析：本摘要由五句话构成。采用的是"总—分"结构。首句对原文首段进行了翻译，使用了现在完成进行时，介词短语放在句尾作时间状语。由此细节，阅卷人员也可以初步看出考生的真实英语水平。第二句翻译的是原文首段的第二句，使用到的时态仍旧是现在完成时，在这句当中，"such"指代"全球化"。第三句是对原文第二段前两句的一个整合，使用了现在完成时，介词短语作后置定语，介词短语作状语，动名词短语作介词之后的宾语。第四句整合原文第三段前两句，运用了现在完成时被动语态，介词短语作后置定语等手段使句型丰富起来。尾句整合原文最后两段，前半句整合第五段，后半句整合第六段，先后运用了并列结构，介词短语作后置定语，过去分词短语作后置定语及介词短语作状语。

摘要当中运用了很多丰富的词汇，包括"fundamental"，"economic globalization"，"progress"，"contribute to"，"advancements in science and technology"，"technical foundation"，"material basis"等。在表达"原因"时，分别用到了"cause"和"factor"；表达"基础"时，"foundation"和"means"进行同义替换；表达"提供"时，运用了 offer 和 provide 实现词汇的变化。以上词汇的同义替换，实现了词汇的多变，从而丰富了表达。

通过本文，可以发现，好的摘要并非只是直译段首句，而是有机地整合全文。同时，文中使用了"firstly"，"meanwhile"等关联词进行连贯衔接，使得结构清晰、逻辑严谨。

【学习指导】

第一，关于摘要写作注意事项。

标题部分：针对考研英语写作，写作 A 节的书信与写作 B 节的短文不用写标题，但是写作 A 节的告示、摘要、备忘录、报告必须有标题。

时态：英文摘要写作应采用第三人称表达方式。在时态方面，大都采用一般现在时。当然考生在能保证语法正确的情况下，也可使用现在完成时或一般过去时。

句型：英文摘要结构严谨，表达精练。英文摘要应尽量使用短句，慎用长句。摘要的句型应力求简单，表意明确。

无需通读全文：通常文章首尾两段及每段的首尾两句，一般就是文章中心。

第二，关于摘要写作步骤。

英语摘要写作步骤可以分为两大步：一是总结中心句（一般用 2 分钟），二是汉译英（一般用 13 分钟）。

总结中心句：抓住文章首尾段，特别是各段首尾句。由此提炼出摘要框架。具体的细节、说明等统统忽略不管。

汉译英：将汉语结构中心句译成英语。

以参考试题为例做一下总结。

标题：经济全球化的主要原因

首段：20世纪50年代初以来，经济全球化获得迅猛发展。其原因主要包括以下几个方面。

第二段：全球化的技术基础。科技进步为全球化快速发展提供了物质基础和技术手段。

第三段：全球化的经济基础。市场经济体制的强势地位不断增强，跨国公司的突飞发展，国际经济组织的不断完善为经济全球化奠定了坚实的经济基础。

第四至六段：首先……其次……最后……（都是对第三段内容的详细说明，可以统统忽略不管）。

第六段末尾：世贸组织（WTO）、国际货币基金组织（IMF）和世界银行（WB）为经济全球化的发展起着制度保障作用。

将上面总结出的段落大意翻译成如下英语表达之后如下。

第一段：Economic globalization has been developing rapidly since the beginning of the 1950s. Several factors contribute to such development.

第二段：Advancements in science and technology have provided the material basis and the technical means for the world rapid progress.

第三段：The market economy which is prevailing over the world; the dramatic development of multinationals; the increasing growth of international economic organizations—all these have laid a solid economic foundation for globalization.

第六段末尾：The ever growing coordinating and controlling power and function exercised by such international economic organizations as WTO, IMF and WB in the international trade and finance.

④ 备忘录。

【文体说明】

备忘录就是上级对下级或同级之间的半正式书信。一般是上司写给下属，或者是同事之间的一种书信。但是因为大家都是同事，所以不是很正式。

【举例说明】

参考题目：

Directions: You are the president of a company. Write a memorandum to Percy Shelly the vice-president on the employee ' s training on computer, telling him the need to train the employees, detailed information, and ask him to write a plan.

范文如下：

Date: January 20, 2010

To: Percy Shelly, Vice President

From: Li Ming, President

Subject: Computer Training of the Staff

As we discussed earlier this week, I agree with you that our firm is faced up with problem of the high rate of computer illiteracy of the staff. We need to make up a plan for training our employees in the new field.

I would like you to design our own in-house computer-training program. We had better classify the employees and put them through the program in turn.

Write up a brief proposal, describing what you think the program should cover. Assume the class runs four hours a week for ten weeks. Also, assume people have no prior computer knowledge or any formal course work in computer science.

范文解析:首先看一下格式。备忘录和书信不一样,备忘录在正文上面要写四行,包括日期、称呼、落款、主题。下面再写正文,正文之后不用写落款。

看一下正文的三段,根据三点提纲各写一段。第一点提纲是培训员工的必要性,首先是"as"引导方式状语从句,"正如我们本周早期所讨论的"使用了过去时。"我同意你的看法"后面加了一个宾语从句。"公司"这一词在题目当中写的是"company",在此改成"firm"进行了同义改写。"我们公司正在面临一个问题,就是员工的计算机盲的比率很高"。此句中,"illiteracy"表示"文盲的",这个词的前缀"il-"是表示否定的前缀,"literacy"表示"认字、识字",这个词的形容词是"literate",表示"认字的,识字的"。第一句话是一个背景交代,即之所以需要培训员工是因为有很多计算机盲。第二句话是备忘录的写作目的,"我们需要制定一个计划,就是在新的领域培训员工"。

第二段写了两句话,用来改写提纲二。第二点提纲展开细节后可写成两点:第一点是把员工分类;第二点是轮流参加培训。第一句话用到了"would like to design...","我希望你制定一个","制定"在第一段第一句话用的是make up,在此同义改写为"design",进行了同义替换。"计划"在第一段第二句用的是"plan",在此替换成"program"。"我们最好……"在这里使用了"had better",因为这是总裁写给副总的备忘录,两人是上下级的关系,所以语气稍强一些。"我们最好把员工分类",动词分类用"classify",其名词形式为"classification"。"并且轮流参加培训","轮流"用的是"in turn"。

最后第三段改写提纲三,"Write up..."是一个省略句、祈使句,没有主语。考研作文一般不要写省略句,但是在此用省略是因为上级写给下级,所以不是特别正式。"写一个简要地计划",第三次出现"计划"用的是"proposal"。"计划"出现了三次,第一次"plan",第二次"program",第三次"proposal"。证明了作者的语言水平比较好。接下来,"写一个简单的计划,描述一下你认为计划应该包括什么?""包括"用到的词是"cover"。第三段也是一个总分结构。后面具体说明怎么写这个计划,分成两点:第一点是这个班一共是10周,每周4个小时;第二点是员工之前没有计算机知识。

【学习指导】

备忘录和书信有两点区别。第一点就是格式不同,书信的格式包括称呼、正文、落款。而备忘录的格式和书信的不一样,备忘录在正文上面要写四行,包括日期、称呼、落款、主题。下面再写正文,正文之后不用写落款。第二点就是写法不同,一般情况下,书信的所有提纲可以都写在第二段,但是备忘录的提纲最好各成一段。由于备忘录是同事间用到的文体,所以自我介绍、感谢等表达在备忘录中就不必写了。

2.6.2 短文写作指导

纵观近些年的考研英语写作部分的题型,短文写作部分(B节)更多地采用了图表或图画提示,目的是考查考生用英语对事物进行抽象思考、归纳、分析的能力。

考生在平时的写作过程当中,要通过阅读优秀范文,积累精彩词汇,掌握精彩句型,熟悉相关写作框架来不断提高自己的写作能力。

1.《考纲》基本信息详解

《考纲》要求考生能写出一般描述性、叙述性、说明性或议论性的文章。

英文写作分为五大文体：应用文、描写文、记叙文、说明文、议论文。写作B节重点考查后四种。具体来说，第一段一般是图画描述或图表描述，属于描写文；第二段一般是意义阐释，第三段是归纳结论或建议措施，都属于论说文。

《考纲》规定，写作B节要求考生“根据提示信息写出一篇160~200词的短文(标点符号不计算在内)。提示信息的形式有主题句、写作提纲、规定情景、图、表等。考生在答题卡2上作答。共20分。”

2.《考纲》考查目标强化指导

(1) 测试要点：内容的完整性；文章的组织连贯性；语法结构和词汇的多样性；语言的准确性。

总体说来，写作A节和B节的差别在于：B节短文写作并没有要求“语域的恰当”。A节对语域却有明确的要求。原因在于写应用文的时候，考生可能会写到私人信件，这时会用到一些口语化的词汇。但是，短文写作无一例外，全都考查的是正式的文体。换言之，短文写作里面不允许出现任何非正式的语言。

(2) 各档范文标准。下边按照一般评分标准，以2009年写作B节考题为例，展示了五个档次的范文，考生以此来规范自己的文章，以争取拿到自己的目标分。

【举例说明】

2009年写作B节考题

Directions:

Write an essay of 160-200 words based on the following drawing. In your essay, you should

1) describe the drawing briefly,

2) explain its intended meaning, and then

3) give your comments.

You should write neatly on ANSWER SHEET 2. (20 points)

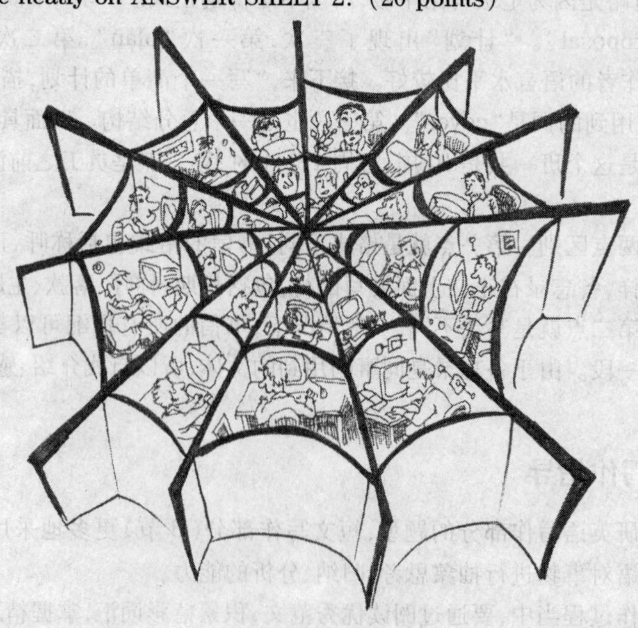

网络的“近”与“远”

① 第五档范文标准。

【规定内容】

要求很好地完成试题规定的以下任务:包含所有内容要点;使用丰富的语法结构和词汇;语言自然流畅,语法错误极少;有效地采用多种衔接手法,文字连贯,层次清晰;格式与语域恰当贴切。

对目标读者(即语言接受对象)完全产生预期的效果。

范文第五档(19 分)如下:

As is illustrated in the cartoon, each person sits in their own work room. In front of them is a computer. Everyone looks at the screen carefully, and communicate with their colleagues through the net instead of talking face to face. Their work places are placed like a net. And below the cartoon, there is a topic which says: the near and far among the Internet.

From the cartoon, we can conclude that the cartoonist wants to convey such a message: with the popularity of computers, people from all over the world become nearer by using the internet to communicate with each other. Meanwhile, people also become far away from their friends. All of us accept the fact that the development of the internet brings lots of conveniences to our daily life, for instance, we can buy a book on the net instead of going to a bookstore. Besides, we can communicate with our friends on the net without going out of home. But we can't ignore the other side of these: the time we spend with friends or family becomes less. And we hardly see them once in a week. It will make us feel lonely if we continue to use the tool on the net to talk with friends instead of talking with them on the phone or going out with them.

To my best understanding, we should use the net to communicate with each other in a proper way. It is just a tool when we really need it to serve us. If we want to keep our friendship more effectively, we should spend more time with them in our real life. Only in this way can we not only make full use of the communication tool on the net but also make our friendship stronger.

评语:该文很好地完成了试题规定的任务,内容完整,既清楚地描述了漫画内容,又指出了其隐含的意思。语言流畅,措辞准确,句型结构有变化,有效使用了连接手段,内容连贯,层次分明。文章易于理解,仅有个别语言错误,字数符合要求。

② 第四档范文标准。

【规定内容】

要求较好地完成试题规定的以下任务:包含所有内容要点,允许漏掉 1 ~2 个次重点;使用较丰富的语法结构和词汇;语言基本准确,只有在试图使用复杂结构或较高级词汇时才有个别错误;采用了适当的衔接手法,层次清晰,组织较严密;格式和语域较恰当。

对目标读者产生预期的效果。

范文第四档(15 分)如下:

As is vividly depicted in the drawing above, we can see clearly that some people are very near by the computer while some people are much long with each other in the net world.

What is conveyed in the picture is most thought-provoking and worth discussing among people, especially the young people. It is a mirror, reflecting the relationships between the people are altering by the Internet. People's opinions differ greatly on this matter. Some people believe that the Internet is very convenient for people who are living in a longer distance to keep connection with each other. Others argue that the Internet make the people living in near areas meet very little. Still others hold that people's facing to face to communicate is reducing to a low level.

It struck me that if nothing is done to solve the social phenomenon, its effect will be soon shown, which inevitably affects the development of the harmonious society. So we should regard the trend rightly. We also should take it into our accounts strictly. We should use the Net more reasonably. On no account should we make the people longer by the computer. Only in this way can we have a good generation foreseen. And a more harmonious society can be built up.

评语:文章较好地完成了试题规定的任务,内容比较完整,既描述了漫画又揭示了隐含的意思,使用了比较丰富的句型结构和词语,使用了一定的连接手段,语言基本通顺,文章结构完整,层次清晰,易于理解,但是有一定数量的语言错误。

③ 第三档范本标准。

【规定内容】

要求基本完成试题规定的任务:虽漏掉一些内容,但包含多数内容要点;应用的语法结构和词汇能满足任务的需求;有一些语法及词汇错误,但不影响理解;采用简单的衔接手法,内容较连贯,层次较清晰;格式和语域基本合理。

对目标群体基本产生预期的效果。

范文第三档(11分)如下:

As the picture vividly depict that internet like a net connect different people in the world. You can communicate with your friends. No matter where they live in, the distance no longer an obstacle in our communication.

The picture reflect a thought-provoking social phenomenon that people in a mounting numbers use internet shopping, work, study and chatting with friends in order to meet each other face and face. There are somewhat reasonable, but you weighing in mind, you can find that distance between our spirit longer than before. On the Internet we can not know each other very well, because some people don't use their real name, even tell lies on internet. On the conterary, if we meet each other face and face, it's better for communication.

Internet make the obstacle of distance vanished, benefit us a lot, we can chating with our friends who live in a city that far from us. However, we should take that serious internet make the distance of our spirit longer than before, internet is a double-edge sword.

评语:该文包含多数内容要点;语法结构与词汇基本能够满足任务要求;有一些严重语法与用词错误,但不影响理解;内容较连贯,层次较清晰。但是,第三部分主要是对第二部分的总结,评论简单。

④ 第二档范文标准。

【规定内容】

未能按要求完成试题规定的任务:漏掉或未能有效阐述一些内容要点,写了一些无关内容;语法结构单调、词汇有限;有较多语法结构或词汇方面的错误,影响了对写作内容的理解;未采用恰当的衔接手法,内容缺少连贯性;格式和语域不恰当。

未能清楚地传达信息给读者。

范文第二档(7分)如下:

As can be seen from the picture, many people are sitting in the front of a computers, who are basing in typing on the keyboard, but they don't immediate communicate with each other though they live near. It looks like a bit pot, everyone has its space, and the computer is necessary for them.

It goes without saying that this picture aims at reavling a common phenomenon in our daily life, that is internet brings conveniences to us, also brings the distance for each other. Nowadays, we must believe that our development can not leave the using of internet. We do any things through the computer instead of saying "hello" to our families or colleagues face to face.

In my opinion, we must realize the importance of the internet and also pay more attentions to communicate with each other face to face. Do not make the computer make a distant between us.

评语:该文遗漏了题目要点,评论不够恰当,语言错误多,有些句子内容表达不清晰,字数不够。

⑤ 第一档范文标准。

【规定内容】

未完成试题规定的任务:明显遗漏主要内容,且有许多不相关的内容;语法项目和词汇的使用单调、重复;语言错误多,有碍读者对内容的理解,语言运用能力差;未使用任何衔接手法,内容不连贯,缺少组织、分段;无格式与语域概念。

未能传达信息给读者。

范文第一档(3 分)如下:

Largely through the influence of many people from different points of the world. The old, the young and the student, they use the computers to constant with another body.

Some people use computer to leare new knowledge, such as the students. Some people use the computer to help them to complete their work. Such as the tank workers. While some people use the computer to play games. For example, some old person like to play game on computer.

Many people on computer is on Monday to Friday. But the player people is everyday more or less. So the world is like a family. Since the computer with us is to enable our to share in a common life we cannot help considering whether or not we are forming the powers of the life's happy.

评语:该文明显遗漏主要内容,不能反映需要表达的观点;语法与用词错误很多,妨碍理解,作者的语言运用能力差;字数不够。

【学习指导】

对于短文的写作要求,可归纳成:内容切题,表达清楚,意思连贯,语言规范。要做到这一点,考生不仅要注意写作前的审题,更重要的是通过平时的训练来提高写作能力。因此,考生应从语言、结构、内容三个方面加强训练。

(1) 语言。

第一,语言应基本正确。基础一般的考生即使使用了小学或中学词汇和句型,只要基本正确,也能得到及格分,即应用文 6 分,短文 12 分,共计 18 分。考生最易犯的语言错误有三类:语法错误、拼写错误和标点错误。最常犯的语法错误包括:随意使用标点、时态错乱、冠词用法错误以及主谓不一致等。以下列出了一些常见错误实例。这些问题只要考生在平时研读范文和练习时稍加注意,就可以避免。

① 随意使用标点:

We couldn't decide upon a new car, there were many attractive models.

分析:根据英语语法规则要求,只要句子成分完整就应用句号断句,或用连接词将其与后句连接。

在此,两句间用了一个逗号,这个错误看似微不足道,但实际上却很严重。此句可修改为:

We couldn't decide upon a new car, for there are many attractive models.

② 主谓不一致:

Many traffic accidents that occurred is the result of carelessness.

分析:根据语法规则,主语和谓语应该保持一致。使用一般现在时的时候,如果主语是单数第三人称或单数名词,那么谓语动词也应该是单数形式。在此句中,主语"accidents"是复数,所以对应的谓语动词应该是复数形式。此句可修改为:

Many traffic accidents that occurred are the result of carelessness.

③ 时态错乱:

It is Mr. Green who made the decision.

分析:在写英语句子的过程中,一定要注意到句子时态前后一致的问题。因此本句应该改为:

It was Mr. Green who made the decision.

另外,考研写作不管是应用文还是短文,都应以现在时为主,尤其是一般现在时。图表描述段和举例论证段可能会用到过去时,即描述过去的年代和数据或列举自己经历过的小事需用过去时。文章尾段展望未来时亦可使用将来时。

第二,语言应丰富多变。基础较好的考生,要想取得考研作文的高分,应做到语言丰富多变,应用文力争获得8分,短文获得16分,共计24分。丰富多变体现在词汇和句型两个方面。同一词语在一句话、一个段落乃至一篇文章中最好不要重复出现,应尽量使用同、近义词替换。句型也不要拘泥于主谓宾句型,可以使用主系表、过去分词和现在分词短语作状语、不定式短语作状语、状语从句等多种句型。

① 词汇的多变。考生在平时的英语学习当中,应该去积累相关词汇的近义词、反义词等。通过词汇的灵活替换,使自己所写的文章表达丰富。以下列出一些词汇替换的具体实例。

think→argue, maintain, consider, assume, in my opinion, to the best of my knowledge, for my part

(as is shown in the) picture→drawing, photo, caricature

important→be of importance, crucial, imperative, fundamental, vital, significant

② 句型的丰富。要提高写作能力,使文章的表达丰富,除了掌握足够的单词之外,还要通过掌握的语法知识使句型丰富起来。以下列出一些精彩句型的具体实例。

形式主语从句、定语从句

It has been universally acknowledged that the ability of teamwork is the most essential qualification that anyone who wants to achieve success should possess.

定语从句、动名词短语、宾语从句:

Those who tried every means to avoid their duty of looking after their elders should bear in mind that they are much indebted to their parents for their birth and growth.

双重否定:

This picture reveals a not-uncommon phenomenon of how elders are treated by their grown-up children in some of the families in China.

系表结构,状语从句:

The real implication of the author is that everyone has to meet difficulties in their life experience, so we have to make adequate preparations for them.

被动语态：

Today, we use machines not only in industry but in other sectors of national economy as well.

提高考研写作成绩的关键是，考生能踏踏实实地提高语言能力，其核心在于多读、多背、多写、多改。

(2) 结构。

英文文章和段落讲究结构清晰，逻辑严谨，通常采用“总—分—总”结构。考研写作一般需写成三段：第一段是总论，提出问题，第二段是分论，分析问题，第三段是总论，总结评论或解决问题。每段内部也是“总—分—总”结构：第一句一般是主题句，总体论述；中间内容是论证部分；最后一句是小结。若不写小结，就是“总—分”结构。阅卷者一般从以下两个方面衡量文章的结构：

① 统一性。所谓统一性，就是指短文主题明确，且整段内容必须围绕主题来扩展，不能出现多个“中心”，不能跑题。

② 连贯性。连贯性指句子与句子之间、段落与段落之间的衔接要自然通畅，主要体现在短文的逻辑发展顺序和过渡词语的使用上。

根据多年命题规律，短文部分考试是考图画作文，而且基本上第一段是图画或图表描述，第二段是意义阐释，第三段是建议措施。结合具体的描述方法，考生需要了解一下统一性和连贯性是如何在具体的写作实践当中得以实现的。

经典段落一：图画/图表描述段。

① 图画描述段。

第1句：总体描述。描述方法：人物/动物/事物+动作+环境，或人物+服装+表情。例如：

As is vividly	revealed depicted	in the	cartoon, drawing,	...

这幅/这些图画生动地描述了……

例句：As is vividly revealed in the cartoon, a hen is making promises. /这幅图画生动地描述一只母鸡正在做出承诺。(1998 年考题写作图示)

再如：

This set of drawings The drawings The pictures The photos	vividly	reflects illustrate that ... reveal show

这幅/这些图画生动地反映了/阐述了/揭示了/展示了……

例句：This set of drawings vividly reflects the destiny of a delicate flower under different circumstances. /这些图画生动地描述了一朵娇弱的花朵在不同环境中的命运。(2003 年考题写作图示)

例句：The picture vividly reveals that a boy is running on the playground. /这幅图画生动地描述一个小男孩在操场上跑步。(2004 年考题写作图示)

又如：

It is vividly	described in the picture illustrated in the cartoon	that ...

这幅(这些)图画生动地反映了(阐述了)……

例句:It is vividly described in the picture that a lamp is lightening in the darkness. /这幅图生动的描述了一盏灯在黑暗之中熠熠生辉。(2001年考题图示)

第2~3句:挖掘细节。一幅图一般直接描述,如果是两幅图则常用到下列句型。例如:

In the first photo, ... In the second picture,...

在第一幅当中……在另一幅当中……

例句:In the first photo, there is a young man with Beckham on his face. In the second picture, there is another young man who is doing Beckham's haircut in a barber's shop./在一幅图当中,一个年轻人把贝克汉姆写在他的脸上。在第二幅当中,另一个年轻人在理发店理了一个小贝头。(2006年考题图示)

再如:

In one picture, ... On the contrary/ By contrast,...

在第一幅当中……与之相反……

例句:In one picture, there were various kinds of fishes and only one fishing-boat in 1900. On the contrary, in 1995 there was only one fish, but a great many fishing-boats. /在一幅图当中,1900年的时候有各种各样的鱼,但只有一条渔船。而与之相反,在1995年的时候,只有一条鱼却有许多条船。(1999年考题图示)

考生在进行第一段图画描述时,可以把图画中的文字说明直接翻译过来作为首段的结尾句,从而使图画描述段落的内容更加丰富。例如:

The caption reads/ indicates that "..."

文字说明显示:"……"。

例句:The caption reads, "Love is like a lamp which is brighter in darker places". /文字说明显示:"爱心是一盏灯,在越黑暗的地方越明亮"。(2001年考题图示)

再如:

We are informed that"..."

文字说明显示:"……"

例句:We are informed that "the flower growing in a greenhouse cannot withstand the test of a storm"./文字说明显示:"温室花朵经不起风雨"。(2003年考题图示)

例句:We are informed that it is a "football game of financially supporting the senior citizen". /文字说明显示:这是一场"养老足球赛"。(2005年考题图示)

图画描述框架总结如下:

This set of drawings above vividly illustrates ... As is shown in the first picture, there is/ are ... The caption reads, "...". On the contrary, there is/ are ... We are informed that "...".

图画描述段落实例如下:

This set of drawings vividly reflects the destiny of a delicate flower under different circumstances. In the first drawing, the flower is placed in a comfortable greenhouse which protects it from the threatening storm. By contrast, when it is exposed to the driving rain, the fragrant flower soon fades and withers, with petals scattering on the ground. We are informed that "the flower growing in a greenhouse cannot withstand the test of a storm". (2003年考题图示)

② 图表描述段。

第1句:概括描述总趋势。例如:

The diagram	show(s)	great changes	in the number of	the GDP	from...to...	in China.
The graph	tell(s)	sharp differences	in the amount of	the scores	between...and...	
The table	describe(s)	sharp contrast	in the percentage of	the salary	among...	
The line chart	is/are about	an upward trend		the temperature		
The bar chart	reveal(s)	a rapid growth		the weight		
The pie chart	display(s)	a sudden rise		the speed		
The figures	demonstrate(s)	a slow increase				
The statistics	exhibit(s)	a sharp fall				
The numbers	illustrate(s)	that...				
The percentage	figure(s)	how...				
The proportion	represent(s)					

再如:

As can be seen from the diagram/chart/graph/table/figures, ...

As (is) shown/described/illustrated/revealed in the diagram/chart/graph/ table/ figures, ...

As we can see from the diagram/chart/graph/table/figures, ...

It can be seen from the figures/statistics that ...

It is clear/apparent/obvious from the figures/statistics that ...

According to the diagram/chart/graph/table, ...

例句:According to the line graph, the U. S. population soared from 2 million to 250 million from 1800 to 1900. /如图表中所示,从1800到1900年,美国人口从200万猛增到2.5亿。

第2~3句:描述细节变化。常用的词汇和词组如下。

a. 增加/上升/提高:

动词:increase, grow, rise, clime, expand, jump, leap, ascend, skyrocket, accumulate, sour

词组:go/push up, gain a momentum, continue its upward trend, on the rise/increase

名词:increase, rise, growth, expansion, pickup, gain, accumulation, ascendance, leap, jump, climb

b. 减少/下降:

动词:decrease, decline, fall, drop, reduce, descend, diminish, dip, slide, shrink, collapse

词组:go down, drop/fall off, take a dip, continue its downward trend, on the decline

名词:decrease, decline, slowdown, slump, shrinkage, dip, drop, fall

c. 剧烈/显著/明显:

副词: dramatically, sharply, considerably, rapidly, suddenly, greatly, alarmingly, significantly, enormously, steeply, massively, incredibly, hugely, amazingly, substantially

词组:at an alarming rate, by leaps and bounds, in big leaps, by a wide margin

d. 缓慢/逐渐:

副词:gradually, steadily, slightly, marginally, slowly, moderately

词组:in a moderate way, by the least amount

e. 保持平稳/不变:

词组：remain stable/ steady/ unchanged, stabilize, level off . . .

f. 起伏/波动：

动词：wave, undulate(波动,起伏), rebound(反弹), recover

词组：rise and fall, fluctuate slightly/ dramatically, fluctuate between . . . and . . . , a minor fluctuation, small rises and falls, small fluctuations

g. 高点值：

peak, reach a peak, reach a high point

h. 低点值：

bottom out, reach the bottom, reach a low point, hit a trough

常用句型如下。

1. The number of ××× + 动词(Verb) + 副词(Adverb) + from. . . to. . . / between . . . and. . .

动词(Verb)：change, increase, jump, rise, decrease, drop, fall, fluctuate, recover(略有回升), jump, climb

副词(Adverb)：clearly, apparently, fast, greatly, rapidly, significantly, suddenly, dramatically, sharply, steeply, abruptly, slowly, gradually, slightly, insignificantly, invisibly, steadily, evenly, smoothly

2. There was a (very) + 形容词(Adjective) + 名词(Noun) + in the number of ××× + from. . . to. . . /between. . . and. . .

形容词(Adjective)：clear, apparent, great, rapid, significant, sudden, dramatic, sharp, steep, abrupt, slow, gradual, slight, insignificant, invisible, steady, even, smooth 等

名词(Noun)：change, increase, jump, rise, decrease, drop, fall, fluctuation

注意：修饰 fluctuation 只能用 wild, gradual, slight, insignificant, invisible, steady, even, smooth 等。

3. The number of ×××	remained steady	from. . . to. . . /between. . . and. . .
	remained stable	
	stayed the same	

There was	little change	in the number of ××× from. . . to. . .
	hardly any change	
	no change	

4. The monthly profit	peaked	in (图表中体现的月份/年)	at	×××(图表中体现的最高值)
The figures	bottom out	at(图表中体现的准确时间点)		×××(图表中体现的最低值).

5. The figure has nearly doubled, compared with that of last year.

和去年相比,数字几乎翻倍。

6. It has increased/ decreased almost three times, compared with . . .

和……相比,增加/下降了几乎三倍。

7. The number is three times as much as that of 1990.

The number is twice more than that of 1990.

数字是 1990 年的三倍。

8. The number was . . . , less than a third of the 1990 total.

数字是……少于1990年总数的1/3。

图表描述框架总结如下：

As is shown in the table/pie chart/line chart/bar chart, the number of ××× + 动词(Verb) + 副词(Adverb) + from... to... / between ... and...

图表描述整段实例如下：

What is shown in the table above indicates that dramatic changes have taken place in the daily expenses in Xi'an from 1995 to 1999. The expenses on food have declined by 30% while those on clothing and recreation have increased respectively by 9% and 7%. The statistics of rise and fall seem to exist in isolation but are closely related to one another.

经典段落二：意义阐述段。

意义阐述段的创作原则是：由表及里、由小见大。

第1句：主题句，应为 Symbolic Meanings，即图画或图表的深层含义。例如：

The symbolic meaning of the picture	is to show us	importance should be attached	to ...
The purpose of the drawer		due attention should be paid	
The purpose of the drawing			

这幅图的象征寓意是/作者的意图是/图画的目的是向我们展示我们应该对……予以重视。

再如：

The picture illustrates the real meaning of ..., by stressing the fact that...

这幅画通过强调……这一事实，阐释了……的真正含义。

例句：The picture illustrates the real meaning of love, by stressing the fact that love is emotional strength, which can support us no matter how dark the world around us becomes. /无论我们周围的世界变得如何黑暗，爱都是能够支撑我们的一种情感力量。这幅图画通过强调这一事实，阐释了爱的真正含义。(2001年考题图示)

又如：

The fact that ... indicates that to some extent ...

这个事实显示了在某种程度上……

例句：The fact that people from different countries are attracted to mysterious Chinese culture indicates that to some extent a culture can be accepted, respected, appreciated and shared internationally. /各国人民被神秘的中国文化所吸引这个事实，显示了在某种程度上，一种文化可以被接受、尊重、欣赏和分享。(2002年考题图示)

又如：

Undoubtedly, the drawings have symbolically revealed a serious problem in our daily life, ...

毫无疑问，这些图画象征性地显示了我们日常生活中的一个严重问题……

例句：Undoubtedly, the drawings have symbolically revealed a serious problem in our daily life, parents' doting care to only children in the current society. /毫无疑问，这些图画象征性地显示了我们日常生活中的一个严重问题：当代社会中父母对独生子女的溺爱。(2003年考题图示)

又如：

The pictures have subtly reflected the social phenomenon that ... is prevalent among the teenagers nowadays.

这幅图画微妙地反映了……在当今青少年中非常盛行这一社会现象。

例句:The pictures have subtly reflected the social phenomenon that idol worship is prevalent among the teenagers nowadays. /这幅图画微妙地反映了偶像崇拜在当今青少年中非常盛行这一社会现象。(2006 年考题图示)

第2~4句:论证。

英语论说文有多种论证手段,最常使用的有因果论证、举例论证以及定义和解释等。

① 因果论证:根据《考纲》,阅卷者在图画作文第二段最希望看到的是分析出现问题的原因,任何问题的出现至少应给出2~3点原因,不能只有一点原因,这是写作的重点。

例句:Owing to the quickening pace of life, competition goes increasingly fierce in all walks of life, stimulating everyone to pursue one goal after another. /随着生活步伐的加快,竞争在各行各业愈演愈烈,由此促使每个人不断去追求一个又一个的目标。(2004 年考题图示)

常用句型:

1. The phenomenon/ change in ... mainly results/ arises from the fact that ...

……方面的现象/变化主要源于……的事实。

2. One may regard the phenomenon as a | sign of / response to | ...

人们可能把这种现象当成……的一种表示/反应。

3. There are many causes/ reasons for the dramatic growth/ decrease. Firstly, ... Secondly, ... Finally, ...

这种急剧的增长/下降有很多原因。首先,……其次,……最后

4. A number of factors can account for the change in ...

很多原因可以解释……方面的变化。

5. Another contributory factor of ... is ...

另一个起作用的因素是……

6. Why ... ? For one thing, ... For another, ... Perhaps the primary reason is ...

为什么? 首先,……其次,……也许最主要的原因是……

7. ... is also responsible for the rise/ decrease in ...

……也是造成……增加或下降的原因。

② 举例论证:通过用具体的例子进行论证,文章更具说服力。回顾以往考试,2001 年考题短文写作的第二段、2004 年考题短文写作的第三段、2007 年考题短文写作的第三段都要求举例论证。当然有些没有要求举例论证的题目,考生们同样可以在第二段的意义阐释段进行举例论证。

整段实例如下:

For instance, when someone is starving to death, just a little food and water from you may save his life. Or when a little girl in a poor rural area drops out of school because of poverty, just a small sum of money from you may support her to finish her schooling and change her life. You have given love which is like a lamp in a dark place where light is most needed. /例如,当有人将要饿死时,你的一点食物和水就能挽救他的生命。又如,当一个乡下的小女孩由于贫困被迫退学时,你的一点钱就能支持她完成学业并且改变她的人生。你给出的爱心正如黑暗中最需要的一盏明灯。(2001 年考题短文写作)

常用句型：

1. Numerous examples can be given, but this/ these will suffice.

可以给出无数的例子,但这个/这些就足够了。

2. I can think of no better illustration than the following one(s).

我想不出比下面这个/这些更好的例子了。

3. This case effectively clarifies the fact that ...

这个例子清楚证明了……的事实。

4. This story tells that ...

这个故事告诉我们……

5. A case in point is ...

一个相关的例子是……

6. As an example of ..., we should remember ...

作为……的实例,我们应该记得……

有时也采用数据论证,例如：

According to the recent survey/ data/ figure/ statistics/ study by the Chinese Academy of Social Science, 70% of teenagers in China worship superstars.

根据中国社会科学院最新的调查,70%的中国青少年崇拜明星。

③ 定义和解释：

a. 定义是采用自问自答的设问形式。

例句：What is idol worship? Idol worship is usually the adolescents' admiration to famous stars. /什么是偶像崇拜？偶像崇拜就是青少年对明星的敬仰。(2006年考题短文写作)

b. 解释是指换个角度把上一句再说一遍,用一次即可。

例句：In other words, a nation's unique culture can become international through worldwide economic and cultural exchanges. /换言之,通过全球经济和文化的交流,一个民族独特的文化能够走向国际化。(2002年考题短文写作)

第5句：小结。将论证的三句话进行总结,与本段主题句首尾呼应。

例句：Briefly speaking, young people are inclined to idolize the people who excel in appearance, intelligence or talent. /简而言之,年轻人倾向于崇拜那些在外貌、智力和才能上十分优秀的人。(2006年考题短文写作)

意义阐释段落实例如下：

The purpose of this picture is to show us that due attention has to be paid to the decrease of ocean resources. Owing to over fishing, the number of fishes has obviously decreased. If we let this situation go as it is, we do not know where fish will be in the future. By that time, our environment will suffer a great destruction. (2000年考题短文写作)

In my opinion, what the picture conveys is far beyond a new fashion trend and carries cultural implications as well. It is clear that a unique culture can be accepted by the international society when its distinctive features are fully expressed. In fact, national cultures have no boundary and may be appreciated and shared by people from other cultural backgrounds. (2002年考题短文写作)

经典段落三：建议措施段

① 结论句(使用1句)。例如：

From what has been discussed above,	we may safely	draw	the conclusion that ...
From the analysis made above		come to	

通过上面讨论的内容/根据上述分析,我们可以得出结论:……

例句:From what has been discussed above, we may safely draw the conclusion that confidence is of great importance to both the individual and a nation. /根据上述讨论,我们得出的结论是:自信心对于个人或者是民族都很重要。(2008 年考题短文写作)

再如:

It is high time we placed great emphasis on ...

我们早就该重视……

例句:It is high time we placed great emphasis on the problem of over-exploitation of ocean resources./我们应该对海洋资源过度开发的问题予以高度的重视。(2000 年考题短文写作)

又如:

Therefore, it is necessary for us to... in a reasonable way and restrain ourselves from overindulgence.

因此,我们必须以合理的方式……避免深陷其中。

例句:Therefore, it is necessary for us to use internet in a reasonable way and restrain ourselves from overindulgence. /因此,我们应该以一个合理的方式去使用因特网而不要过度沉迷。(2009 年考题短文写作)

② 两个方面提建议(使用2句)。例如:

1. To begin with, relevant laws and regulations should be made to severely punish those who... In addition, we should cultivate the awareness of the young that ...

一方面,我们应该指定相关的法律法规严惩那些……的人。另一方面,我们应该培养人们的意识:……

2. On the one hand, we should appeal to the authorities to make strict laws to control this problem. On the other hand, we should enhance/cultivate the awareness of people that this issue is vital for us.

一方面,我们应该呼吁政府制定严格的法律来控制这个问题;另一方面,我们应该提高/培养人们的意识:这个问题对我们很重要。

③ 包装结尾,展望未来(使用1句)。

常用句型:

1. I believe we humans can overcome this difficulty and we will have a brighter future.

我相信人类能够克服这个问题,并能拥有更美好的未来。

2. Only in this way can we solve the problem. (倒装句)

3. In conclusion, it is ... that ... (强调句)

4. It is high time that we placed great emphasis on this phenomenon.

我们早应该对这个问题给予高度重视了。

建议措施段段落实例如下:

1. Therefore, it is imperative for us to take drastic measures. For one thing, we should appeal to the authorities to make strict laws to control commercial fishing. For another, we should

enhance the awareness of people that the ocean resources are vital to us. Only in this way can we protect our ocean resources. Also I believe that we humans can overcome this difficulty, and that we will have a brighter future.（2000 年考题短文写作）

2. To sum up, we should offer our help to all the needed. We expect to get love from others and we also give love to others. So when you see someone in difficulty or in distress and in need of help, don't hesitate to give your love to him (her). I believe that the relationship between people will be harmonious and that our society will be a better place for us to live in.（2001 年考题短文写作）

3. Accordingly, it is vital for us to derive positive implications from these thought-provoking drawings. On the one hand, we can frequently use them to enlighten the youth to be more independent in life. On the other hand, parents should be sensible enough to give their children more freedom to deal with troubles and problems. Only by undergoing more challenges and toils in adversity can young people cultivate strong personality and ability, and only in this way can they become winners in this competitive world.（2003 年考题短文写作）

4. Having considered both sides of the argument, I have come to the conclusion that the advantages of owning a car outweigh the disadvantages. Therefore, it seems to me that China should increase its output of automobiles and enlarge the private car market. The result would be that cars would become cheaper, while at the same time the extra demand would encourage the auto industry to produce more efficient and family-oriented vehicles.

5. From the analysis made above, we may come to the conclusion that people's living standards in Xi'an have been constantly improved between 1995 and 1999. With the further growth in economy and more changes in life style, the tendency indicated in the table will continue in the better direction.

（3）内容。

内容是考生观点和思维的体现。考研写作究其实质是对语言的考查。所以考生的观点不必是独一无二的，只要切题，并能自圆其说即可。有的考生在看到题目后，不知从何写起，这种现象的根源在于缺乏思维方面的训练。考生在平时可以通过阅读优秀范文，阅读英文报刊去积累精彩的观点，让思维得到有效的锻炼。

第3部分 试题分析

3.1 2009年研究生入学统一考试英语试题

Section Ⅰ Use of English

Directions:

Read the following text. Choose the best word(s) for each numbered blank and mark A, B, C or D on ANSWER SHEET 1. (10 points)

Research on animal intelligence always makes us wonder just how smart humans are. ____1____ the fruit-fly experiments described by Carl Zimmer in the *Science Times*. Fruit flies who were taught to be smarter than the average fruit fly ____2____ to live shorter lives. This suggests that ____3____ bulbs burn longer, that there is a(n) ____4____ in not being too bright.

Intelligence, it ____5____, is a high-priced option. It takes more upkeep, burns more fuel and is slow ____6____ the starting line because it depends on learning — a(n) ____7____ process — instead of instinct. Plenty of other species are able to learn, and one of the things they've apparently learned is when to ____8____.

Is there an adaptive value to ____9____ intelligence? That's the question behind this new research. Instead of casting a wistful glance ____10____ at all the species we've left in the dust I. Q.-wise, it implicitly asks what the real ____11____ of our own intelligence might be. This is ____12____ the mind of every animal we've ever met.

Research on animal intelligence also makes us wonder what experiments animals would ____13____ on humans if they had the chance. Every cat with an owner, ____14____, is running a small-scale study in operant conditioning. We believe that ____15____ animals ran the labs, they would test us to ____16____ the limits of our patience, our faithfulness, our memory for locations. They would try to decide what intelligence in humans is really ____17____, not merely how much of it there is. ____18____, they would hope to study a(n) ____19____ question: Are humans actually aware of the world they live in? ____20____ the results are inconclusive.

1. [A] Suppose	[B] Consider	[C] Observe	[D] Imagine
2. [A] tended	[B] feared	[C] happened	[D] threatened
3. [A] thinner	[B] stabler	[C] lighter	[D] dimmer
4. [A] tendency	[B] advantage	[C] inclination	[D] priority
5. [A] insists on	[B] sums up	[C] turns out	[D] puts forward
6. [A] off	[B] behind	[C] over	[D] along
7. [A] incredible	[B] spontaneous	[C] inevitable	[D] gradual
8. [A] fight	[B] doubt	[C] stop	[D] think
9. [A] invisible	[B] limited	[C] indefinite	[D] different

10. [A] upward	[B] forward	[C] afterward	[D] backward
11. [A] features	[B] influences	[C] results	[D] costs
12. [A] outside	[B] on	[C] by	[D] across
13. [A] deliver	[B] carry	[C] perform	[D] apply
14. [A] by chance	[B] in contrast	[C] as usual	[D] for instance
15. [A] if	[B] unless	[C] as	[D] lest
16. [A] moderate	[B] overcome	[C] determine	[D] reach
17. [A] at	[B] for	[C] after	[D] with
18. [A] Above all	[B] After all	[C] However	[D] Otherwise
19. [A] fundamental	[B] comprehensive	[C] equivalent	[D] hostile
20. [A] By accident	[B] In time	[C] So far	[D] Better still

1.【参考答案】B

【考查目标】动词辨析题

【答案解析】本题目选择动词,放在祈使句句首。文章开篇指出:"Research on animal intelligence always makes us wonder just how smart humans are.""对动物智慧的研究总是让我们对人类到底有多聪明感到好奇"。接着举了果蝇的例子,由概括到具体,选"consider"意为"让读者考虑一下(果蝇实验)",从而引出下文具体的例子。

选项中"suppose"表示"认为,假定","imagine"表示"想象","observe"意为"观察",三个选项代入文中都不能与上句语意正确衔接。

2.【参考答案】A

【考查目标】动词短语题

【答案解析】本题目选择动词(过去式),与介词"to"构成动词短语搭配,在句子中充当谓语。"Fruit flies who were taught to be smarter than the average fruit fly... to live shorter lives."原文讲述的是在实验中经常发生的一种情况,即"通过训练变得更聪明的果蝇,其寿命往往比普通果蝇短",故选[A]项。

其他三个选项"feared to"表示"害怕做某事";"happened to"表示"碰巧做某事";"threatened to"表示"威胁要做某事",都可接不定式结构做宾语,构成"... to do sth."结构,符合句子的语法要求。但"fear to do sth."和"threaten to do sth."与主语"Fruit flies"语义不搭配,造成句子不合逻辑。"happen to do sth."不符合上下文所给的信息,无法构成上下文的合理衔接,故排除。

3.【参考答案】D

【考查目标】形容词辨析题

【答案解析】本题目选择形容词比较级,在句中作定语修饰"bulbs"。"This suggests that bulbs burn longer..."(这让人想起……的灯泡照明时间比较长……)。上句讲到"聪明的果蝇寿命往往较短",这句接着用灯泡作类比,与上句对应,应该是较暗的灯泡使用时间较长,所以选[D] dimmer"较暗的"。

其他三个选项"lighter"意为"更亮的",与前文意思相悖,排除掉;"thinner"意为"更薄的,更瘦的",侧重形状;"stable"意为"更稳定的",强调亮度。只有结合上下文所提供的信息才能排除干扰项。

4.【参考答案】B

【考查目标】名词辨析题

【答案解析】本题目选择名词，并能与"in"搭配。"advantage"表示"优势"，后常接介词"in"，即"an advantage in sth."（在某方面具有优势）；从上下文信息来看，前面说聪明的果蝇寿命短，越不亮的灯泡使用时间越长，所以这里应该推断出"不太聪明（灯泡不太亮）是有优势的"，故[B]为正确选项。注意，"bright"在此处是一语双关，既可表示"灯泡的亮"，也可表示"人的聪明"。

其他三个选项，"tendency"表示"趋势，倾向"，后面常接介词"for"或动词不定式，"inclination"表示"倾向，意愿，倾斜度"，后常接介词"for"或动词不定式；"priority"表示"优先权"，后常接"over"。此三项介词搭配都不正确，故排除。

5.【参考答案】C

【考查目标】动词短语题

【答案解析】本题目要选择动词短语，使插入语完整。从上文可知，"聪明的果蝇寿命往往较短"，以及"不太聪明是有优势的"，由此推出的结果是：聪明也是要付出代价的。"turn out"意为"原来是，证明是，结果是……"，把"it turns out"用作插入语，使该句与上段内容紧紧联系起来，因此选[C]项。

其他三个选项"insist on"意为"坚持"；"sum up"意为"总计，总结"；"put forward"意为"提出"。此三项均不能与上下文语意对应，所以排除。

6.【参考答案】A

【考查目标】介词题

【答案解析】本题目选择介词，体现与"the starting line"（起跑线）的逻辑关系。本句的逻辑主语是"it"，指代前面的"intelligence"，选项"off"有"离开"之意，"slow off the starting line"表示"（智力）离开起跑线的速度慢"，紧接着后面"because"引导的从句解释了智力起步慢的原因，前后逻辑一致，故选[A]项。

"behind"和"over"可以首先排除，因为这里没有涉及空间位置关系；"along"表示"沿着起跑线"之意，这与后面的"process"意思不符，所以排除。

7.【参考答案】D

【考查目标】形容词辨析题

【答案解析】本题目选择形容词，做"process"的定语。破折号表示对前面内容即"learning"的解释。这里把"learning"（学习）与"instinct"（本能）作对比，结合前文的"slow"，以及学习自身的特点可知，只有"gradual"（渐进的）符合题意。故本题答案为[D]项。

其他三个选项"incredible"意为"难以置信的"；"spontaneous"意为"自发的"；inevitable 意为"不可避免的"；这三项都可以修饰"process"，但都不能说明导致"智力起步慢"的学习特点，以及学习不同于本能的特点，故排除。

8.【参考答案】C

【考查目标】动词辨析题

【答案解析】"Plenty of other species are able to learn, and one of the things they've apparently learned is when to..."意为"许多其他物种都能够学习，它们显然已经学会的一件事就是何时……"由上文信息可知，聪明需要学习，很多物种都能够学习，但都没有变聪明，这是因为它们还学会了适时停止学习，因此选[C]项。

其他三个选项都是简单动词，"fight"对"stop"构成了翻译干扰，"doubt"和"think"都是思维词汇，虽然与句中关键词有关联，但在语义上讲不通，所以不选。

9.【参考答案】B

【考查目标】形容词辨析题

【答案解析】本题目选择形容词,作定语修饰"intelligence"。由上文可知,"智力需要付出高昂的代价",本句承接上文,提出了一个疑问:"……的智力有适应价值吗?"从上文来看,作者一直在论述智力的不利方面。因此"有限的智力对生物有适应价值",与上下文语义衔接。选项中"limited"表示"有限的,不多的",符合题意,故选[B]项。

其他三个选项"invisible"意为"看不见的";"indefinite"意为"不确定的";"different"意为"不同的"。这三项均与数量多少无关,所以排除。

10.【参考答案】D

【考查目标】副词辨析题

【答案解析】本题目选择副词以表明逻辑关系。"we've left in the dust I. Q. -wise"是定语从句,修饰"the species"。"cast a glance at..."意为"对……投以目光";"leave sb. in the dust"是固定搭配,是"将某人远远抛在后面"的意思;"I. Q. -wise"是派生词,后缀"-wise"表示方式,意为"在I. Q. 方面"。这句话是说"该研究不是要我们对那些在智力方面已被人类远远抛在后面的物种投以悲怜的眼光。"人类看这些被抛在后面的物种,自然是往后看了,所以"backward"为正确选项。

其他三个选项与"backward"相同,都是后缀"-ward"构成的副词。"upward"意为"向上";"forward"意为"向前";"afterward"意为"之后,后来(表时间)"。该三项均不符合上下文语义,应排除。

11.【参考答案】D

【考查目标】名词辨析题

【答案解析】本题目选择名词,做宾语从句的主语。"...it implicitly asks what the real... of our own intelligence might be."意为"这项实验含蓄地提出一个问题:人类智慧的真正……可能是什么。"前文已经提到"Intelligence... is a high priced option"。因此,"人类智力的代价"最符合上下文意,应选[D]项。

其他选项"features"意为"特征";"influences"意为"影响";"results"意为"结果","results"干扰较大,但"结果"是中性词,不能体现"智力"的不利方面,故排除。

12.【参考答案】B

【考查目标】固定搭配题

【答案解析】本题目选择介词,与"mind"搭配。"on one's mind"或"on the mind of sb."是固定短语,意为"有心事,总是想着",代入文中,所在句子的含义为"我们所遇到的每种动物都惦记着这个问题",即人类智力的真正代价是什么。这与下文"如果动物有计划的话,它们会对人类做什么样的实验"语义衔接。

其他选项"outside"表示"在……外";"by"表示"被……";"across"表示"越过……",都不能与"mind"构成固定搭配,应排除。

13.【参考答案】C

【考查目标】动词搭配题

【答案解析】本题目选择动词,作为"wonder"引导的宾语从句的谓语。空格所在部分是"what"引导的宾语从句,其正常语序是"animals would... what experiments on huamns if they had the chance",意为"如果动物有机会,它们将对人类……什么实验"。"perform experiments on huamans"指"对人类做实验",符合文意,故选[C]项。

其他三个选项"deliver"意为"递送",还有"履行(诺言),不负(所望)";"apply"意为"应用",与"to"搭配使用。两者均不能与"experiments"搭配。若用"carry",则为"carry out experiments",所以应排除。

14.【参考答案】D

【考查目标】逻辑关系题

【答案解析】本题目选择介词短语在句中做插入语,表明逻辑关系。前文已经讲到作者很好奇,如果动物有机会的话,会对人类进行何种实验。本句接着说"每一只有主人的猫都在进行一项有关操作性条件反射的小规模研究。"这是以"cat"为例进一步论述动物对人进行实验,因此应选择表示举例的介词短语,故选[D]项"for instance"。

其他选项"by chance"意为"偶然";"as usual"意为"像往常一样";均不符合题意。而"in contrast"意为"与……相比";虽然也是表示上下文逻辑关系的逻辑词,但无法与上下文衔接,应排除。

15.【参考答案】A

【考查目标】逻辑关系题

【答案解析】本题目选择连词,体现句子之间的逻辑关系。由"believe that... ran... would test..."判断本句使用了虚拟语气,是对动物可能对人类进行实验进行了假设,故选[A]项。

其他三个选项都是可以引导从句的连词,选项"unless"意为"除非";"as"意为"因为,当……的时候,随着……";"lest"意为"唯恐,以免"。这三项均不符合题意,应排除。

16.【参考答案】C

【考查目标】动词辨析题

【答案解析】本题目选择动词,与"limits"搭配,作为"test"的目的,即"test sb. to do sth.",所在部分的含义是:它们(动物)会对我们进行测验,以……我们的忍耐极限、忠诚度以及对地形的记忆力。填入的动词需要与三个并列的名词短语"limits... faithfulness... memory"构成动宾搭配,而且其逻辑主语为句子主语"they"(animals),符合要求的只有选项[C]determine,说明动物进行测验的目的。

其他三个选项,"moderate"意为"缓和",是脱离上下文设置的干扰;"overcome"意为"克服","reach"意为"达到",这两个词都可以与"limits"构成常见的动宾搭配,但它们与"faithfulness"和"memory"则不搭配,故排除。

17.【参考答案】B

【考查目标】介词题

【答案解析】本题目选择介词,体现逻辑关系。该句承接上一句,继续论述假设动物对人类进行实验的内容。只有选项[B]for 表示"目的",构成"what... for"符合语境,表明动物们想了解人类智慧是用来干什么的。

其他选项都是常用的介词,含义丰富,都可接"what"做宾语,因此需要通过上下文排除。"at"与"after"需与动词连用,才可以表示"目的,目标",如"aim at"(目的是),"seek after"(追求)。"with"表示伴随、工具等,也可表示"关于,对于",但意思不能与上下文衔接,应排除。

18.【参考答案】A

【考查目标】逻辑关系题

【答案解析】本题目选择逻辑关系词,体现前后句子之间的逻辑关系。前面两句解释了假设动物对人类进行实验会进行的内容:它们想了解人类的某些极限,想知道人类智慧的用途。本句与前两句构成并列排比,"they would hope to study a(n)... question"(它们希望研究一个……问题),与前两句应为顺承关系,表示强调或递进,只有"above all"(首先,尤其是)符合题意。

其他选项都是常用的逻辑关系连接词。“after all”意为“毕竟”,与“above all”形近,但含义完全不同;“however”意为“但是”,表示转折;“otherwise”意为“否则”,引出一种假设的结果。三者均不符合题意,故排除。

19.【参考答案】A

【考查目标】形容词辨析题

【答案解析】本题目选择形容词,作定语修饰“question”。仅从问题本身无法判断它到底是一个什么样的问题。但由下文可知,这个“question”是“Are humans actually aware of the world they live in?”(人类是否真正了解他们生活的这个世界?)这应该是个最基本的问题,故选[A]项。

其他选项都是脱离上下文语境设置的搭配。“comprehensive”意为“综合的”;“equivalent”意为“相等的”;“hostile”意为“敌对的”。三者都不符合题意,应排除。

20.【参考答案】C

【考查目标】逻辑关系题

【答案解析】本题目选择短语体现与前面句子的逻辑关系。前面句子提出一个问题,本句讲“... the results are inconclusive”(……结果是不确定的)。因此,选项[C]项“so far”(迄今为止)最符合题意。

其他选项都是脱离上下文设置的短语。“by accident”意为“偶然”;“in time”意为“及时”;“better still”意为“更好”。把它们代入文中,都无法与上下文衔接,所以排除。

Section Ⅱ Reading Comprehension

Part A

Directions:

Read the following four texts. Answer the questions below each text by choosing A, B, C or D. Mark your answers on ANSWER SHEET 1. (40 points)

Text 1

Habits are a funny thing. We reach for them mindlessly, setting our brains on auto-pilot and relaxing into the unconscious comfort of familiar routine. "Not choice, but habit rules the unreflecting herd," William Wordsworth said in the 19th century. In the ever-changing 21st century, even the word "habit" carries a negative implication.

So it seems paradoxical to talk about habits in the same context as creativity and innovation. But brain researchers have discovered that when we consciously develop new habits, we create parallel paths, and even entirely new brain cells, that can jump our trains of thought onto new, innovative tracks.

Rather than dismissing ourselves as unchangeable creatures of habit, we can instead direct our own change by consciously developing new habits. In fact, the more new things we try—the more we step outside our comfort zone—the more inherently creative we become, both in the workplace and in our personal lives.

But don't bother trying to kill off old habits; once those ruts of procedure are worn into the brain, they're there to stay. Instead, the new habits we deliberately press into ourselves create parallel pathways that can bypass those old roads.

"The first thing needed for innovation is a fascination with wonder," says Dawna Markova, author of *The Open Mind*. "But we are taught instead to 'decide', just as our president calls himself 'the Decider'." She adds, however, that "to decide is to kill off all possibilities but one. A good innovational thinker is always exploring the many other possibilities."

All of us work through problems in ways of which we're unaware, she says. Researchers in the late 1960s discovered that humans are born with the capacity to approach challenges in four primary ways: analytically, procedurally, relationally (or collaboratively) and innovatively. At the end of adolescence, however, the brain shuts down half of that capacity, preserving only those modes of thought that have seemed most valuable during the first decade or so of life.

The current emphasis on standardized testing highlights analysis and procedure, meaning that few of us inherently use our innovative and collaborative modes of thought. "This breaks the major rule in the American belief system—that anyone can do anything," explains M. J. Ryan, author of the 2006 book *This Year I Will...* and Ms. Markova's business partner. "That's a lie that we have perpetuated, and it fosters commonness. Knowing what you're good at and doing even more of it creates excellence." This is where developing new habits comes in.

21. In Wordsworth's view, "habits" is characterized by being

[A] casual. [B] familiar. [C] mechanical. [D] changeable.

22. Brain researchers have discovered that the formation of new habits can be

[A] predicted. [B] regulated. [C] traced. [D] guided.

23. The word "ruts" (Paragraph 4) is closest in meaning to

[A] tracks. [B] series. [C] characteristics. [D] connections.

24. Dawna Markova would most probably agree that

[A] ideas are born of a relaxing mind.

[B] innovativeness could be taught.

[C] decisiveness derives from fantastic ideas.

[D] curiosity activates creative minds.

25. Ryan's comments suggest that the practice of standardized testing

[A] prevents new habits from being formed.

[B] no longer emphasizes commonness.

[C] maintains the inherent American thinking mode.

[D] complies with the American belief system.

21.【参考答案】C

【考查目标】理解文中的具体信息

【答案解析】根据题干中的关键词"Wordsworth"定位到第一段第三句。引文中"unreflecting"(缺乏思考的)一词说明 William Wordsworth 对习惯持否定态度。此外,引文是上面一句的递进,因此"mindlessly","auto-pilot","unconscious"都代表着他的观点。"mechanical"(机械的)恰好可以概括这些词说明习惯的特点,因此[C]为正确答案。

[A]、[B]和[D]项利用第一段的个别词汇设置干扰。"casual","familiar","changeable"分别

源于第二句的“mindlessly”,“familiar”以及末句的“ever-changing”。

22.【参考答案】D

【考查目标】理解文中的具体信息

【答案解析】根据题干中的关键词“Brain researchers”将答案定位到第二段第二句。该句指出,脑研究者发现,有意识地培养新习惯可以促进创新思维的发展。由此可知新习惯的形成是可以引导的,因此[D]为正确答案。此外,第三段首句中的“direct our own change by consciously developing new habits”(有意识地培养新习惯来做出改变)也可验证[D]项为正确答案。

[A]项“习惯的形成可预测”是无关干扰项。[B]项利用常识进行干扰。[C]项利用第二段中的词语“paths”和“tracks”进行干扰。

23.【参考答案】A

【考查目标】根据上下文推测生词的词义

【答案解析】“ruts”所在句是一个由分号连接的并列复合句,两个分句之间存在因果关系。该句说明了旧习惯的特点:不必费力地抹去旧有的习惯,因为那些旧习惯流程的……一旦形成很难消除。“instead”引导的第二句与首句形成对比,说明新习惯的形成特点:在大脑中绕过那些旧路线生成相应的新路线。因此“ruts”与下文的“pathways”和“roads”应该是同义替换,因此[A]项“trace”(小道,踪迹,车辙)是正确选项。

[B]、[C]、[D]项都是脱离上下文的无关干扰项。

24.【参考答案】D

【考查目标】理解文中的具体信息

【答案解析】根据题干中的人名关键词“Dawna Markova”定位到第五段。第五段首句“The first thing needed for innovation is a fascination with wonder”可以说明 Markova 认为创新的首要条件就是满怀好奇。选项[D]是该段首句的同义改写,因此是正确答案。

文章只是在首段提到习惯的话题时用到了“relaxing”一词,指的是大脑放松地进入到无意识舒服状态,而没有提到思想和放松的大脑的关系,故排除[A]。[B]、[C]项均属偷换概念。[B]项将第五段第二句的“做决定能够被传授”偷换成“创新力能够被传授”;[C]项将第五段首句的“创新源于新奇的想法”偷换成“果断源于新奇的想法”。

25.【参考答案】A

【考查目标】进行有关的判断、推理和引申

【答案解析】文章最后一段第一句谈到当前的标准化测试的注重就是鼓励分析和流程法,这意味着我们当中只有少数人会本能地使用创新和合作的思考模式。这说明标准测试忽略了创新和合作的思考模式。而文章第二段已经表明了创新与习惯的关系——培养新习惯是为了促进创新思维。因此,忽略了创新思考模式的标准测试,当然就阻碍了新习惯的形成,故答案为[A]。

[B]项中的“no longer emphasizes commonness”恰与 Ryan 所认为的“it fosters commonness”相反,故排除。[C]项中的“maintains”与文章最后一段第一句中的“few of us use”相反,也排除。[D]项中的“complies with”与 Ryan 评价中的“breaks”相矛盾,故也排除。所以这三项全是反义干扰。

Text 2

It is a wise father that knows his own child, but today a man can boost his paternal

(fatherly) wisdom—or at least confirm that he's the kid's dad. All he needs to do is shell out $30 for a paternity testing kit (PTK) at his local drugstore—and another $120 to get the results.

More than 60,000 people have purchased the PTKs since they first became available without prescriptions last year, according to Doug Fogg, chief operating officer of Identigene, which makes the over-the-counter kits. More than two dozen companies sell DNA tests directly to the public, ranging in price from a few hundred dollars to more than $2,500.

Among the most popular: paternity and kinship testing, which adopted children can use to find their biological relatives and families can use to track down kids put up for adoption. DNA testing is also the latest rage among passionate genealogists—and supports businesses that offer to search for a family's geographic roots.

Most tests require collecting cells by swabbing saliva in the mouth and sending it to the company for testing. All tests require a potential candidate with whom to compare DNA.

But some observers are skeptical. "There's a kind of false precision being hawked by people claiming they are doing ancestry testing," says Troy Duster, a New York University sociologist. He notes that each individual has many ancestors—numbering in the hundreds just a few centuries back. Yet most ancestry testing only considers a single lineage, either the Y chromosome inherited through men in a father's line or mitochondrial DNA, which is passed down only from mothers. This DNA can reveal genetic information about only one or two ancestors, even though, for example, just three generations back people also have six other great-grandparents or, four generations back, 14 other great-great-grandparents.

Critics also argue that commercial genetic testing is only as good as the reference collections to which a sample is compared. Databases used by some companies don't rely on data collected systematically but rather lump together information from different research projects. This means that a DNA database may have a lot of data from some regions and not others, so a person's test results may differ depending on the company that processes the results. In addition, the computer programs a company uses to estimate relationships may be patented and not subject to peer review or outside evaluation.

26. In Paragraphs 1 and 2, the text shows PTK's
[A] easy availability. [B] flexibility in pricing.
[C] successful promotion. [D] popularity with households.

27. PTK is used to
[A] locate one's birth place. [B] promote genetic research.
[C] identify parent-child kinship. [D] choose children for adoption.

28. Skeptical observers believe that ancestry testing fails to
[A] trace distant ancestors. [B] rebuild reliable bloodlines.
[C] fully use genetic information. [D] achieve the claimed accuracy.

29. In the last paragraph, a problem commercial genetic testing faces is
[A] disorganized data collection. [B] overlapping database building.
[C] excessive sample comparison. [D] lack of patent evaluation.

30. An appropriate title for the text is most likely to be

[A] Fors and Againsts of DNA Testing.　　[B] DNA Testing and Its Problems.

[C] DNA Testing Outside the Lab.　　[D] Lies Behind DNA Testing.

26.【参考答案】A

【考查目标】理解文中的具体信息

【答案解析】文章第一段和第二段提到,只需花30元即可从住处附近的药店购买PTK;不需要医师处方即可购买;购买者人数众多;20多家公司直接向公众出售基因检测服务。由此可见容易获得是其特点,因此正确选项是[A]。

文中已经明确指出PTK的价格为30美元,因此排除[B]项。前两段只提到了PTK的销售结果,并没有提到促销手段,排除[C]项。第二段首句只提到购买者人数多达"more than 60,000 people",[D]项却将购买者具体为家庭,因此排除。

27.【参考答案】C

【考查目标】理解文中的具体信息

【答案解析】文章第一段段首在引出PTK时说"父贤知其子",但现在的男人可以增强其为人父的智慧——或者至少确认自己是孩子的爸爸。他所需要做的是花费30美元在当地药店做一个PTK测试。由此可见PTK是用于父子关系的检查手段,故正确答案为[C]。

[A]、[B]、[D]三项不仅将文章第三段介绍的基因检测的其他用途说成是PTK的用途,而且还偷换了文中的重要概念:[A]项将"为家族寻找地域根源"偷换成"确定出生地";[B]项将"成为谱系学研究的最新手段"偷换成"促进基因研究";[D]项将"追查被领养孩子的下落"偷换成"选择领养的孩子"。

28.【参考答案】D

【考查目标】理解文中的具体信息

【答案解析】根据题干中的关键词"Skeptical observers"和"ancestry testing"定位到第五段第一、二句。第二句引用一位持怀疑态度的观察家的话指出,声称自己在做家谱检测的人们正在吹嘘一种虚假的准确性,故正确答案为[D]。

[A]、[B]、[C]三项均偷换了文中的重要信息。文章第五段第四句提到"only considers a single lineage"(只追溯单一谱系的祖先),但[A]项将其偷换成"fail to trace distant ancestors"(不能追溯年代久远的祖先)。[B]项将文中"不能重建完整的血统谱系"偷换成"不能重建可靠的血统谱系"。[C]项将文中的"只能揭示少量基因信息"偷换成"未能充分利用基因信息"。

29.【参考答案】A

【考查目标】理解文中的具体信息

【答案解析】末段第二句指出,一些商业基因检测公司采用的数据库并非基于系统的数据收集,而是将多个研究项目的数据堆砌在一起。[A]项概括了商业基因检测存在的第一个问题,是第六段第二句话中"don't rely on data collected systematically"的同义替换,因此是正确答案。

[B]项是对末段第二句的过度引申。该段首句提到"…the reference collections to which a sample is compared",只提到同样本进行比较,并未提及"excessive",因此排除[C]。[D]项将末句提到的计算机程序的问题说成是商业基因检测的问题,因此也排除。

30.【参考答案】B

【考查目标】理解主旨要义

【答案解析】纵观全文,文章第一段引出DNA测试的话题,第二段到第四段介绍了DNA测试的特点、用途及要求,最后两段从“observers”和“critics”的观点出发说明了DNA测试的问题所在。[B]项完整、准确地概括了文章内容,为恰当的题目。

本文只论述了DNA检测的局限性,没有明确论述它的优点,因此[A]项不能很好地概括全文。[C]项过于笼统,没有揭示出议论的范围,而且文中也并未指出商业基因检测就是实验室外的基因测试,故排除。文章后两段着重讨论DNA检测的问题,但这只是文中的一部分内容,而且把问题说成“lies”属于过度推断,因此排除[D]项。

Text 3

The relationship between formal education and economic growth in poor countries is widely misunderstood by economists and politicians alike. Progress in both areas is undoubtedly necessary for the social, political, and intellectual development of these and all other societies; however, the conventional view that education should be one of the very highest priorities for promoting rapid economic development in poor countries is wrong. We are fortunate that it is, because building new educational systems there and putting enough people through them to improve economic performance would require two or three generations. The findings of a research institution have consistently shown that workers in all countries can be trained on the job to achieve radically higher productivity and, as a result, radically higher standards of living.

Ironically, the first evidence for this idea appeared in the United States. Not long ago, with the country entering a recession and Japan at its pre-bubble peak, the U. S. workforce was derided as poorly educated and one of the primary causes of the poor U. S. economic performance. Japan was, and remains, the global leader in automotive-assembly productivity. Yet the research revealed that the U. S. factories of Honda, Nissan, and Toyota achieved about 95 percent of the productivity of their Japanese counterparts—a result of the training that U. S. workers received on the job.

More recently, while examining housing construction, the researchers discovered that illiterate, non-English-speaking Mexican workers in Houston, Texas, consistently met best-practice labor productivity standards despite the complexity of the building industry's work.

What is the real relationship between education and economic development? We have to suspect that continuing economic growth promotes the development of education even when governments don't force it. After all, that's how education got started. When our ancestors were hunters and gatherers 10,000 years ago, they didn't have time to wonder much about anything besides finding food. Only when humanity began to get its food in a more productive way was there time for other things.

As education improved, humanity's productivity potential increased as well. When the competitive environment pushed our ancestors to achieve that potential, they could in turn afford more education. This increasingly high level of education is probably a necessary, but not a sufficient, condition for the complex political systems required by advanced economic performance. Thus poor countries might not be able to escape their poverty traps without political changes that may be possible only with broader formal education. A lack of formal education, however, doesn't constrain the ability of the developing world's workforce to substantially improve productivity for the foreseeable future. On the contrary, constraints on improving productivity explain why education isn't developing more quickly there than it is.

31. The author holds in Paragraph 1 that the importance of education in poor countries

[A] is subject to groundless doubts. [B] has fallen victim of bias.

[C] is conventionally downgraded. [D] has been overestimated.

32. It is stated in Paragraph 1 that the construction of a new educational system

[A] challenges economists and politicians. [B] takes efforts of generations.

[C] demands priority from the government. [D] requires sufficient labor force.

33. A major difference between the Japanese and U. S. workforces is that

[A] the Japanese workforce is better disciplined.

[B] the Japanese workforce is more productive.

[C] the U. S. workforce has a better education.

[D] the U. S. workforce is more organized.

34. The author quotes the example of our ancestors to show that education emerged

[A] when people had enough time.

[B] prior to better ways of finding food.

[C] when people no longer went hungry.

[D] as a result of pressure on government.

35. According to the last paragraph, development of education

[A] results directly from competitive environments.

[B] does not depend on economic performance.

[C] follows improved productivity.

[D] cannot afford political changes.

31.【参考答案】D

【考查目标】理解作者的意图、观点和态度

【答案解析】作者在文章第一段首句开门见山地指出"贫穷国家正式教育和经济增长之间的关系被误解了"。第二句"however"之后的分句指出"在促进贫困国家经济快速发展中,教育应该放在最优先的地位,这一传统观点是错误的"。既然教育作为促进经济发展的第一要务是一种错误看法,那么可推断出:传统上教育的重要性受到了过度的重视,即被高估了。故正确答案为[D]项。

[A]项错在"groundless"(没有根据的),作者提出其观点是有根据的。第三句指出,通过教育提高经济效益需要漫长的时间;第四句指出,研究表明通过对个人在岗培训可以从根本上提高生产率。[B]项夸大其词,将文章中的"conventional view"(传统观点)夸大为"bias"(偏见)。[C]项为反向干扰。

32.【参考答案】B

【考查目标】理解文中的具体信息

【答案解析】根据题干关键词"a new education system"定位到首段第三句,"…because building new educational systems there and putting enough people through them to improve economic performance would require two or three generations”，即建立新的教育体系并且让足够多的人接受教育来提高经济水平需要几代人的努力。因此正确答案为[B]项。题干中的“the construction of a new education system”是第三句中“building new educational systems”的同义替换；正确选项[B]中“takes efforts of generations”是第三句中“require two or three generations”的同义替换。

[A]项利用首段首句中的词语“economists and politicians”作干扰；[C]项是传统观点，不是作者观点；[D]项也是利用文中个别词汇编造出来的选项，也不符合常识。

33.【参考答案】B

【考查目标】理解文中的具体信息

【答案解析】根据题干中的“the Japanese and U.S workforces”定位到文章第二段。该段首句承上启下，“this idea”指的就是第一段末句提出的观点“研究表明通过对个人在岗培训可以从根本上提高生产率”，“the first evidence”表明第二段在举例证明该观点。下面三句是具体的例子。第二句指出，“美国劳动力被嘲笑为受教育水平低，而这种教育情况被看做是其经济水平不好的主要原因之一”；第三句讲“日本在自动化生产效率方面是全球的领导者，水平很高”；第四句转折后指出，“一些日本企业的美国工厂的工人通过在岗培训，达到了与日本本土工人差不多的生产率”。由此，通过美国工人与日本工人的生产率的对比证明了第一段末句的观点。题目问日本和美国劳动力的主要区别，考查例子本身，而例子是为证明观点服务的，[B]项提到了关键词“productive”，且与第二段第三句的事实相符，故为正确答案。

[A]项和[D]项中的“better disciplined”和“more organized”属无中生有，且与文中论述的工人的“productivity”(劳动生产率)无关，故排除；[C]项与第二段第二句谈到的事实不符。

34.【参考答案】C

【考查目标】区分论点和论据

【答案解析】根据题干中的“our ancestors”定位到文章第四段。第四段首句以问句的形式引出论点，第二句给出观点“经济持续增长促进教育的发展”，第三句引起例证“教育就是这样产生的”，后面的例子(第四句和第五句)具体讲教育是如何产生的，均为论据。论据是来证明论点的。所以，浏览选项，可以确定[C]项为正确答案。“education emerged when people no longer went hungry”既说明了教育产生的原因，又形象地说明了教育与经济的关系，论证了第二句提出的观点。

[A]项是本题最大的干扰项，第四段第五句具体讲到“只有当人类祖先开始更有效率地获取食物后，他们才有时间考虑猎取食物以外的其他事情(即教育)”，所以[A]项表面上看似正确的，但是要注意，这个选项停留在例子本身，没有反映前面的论点，故不能选。[B]项则和文章内容相反；[D]项曲解了“even when governments don’t force it”。

35.【参考答案】C

【考查目标】理解作者的意图、观点或态度

【答案解析】文章最后一段第一句及二句谈到：随着教育的改善，人类的生产率潜能也得到了提高。当竞争环境促使我们的祖先去实现这种潜能(即更高的生产率)时，他们反过来又能负担更多的教育。由此可以看出，教育促进经济的发展，而经济发展则反过来又能促进教育发展，两者之间是一种相互促进的作用，故本题答案为[C]。

[A]项断章取义，错在“直接”两个字上，第二句讲，竞争环境促使人们实现更高的生产率，从而

间接促进教育发展。[B]项是反向干扰，第二句就谈到，生产率提高促进教育的发展，所以教育的发展依赖经济表现。[D]项提到了政治变革。文章最后一段的第三句及第四句提到了政治变革，第三句提到提高教育水平是建立政治体制的必要而非充分条件，第四句提到政治变革只能通过较广泛的正式教育来实现。通过这两个信息，排除 D 项。

Text 4

The most thoroughly studied intellectuals in the history of the New World are the ministers and political leaders of seventeenth-century New England. According to the standard history of American philosophy, nowhere else in colonial America was "so much importance attached to intellectual pursuits." According to many books and articles, New England's leaders established the basic themes and preoccupations of an unfolding, dominant Puritan tradition in American intellectual life.

To take this approach to the New Englanders normally means to start with the Puritans' theological innovations and their distinctive ideas about the church—important subjects that we may not neglect. But in keeping with our examination of southern intellectual life, we may consider the original Puritans as carriers of European culture, adjusting to New World circumstances. The New England colonies were the scenes of important episodes in the pursuit of widely understood ideals of civility and virtuosity.

The early settlers of Massachusetts Bay included men of impressive education and influence in England. Besides the ninety or so learned ministers who came to Massachusetts churches in the decade after 1629, there were political leaders like John Winthrop, an educated gentleman, lawyer, and official of the Crown before he journeyed to Boston. These men wrote and published extensively, reaching both New World and Old World audiences, and giving New England an atmosphere of intellectual earnestness.

We should not forget, however, that most New Englanders were less well educated. While few craftsmen or farmers, let alone dependents and servants, left literary compositions to be analyzed, it is obvious that their views were less fully intellectualized. Their thinking often had a traditional superstitious quality. A tailor named John Dane, who emigrated in the late 1630s, left an account of his reasons for leaving England that is filled with signs. Sexual confusion, economic frustrations, and religious hope—all came together in a decisive moment when he opened the Bible, told his father that the first line he saw would settle his fate, and read the magical words: "Come out from among them, touch no unclean thing, and I will be your God and you shall be my people." One wonders what Dane thought of the careful sermons explaining the Bible that he heard in Puritan churches.

Meanwhile, many settlers had slighter religious commitments than Dane's, as one clergyman learned in confronting folk along the coast who mocked that they had not come to the New World for religion. "Our main end was to catch fish."

36. The author holds that in the seventeenth-century New England

[A] Puritan tradition dominated political life.

[B] intellectual interests were encouraged.

[C] politics benefited much from intellectual endeavors.

[D] intellectual pursuits enjoyed a liberal environment.

37. It is suggested in Paragraph 2 that New Englanders

[A] experienced a comparatively peaceful early history.

[B] brought with them the culture of the Old World.

[C] paid little attention to southern intellectual life.

[D] were obsessed with religious innovations.

38. The early ministers and political leaders in Massachusetts Bay

[A] were famous in the New World for their writings.

[B] gained increasing importance in religious affairs.

[C] abandoned high positions before coming to the New World.

[D] created a new intellectual atmosphere in New England.

39. The story of John Dane shows that less well-educated New Englanders were often

[A] influenced by superstitions.

[B] troubled with religious beliefs.

[C] puzzled by church sermons.

[D] frustrated with family earnings.

40. The text suggests that early settlers in New England

[A] were mostly engaged in political activities.

[B] were motivated by an illusory prospect.

[C] came from different intellectual backgrounds.

[D] left few formal records for later reference.

36. 【参考答案】B

【考查目标】理解作者的意图、观点或态度

【答案解析】根据题干中的关键词"in the seventeenth-century New England"定位到第一段。该段的第二句指出新英格兰的一大特点在于"so much importance attached to intellectual pursuits"，可见新英格兰重视知识的追求。因此[B]项"知识兴趣受到鼓励"为正确答案。[B]项中的"intellectual interests"是该句中"intellectual pursuits"的同义改写，"encouraged"是"attach importance to"的同义改写。

文中探讨的是清教传统与知识追求的关系，而不是与政治追求的关系，故[A]项错误。[C]项无中生有。[D]项反向干扰。第一段第三句说，英格兰的领袖确立了美国知识生活的基本主题，长久以来占统治地位的清教传统先入为主。由此可见，新英格兰地区的求知环境是有限制的，并非是"liberal"(宽松自由的)。

37. 【参考答案】B

【考查目标】进行有关的判断、推理和引申

【答案解析】第二段第二句提到，"... we may consider the original Puritans as carriers of European culture, adjusting to New World circumstances"，即我们可以把最早的清教徒们视为欧洲文化的使者，他们在适应新大陆的环境。其中的"original Puritans"指的就是第二段第一句中的"New Englanders"。由此可知，[B]项"带来了旧大陆的文化"正确，是第二句中"carriers of European culture"的同义改写。"the Old World"(旧大陆)即欧洲大陆，是相对于北美新大陆而

言的。

[A]项错在“peaceful”一词上。第二段末句说,新英格兰是早期移民开创文明的重要地区,从中体会不到“peaceful”所表达的和平的、平静的含义。第二段第二句提到了“examination of southern intellectual life”,但其主语是作者,而非“New Englanders”,故[B]项错误。第二段首句提到了“start with the Puritans' theological innovations”,也是在提及作者对“New Englanders”的研究,完全推断不出[D]项谈到的“新英格兰人被宗教创新所缠绕”。

38.【参考答案】D

【考查目标】理解文中的具体信息

【答案解析】根据题干中的关键词“Massachusetts Bay”定位到文章第三段。该段末句提到,“These men wrote and published extensively, reaching both New World and Old World audiences, and giving New England an atmosphere of intellectual earnestness”,即这些人(上句提到的牧师和政治领袖)广泛著书并出版,其读者覆盖了新旧大陆,为新英格兰营造了一种求知的氛围。故答案为[D]项。[D]项是末句“giving New England an atmosphere of intellectual earnestness”的同义改写。

[A]项中的“in the new world”范围缩小,原文指出他们的读者来自新旧两个世界。[B]项偷换概念,文中提到的是他们在知识文化方面的影响,而非宗教事务中的影响。[C]项过度推理,文中只提到John Winthrop在来波士顿层担任王室官员,属于个例,推断不出[C]项。还有一点要注意,考研阅读考查“理解文中的具体信息”时,往往考查文中的重要信息和细节,而非细枝末节的信息,[A]、[B]和[C]项都是文中的细节信息。

39.【参考答案】A

【考查目标】区分论点和论据

【答案解析】根据题目中的“John Dane”定位在文章第四段。John Dane的故事位于该段后半部分,这个故事是作为论据,论证其前面第三句提到的论点“Their thinking often had a traditional superstitious quality”,即“他们(未受到良好教育的新英格兰人)的思想一般来说还是带有传统的迷信色彩”。故[A]项为正确答案,是对该段第三句的同义改写。

本题是对论据设题,考查考生对论据作用的理解。论据是为了证明论点,故这类题的答案一定要在举例前后的观点的表述中找答案。[B]、[C]、[D]项都是根据例子本身的细节信息“Sexual confusion, economic frustrations, and religious hope”设置的干扰项,不能入选。

40.【参考答案】C

【考查目标】进行有关的判断、推理和引申

【答案解析】这道题目需要通读全文归纳总结得出答案。第三段首句提到,“The early settlers of Massachusetts Bay included men of impressive education and influence in England”,即“马萨诸塞州海湾的早期移民中有不少人在英国接受了教育,深受其文化的影响”;第四段提到,“...most New Englanders were less well educated. ... Their thinking often had a traditional superstitious quality”,即“大多数新英格兰人都没有接受过良好的教育……他们的思想一般来说还带有传统的迷信色彩”;第五段提到,“...many settles had slighter religious commitments than Dane's, ...they had not come to the New World for religion”,即“还有很多移民没有虔诚的宗教信仰”。可见,早期的移民背景多样、知识程度差异显著,故[C]项正确。

[A]项“political activities”文中没有涉及。[B]项和[D]项都是第四段提到的未受过良好教育的新英格兰人的特点,而不是所有新英格兰早期移民的特点,犯了以偏概全的错误。

Part B

Directions:

In the following text, some segments have been removed. For Questions 41–45, choose the most suitable one from the list A–G to fit into each of the numbered blanks. There are two extra choices, which do not fit in any of the blanks. Mark your answers on ANSWER SHEET 1. (10 points)

Coinciding with the groundbreaking theory of biological evolution proposed by British naturalist Charles Darwin in the 1860s, British social philosopher Herbert Spencer put forward his own theory of biological and cultural evolution. Spencer argued that all worldly phenomena, including human societies, changed over time, advancing toward perfection. (41) ________

American social scientist Lewis Henry Morgan introduced another theory of cultural evolution in the late 1800s. Morgan helped found modern anthropology—the scientific study of human societies, customs and beliefs—thus becoming one of the earliest anthropologists. In his work, he attempted to show how all aspects of culture changed together in the evolution of societies. (42) ________

In the early 1900s in North America, German-born American anthropologist Franz Boas developed a new theory of culture known as historical particularism. Historical particularism, which emphasized the uniqueness of all cultures, gave new direction to anthropology. (43) ________

Boas felt that the culture of any society must be understood as the result of a unique history and not as one of many cultures belonging to a broader evolutionary stage or type of culture. (44) ________

Historical particularism became a dominant approach to the study of culture in American anthropology, largely through the influence of many students of Boas. But a number of anthropologists in the early 1900s also rejected the particularist theory of culture in favor of diffusionism. Some attributed virtually every important cultural achievement to the inventions of a few, especially gifted peoples that, according to diffusionists, then spread to other cultures. (45) ________

Also in the early 1900s, French sociologist Émile Durkheim developed a theory of culture that would greatly influence anthropology. Durkheim proposed that religious beliefs functioned to reinforce social solidarity. An interest in the relationship between the function of society and culture became a major theme in European, and especially British, anthropology.

[A] Other anthropologists believed that cultural innovations, such as inventions, had a single origin and passed from society to society. This theory was known as diffusionism.

[B] In order to study particular cultures as completely as possible, he became skilled in linguistics, the study of languages, and in physical anthropology, the study of human biology and anatomy.

[C] He argued that human evolution was characterized by a struggle he called the "survival of the fittest," in which weaker races and societies must eventually be replaced by stronger, more advanced races and societies.

[D] They also focused on important rituals that appeared to preserve a people's social structure, such as initiation ceremonies that formally signify children's entrance into adulthood.

[E] Thus, in his view, diverse aspects of culture, such as the structure of families, forms of marriage, categories of kinship, ownership of property, forms of government, technology, and systems of food production, all changed as societies evolved.

[F] Supporters of the theory viewed culture as a collection of integrated parts that work together to keep a society functioning.

[G] For example, British anthropologists Grafton Elliot Smith and W. J. Perry incorrectly suggested, on the basis of inadequate information, that farming, pottery making, and metallurgy all originated in ancient Egypt and diffused throughout the world. In fact, all of these cultural developments occurred separately at different times in many parts of the world.

41.【参考答案】C

【考查目标】段落的连贯性

【答案解析】空格设在第一段末,所填信息一定要与上文保持连贯与一致。空格前的核心信息谈到Spencer的理论特点,人类社会的进化类似于达尔文的进化论,是一个不断进步的过程。浏览七个选项,[C]项的内容正好与此吻合,“He argued”承接了空格前的“Spencer argued”。[C]项讲到的适者生存、弱小的民族和社会最终必将被更强大、更先进的民族和社会所取代与空格前的“advancing toward perfection”表达了相同的意思,故答案为[C]。

42.【参考答案】E

【考查目标】段落的连贯性

【答案解析】该段空格前的中心内容谈到Morgan的文化进化论,空格前的句子讲到在他的研究中,他试图阐明文化的所有方面是如何随着社会的变化而变化,空格处填入的信息也必然与此相关,比对剩下的选项,[E]项基本上是重复了空格前的内容,[E]项中的“diverse aspects of culture...”是原文“all aspects of culture...”的同义转换,故[E]为答案。

43.【参考答案】A

【考查目标】段落的连贯性

【答案解析】该段空格前主要介绍了Franz Boas的历史特殊论。依据语篇衔接的连贯性可以推出空格处填入的信息要么会继续介绍历史特殊论要么会转向其他相关内容的介绍上,浏览剩余的选项,发现[A]项主要介绍了另一种理论——传播论,而这一理论的观点与特殊论是相对的,由此可知,[A]项在语意上与空格前信息形成了对比关联。再者,[A]项中的“Other anthropologists”呼应了原文中的“American Anthropologist”,“diffusionism”呼应了原文中的“particularism”。因此[A]为答案。

44.【参考答案】B

【考查目标】段落的一致性

【答案解析】该段空格前的中心内容是接着讲Boas的理论,他认为,任何社会的文化都必须被理解为某一独特历史的结果,而不是属于某一更广义的进化阶段或者文化类型的许多文化之一。浏览剩下的选项,应首先寻找是否存在符合此主旨要义的选项,可以发现[B]项的内容与空格前的信息紧密衔接，而且[B]项中的"he"指代的正是空格前的"Boas"，"particular cultures"正是与原文"a unique history and not as one of many cultures"的同义转换，由此可知，[B]为答案。

45.【参考答案】G

【考查目标】段落的一致性

【答案解析】空格设在本段末句。需通过本段的中心内容及空格前一句来确定本题的答案。该段由第二句的"But"引出了本段谈论的中心内容是"diffusionism"这一理论，空格前的一句话论述了传播论的观点：每项重要的文化成就都是少数特别有天赋的民族的发明创造，并传播到其他文化中。浏览剩下的选项，[G]项是围绕这一话题在论说，[G]项通过举例，从反面论证了传播论者观点的错误，而且[G]项中的"farming, pottery making, and metallurgy"呼应了原文的"every important cultural achievement"，"diffused throughout the world"呼应了原文的"spread to other cultures"，故[G]为答案。

Part C

Directions:

Read the following text carefully and then translate the underlined segments into Chinese. Your translation should be written clearly on ANSWER SHEET 2. (10 points)

There is a marked difference between the education which every one gets from living with others and the deliberate educating of the young. In the former case the education is incidental; it is natural and important, but it is not the express reason of the association. (46) It may be said that the measure of the worth of any social institution is its effect in enlarging and improving experience. but this effect is not a part of its original motive. Religious associations began, for example, in the desire to secure the favor of overruling powers and to ward off evil influences; family life in the desire to gratify appetites and secure family perpetuity; systematic labor, for the most part, because of enslavement to others, etc. (47) Only gradually was the by-prodcut of the institution noted, and only more gradually still was this effect considered as a directive factor in the conduct of the institution. Even today, in our industrial life, apart from certain values of industriousness and thrift, the intellectual and emotional reaction of the forms of human association under which the world's work is carried on receives little attention as compared with physical output.

But in dealing with the young, the fact of association itself as an immediate human fact, gains in importance. (48) While it is easy to ignore in our contact with tmen the effect of our acts upon their disposition, it is not so easy as in dealing with adults. The need of training is too evident and the pressure to accomplish a change in their attitude and habits is too urgent to leave these consequences wholly out of account. (49) Since our chief business with them is to enable them to share in a common life we cannot help considering wherther or not we are forming the powers which will secure this ability. If humanity has made some headway in realizing that the ultimate value of every institution is its distinctively human effect we may well believe that this lesson has been learned largely through dealings with the young.

(50) We are thus led to distinguish, within the broad educational process which we have been so far considering, a more formal kind of education—that of direct trition of schooling. In

undeveloped social groups, we find very little formal teaching and training. Savage groups mainly rely for instilling needed dispositions into the young upon the same sort of association which keeps adults loyal to their group.

46.【英文原句】It may be said that the measure of the worth of any social institution is its effect in enlarging and improving experience, but this effect is not a part of its original motive.

【考查目标】主语从句,被动语态

【答案解析】主语从句无需调整语序;"it"做形式主语,而主句的谓语动词是被动语态,按照被动语态的翻译方法,可译为"据说"或"我们可以说"。

【参考译文】虽然我们可以说衡量任何一个社会机构价值的标准是其在丰富和完善人生(经验)方面所起的作用,但这种作用并不是我们最初动机的组成部分。

47.【英文原句】Only gradually was the by-product of the institution noted, and only more gradually still was this effect considered as a directive factor in the conduct of the institution.

【考查目标】倒装句,被动语态

【答案解析】该句是"and"连接的并列倒装句,为了便于翻译可以将其调整为正常语序:"the by-product of the institution was only gradually noted and this effect was considered only more gradually still as a directive factor in the conduct of the institution";此句中所含的被动语态可以直接处理成"被"字句,也可以通过增加主语"人们"以及运用汉语词汇"把"等来翻译。

【参考译文】人们只是逐渐地才注意到机构的这一副产品,而人们把这种作用视为机构运作的指导性因素的过程则更为缓慢。

48.【英文原句】While it is easy to ignore in our contact with them the effect of our acts upon their disposition, it is not so easy as in dealing with adults.

【考查目标】状语从句,代词指代

【答案解析】"while"引导让步状语从句,从句的部分可以翻译为"尽管……";"them"为代词,意思模糊,翻译时还原为"年轻人"。

【参考译文】在与年轻人的接触中,我们很容易忽视自己的行为对他们的性情所产生的影响,然而在与成年人打交道时这种情况就不那么容易发生了。

49.【英文原句】Since our chief business with them is to enable them to share in a common life we cannot help considering whether or not we are forming the powers which will secure this ability.

【考查目标】原因状语从句,定语从句

【答案解析】"Since"引导的原因状语从句位于句首,翻译时句序不必调整;"which"引导的定语从句修饰"powers",较短小,可采用前置法,翻译到所修饰的"powers"之前。

【参考译文】由于我们对年轻人所做的首要工作在于使他们能够在共同生活中彼此相融,因此我们不禁要考虑自己是否在形成让他们获得这种能力的力量。

50.【英文原句】We are thus led to distinguish, within the broad educational process which we have been so far considering, a more formal kind of education—that of direct tuition or schooling.

【考查分析】被动语态,定语从句。

【答案解析】本句的主干为被动结构："we are thus led to distinguish..."，可译为汉语的主动语态，即将主语译为宾语，并且为了与上文更好的衔接，增译主语"这"；"which"引导的定语从句修饰"process"，根据定语从句的翻译方法可以把定语从句置于"process"之前。

【参考译文】这就使我们得以在一直讨论的广义的教育过程中进一步区分出一种更为正式的教育形式，即直接讲授或学校教育。

Section Ⅲ Writing

Part A

51. **Directions**:

Restrictions on the use of plastic bags have not been so successful in some regions. "White Pollution" is still going on.

Write a letter to the editor(s) of your local newspaper to

1) give your opinions briefly, and

2) make two or three suggestions.

You should write about 100 words on ANSWER SHEET 2.

Do not sign your own name at the end of the letter. Use "Li Ming" instead.

Do not write the address. (10 points)

【考查分析】考查的是书信中的建议信，是一封公务信函。考生在写作的过程中，要注意书信的基本格式，恰当的语域、不要遗漏写作指导部分提纲中的要点，另外可以灵活的套用建议信中常常用到的固定表达方式。另外建议信最重要的一点是不要光提出问题，不给出建议，那样就成了投诉信。

【审题谋篇】题目要求考生写一封建议信，大意是某些地区禁止塑料袋使用，但不是很成功，白色污染仍然在继续，就此给当地报纸的编辑写一封信，表明考生对此的看法并提出2~3条建议。

该信函可以通过三段展开。在第一段中，直接点明主题，开门见山地说出写作意图，可以笼统地提出当前"白色污染"的现状及危害。第二段则要发挥想象力，从2~3个方面点出怎样杜绝塑料袋的使用，减少"白色污染"。在写第二段时，一定要打开思路，可写的建议多种多样，如政府需要制定法律，人民群众需要提高意识。具体来说，可写一次性塑料袋应该严禁使用。最后一段提出希望采纳建议，并表示谢意，期盼回复。在写该段时，完全可套用经典句型来完成文章的写作。

【高分作文】

Dear editor(s),

I am writing this letter to draw your attention on "White Pollution". Our country has officially enacted the law of plastic bag restriction, but it is observed in vain in several places, thus resulting in the continuing of "White Pollution".

To address this problem, I would like to make some conductive recommendations. On the one hand, the authorities should set up rules and regulations to control the productivity and circulation of the plastic bags. On the other hand, people should realize the significance of protecting our environment and not use too many plastic bags.

I sincerely hope you will find these proposals useful. Your prompt attention to my recommendations will be highly appreciated.

Yours sincerely,

Li Ming

Part B

52. **Directions**:

Write an essay of 160 - 200 words based on the following drawing. In your essay, you should

1) describe the drawing briefly,

2) explain its intended meaning, and then

3) give your comments.

You should write neatly on ANSWER SHEET 2. (20 points)

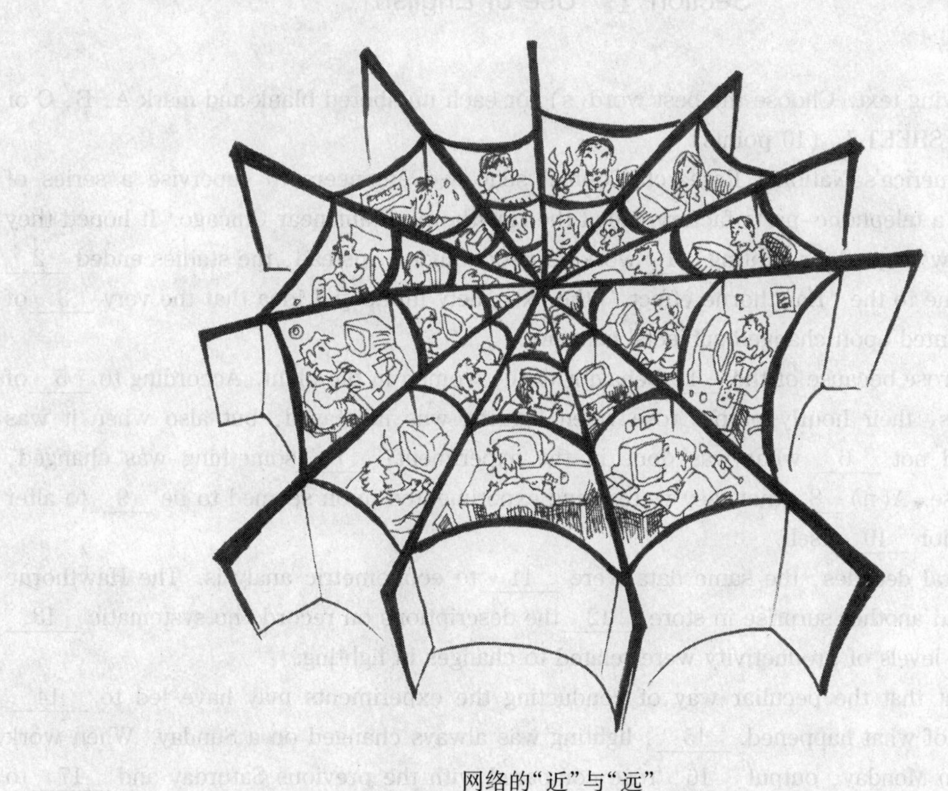

网络的“近”与“远”

【考查分析】短文写作部分考到的依旧是图画题,考生在写作过程中应该准确把握图画所反映的主旨,然后完成三段的写作任务。

【审题谋篇】本题属于图画作文中的现象阐释题型。一种普遍的现象通过漫画展示出来,而且在漫画的下方有明确的文字说明,揭示了漫画中的现象是利弊共存的,在行文时需在说明现象的同时充分分析其利弊,再给出对现象的评论并表明态度。

在看到这一作文题目时,仔细审题很关键。考生一看图,映入眼帘的是张大网,网被分成许多格子,每个格子里有一个人,坐在电脑前,下面标着一行汉字——网络的:“近与远”。这行汉字提示该作文的主题是“网络拉近了人们之间的距离,还是拉大了人们之间的距离”。由于图中最突出的是格子,所以文章除了要写网络可以缩短人们之间的距离,也要突出网络给人们造成的隔阂以及网络疏远了人们的关系,减少了人与人之间面对面的交往。

这篇文章遵循三段论。第一段描写图画,说明很多人在被网络分割成的格子里上网。第二段点题,讨论图画意义,可以采用固定的套路"一分为二"的分析网络带来的利弊。第三段谈自己对此的观点。

【高分作文】

请参考本书第2部分第五档范文标准。

3.2 2010年研究生入学统一考试英语试题

Section Ⅰ Use of English

Directions:

Read the following text. Choose the best word(s) for each numbered blank and mark A, B, C or D on ANSWER SHEET 1. (10 points)

In 1924 America's National Research Council sent two engineers to supervise a series of experiments at a telephone-parts factory called the Hawthorne Plant near Chicago. It hoped they would learn how shop-floor lighting __1__ workers' productivity. Instead, the studies ended __2__ giving their name to the "Hawthorne effect," the extremely influential idea that the very __3__ of being experimented upon changed subjects' behavior.

The idea arose because of the __4__ behavior of the women in the plant. According to __5__ of the experiments, their hourly output rose when lighting was increased, but also when it was dimmed. It did not __6__ what was done in the experiment; __7__ something was changed, productivity rose. A(n) __8__ that they were being experimented upon seemed to be __9__ to alter workers' behavior __10__ itself.

After several decades, the same data were __11__ to econometric analysis. The Hawthorne experiments had another surprise in store. __12__ the descriptions on record, no systematic __13__ was found that levels of productivity were related to changes in lighting.

It turns out that the peculiar way of conducting the experiments may have led to __14__ interpretations of what happened. __15__, lighting was always changed on a Sunday. When work started again on Monday, output __16__ rose compared with the previous Saturday and __17__ to rise for the next couple of days. __18__, a comparison with data for weeks when there was no experimentation showed that output always went up on Mondays. Workers __19__ to be diligent for the first few days of the week in any case, before __20__ a plateau and then slackening off. This suggests that the alleged "Hawthorne effect" is hard to pin down.

1. [A] affected [B] achieved [C] extracted [D] restored
2. [A] at [B] up [C] with [D] off
3. [A] truth [B] sight [C] act [D] proof
4. [A] controversial [B] perplexing [C] mischievous [D] ambiguous
5. [A] requirements [B] explanations [C] accounts [D] assessments
6. [A] conclude [B] matter [C] indicate [D] work

7. [A] as far as [B] for fear that [C] in case that [D] so long as
8. [A] awareness [B] expectation [C] sentiment [D] illusion
9. [A] suitable [B] excessive [C] enough [D] abundant
10. [A] about [B] for [C] on [D] by
11. [A] compared [B] shown [C] subjected [D] conveyed
12. [A] Contrary to [B] Consistent with [C] Parallel with [D] Peculiar to
13. [A] evidence [B] guidance [C] implication [D] source
14. [A] disputable [B] enlightening [C] reliable [D] misleading
15. [A] In contrast [B] For example [C] In consequence [D] As usual
16. [A] duly [B] accidentally [C] unpredictably [D] suddenly
17. [A] failed [B] ceased [C] started [D] continued
18. [A] Therefore [B] Furthermore [C] However [D] Meanwhile
19. [A] attempted [B] tended [C] chose [D] intended
20. [A] breaking [B] climbing [C] surpassing [D] hitting

1.【参考答案】A

【考查目标】动词辨析题

【答案解析】本题目选择动词。空格处所填的词说明工厂的照明与工人劳动生产率之间的关系,显然这里需要的意思是"影响"。"affected"意为"影响",符合题意,故本题答案为选项[A]。此句要表达的意思是"工厂的照明如何影响工人的劳动生产率"。

其他三个选项,[B]achieve 表示"达到,完成";[C]extract 表示"提取;榨出";[D]restore 表示"恢复,使修复"。虽然都能与空格前后的主语"shop-floor lighting"和宾语"workers' productivity"连用,但是放在这里,句意不通顺,所以排除。

2.【参考答案】B

【考查目标】介词搭配题

【答案解析】"end up doing sth."表示"最终达到某种状态或采取某种行动(尤指经过一个漫长的过程)"。填入空格处后,句子的意思为:这些研究最终以得到一个被冠之以"霍桑效应"的结论而告终,故本题选[B]项。

其他选项中首先可排除 at,因为"end"和"at"不能形成固定搭配;"end with"意为"以……告终",后常接名词或名词词组,如"Life does not end with death",故排除"with";"end"与"off"连用时,结构为"end sth. off"(妥当或顺利地结束某事物),所以"off"也不符合题意。

3.【参考答案】C

【考查目标】名词辨析题

【答案解析】分析句子结构可知,"the extremely influential idea..."是对"Hawthorne effect"的补充说明,可看作其同位语;"idea"后的"that"又引导同位语从句,进一步说明"idea"的内容。不难看出,从句的主干为"the very...changed subject's behavior"。"of being experimented upon"作本题所填词的定语。根据上下文的语义可知选项[C]为本题正确答案。本题所在的部分大意为:这个十分具有影响力的结论认为,仅仅是被试验这一行为就足以使实验客体的表现发生变化。

其他三项,[A]truth 意为"事实";[B]sight 意为"景象,视觉,视野";[D]proof 意为"证据,证明",从语法上都能与"of being experimented upon"连用,但放入空格中语义不通,故排除。

4.【参考答案】B

【考查目标】形容词辨析题

【答案解析】该题需要结合上下文来解答。后文的意思是，无论照明灯变亮还是变暗，女工的生产效率都会提高，因此这个现象是"令人费解的"，只有"perplexing"有此意，故本题的正确答案是选项[B]。

而其他三个选项，[A] controversial 意为"有争议的；有争论的"；[C] mischievous 意为"恶作剧的；淘气的"；[D] ambiguous 意为"引起歧义的，模糊不清的"，都可以修饰空后的"behavior"，但与全文信息不符，因为上下文没有涉及妇女们的行为是"有争议的"、"恶作剧的"或"引起歧义的"，故排除。

5.【参考答案】C

【考查目标】名词辨析题

【答案解析】该句的意思是"根据实验报告的……灯光增强时，工人的单位生产率就会提高；但是，灯光减弱时工人的单位生产率也会提高"。空格后面是实验的具体描述，四个选项中[C] account 作名词时，表示"理解，解释"或"账目，账单"，但它还有特殊含义，表示"报告；描述"，故正确答案为选项[C]。

其他选项[A] requirements 意为"要求"；[B] explanations 意为"解释；说明"；[D] assessments 意为"评定；估价"，虽然都能与后文中的介词"of"搭配，但在语义上并不能衔接，故排除。

6.【参考答案】B

【考查目标】固定搭配题

【答案解析】根据第4题的分析得出，该句表达的意思是，"在实验室中做什么并不重要"，因此，使用固定搭配"It didn't matter ..."。本题考查了"It doesn't /didn't matter..."意为"……不重要"，其中"it"为形式主语，真正的主语为后面的从句。所以本题的正确答案为选项[B]。

其他三个干扰选项都能与空格前的"It did not"连用。其中[A] conclude 和[C] indicate 为及物动词，如果填入空格，后面的"what"从句只能作宾语，这样一来句首的"it"应该有所指；但在上下文中，找不到能衔接上下文的"it"所指代的对象，故排除这两项。[D] work 表示"起作用"时，是不及物动词，但填入后与上下文信息不符，故排除。

7.【参考答案】D

【考查目标】逻辑关系题

【答案解析】联系前面的分析，本空所填句的意思是"在实验中做什么并不重要；只要有改变，劳动生产率就会提高"。此处句中的分号表明分号前后的句子在语法上是独立的；所填入的短语只要能正确表达"something was changed"和"productivity rose"之间的逻辑条件关系即可。[D] so long as 表示"只要"，常用于引导条件状语从句，表明主句发生的动作以从句谈论的情况为前提。故选项[D]为正确答案。

其他三个选项中的短语都能引导状语从句。[C] in case that 中的"that"可以省略，该短语有两种用法：① 用作连词，表示条件，其意为"如果，万一"；② 用作连词表示目的，其意为"以防，免得"。[B] for fear that 其后所接的从句多为虚拟语气；[A] as far as 意思比较多，填入空中，语义都不通顺，所以排除。

8.【参考答案】A

【考查目标】名词辨析题

【答案解析】分析句子结构可知，空后的"that"从句作空格处所填名词的同位语。也就是说，所填名词表示一个抽象的概念，而“they were being experimented upon”（他们是实验的对象）正是对这个概念的具体说明。由此看出，只有[A]awareness“意识”符合上下文语义和语境。该句表达的意思是，只要人们意识到自己是实验对象，这一意识本身似乎就足以改变他们的行为了。故本题选[A]项。

其他三个选项[B]expectation表示“预期，期望”；[C]sentiment表示“感情，情绪”；[D]illusion表示“幻觉，错觉”，填入空格中与文意不符，故排除。

9.【参考答案】C

【考查目标】固定搭配题

【答案解析】判定形容词可以根据前面的主语“awareness”和句中的固定搭配“be +形容词+ to”。再根据上下文所提供的信息，可以判断这里要表达的含义是“工人感觉被实验的意识似乎已经足够改变她们的行为”，故本题选[C]enough，短语“be enough to do sth.”（足够做某事）是常考结构。

其他三个选项，[A]suitable也可用于“be…to do”的结构，形成搭配干扰，但填入该项后，上下文语义不衔接。[B]excessive意为“过分的，极度的”，填入后句意不通。[D]abundant意为“充裕的，丰富的”形成近义干扰，但该词不用于“be…to do”结构，“abundant”大多数情况下是指某一地区资源的丰富程度，放在本空中，明显不合适，故排除。

10.【参考答案】D

【考查目标】固定搭配题

【答案解析】本题考查的是“介词+oneself”的用法。反身代词与不同的介词连用，可表达不同的意思。本题的关键是在于明白“itself”所指代的对象。本题所在的句子是“An awareness seemed to be enough to alter worker's behavior…itself”。“itself”代指句子的主语“awareness”。结合前两个题的分析，本句的大致意思是：仅凭意识本身，就足以改变工人们的行为了。故本题的正确答案是选项[D]。

其他三个选项中，[C]on首先排除，该词不能与“oneself”构成固定搭配；[A]about和[B]for两项代入原文后，句子意思不通顺，故也排除。

11.【参考答案】C

【考查目标】动词辨析题

【答案解析】空格所在的主语是“the same data”，介词“to”后面的宾语为：“economic analysis”。在语义上，二者之间的关系理应为“……数据被用于……分析”。联系上下文可知，“the same data”指代前面提到的实验数据。因此本题所在句的意思是：几十年后，上述实验的数据接受了计量经济学分析，符合句意的只有选项[C]，“(be) subjected (to)”意为“受到……，接受……”。

其他三个选项，[A](be) compared (to)意为“被比作……”；[B](be) shown (to)意为“被展示出来”；[D](be) conveyed (to)意为“被传达；被表达”，都不能与上下文很好的衔接，应排除。

12.【参考答案】A

【考查目标】逻辑关系题

【答案解析】根据本空之前的句子“霍桑实验还有另外一个让人意想不到的结果”得知，下面所说的内容应该是与记录中的一些描述相悖，因此需要一个表示转折关系的连接词，只有[A]项“contrary to”表示“与……相反”，符合文意。

其他三个选项，“consistent with”意为“与……一致”；“parallel with”意为“与……平行”；

"peculiar to"意为"是……特有的,是……独有的"。这三项都是常用的词组,只从含义上并不能排除任何一项,只有结合上下文语境来排除。

13.【参考答案】A

【考查目标】名词辨析题

【答案解析】根据同位语从句及修饰限定词"systematic"判断此处需要一个比较确凿的"证据",同时要与动词"find"构成动宾搭配。只有[A]项"evidence"(证据,迹象)符合要求。

其他选项,"guidance"意为"引导,指导";"implication"意为"暗示,含义";"source"意为"来源,原始资料"。这三项语义上不能准确的衔接,故排除。

14.【参考答案】D

【考查目标】形容词辨析题

【答案解析】本题处于文章末段首句,是对上文的进一步展开和总结,并且所填形容词修饰"interpretations of what happened"。符合条件的只有"misleading",该词既能概括对上文研究结果的看法,又能引出下文的例子,并且表示"对已发生现象的错误解释",故选[D]项。

根据题意首先排除"enlightening"(引导,指导)和"reliable"(可靠的)。前面并没有谈到对于所发生事情的任何"有争议"的结论,如果选择"disputable"(有争议的),则后面应该阐述引起争议的观点,故排除。

15.【参考答案】B

【考查目标】逻辑关系题

【答案解析】本题考查了句间逻辑关系。段落首句总述,接着后面的内容举例子进行说明。显然是从"概括"到"具体"的关系。故正确答案为选项[B]for example 意为"例如"。

其他三个选项中,首先可排除[D]As usual 表示"通常;照例",与后面的"always"矛盾;而[A]In contrast"与此相反",表示对比;[C]In consequence 表示"结果",表明前后句为"因"与"果"的关系,均不符合题意,应排除。

16.【参考答案】A

【考查目标】副词辨析题

【答案解析】空格中要求填入的副词用来修饰"产出如何上升"。根据文中前后信息可以判断:产出上升和灯光变化没有关系,它是一个比较有规律的现象。选项[A]duly 表示"适时地,按时地",代入文中符合上下文信息,故[A]为正确选项。

其他选项[B]accidentally 意为"偶然地",[C]unpredictably 意为"无法预言地",[D]suddenly 意为"突然地",都不能表达很通顺的逻辑关系,故排除。

17.【参考答案】D

【考查目标】动词辨析题

【答案解析】所填空格之前是并列连词"and",同时根据前半句的"duly rose"可知,该处需要的是与原文一致性的概念。而[D]continue 表示"继续",具有递进的关系。因此,选项[D]为正确。

其他选项[A]failed (to do)意为"未能";[B]ceased (to do)意为"停止";[C]started (to do)意为"开始",语义上不能很好地衔接,故排除。

18.【参考答案】C

【考查目标】逻辑关系题

【答案解析】本题旨在考查本段第二句、第三句和第四句之间的逻辑关系。抓住"实验期间"得出的数据和"没有进行实验时"得出的数据之间的对比就找到了本题的突破口。本句的意思为"当对没有实验的周进行数据对比时,发现产出经常在周一时上升"。显然与前句"当星期一复工时,产出当然比光照改变前的星期六高,并会持续上升一些日子"在意义上发生了转折,故本题的正确选项是[C]However。

其他三个选项[A]Therefore 意为"因此",表示因果关系;[B]Furthermore 意为"此外",表示递进关系;[D]Meanwhile 意为"与此同时",表示并列。这三项都不能表示转折关系,故排除。

19.【参考答案】B

【考查目标】动词辨析题

【答案解析】根据句中的时间"for the first few days"和前句中的"when"可以看出,本题是在说明一种常规的事实,四个选项中动词"tend"表示"趋向,倾向","tend to do sth."在这里译作"常常……"。填入后该部分的意思为"无论情况如何,工人们常常在每周前几天努力工作……"正文选项(B)tended 为正确选项。

其他三项代入原文后,语义上不通顺。[A]attempted (to)意为"企图,试图";[C]chose (to)意为"选择";[D]intended (to) 意为"打算,准备",应排除。

20.【参考答案】D

【考查目标】动词辨析题

【答案解析】本题所要求填入的分词与"a plateau"构成动宾搭配。"plateau"在此取其"稳定状态"之意。本题所在的句子曾谈到"工人们常在每周前几天努力工作";接着用"before"引出句子的状语,"before"在此意为"在……之前,随后",其后跟了两个含先后顺序的动名词结构。既然有"接着松懈下来(then slacking off)"这一情况出现,说明,在这之前有一个"紧张"的过程,由此可推测"... a plateau"所要表达的含义。故本题的正确答案是选项[D]。"hitting"意为"达到,到达"。

其他三个选项,[A]breaking (a plateau)意为"打破一种稳定状态"与句中的"diligent"在感情色彩上相矛盾,故排除;[B]climbing 强调的是"艰辛、费力地往上爬"或"(价格)上涨",用在此也不合适;[C]surpassing (a plateau)表示"超过一种稳定状态"也不合适,故排除。

Section Ⅱ Reading Comprehension

Part A

Directions:

Read the following four texts. Answer the questions below each text by choosing A, B, C or D. Mark your answers on ANSWER SHEET 1. (40 points)

Text 1

Of all the changes that have taken place in English-language newspapers during the past quarter-century, perhaps the most far-reaching has been the inexorable decline in the scope and seriousness of their arts coverage.

It is difficult to the point of impossibility for the average reader under the age of forty to imagine a time when high-quality arts criticism could be found in most big-city newspapers. Yet a considerable number of the most significant collections of criticism published in the 20th century consisted in large part of newspaper reviews. To read such books today is to marvel at the fact that their learned contents were once deemed suitable for publication in general-circulation dailies.

We are even farther removed from the unfocused newspaper reviews published in England between the turn of the 20th century and the eve of World War II, at a time when newsprint was dirt-cheap and stylish arts criticism was considered an ornament to the publications in which it appeared. In those far-off days, it was taken for granted that the critics of major papers would write in detail and at length about the events they covered. Theirs was a serious business, and even those reviewers who wore their learning lightly, like George Bernard Shaw and Ernest Newman, could be trusted to know what they were about. These men believed in journalism as a calling, and were proud to be published in the daily press. "So few authors have brains enough or literary gift enough to keep their own end up in journalism," Newman wrote, "that I am tempted to define 'journalism' as 'a term of contempt applied by writers who are not read to writers who are'."

Unfortunately, these critics are virtually forgotten. Neville Cardus, who wrote for the *Manchester Guardian* from 1917 until shortly before his death in 1975, is now known solely as a writer of essays on the game of cricket. During his lifetime, though, he was also one of England's foremost classical-music critics, and a stylist so widely admired that his *Autobiography* (1947) became a best-seller. He was knighted in 1967, the first music critic to be so honored. Yet only one of his books is now in print, and his vast body of writings on music is unknown save to specialists.

Is there any chance that Cardus's criticism will enjoy a revival? The prospect seems remote. Journalistic tastes had changed long before his death, and postmodern readers have little use for the richly upholstered Vicwardian prose in which he specialized. Moreover, the amateur tradition in music criticism has been in headlong retreat.

21. It is indicated in Paragraphs 1 and 2 that
 [A] arts criticism has disappeared from big-city newspapers.
 [B] English-language newspapers used to carry more arts reviews.
 [C] high-quality newspapers retain a large body of readers.
 [D] young readers doubt the suitability of criticism on dailies.

22. Newspaper reviews in England before World War II were characterized by
 [A] free themes.
 [B] casual style.
 [C] elaborate layout.
 [D] radical viewpoints.

23. Which of the following would Shaw and Newman most probably agree on?
 [A] It is writers' duty to fulfill journalistic goals.
 [B] It is contemptible for writers to be journalists.
 [C] Writers are likely to be tempted into journalism.
 [D] Not all writers are capable of journalistic writing.

24. What can be learned about Cardus according to the last two paragraphs?
 [A] His music criticism may not appeal to readers today.
 [B] His reputation as a music critic has long been in dispute.
 [C] His style caters largely to modern specialists.
 [D] His writings fail to follow the amateur tradition.

25. What would be the best title for the text?

[A] Newspapers of the Good Old Days

[B] The Lost Horizon in Newspapers

[C] Mournful Decline of Journalism

[D] Prominent Critics in Memory

21.【参考答案】B

【考查目标】理解主旨要义

【答案解析】本题的答案需要通过总结概括文章前两段内容得出。首段主要是讲，在过去的25年里，英语报纸发生的影响最为深远的变化是“文艺报道的范围和严肃性方面的大幅衰落”；第二段具体论证以前的报纸高质量的艺术评论很多。综合起来，可以发现选项[B]“英语报纸过去载有更多的文艺批评”为正确选项。

选项[A]错在“has disappeared”一词上，文中用的是“decline”意为“数量减少”，而不是消失。文中根本没有传达选项[C]的含义。选项[D]错在“doubt”一词，感情色彩不对，因为文章第二段末句讲“在今天读这些书，我们会惊讶于如此有学问的文章在过去竟然被认为适合在大众阅读的日报上发表”，“marvel”一词含有赞扬的意思。

22.【参考答案】A

【考查目标】理解文中的具体信息

【答案解析】根据题干中的“World War Ⅱ”，可以定位在第三段首句。该句提到“unfocused newspaper reviews published in England between the turn of the 20th century and the eve of World War Ⅱ”，所以二战前英国报纸评论文章的特点应该是“unfocused”（不聚焦的，不集中的），具体到“newspaper reviews”指“主题不集中的、发散的、自由的”。故正确答案为选项[A]“自由的主题”。“free”是“unfocused”的同义替换。

选项[B]错在“casual”一词上，第三段后面提到了“a serious business”，与“casual”正好相反。选项[C]与原文含义有出入，文中提到了“stylish arts criticism was considered an ornament to the publications”，其中的“stylish”在文中是“风格独特的”含义，而不是讲文章的编排，故选项[C]为干扰项。选项[D]错在“radical”（根本的，激进的）一词上，文章提到了“serious”，但“radical”一词属于过度引申。

23.【参考答案】D

【考查目标】进行有关的判断、推理和引申

【答案解析】根据题干中的“Shaw and Newman”定位在第三段的后半部分。文中提到，“他们深信新闻业是一个天职，并为自己能够在日报上发表文章而感到自豪”。后面引号中的句子直接体现了Newman的观点，“没有几个作家有足够的智慧和文学天赋坚持在报纸上发表文章，以至于我不由得要把‘新闻’定义为‘那些没有学识的作家对有学识的作家的蔑称’”。由此推断出选项[D]“并不是所有的作家都有能力从事新闻写作”是正确的。

选项[A]错在“duty”一词上，文中并未提及作家有完成新闻目标的职责。选项[B]错在“contemptible”（可鄙的）一词上，这是对第三段最后一句话的误解，且与原文中的“proud”（自豪的）相反。选项[C]明显是错误的，在原文没有对应信息。

24.【参考答案】A

【考查目标】进行有关的判断、推理和引申

【答案解析】本题的答案来自于文章最后两段。第四段讲，Cardus是一个音乐评论家，写作风格独特,享有盛名,但是现在他所有的著作中只有一本书还在出版,他在音乐领域的大量著作除专家之外无人知晓。第五段讲,Cardus 评论文章复苏兴盛的前景并不明朗,新闻业的口味已经发生了变化,后现代读者很少阅读他所擅长的散文。综合起来,选项[A]"他的音乐评论文章可能对现在的读者没有吸引力"为正确答案。

选项[B]错在"in dispute"一词上,第四段中"one of England's foremost classical-music critics, and a stylist so widely admired... the first music critic to be so honored"等都表明,他作为音乐批评家的名声没有争议。选项[C]在原文的基础上过度推理,第四段末句说,"他在音乐领域的大量著作除专家之外无人知晓",据此无法推断出"他的风格在很大程度上迎合了现代的专家"。选项[D]是就第五段末句中的"the amateur tradition"编造的干扰选项。

25.【参考答案】B

【考查目标】理解主旨要义

【答案解析】本文在第一段提出文章中心,在过去的25年里,英语报纸发生的影响最为深远的变化是"文艺报道的范围和严肃性方面的大幅衰落"。下面围绕此中心进行具体阐述,英语报纸过去有大量的文艺评论,主题自由,风格严肃,作家有足够的智慧和文学天赋才可以在报纸上发表评论文章。第四段和第五段通过 Cardus 的例子说明过去的评论文章对现在的读者没有吸引力了,业余评论传统在迅速衰退。综上所述,选项[B]"报纸中消失的领域"为文章的最佳标题。

选项[A]的中心词是"newspapers",主题概括太宽泛,并且文章的重点不是回顾过去的美好,而是指出现在的问题。选项[C]的中心词是"journalism",也扩大了范围,文章讨论的不是新闻业的衰落,而是报纸上文艺评论文章的衰落。选项[D]"记忆中的卓越批评家",偏离了文章中心。

Text 2

Over the past decade, thousands of patents have been granted for what are called business methods. Amazon. com received one for its "one-click" online payment system. Merrill Lynch got legal protection for an asset allocation strategy. One inventor patented a technique for lifting a box.

Now the nation's top patent court appears completely ready to scale back on business-method patents, which have been controversial ever since they were first authorized 10 years ago. In a move that has intellectual-property lawyers abuzz, the U. S. Court of Appeals for the Federal Circuit said it would use a particular case to conduct a broad review of business-method patents. *In re Bilski*, as the case is known, is "a very big deal," says Dennis D. Crouch of the University of Missouri School of Law. It "has the potential to eliminate an entire class of patents."

Curbs on business-method claims would be a dramatic about-face, because it was the Federal Circuit itself that introduced such patents with its 1998 decision in the so-called State Street Bank case, approving a patent on a way of pooling mutual-fund assets. That ruling produced an explosion in business-method patent filings, initially by emerging Internet companies trying to stake out exclusive rights to specific types of online transactions. Later, more established companies raced to add such patents to their files, if only as a defensive move against rivals that might beat them to the punch. In 2005, IBM noted in a court filing that it had been issued more than 300 business-method patents, despite the fact that it questioned the legal basis for granting them. Similarly, some Wall Street investment firms armed themselves with patents for financial products, even as they took positions in court cases opposing the practice.

The Bilski case involves a claimed patent on a method for hedging risk in the energy market. The Federal Circuit issued an unusual order stating that the case would be heard by all 12 of the court's judges, rather than a typical panel of three, and that one issue it wants to evaluate is whether it should "reconsider" its State Street Bank ruling.

The Federal Circuit's action comes in the wake of a series of recent decisions by the Supreme Court that has narrowed the scope of protections for patent holders. Last April, for example, the justices signaled that too many patents were being upheld for "inventions" that are obvious. The judges on the Federal Circuit are "reacting to the anti-patent trend at the Supreme Court," says Harold C. Wegner, a patent attorney and professor at George Washington University Law School.

26. Business-method patents have recently aroused concern because of

[A] their limited value to businesses.

[B] their connection with asset allocation.

[C] the possible restriction on their granting.

[D] the controversy over their authorization.

27. Which of the following is true of the Bilski case?

[A] Its ruling complies with the court decisions.

[B] It involves a very big business transaction.

[C] It has been dismissed by the Federal Circuit.

[D] It may change the legal practices in the U. S.

28. The word "about-face" (Para. 3) most probably means

[A] loss of goodwill.

[B] increase of hostility.

[C] change of attitude.

[D] enhancement of dignity.

29. We learn from the last two paragraphs that business-method patents

[A] are immune to legal challenges.

[B] are often unnecessarily issued.

[C] lower the esteem for patent holders.

[D] increase the incidence of risks.

30. Which of the following would be the subject of the text?

[A] A looming threat to business-method patents.

[B] Protection for business-method patent holders.

[C] A legal case regarding business-method patents.

[D] A prevailing trend against business-method patents.

26.【参考答案】C

【考查目标】理解文中的具体信息

【答案解析】根据题干中的"recently"一词和时态将该题定位在第二段首句。该句提到,现在国家最高专利法庭已准备好要缩减商业方法专利的规模。这种变化引起了人们的关注,也是本文的中心。所以本题答案为选项[C]"授予这种专利可能会受到限制"。

选项[A]文中未提及。选项[B]是根据首段第三句中的“asset allocation”编造的一个干扰选项。选项[D]为最大的干扰项,它是根据第二段首句中“which”引导的定语从句编制出来。该定语从句意为“商业方法专利自从十年前第一个专利被授予以来就饱受争议”。但是本题问的是商业方法专利最近引起人们关注的原因,故选项[D]答非所问。

27.【参考答案】D

【考查目标】进行有关的判断、推理和引申

【答案解析】根据题干中的“the Bilski case”定位到第二段后半部分。文中说,美国联邦巡回上诉法庭提出将用一个特定的案例来对商业方法专利进行全面的评估。Dennis D. Crouch 指出,“the Bilski case”是一个“大案子”,此案“有可能使得这类专利(商业方法专利)被废除”。由此推出,选项[D]“此案可能改变美国的法律实践”为正确答案。

选项[A]与文中事实不符,文中说“it would use a particular case to...”,可见该案还没有宣判。选项[B]是对文中“a very big deal”的曲解,用其表面含义代替了在文章中的含义。选项[C]属于无中生有。

28.【参考答案】C

【考查目标】根据上下文推测生词的含义

【答案解析】“about-face”一词位于第三段首句,该句说,“对于商业方法专利的限制将会是一种巨大的……因为正是联邦法院在1998年的美国道富银行一案中引入了这种专利”。在此句中可以发现,联邦法院首先引入了这种专利,现在又对其限制,这是一种态度的转变。故本题正确答案为选项[C]。

选项[A]“好意的失去”、选项[B]“敌意的增加”和选项[D]“尊严的增强”代入进去都不符合句意逻辑,故排除。

29.【参考答案】B

【考查目标】进行有关的判断、推理和引申

【答案解析】第四段提到,法庭要评估是否应该“重新考虑”对美国道富银行一案的判决。第五段谈到,此前,高等法院最近已经作出了一系列的决定,旨在缩小对专利持有者的保护范围。例如,去年四月,法官们指出有太多的专利在保护那些显而易见的“发明”。综合分析,选项[B]“商业方法专利的颁发经常是不必要的”为正确答案,正好对应文中的“too many patents were being upheld for ‘inventions’ that are obvious”。

选项[A]与文意相反。选项[C]属于无中生有,文中没有提及“esteem”(尊重)。选项[D]是根据第四段首句中的“hedging risks”编造的选项。

30.【参考答案】A

【考查目标】理解主旨要义

【答案解析】本文的第二段首句即提出全文中心思想,“现在国家最高专利法庭已准备好要缩减商业方法专利的规模”。下面对此中心思想进行具体阐述,举了Bilski的案例,指出此案有可能使得这类专利被废除,并指出联邦巡回法庭改变态度,对商业方法专利进行限制,缩小对专利持有者的保护范围,认为很多专利的颁发是不必要的。所有这些都表明威胁正在临近商业方法专利,故正确答案为选项[A]“商业方法专利面临的威胁”。

选项[B]与文意相反,文章谈及的是对商业方法专利的限制,而不是保护。选项[C]只是文中论述的例子,不是文章主题。选项[D]的干扰性最强,错在“prevailing”一词,二段末句提到了“potential”,四段末句提到了“whether it should ‘reconsider’ its State Street Bank ruling”,商业方法专利规模的缩减还处在讨论和准备阶段，故选项[D]为干扰项。

Text 3

In his book *The Tipping Point*, Malcolm Gladwell argues that "social epidemics" are driven in large part by the actions of a tiny minority of special individuals, often called influentials, who are unusually informed, persuasive, or well connected. The idea is intuitively compelling, but it doesn't explain how ideas actually spread.

The supposed importance of influentials derives from a plausible-sounding but largely untested theory called the "two-step flow of communication": Information flows from the media to the influentials and from them to everyone else. Marketers have embraced the two-step flow because it suggests that if they can just find and influence the influentials, those select people will do most of the work for them. The theory also seems to explain the sudden and unexpected popularity of certain looks, brands, or neighborhoods. In many such cases, a cursory search for causes finds that some small group of people was wearing, promoting, or developing whatever it is before anyone else paid attention. Anecdotal evidence of this kind fits nicely with the idea that only certain special people can drive trends.

In their recent work, however, some researchers have come up with the finding that influentials have far less impact on social epidemics than is generally supposed. In fact, they don't seem to be required at all.

The researchers' argument stems from a simple observation about social influence: With the exception of a few celebrities like Oprah Winfrey—whose outsize presence is primarily a function of media, not interpersonal, influence—even the most influential members of a population simply don't interact with that many others. Yet it is precisely these non-celebrity influentials who, according to the two-step-flow theory, are supposed to drive social epidemics, by influencing their friends and colleagues directly. For a social epidemic to occur, however, each person so affected must then influence his or her own acquaintances, who must in turn influence theirs, and so on; and just how many others pay attention to each of *these* people has little to do with the initial influential. If people in the network just two degrees removed from the initial influential prove resistant, for example, the cascade of change won't propagate very far or affect many people.

Building on the basic truth about interpersonal influence, the researchers studied the dynamics of social influence by conducting thousands of computer simulations of populations, manipulating a number of variables relating to people's ability to influence others and their tendency to be influenced. They found that the principal requirement for what is called "global cascades"—the widespread propagation of influence through networks—is the presence not of a few influentials but, rather, of a critical mass of easily influenced people.

31. By citing the book *The Tipping Point*, the author intends to

[A] analyze the consequences of social epidemics.

[B] discuss influentials' function in spreading ideas.

[C] exemplify people's intuitive response to social epidemics.

[D] describe the essential characteristics of influentials.

32. The author suggests that the "two-step-flow theory"

[A] serves as a solution to marketing problems.

[B] has helped explain certain prevalent trends.

[C] has won support from influentials.

[D] requires solid evidence for its validity.

33. What the researchers have observed recently shows that

[A] the power of influence goes with social interactions.

[B] interpersonal links can be enhanced through the media.

[C] influentials have more channels to reach the public.

[D] most celebrities enjoy wide media attention.

34. The underlined phrase "*these* people" in Paragraph 4 refers to the ones who

[A] stay outside the network of social influence.

[B] have little contact with the source of influence.

[C] are influenced and then influence others.

[D] are influenced by the initial influential.

35. What is the essential element in the dynamics of social influence?

[A] The eagerness to be accepted.

[B] The impulse to influence others.

[C] The readiness to be influenced.

[D] The inclination to rely on others.

31.【参考答案】B

【考查目标】理解主旨要义

【答案解析】本文作者开篇引用了"*The tipping point*"这本书中的观点:"'social epidemics' are driven in large part by the actions of a tiny minority of special individuals, often called influentials",即社会潮流在很大程度上是由一小部分有影响力的人推动的。首段末句提到,这一观点本身非常具有吸引力,但是这不能解释新想法实际上如何传播的。由此可见,作者引用这本书中的观点,是引出"探讨有影响力的人在新想法传播过程中起到的作用"这一话题。浏览选项,发现选项[B]概括正确。

选项[A]错在"consequence"一词上,文章谈及的是社会潮流的推动力(driven)和方式(how),而非结果。选项[C]"表明人们对于社会潮流的本能反应"也偏离了首段话题,是利用首段中的个别词汇"intuitively"及"social epidemics"编造的选项。选项[D]是首段的细节信息,不是作者引用此书的目的。

32.【参考答案】D

【考查目标】理解作者的意图、观点或态度

【答案解析】根据"two-step-flow theory"把这道题定位在第二段首句,该句提到,人们总是默认有影响力的人非常重要,这种想法来源于一个听起来有道理但却没有经过实践检验的理论(a plausible-sounding but largely untested theory)即所谓的"两级传播"理论。首段末句总结到,这种轶事般的证据(anecdotal evidence of this kind)能很好地佐证这一想法,那就是只有某一些人能够推动潮流发展。由此可见,这种理论还没有足够的证据。选项[D]"两级传播"理论"需要确凿的证据来保证其效力"为正确答案。

选项[A]是针对第二段第二句设置的选项。营销人员认为"两级传播"理论是针对市场问题的解决方案,但事实上本段开头就说,这一理论看似合理但并未经过证实。选项[B]是针对第二段第三句和第四句设置的选项,文中说"The theory seems to explain..."(看起来能够解释),"a cursory search"(匆促的调查)都暗示了解释可能存在的漏洞,故选项[B]错误。选项[C]属于无中生有。

33.【参考答案】A

【考查目标】进行有关的判断、推理和引申

【答案解析】本题问研究者的最新发现,文章在第二段驳斥了传统的"两级传播"理论以后,从第三段开始讲最新的研究成果。第三段提到,"最近一些研究者发现,有影响力的人对于社会潮流的影响力远远没有人们默认的那么大,实际上,要传播社会潮流看起来并不需要这些人"。第四段作进一步阐释。前两句指出:"研究者的这种观点源于对社会影响力的简单观察,除了一些个别的例子,即使是社会上最有影响力的人,他们也并不与很多人交往"。"Yet"转折后指出,正是这些非名人而有影响力的人们通过直接影响他们的朋友和同事推动社会潮流。可见,作者认为,影响力和人与人之间的社会互动密切相关。故选项[A]为本题正确答案。

选项[B]属于偷换概念,第四段第一句中提到,Oprah Winfrey 的名声和影响力(outsize presence)主要是由于媒体的作用,选项[B]改为人际关系(interpersonal links)。选项[C]与文中事实不符,第四段第一句说,即使是社会上最有影响力的人,他们也并不与很多人交往。选项[D]则属于无中生有。

34.【参考答案】C

【考查目标】理解文中的具体信息

【答案解析】根据画线部分"these people"把该题定位在第四段第三句。这句话提到,如果一种东西要在社会上盛行,那么每一个受到影响的人都必须接着影响他们的熟人,后者又接着影响他们的熟人,以此类推;有多少人关注"这些人"已经和最初发起流行的那些有影响力的人没有多大关系了。可见,这些人不会是最初发起流行的那些有影响力的人,而是被影响继而影响别人的人,因此选项[C]为本题正确答案。

选项[A]、[B]和[D]带入原文后,均不能构成正确的语义衔接。

35.【参考答案】C

【考查目标】理解文中的具体信息

【答案解析】根据题干中的"dynamics of social influence"定位到文章末段。末段末句提到,实现风靡全球的影响的最重要因素不是那些有影响力的人,而是一大群易受影响的人。由此得出,选项[C]为正确答案。

选项[A]、[B]和[D]文中都没有提到。

Text 4

Bankers have been blaming themselves for their troubles in public. Behind the scenes, they have been taking aim at someone else: the accounting standard-setters. Their rules, moan the banks, have forced them to report enormous losses, and it's just not fair. These rules say they must value some assets at the price a third party would pay, not the price managers and regulators would like them to fetch.

Unfortunately, banks' lobbying now seems to be working. The details may be unknowable, but the independence of standard-setters, essential to the proper functioning of capital markets, is being compromised. And, unless banks carry toxic assets at prices that attract buyers, reviving the banking system will be difficult.

After a bruising encounter with Congress, America's Financial Accounting Standards Board (FASB) rushed through rule changes. These gave banks more freedom to use models to value illiquid assets and more flexibility in recognizing losses on long-term assets in their income statements. Bob Herz, the FASB's chairman, cried out against those who "question our motives." Yet bank shares rose and the changes enhance what one lobbying group politely calls "the use of judgment by management."

European ministers instantly demanded that the International Accounting Standards Board (IASB) do likewise. The IASB says it does not want to act without overall planning, but the pressure to fold when it completes its reconstruction of rules later this year is strong. Charlie McCreevy, a European commissioner, warned the IASB that it did "not live in a political vacuum" but "in the real world" and that Europe could yet develop different rules.

It was banks that were <u>on the wrong planet</u>, with accounts that vastly overvalued assets. Today they argue that market prices overstate losses, because they largely reflect the temporary illiquidity of markets, not the likely extent of bad debts. The truth will not be known for years. But banks' shares trade below their book value, suggesting that investors are skeptical. And dead markets partly reflect the paralysis of banks which will not sell assets for fear of booking losses, yet are reluctant to buy all those supposed bargains.

To get the system working again, losses must be recognized and dealt with. America's new plan to buy up toxic assets will not work unless banks mark assets to levels which buyers find attractive. Successful markets require independent and even combative standard-setters. The FASB and IASB have been exactly that, cleaning up rules on stock options and pensions, for example, against hostility from special interests. But by giving in to critics now they are inviting pressure to make more concessions.

36. Bankers complained that they were forced to

[A] follow unfavorable asset evaluation rules.

[B] collect payments from third parties.

[C] cooperate with the price managers.

[D] reevaluate some of their assets.

37. According to the author, the rule changes of the FASB may result in

[A] the diminishing role of management.

[B] the revival of the banking system.

[C] the banks' long-term asset losses.

[D] the weakening of its independence.

38. According to Paragraph 4, McCreevy objects to the IASB's attempt to

[A] keep away from political influences.

[B] evade the pressure from their peers.

[C] act on their own in rule-setting.

[D] take gradual measures in reform.

39. The author thinks the banks were "on the wrong planet" in that they

[A] misinterpreted market price indicators.

[B] exaggerated the real value of their assets.

[C] neglected the likely existence of bad debts.

[D] denied booking losses in their sale of assets.

40. The author's attitude towards standard-setters is one of

[A] satisfaction. [B] skepticism. [C] objectiveness. [D] sympathy.

36.【参考答案】A

【考查目标】理解文中的具体信息

【答案解析】由题干关键词"complained"和"were forced"将信息定位于第一段最后两句,"银行抱怨会计准则设立者设立的规则,这迫使银行不得不报道大量的损失,这些规则要求,银行必须以第三方愿意支付的价格来估量某些资产"。因此,选项[A]为正确答案,该选项中的"unfavorable"和"asset evaluation"分别是对原文中"not fair"和"value some assets"的同义替换。

选项[B]是对文中"they must value some assets at the price a third party would pay"的曲解。选项[C]错在"price managers",文中并未出现这个概念,这是对首段末句定语从句的误解,"managers and regulators would like them to fetch"是"price"的定语从句,命题人在考查考生的断句能力。选项[D]"reevaluate"文中未提到,属于无中生有。

37.【参考答案】D

【考查目标】理解作者的意图、观点或态度

【答案解析】文章第二段的前两句提到,银行的游说似乎起到了作用,标准制定者(standard-setters)的独立性开始受到损害。第三段第一句提到,"在经历了与国会的不快遭遇后,FASB的规则很快作出了改变"。FASB属于标准制定者,故FASB规则的改变可能会引起其独立性的减弱,选项[D]为正确答案。

选项[A]中的"diminish"与第三段尾句中的"enhance"相矛盾。第二段末句提到银行的复苏将会非常困难,所以选项[B]不对。选项[C]断章取义,是针对第三段第二句中"losses on long-term assets"编造的选项。

38.【参考答案】C

【考查目标】理解文中的具体信息

【答案解析】根据题干中的"McCreevy objects to"定位到第四段。第四段提到欧洲的部长们要求IASB立即根据美国的变化做出一样的反应,而IASB不想在没有全面计划的前提下采取行动,McCreevy警告IASB"不是处在政治真空中"而是在"现实世界里"。综上可以判断出,IASB不像FASB那样在压力下匆匆修改规则,想自己独立制定规则。故正确答案是选项[C]"按照自己的意愿制定规则",与FASB独立性减弱的情形形成对照。

选项[A]干扰性非常强,属于对"not live in a political vacuum"的曲解,这里加了引号,要理解其言外之意,这不是说IASB远离政治影响,而是McCreevy反对IASB按照自己的意愿行事;选项[B]和[D]属于无中生有,文中未提到来自同行的压力和渐进的改革。

39.【参考答案】B

【考查目标】理解作者的意图、观点或态度

【答案解析】根据题干信息,可以定位到第五段首句。这是一个强调结构,"with..."解释"banks that were on the wrong planet"的原因,即银行账目将资产估价过高。故选项[B]为正确答案。

选项[A]属于无中生有。选项[C]是利用第二句中的“the likely extent of bad debts”编造出来的干扰选项。原文在第五段末句提到,银行因为担心账面损失而不愿意出售资产,可见选项[D]的表述并不准确。

40.【参考答案】D

【考查目标】理解作者的意图、观点或态度

【答案解析】文章在第二段提到在银行的游说下,制度制定者的独立性开始受到损害,第三段提到FASB在银行的压力下匆匆修改了规则,第四段提到IASB也面临着巨大的压力。文章末段作者更是直接发表评论,成功的市场需要独立甚至是具有斗争性的准则制定者,FASB和IASB过去正是那样对抗特殊利益集团的,但是,由于向批评者屈服,他们反而引来更多迫使其让步的压力。这些都表明了作者对制度制定者的同情。故选项[D]为正确答案。

选项[A]中的“满意”显然是错误的,制度制定者的妥协态度不是作者所希望的。选项[B]表示出“怀疑”,作者并不怀疑制度制定者独立制定的规则,只是对其压力下的妥协表示同情。选项[C]表示出“客观”,文章明确表达了作者对制度制定者的同情,故立场不再是客观的了。

Part B

Directions:

For questions 41-45, choose the most suitable paragraphs from the list A-G and fill them into the numbered boxes to form a coherent text. **Paragraph E** has been correctly placed. There is one paragraph which does not fit in with the text. Mark your answers on ANSWER SHEET 1. (10 points)

[A] The first and more important is the consumer's growing preference for eating out: the consumption of food and drink in places other than homes has risen from about 32 percent of total consumption in 1995 to 35 percent in 2000 and is expected to approach 38 percent by 2005. This development is boosting wholesale demand from the food service segment by 4 to 5 percent a year across Europe, compared with growth in retail demand of 1 to 2 percent. Meanwhile, as the recession is looming large, people are getting anxious. They tend to keep a tighter hold on their purse and consider eating at home a realistic alternative.

[B] Retail sales of food and drink in Europe's largest markets are at a standstill, leaving European grocery retailers hungry for opportunities to grow. Most leading retailers have already tried e-commerce, with limited success, and expansion abroad. But almost all have ignored the big, profitable opportunity in their own backyard: the wholesale food and drink trade, which appears to be just the kind of market retailers need.

[C] Will such variations bring about a change in the overall structure of the food and drink market? Definitely not. The functioning of the market is based on flexible trends dominated by potential buyers. In other words, it is up to the buyer, rather than the seller, to decide what to buy. At any rate, this change will ultimately be acclaimed by an ever-growing number of both domestic and international consumers, regardless of how long the current consumer pattern will take hold.

[D] All in all, this clearly seems to be a market in which big retailers could profitably apply their gigantic scale, existing infrastructure, and proven skills in the management of product ranges, logistics, and marketing intelligence. Retailers that master the intricacies of wholesaling in Europe may well expect to rake in substantial profits thereby. At least, that is how it looks as a whole. Closer inspection reveals important differences among the biggest national markets, especially in their customer segments and wholesale structures, as well as the competitive dynamics of individual food and drink categories. Big retailers must understand these differences before they can identify the segments of European wholesaling in which their particular abilities might unseat smaller but entrenched competitors. New skills and unfamiliar business models are needed too.

[E] Despite variations in detail, wholesale markets in the countries that have been closely examined—France, Germany, Italy, and Spain—are made out of the same building blocks. Demand comes mainly from two sources: independent mom-and-pop grocery stores which, unlike large retail chains, are too small to buy straight from producers, and food service operators that cater to consumers when they don't eat at home. Such food service operators range from snack machines to large institutional catering ventures, but most of these businesses are known in the trade as "horeca": hotels, restaurants, and cafés. Overall, Europe's wholesale market for food and drink is growing at the same sluggish pace as the retail market, but the figures, when added together, mask two opposing trends.

[F] For example, wholesale food and drink sales came to $268 billion in France, Germany, Italy, Spain, and the United Kingdom in 2000—more than 40 percent of retail sales. Moreover, average overall margins are higher in wholesale than in retail; wholesale demand from the food service sector is growing quickly as more Europeans eat out more often; and changes in the competitive dynamics of this fragmented industry are at last making it feasible for wholesalers to consolidate.

[G] However, none of these requirements should deter large retailers (and even some large food producers and existing wholesalers) from trying their hand, for those that master the intricacies of wholesaling in Europe stand to reap considerable gains.

41. → 42. → 43. → 44. → E → 45.

41.【参考答案】B

【考查目标】文章结构

【答案解析】由于本题首段未给出,可依据篇章结构特点及运用排除法首先确定本题的答案。既然需填入的是文章的首段,尤其要注意哪个段落可以作为一个篇章的起始段落。比对各个选项,[A]、[C]和[D]项的首句中分别以"The first and more..."、"will such..."以及"All in all, this..."开头。这说明是对上文已提及内容的指代衔接。[E]和[G]项的首句分别以"Despite..."和"However..."开头,这说明应与上段已提及的内容构成转折衔接。[F]项首句中的"For example"表明这应是对上文某观点或某一现象的例证衔接。由此可知,以上几个选项均不是第一段,均可排除,因此只剩下选项[B],其首句提出了欧洲食品零售所面临的问题,这显然是率先提出了问题,符合篇章结构特点中首段提出话题的写作原则,故[B]为正确答案。

42.【参考答案】F

【考查目标】段落的连贯性

【答案解析】首段末句指出首段的核心信息:食品和饮料的批发行业正是零售商所需要的。由此可见,此处只是笼统地提出了一种看法,依据篇章展开的逻辑,下文会就这一看法展开进一步的阐述,而[F]以提示词"For example"举例说明法国、德国、意大利等国家的食品批发产业的市场规模比食品零售产业要大40%。而且在"moreover"后又进一步说明批发的利润比零售大很多。由此可见[F]项和[B]项是明显的观点与例证的语意关联,故[F]为本题答案。

43.【参考答案】D

【考查目标】段落的连贯性

【答案解析】上段的主旨要义是介绍了食品批发商的优势,而[D]第一句讲到:总之,显然在这一市场中大的零售商可以利用其庞大规模、现有基础设施,以及在产品范围、物流、营销情报方面出色的管理技能,从而获利。显然这是在对上文的内容进行总结,其中"All in all"是明显对[F]举例内容进行总结的提示词,"this"指代上文提到的具有优势的食品批发业。因此[D]为本题答案。

44.【参考答案】G

【考查目标】段落的连贯性

【答案解析】上段最后一句提出的"particular abilities"以及"New skills and unfamiliar business models are needed"(零售商需要新的技能以及不熟悉的商业模式)表明这句是对大型零售商提出的要求。而[G]项第一句提到的"these requirements"(这些要求)正好能与上段段尾呼应,形成顺畅合理的语意衔接,此外,[G]项首句的 requirements 呼应了[D]项末的"needed",[G]项后半句话"those... reap considerable gains"与[D]项第二句"Retailers... rake in substantial profits thereby"表达了同样的意思,这也证明了两段前后的衔接关系。故[G]为本题答案。

45.【参考答案】A

【考查目标】段落的一致性

【答案解析】从此题前文的已知段落[E]中的最后一句"two opposing trends"可以推测接下来的段落可能会对这两种趋势进行说明。这两种趋势在[A]项中得到了体现,即一方面由于人们选择在外就餐而扩大了食品批发的需求,而另一方面人们又开始感到"anxious"。而[C]项第一句提到的"such variations"在上文中并没有得到体现,因此可以断定[A]为正确答案。

Part C

Directions:

Read the following text carefully and then translate the underlined segments into Chinese. Your translation should be written clearly on ANSWER SHEET 2. (10 points)

One basic weakness in a conservation system based wholly on economic motives is that most members of the land community have no economic value. Yet these creatures are members of the biotic community and, if its stability depends on its integrity, they are entitled to continuance.

When one of these noneconomic categories is threatened and, if we happen to love it, we invent excuses to give it economic importance. At the beginning of the century songbirds were supposed to be disappearing. (46) Scientists jumped to the rescue with some distinctly shaky evidence to the effect that insects would eat us up if birds failed to control them. The evidence had to be economic in order to be valid.

It is painful to read these roundabout accounts today. We have no land ethic yet, (47) but we have at least drawn nearer the point of admitting that birds should continue as a matter of intrinsic right, regardless of the presence or absence of economic advantage to us.

A parallel situation exists in respect of predatory mammals and fish-eating birds. (48) Time was when biologists somewhat overworked the evidence that these creatures preserve the health of game by killing the physically weak, or that they prey only on "worthless" species. Here again, the evidence had to be economic in order to be valid. It is only in recent years that we hear the more honest argument that predators are members of the community, and that no special interest has the right to exterminate them for the sake of a benefit, real or fancied, to itself.

Some species of trees have been "read out of the party" by economics-minded foresters because they grow too slowly, or have too low a sale value to pay as timber crops. (49) In Europe, where forestry is ecologically more advanced, the noncommercial tree species are recognized as members of the native forest community, to be preserved as such, within reason. Moreover, some have been found to have a valuable function in building up soil fertility. The interdependence of the forest and its constituent tree species, ground flora, and fauna is taken for granted.

To sum up: a system of conservation based solely on economic self-interest is hopelessly lopsided. (50) It tends to ignore, and thus eventually to eliminate, many elements in the land community that lack commercial value, but that are essential to its healthy functioning. It assumes, falsely, that the economic parts of the biotic clock will function without the uneconomic parts.

46.【英文原句】Scientists jumped to the rescue with some distinctly shaky evidence to the effect that insects would eat us up if birds failed to control them.

【考查目标】同位语从句和条件状语从句的翻译

【答案解析】此处"that"引导的同位语从句与"to the effect"(大意是,大致说的是)搭配,无需调整顺序,直接翻译成"其大意是,大致说的是……"即可;"if"条件状语从句修饰"that"从句,根据汉语表达习惯,调整到所修饰的"that"从句前面翻译。

【参考译文】科学家们立即拿出某些明显站不住脚的证据前来救驾,大致说的是,如果鸟儿不能控制害虫的话,害虫就会把我们(的一切)吃掉。

47.【英文原句】but we have at least drawn nearer the point of admitting that birds should continue as a matter of intrinsic right, regardless of the presence or absence of economic advantage to us.

【考查目标】宾语从句,让步状语

【答案解析】"that"引导的是"admitting"的宾语,按照原文顺序翻译即可;"regardless of..."为"that"从句的让步状语,根据汉语习惯将其置于"that"从句的前面翻译,使译文更通顺。此外,介词短语"of admitting that..."修饰"the point",鉴于修饰成分繁杂,翻译时可以先翻"point"之前的内容,再翻"of"之后的内容。另外,可以将"the point of admitting"(承认……观点)翻译出来,加个冒号,再翻后面的内容,这样更通顺。

【参考译文】但是我们至少几乎承认了这样一种观点:不管鸟类对我们是否有经济价值,生存都是它们的固有权利。

48.【英文原句】Time was when biologists somewhat overworked the evidence that these creatures preserve the health of game by killing the physically weak, or that they prey only on "worthless" species.

【考查目标】表语从句,同位语从句

【答案解析】"when"表语从句无须调整顺序。将"Time was when"(曾经,曾几何时)看成一个整体更好翻译。两个"that"同位语从句采用冒号翻译法,即翻译完主句后,后面加冒号,引出两个"that"从句的具体内容。

【参考译文】曾几何时,生物学家总是滥用以下的这条证据:这些生物通过杀死体弱者来保持种群的健康,或者说它们仅仅去捕食"没有价值的"物种。

49.【英文原句】In Europe, where forestry is ecologically more advanced, the non-commercial tree species are recognized as members of native forest community, to be preserved as such, within reason.

【考查目标】定语从句,被动语态

【答案解析】"where"定语从句的先行词为"Europe",可以采用前置法,将其翻译到先行词之前,即"在生态林业较为先进的欧洲";还可以将先行词与从句进行融合,即"欧洲的林业从生态上讲较为先进";被动语态"are recognized as..."的逻辑主语为"Europe",根据被动语态的翻译方法,此处可还原主语翻译成主动语态,即"欧洲把……视为……";被动语态"to be preserved as",根据被动语态的翻译方法,运用词汇翻译为主动语态,即"加以保护"。

【参考译文】欧洲的林业从生态上讲较为先进,它把没有成为商业化对象的树种视为当地森林群落的成员而适当地加以保护。

50.【英文原句】It tends to ignore, and thus eventually to eliminate, many elements in the land community that lack commercial value, but that are essential to its healthy functioning.

【考查目标】代词指代,定语从句

【答案解析】"it"为指示代词,在此句中做主语,为了使本句语义表述清晰,需要把代词还原。回到原文不难发现,"it"所指代的就是上一句话中的"system"。所以把代词还原为"这一体系"即可;"and"并列的两个"that"所引导的定语从句修饰"many elements",根据定语从句的翻译方法,可以采用前置法,把定语从句直接置于所修饰的词之前。

【参考译文】这一体系容易忽视并最终导致灭绝那些陆地生物群落中很多缺乏商业价值的物种,然而这些物种对于整个生物群落的健康运行是至关重要的。

Section Ⅲ Writing

Part A

51. **Directions**:

You are supposed to write for the Postgraduates' Association a notice to recruit volunteers for an international conference on globalization. The notice should include the basic qualifications for applicants and other information which you think is relevant.

You should write about 100 words on ANSWER SHEET 2.

Do not sign your own name at the end of the notice. Use "Postgraduates' Association" instead. (10 points)

【考查分析】本次在考研应用文当中考到了通知。考生在写作的过程中,要注意通知的基本格式,不要遗漏写作指导部分提纲中的要点。其实,通知这种文体在英语四、六级考试当中都考过,所以考生应对这种文体格外关注。

【审题谋篇】应用文写作要求考生以研究生会的名义写一封通知,通知的内容是为全球化的国际会议招募志愿者,而且还说明了这个通知必须包括申请者的基本职位要求及考生认为相关的其他信息。

“通知”这一事务公文，目的在于督促或通知对方参加活动，具体来讲，此次作文题目涉及招募志愿者。格式上，题目、正文以及署名是必不可少的部分。标题应放在首行正中央；正文应写1~3段，5~7句即可；落款写在中间偏后位置，与正文之间不需空行；告示类中通知的日期应放在题目的右下方。语言上，除了注意正确性外，还应在表达上直截了当、简洁明了，可适当使用被动句表达。内容上，题目要求写招募职位以及相关信息。关于职位，可写涉及前台接待、会场指引、乘车指引、英文翻译等服务的岗位。此外，还可以对志愿者提出要求：志愿者应该工作认真负责、积极主动并具有团队合作精神，还需要沟通能力强，具有较好的英语口语和听力水平等。其他相关信息，可以提及会议时间、地点以及将怎样安排志愿者等。

【高分作文】

Notice

July 1, 2009

The International Conference of Global Integration will be held on September 23rd in China Institute of International Studies, and twenty volunteers are wanted among the students in our school.

The positions recruited include receptionist, conference guider, transportation guider and English interpreter, and the volunteers are requested to speak fluent English and are expected to be active, open-minded and conscientious. All the volunteers will be trained for 5 days before the conference and provided with free transportation and meal.

For those who are interested in taking part in the activity, please send your resume to the email address: postgraduates@ zju. cn before August 1st.

Postgraduates' Association

Part B

52. **Directions:**

Write an essay of 160-200 words based on the following drawing. In your essay, you should

1) describe the drawing briefly,

2) explain its intended meaning, and

3) give your comments.

You should write neatly on ANSWER SHEET 2. (20 points)

【考查分析】本次短文写作部分考到的依旧是图画题，考生在写作过程中应该准确把握图画所反映的主旨，然后完成三段的写作任务。

【审题谋篇】本题为图画作文中的现象阐释题型，图画上是一个热气腾腾的火锅，里面包括诸如“功夫”、“儒”、“道”、“京剧”、“老舍”、“解构”、“莎士比亚”等标志着东西方文化的词。很明显，图画的含义是关于文化交流的，有交流就有冲突，但是图画下面的文字“文化‘火锅’，既美味又营养”揭示了这幅图积极向上的寓意，即各种各样的东西方文化元素交汇融合，民族的文化可以成为世界的，这一趋势有利于人类发展。由此可见，本次作文的主题是文化融合。

提纲包括三点，一是描述图片，二是解释含义，三是对此现象作出评论。文章也遵循三段式，第一段描述图片中的各类文化元素。第二段点题，阐释图画的含义，最好在段首设置主题句，然后围绕主题句展开，最后再稍作总结，也就是用总分总的结构。第三段对此现象进行评论，可以提出建议，也可以写世界文化的融合、交流是时代的潮流，同时要继续保持和振兴各民族文化。

文化“火锅”,既美味又营养

【高分作文】

As is portrayed in the enlightening picture, a hot pot, with numerous ingredients in it, includes such domestic and alien cultures as literature, moral values and performing arts. It seems that the hot pot tastes very delicious because of the rich nutrition of the multi-cultures.

Obviously, the picture characterizes the present situation of Chinese society in which Chinese and Western culture conflict with each other but also merge into a unique form to a certain degree. Since China has opened its door widely to the outside world, many people from different countries have been deeply fascinated by Chinese culture. They will accept and love the Chinese culture as a whole. In addition, Chinese culture should be well shared with foreign people, who have shown their enthusiasm towards China. Meanwhile, the Chinese people are also exposed to foreign cultures when more foreign people come to this oriental country. In this way people from various nations in the world will be able to acquire better understanding of each other and live peacefully in this world.

As far as I am concerned, the culture of any nation is a kind of precious heritage, and belongs to the whole mankind. With economic globalization, the blending of different cultures has become inevitable trend of the time. No country is an isolated island, be it China or the western world. The clearer we grasp the current situation, the more it would be beneficial to the global villagers.

3.3 2011年研究生入学统一考试英语试题

Section Ⅰ Use of English

Directions:

Read the following text. Choose the best word(s) for each numbered blank and mark A, B, C or D on ANSWER SHEET 1. (10 points)

Ancient Greek philosopher Aristotle viewed laughter as “a bodily exercise precious to health.” But ___1___ some claims to the contrary, laughing probably has little influence on physical fitness. Laughter does __2__ short-term changes in the function of the heart and its blood vessels, __3__ heart rate and oxygen consumption. But because hard laughter is difficult to __4__, a good laugh is unlikely to have __5__ benefits the way, say, walking or jogging does.

__6__, instead of straining muscles to build them, as exercise does, laughter apparently accomplishes the __7__. Studies dating back to the 1930s indicate that laughter __8__ muscles, decreasing muscle tone for up to 45 minutes after the laugh dies down.

Such bodily reaction might conceivably help __9__ the effects of psychological stress. Anyway, the act of laughing probably does produce other types of __10__ feedback that improve an individual's emotional state. __11__ one classical theory of emotion, our feelings are partially rooted __12__ physical reactions. It was argued at the end of the 19th century that humans do not cry __13__ they are sad but that they become sad when the tears begin to flow.

Although sadness also __14__ tears, evidence suggests that emotions can flow __15__ muscular responses. In an experiment published in 1988, social psychologist Fritz Strack of the University of Würzburg in Germany asked volunteers to __16__ a pen either with their teeth-thereby creating an artificial smile-or with their lips, which would produce a(n) __17__ expression. Those forced to exercise their smiling muscles __18__ more enthusiastically to funny cartoons than did those whose mouths were contracted in a frown, __19__ that expressions may influence emotions rather than just the other way around. __20__, the physical act of laughter could improve mood.

1. [A] among [B] except [C] despite [D] like
2. [A] reflect [B] demand [C] indicate [D] produce
3. [A] stabilizing [B] boosting [C] impairing [D] determining
4. [A] transmit [B] sustain [C] evaluate [D] observe
5. [A] measurable [B] manageable [C] affordable [D] renewable
6. [A] In turn [B] In fact [C] In addition [D] In brief
7. [A] opposite [B] impossible [C] average [D] expected
8. [A] hardens [B] weakens [C] tightens [D] relaxes
9. [A] aggravate [B] generate [C] moderate [D] enhance
10. [A] physical [B] mental [C] subconscious [D] internal
11. [A] Except for [B] According to [C] Due to [D] As for
12. [A] with [B] on [C] in [D] at
13. [A] unless [B] until [C] if [D] because
14. [A] exhausts [B] follows [C] precedes [D] suppresses
15. [A] into [B] from [C] towards [D] beyond
16. [A] fetch [B] bite [C] pick [D] hold
17. [A] disappointed [B] excited [C] joyful [D] indifferent
18. [A] adapted [B] catered [C] turned [D] reacted
19. [A] suggesting [B] requiring [C] mentioning [D] supposing
20. [A] Eventually [B] Consequently [C] Similarly [D] Conversely

1.【参考答案】C

【考查目标】逻辑关系题

【答案解析】第一段第一句意思是:古希腊哲学家亚里士多德把笑看做是"有益于健康的身体运动",由连词"but"可知,第二句与第一句形成语义转折,即一些人提出相反的观点:笑不利于身体健康。第二句逗号之后又提出:笑可能对身体健康几乎没有影响。这是对前两种观点的否定,由此判断第二句的句内逻辑是转折关系,[A]、[B]、[C]、[D]四个选项中只有[C]despite 意为"尽管"表示转折,所以是正确答案。

2.【参考答案】D

【考查目标】动词辨析题

【答案解析】上下文语境是"笑确实能对心血管功能……短期的改变",具体说明笑对身体产生的影响。所选动词要与后面的"changes"构成动宾关系,并且带有"发生……作用,产生……效果"的含义。四个选项中[A] reflect 意为"反映",[B] demand 意为"要求",[C] indicate 意为"表明,暗示",[D] produce 意为"产生、引起",只有[D] 选项符合本句语境,所以是正确答案。

3.【参考答案】B

【考查目标】动词辨析题

【答案解析】文中提到"笑能够……心律速率和氧气摄取量。"[A] stabilizing 意为"安定,稳定",[B] boosting 意为"促进,推进",[C] impairing 意为"损害,削弱",[D] determining 意为"决定"。根据具体语境判断应该是"笑能够促进心律",所以[B]为正确答案。

4.【参考答案】B

【考查目标】动词辨析题

【答案解析】这句话意思是"但是因为大笑很难……一次大笑不可能像走路或者慢跑那样产生……益处",可知这里将"laughter"与"walking"和"jogging"进行比较,"walking"和"jogging"的特点是可以持续比较长的时间,由此可推出前半句话的意思:laughter 很难持续很长的时间。四个选项[A] transmit 意为"传播",[B] sustain 意为"维持",[C] evaluate 意为"评估",[D] observe 意为"观察"。只有[B]符合上下文语境,是正确答案。

5.【参考答案】A

【考查目标】形容词辨析题

【答案解析】本句话意思是"一次大笑不可能像走路或者慢跑那样对心血管功能产生……益处"。[A] 意为 measurable"可测量的,重大的,重要的",[B] 意为 manageable"易控制的",[C] affordable 意为"负担得起的",[D] renewable 意为"可再生的"。四个选项中能和"益处"形成搭配关系的只有[A],用于说明"benefits"的程度,故是正确答案。

6.【参考答案】B

【考查目标】逻辑关系题

【答案解析】第二段首句的意思是"……不像其他的锻炼可以拉紧肌肉,笑很显然起到了……作用",从"instead of"和"apparently"可以判断本句与上文有承接和转折的关系,空格要求填入表示逻辑转折关系的词。四个选项中[A] In turn 意为"轮流",[C] In addition 意为"另外",[D] In brief 意为"简而言之",都不符合语境,只有[B] In fact 意为"事实上"含有转折关系,符合上下文语境,是正确答案。

7.【参考答案】A

【考查目标】形容词辨析题

【答案解析】根据上题分析,从"instead of"和"apparently"可以判断:笑的作用和其他锻炼的作用是相反的。四个选项中[B] impossible 意为"不可能的",[C] average 意为"平均的",[D] expected 意为“预期的”，都不符合语境，所以[A] opposite 意为“相反的”是正确答案。

8.【参考答案】D

【考查目标】动词辨析题

【答案解析】空格所在句子是“笑……肌肉”，所选动词与“muscles”形成动宾关系，并且要与后半句话“decreasing muscle tone for up to 45 minutes after the laugh dies down”语义保持一致，四个选项中[A] hardens 意为“使变硬”，[B] weakens 意为“使变弱”，[C] tightens 意为“使变紧”，[D] relaxes 意为“使松弛”，把[D]代入空中，表示笑使肌肉放松，与前一句“不像其他的锻炼可以拉紧肌肉，笑很显然起到了相反的作用”语义一致，故[D]正确。

9.【参考答案】C

【考查目标】动词辨析题

【答案解析】本句话的意思是“这样的身体反应可能会有助于……心理紧张状态的影响”。根据文中“such bodily reaction”是指上一段中“可以放松肌肉的大笑”，由此推断这里的意思是：减轻心理压力。四个选项中[A] aggravate 意为“加剧，恶化”，[B] generate 意为“使形成，发生”，[D] enhance 意为“增加”，不符合语境，只有[C] moderate 意为“减轻，缓和”，符合语境，是正确答案。

10.【参考答案】A

【考查目标】形容词辨析题

【答案解析】本句话的意思是“笑的行为可能会产生其他形式的……反馈来改善个人的情绪状态”。这里要求填入一个形容词，修饰紧跟其后的名词“feedback”，这个名词性短语由主语“the act of laughing”发出，并受到后面“that”从句的修饰限制。主语“笑的行为”是一种身体上的行为，与后面“other types of... feedback”相呼应，所以[A] physical 意为“身体上的”是正确答案，其他选项[B] mental 意为“精神上的”，[C] subconscious 意为“潜意识的”，[D] internal 意为“内在的”，均不符合语境。故排除。

11.【参考答案】B

【考查目标】固定搭配题

【答案解析】本句话的意思是“……一个经典的情绪理论，我们的感情一部分是起因于身体的反应”。由前后句义判断这里应该是“根据一个经典的情绪理论……”[A] Except for 表示“除了……”，它引出一个与前面的词相反的原因或者事例。[B] According to 意为“根据，按照”，表示依据，后面常跟表示理论、思想之类的词，是正确答案。[C] Due to 意为“由于，因为”，后面跟一般原因。[D] As for 意为“至于，就……方面说”，用以转换话题和表现态度，故排除。

12.【参考答案】C

【考查目标】介词搭配题

【答案解析】“be rooted in”是固定词组，表示“根源在于”或“来源于……”，代入空格中表示“我们的感情一部分是起因于身体的反应”。其他选项均不能跟“be rooted”搭配使用，故排除。

13.【参考答案】D

【考查目标】逻辑关系题

【答案解析】本句话的意思是“人们不是……伤心而流泪，而是当开始流泪时他们才变得伤心”，具体解释情绪与身体反应之间的逻辑关系。由转折连接词“but”可知前后两个分句表达的内容是相反的，第二个分句表示流泪引起伤心。由此推出，第一个分句应是伤心引起流泪，伤心和流泪之间是因果关系。四个选项中[A] unless 意为“除非，如果不”，[B] until 意为“到……为止”，[C] if 意为“假如”，均不符合语境。[D] because 表示因果关系，故是正确答案。

14.【参考答案】C

【考查目标】动词辨析题

【答案解析】本句承接上一段,上文提到"当人们流泪时会伤心",所以伤心在流泪之后。但本句出现表示转折关系的"Although",由此判断这里要说明另一种情况"伤心也会在流泪之前"。四个选项中[A] exhausts 意为"使筋疲力尽,使疲惫不堪",[B] follows 意为"跟随",[D] suppresses 意为"压制,阻止,抑制",均不符合语境。[C] precedes 意为"先于,表示在……之前发生(或出现)"是正确答案。

15.【参考答案】B

【考查目标】介词搭配题

【答案解析】由"Although"可以判断本句前半部分和后半部分是转折让步的关系,前半句说"伤心在流泪之前",那么后半句应该是"伤心在流泪之后",也就是"情绪是肌肉反映的结果"。[A] into 意为"进入……中,到……里",[C] towards 意为"向,朝",[D] beyond 意为"超出,超过",均不符合语境。[B] from 意为"来自"表原因,符合表达需要,故为正确答案。

16.【参考答案】D

【考查目标】动词辨析题

【答案解析】空格要求填入动词,并且要与后面的"a pen"构成动宾搭配,同时这个动作的实现方式是"with their teeth ... or with their lips"。四个选项中[A] fetch 意为"取来",[B] bite 意为"咬,叮",[C] pick 意为"采,摘",[D] hold 意为"拿,抱,握住"。根据具体语境可知,该实验要求志愿者用牙咬住或者用嘴含住一支笔,"hold"的意思最符合,故为正确答案。

17.【参考答案】A

【考查目标】形容词辨析题

【答案解析】这里要求填入一个形容词,修饰后面的"expression",并且这种表情是"当用嘴唇含住一支笔时"产生的。根据上下文可知两组志愿者的表情是相反的,并且"当用牙咬住一支笔时可以制造一种假笑",由此可推断"当用嘴唇含住一支笔时会产生一种失望的表情",这与后文中提到的"那些闭着嘴的志愿者"相呼应。四个选项中[B] excited 意为"兴奋的",[C] joyful 意为"快乐的",[D] indifferent 意为"漠不关心的",都不符合语境,故排除。[A] disappointed 意为"失望的",符合句子的需要,是正确答案。

18.【参考答案】D

【考查目标】动词辨析题

【答案解析】这里要求填入一个动词,并且与后面的"to"构成固定搭配。本句的意思是"在观看有趣的动画片时,那些被强制锻炼笑肌的志愿者比那些闭着嘴巴、皱着眉头的志愿者……更加热情"。即用牙咬住一支笔的志愿者对动画片的反应更加热情。四个选项中[A] adapted (to)意为"变得习惯于……,使适应于……",[B] catered (to)意为"迎合、满足某种需要或要求",[C] turned(... to)意为"转向",均不符合语境。[D] reacted (to)意为"对……做出反应",是正确答案。

19.【参考答案】A

【考查目标】动词辨析题

【答案解析】根据句意可以判断空格前是实验的结果,即:在观看有趣的动画片时,那些被强制锻炼笑肌的志愿者比那些闭着嘴巴、皱着眉头的志愿者反应更加热情。空格后是实验推出的结论"表情会影响情绪,而不是情绪影响表情"。所选动词要能体现二者的关系,四个选项中[B] requiring 意为"需要,要求",[C] mentioning 意为"提到",[D] supposing 意为"假定,假设"都不符合上下文语境,故排除。[A] suggesting 意为"表明",后接结论的句子,符合要求,故为正确答案。

20.【参考答案】C

【考查目标】逻辑关系题

【答案解析】上文提到了"表情会影响情绪,而不只是情绪影响表情",后文又提到了"笑这一行为可以使心情好转",前后两句解释的是同一种情况,表示从一般到具体的逻辑关系。[A] Eventually 和[B] Consequently,都是作为"总结"的副词,[D] Conversely 表示"相反",只有[C] Similarly 意为"同样地",符合上下文逻辑,是正确选项。

Section Ⅱ Reading Comprehension

Part A

Directions:

Read the following four texts. Answer the questions below each text by choosing A, B, C or D. Mark your answers on ANSWER SHEET 1. (40 points)

Text 1

The decision of the New York Philharmonic to hire Alan Gilbert as its next music director has been the talk of the classical-music world ever since the sudden announcement of his appointment in 2009. For the most part, the response has been favorable, to say the least. "Hooray! At last!" wrote Anthony Tommasini, a sober-sided classical-music critic.

One of the reasons why the appointment came as such a surprise, however, is that Gilbert is comparatively little known. Even Tommasini, who had advocated Gilbert's appointment in the *Times*, calls him "an unpretentious musician with no air of the formidable conductor about him." As a description of the next music director of an orchestra that has hitherto been led by musicians like Gustav Mahler and Pierre Boulez, that seems likely to have struck at least some *Times* readers as faint praise.

For my part, I have no idea whether Gilbert is a great conductor or even a good one. To be sure, he performs an impressive variety of interesting compositions, but it is not necessary for me to visit Avery Fisher Hall, or anywhere else, to hear interesting orchestral music. All I have to do is to go to my CD shelf, or boot up my computer and download still more recorded music from iTunes.

Devoted concertgoers who reply that recordings are no substitute for live performance are missing the point. For the time, attention, and money of the art-loving public, classical instrumentalists must compete not only with opera houses, dance troupes, theater companies, and museums, but also with the recorded performances of the great classical musicians of the 20th century. These recordings are cheap, available everywhere, and very often much higher in artistic quality than today's live performances; moreover, they can be "consumed" at a time and place of the listener's choosing. The widespread availability of such recordings has thus brought about a crisis in the institution of the traditional classical concert.

One possible response is for classical performers to program attractive new music that is not yet available on record. Gilbert's own interest in new music has been widely noted: Alex Ross, a classical-music critic, has described him as a man who is capable of turning the Philharmonic into "a markedly different, more vibrant organization." But what will be the nature of that difference? Merely expanding the orchestra's repertoire will not be enough. If Gilbert and the Philharmonic are to succeed, they must first change the relationship between America's oldest orchestra and the new audience it hopes to attract.

21. We learn from Paragraph 1 that Gilbert's appointment has

[A] incurred criticism. [B] raised suspicion.

[C] received acclaim. [D] aroused curiosity.

22. Tommasini regards Gilbert as an artist who is

[A] influential. [B] modest. [C] respectable. [D] talented.

23. The author believes that the devoted concertgoers

[A] ignore the expenses of live performances.

[B] reject most kinds of recorded performances.

[C] exaggerate the variety of live performances.

[D] overestimate the value of live performances.

24. According to the text, which of the following is true of recordings?

[A] They are often inferior to live concerts in quality.

[B] They are easily accessible to the general public.

[C] They help improve the quality of music.

[D] They have only covered masterpieces.

25. Regarding Gilbert's role in revitalizing the Philharmonic, the author feels

[A] doubtful. [B] enthusiastic. [C] confident. [D] puzzled.

21.【参考答案】C

【考查目标】进行有关的判断、推理和引申

【答案解析】根据题干可以定位到文章第一段第二句"For the most part, the response has been favorable, to say the least"和第三句"Hooray! At last!",由此句中的"favorable"和"Hooray"可知,人们对这一任命的回应是积极的,因此只有选项[C]是正确答案。

22.【参考答案】B

【考查目标】理解文中的具体信息

【答案解析】根据题干,可以定位到文章第二段 Tommasini 对 Gilbert 的评论"an unpretentious musician with no air of the formidable conductor about him"。其中"unpretentious"意思是"不做假的,不虚饰或矫揉造作的","with no air of the formidable conductor about him,"意思是"他没有指挥家那种强大的、令人敬畏的气势",四个选项中,只有选项[B]最接近此意。

选项[A]、选项[C]、选项[D]在文中找不到依据,故排除。

23.【参考答案】D

【考查目标】进行有关的判断、推理和引申

【答案解析】本题考查作者对于现场音乐会虔诚的追随者的观点。第四段开头作者提到,"现场音乐会虔诚的追随者认为录音不能代替现场表演",但作者认为"Devoted concertgoers ... are missing the point"(现场音乐会虔诚的追随者没有切中要害),之后是论据,用来支持作者的观点,作者认为"These recordings are cheap, available everywhere, and very often much higher in artistic quality than today's live performances"(这些唱片价格低廉,随处可以买到,而且在艺术品质上往往高于现今的现场表演)。选项[D]高度概括了作者对"devoted concertgoers"的看法,故为正确答案。

原文虽然提到"These recordings are cheap",但这是作者的看法,文章并未提到音乐会的虔诚追随者忽视了现场表演的费用,故排除选项[A]。选项[B]选项没有概括出作者对于"devoted concertgoers"的观点态度,太浅显,且与原文的描述"Devoted concertgoers who reply that recordings are no substitute for live performance ..."存在误差。选项[C]原文没有提到。

24.【参考答案】B

【考查目标】进行有关的判断、推理和引申

【答案解析】根据题干,可以定位到文章第四段。通过第四段第三句"These recordings are cheap, available everywhere..."和第四段最后一句"The widespread availability of such recordings has thus brought ..."很容易推断出选项[B] They are easily accessible to the general public(大众很容易就能得到这些唱片)为正确答案。

由第四段第三句"These recordings are cheap... very often much higher in artistic quality than today's live performances"可知选项[A]是错误的。文中谈到"这些唱片价格低廉,随处可以买到,而且在艺术品质上往往高于现今的现场表演",并不是说"他们帮助提高了音乐的品质",故不能选选项[C]。选项[D]太绝对,无法从文中推出。

25.【参考答案】A

【考查目标】理解作者的意图、观点或态度

【答案解析】根据题干,可以定位到文章最后一段,尤其是最后三句提到,"But what will be the nature of that difference? Merely expanding the orchestra's repertoire will not be enough. If Gilbert and the Philharmonic are to succeed, they must first change the relationship between America's oldest orchestra and the new audience it hopes to attract"。很明显,作者认为"Gilbert 与众不同的实质仅仅是增加了管弦乐队的节目,这是不够的","Gilbert 和 Philharmonic 要想成功,还必须做……"由此可知,作者不满意 Gilbert 在振兴交响乐团中的作用。故选项[A]为正确答案。

选项[B]和选项[C]为反向干扰。选项[D]不符合常识,作者不可能对其论述的内容迷惑不解,故排除。

Text 2

When Liam McGee departed as president of Bank of America in August, his explanation was surprisingly straight up. Rather than cloaking his exit in the usual vague excuses, he came right out and said he was leaving "to pursue my goal of running a company." Broadcasting his ambition was "very much my decision," McGee says. Within two weeks, he was talking for the first time with the board of Hartford Financial Services Group, which named him CEO and chairman on September 29.

McGee says leaving without a position lined up gave him time to reflect on what kind of company he wanted to run. It also sent a clear message to the outside world about his aspirations. And McGee isn't alone. In recent weeks the No. 2 executives at Avon and American Express quit with the explanation that they were looking for a CEO post. As boards scrutinize succession plans in response to shareholder pressure, executives who don't get the nod also may wish to move on. A turbulent business environment also has senior managers cautious of letting vague pronouncements cloud their reputations.

As the first signs of recovery begin to take hold, deputy chiefs may be more willing to make the jump without a net. In the third quarter, CEO turnover was down 23% from a year ago as nervous boards stuck with the leaders they had, according to Liberum Research. As the economy picks up, opportunities will abound for aspiring leaders.

The decision to quit a senior position to look for a better one is unconventional. For years executives and headhunters have adhered to the rule that the most attractive CEO candidates are the ones who must be poached. Says Korn/Ferry senior partner Dennis Carey: "I can't think of a single search I've done where a board has not instructed me to look at sitting CEOs first."

Those who jumped without a job haven't always landed in top positions quickly. Ellen Marram quit as chief of Tropicana a decade ago, saying she wanted to be a CEO. It was a year before she became head of a tiny Internet-based commodities exchange. Robert Willumstad left Citigroup in 2005 with ambitions to be a CEO. He finally took that post at a major financial institution three years later.

Many recruiters say the old disgrace is fading for top performers. The financial crisis has made it more acceptable to be between jobs or to leave a bad one. "The traditional rule was it's safer to stay where you are, but that's been fundamentally inverted," says one headhunter. "The people who've been hurt the worst are those who've stayed too long."

26. When McGee announced his departure, his manner can best be described as being

[A] arrogant. [B] frank. [C] self-centered. [D] impulsive.

27. According to Paragraph 2, senior executives' quitting may be spurred by

[A] their expectation of better financial status.

[B] their need to reflect on their private life.

[C] their strained relations with the boards.

[D] their pursuit of new career goals.

28. The word "poached" (Paragraph 4) most probably means

[A] approved of. [B] attended to. [C] hunted for. [D] guarded against.

29. It can be inferred from the last paragraph that

[A] top performers used to cling to their posts.

[B] loyalty of top performers is getting out-dated.

[C] top performers care more about reputations.

[D] it's safer to stick to the traditional rules.

30. Which of the following is the best title for the text?

[A] CEOs: Where to Go?

[B] CEOs: All the Way Up?

[C] Top Managers Jump without a Net

[D] The Only Way Out for Top Performers

26.【参考答案】B

【考查目标】理解文中的具体信息

【答案解析】文章首段首句提到，"When Liam McGee departed …, his explanation was surprisingly straight up”,即“当Liam McGee离开时,他给出的解释出乎意料的坦率”,后文具体描述时还提到,“Rather than cloaking his exit in the usual vague excuses, he came right out and said...”,即“他不是借助一些惯用的闪烁其词来掩饰他的离职,而是直截了当地说……”,选项[B] frank是对文中“straight up”和“right out”的同义替换,所以为正确答案。

选项[A]是利用文中首段第二句的引言处设置的干扰;选项[C]是从“was very much my decision”主观臆断来的,不能选;选项[D]是近义干扰,但是与文意不符,文中明确谈到“to pursue my goal of running a company”,可见这个离职有明确目的,不是冲动的。

27.【参考答案】D

【考查目标】理解文中的具体信息

【答案解析】本题问高级管理人员离职的可能原因。文章第二段首先谈到,McGee离职后思考他想要经营什么样的公司,他的离职给外界传递了他的抱负,即首段提到的“to pursue my goal of running a company”。第三句谈到“And McGee isn't alone”(不光McGee是这种情况),表明论述从McGee的具体案例转到高级管理人员的一般情况,下面举例谈到“the No. 2 executives at Avon and American Express quit with the explanation that they were looking for a CEO post”,即“高管辞职是因为他们有新的抱负,追求新的职业目标”。故选项[D]为正确答案。

选项[A]中的“financial status”文中未提及;选项[B]中的“reflect on their private life”是对文中“reflect on what kind of company he wanted to run”的严重曲解;选项[C]是根据第二段倒数第二句的推理而来的选项,根据该句可以推断:没有继任更好职位的管理者可能会辞职,但无法推断出“他们与董事会关系紧张”。

28.【参考答案】C

【考查目标】根据上下文推测生词的含义

【答案解析】第四段首句是该段中心句,该句指出:辞去高级职位后再寻找更好职位的决定不是常规做法。后文围绕该中心句论述。要推断的词“poached”出现在该段第二句中:“For years executives and headhunters have adhered to the rule that the most attractive CEO candidates are the ones who must be poached”。意思是“多年来高管和猎头们一直都奉行这一原则:最有魅力的CEO候选人必须被……”,下文的引言来证明这个观点“I can't think of a single search I've done where a board has not instructed me to look at sitting CEOs first”,意思是说董事会要求从那些在任的CEO中寻找人选。由此我们推断出“be poached”的含义为“被猎取”,有被挖墙脚的意思。故选项[C]为正确答案。文中出现的“headhunters”、“search”和“to look at sitting CEOs first”均提供了确凿证据。

选项[A]、选项[B]含义不符合语境。选项[D]与原文意思相反。

29.【参考答案】A

【考查目标】进行有关的判断、推理和引申

【答案解析】最后一段第二句提到“The financial crisis has made it more acceptable to be between jobs or to leave a bad one”,意思是“金融危机让人们更容易接受失业或辞掉一份糟糕的工作”。后面引用一个猎头的话进一步证明这一观点,猎头说:“传统的原则认为待在现在的位置上更为安全,但是这一原则已经被彻底颠覆了。那些受到最大伤害人的往往是那些在一个位置上待太久的人”。选项[A]是对文中“The traditional rule was it's safer to say where you are, but that's been fundamentally inverted”的同义替换。

选项[B]中提到的“loyalty”(忠诚)一词是原文没有的概念,“不待在原岗位”与“忠诚过时”不是同一个概念。选项[C]是根据该段首句改编的选项,但与首句含义相反。选项[D]与本段的核心信息相反。

30.【参考答案】C

【考查目标】理解主旨要义

【答案解析】本文以 McGee 的故事开头,他宣布离职的方式非常坦率,两周后找到了新职位。第二段继续谈到,McGee 在没有找到新职位的情况下离开,这给了他思考未来的时间,同他一样,高管们离职的原因是要去追求新的职业目标。第三段的中心意思是,高管们更愿意在没有新职位的情况下跳槽。第四段的大意是,辞去高级职位然后去寻找更好的工作不是常规做法。第五段谈到没有工作就跳槽的高管们并不总是能很快找到高职位。第六段讲如今人们更容易接受失业或辞掉一份糟糕的工作。文章一直在重复一个主题"高管们辞职后再去找新工作",故选项[C]为正确答案。文中的"McGee leaving without a position lined up","deputy chiefs may be more willing to make the jump without a net","to quit a position to look for a better one"以及"jump without a job"都在重复这个主题。

文中并没有谈及 CEO 们的出路问题,故选项[A]不能概括文章主旨;选项[B]很宽泛,不能准确反映中心思想;选项[D]太过绝对,不能成为文章主旨。

Text 3

The rough guide to marketing success used to be that you got what you paid for. No longer. While traditional "paid" media—such as television commercials and print advertisements—still play a major role, companies today can exploit many alternative forms of media. Consumers passionate about a product may create "earned" media by willingly promoting it to friends, and a company may leverage "owned" media by sending e-mail alerts about products and sales to customers registered with its Web site. The way consumers now approach the process of making purchase decisions means that marketing's impact stems from a broad range of factors beyond conventional paid media.

Paid and owned media are controlled by marketers promoting their own products. For earned media, such marketers act as the initiator for users' responses. But in some cases, one marketer's owned media become another marketer's paid media—for instance, when an e-commerce retailer sells ad space on its Website. We define such sold media as owned media whose traffic is so strong that other organizations place their content or e-commerce engines within that environment. This trend, which we believe is still in its infancy, effectively began with retailers and travel providers such as airlines and hotels and will no doubt go further. Johnson & Johnson, for example, has created BabyCenter, a stand-alone media property that promotes complementary and even competitive products. Besides generating income, the presence of other marketers makes the site seem objective, gives companies opportunities to learn valuable information about the appeal of other companies' marketing, and may help expand user traffic for all companies concerned.

The same dramatic technological changes that have provided marketers with more (and more diverse) communications choices have also increased the risk that passionate consumers will voice their opinions in quicker, more visible, and much more damaging ways. Such hijacked media are the opposite of earned media: an asset or campaign becomes hostage to consumers, other stakeholders, or activists who make negative allegations about a brand or product. Members of social networks, for instance, are learning that they can hijack media to apply pressure on the businesses that originally created them.

If that happens, passionate consumers would try to persuade others to boycott products, putting the reputation of the target company at risk. In such a case, the company's response may not be sufficiently quick or thoughtful, and the learning curve has been steep. Toyota Motor, for example, alleviated some of the damage from its recall crisis earlier this year with a relatively quick and well-orchestrated social-media response campaign, which included efforts to engage with consumers directly on sites such as Twitter and the social-news site Digg.

31. Consumers may create "earned" media when they are

[A] obsessed with online shopping at certain Web sites.

[B] inspired by product-promoting e-mails sent to them.

[C] eager to help their friends promote quality products.

[D] enthusiastic about recommending their favorite products.

32. According to Paragraph 2, sold media feature

[A] a safe business environment. [B] random competition.

[C] strong user traffic. [D] flexibility in organization.

33. The author indicates in Paragraph 3 that earned media

[A] invite constant conflicts with passionate consumers.

[B] can be used to produce negative effects in marketing.

[C] may be responsible for fiercer competition.

[D] deserve all the negative comments about them.

34. Toyota Motor's experience is cited as an example of

[A] responding effectively to hijacked media.

[B] persuading customers into boycotting products.

[C] cooperating with supportive consumers.

[D] taking advantage of hijacked media.

35. Which of the following is the text mainly about?

[A] Alternatives to conventional paid media.

[B] Conflict between hijacked and earned media.

[C] Dominance of hijacked media.

[D] Popularity of owned media.

31.【参考答案】D

【考查目标】理解文中的具体信息

【答案解析】根据题干,定位到文章第一段第四句。该句指出,迷恋某种产品的消费者可能自愿将产品推荐给朋友,从而创建出"免费"媒体。而选项[D]恰是对这一点的正确表述,是对原文中"willingly promoting it to friends"的同义替换。

选项[A]中"online shopping"属于无中生有的信息。选项[B],是与"自有"媒体相关的信息。另外,原文指出"一些公司通过邮件向其网站的注册用户发送产品和销售提示",但并没有说明消费者受到邮件的激励,因此选项[B]与原文信息不符。选项[C]"帮助朋友推销产品"与原文信息不符,属于无中生有。

32.【参考答案】C

【考查目标】理解文中的具体信息

【答案解析】根据题干中的"sold media",定位到第二段第四句,该句指出,我们将这种"售出"媒体定义为因流量很大而吸引其他机构纷纷前来投放他们的内容或电子商务引擎的"自有"媒体。选项[C]正好对应文中信息"whose traffic is so strong",属于同义替换。

选项[A]、选项[B]、选项[D]三个选项内容,均属于无中生有。

33.【参考答案】B

【考查目标】进行有关的判断、推理和引申

【答案解析】本题考查"earned media"给商业带来的影响。由第三段第一句和第二句的逻辑关系来看,"免费"媒体可以变为与之对立的"劫持"媒体。该段第二句冒号之后具体解释了"劫持"媒体,即一种资产或活动被消费者、其他股东或者激进分子所劫持。第三句举例指出有些人就会认为自己可以要挟媒体对商业施加压力。由此可见,"免费"媒体可能对商业造成危害。选项[B]正好是对这些内容的概括,故为正确答案。

选项[A]中"constant conflicts"说法过于绝对。选项[C]中"fiercer competition"属于无中生有的信息。选项[D]中的说法也过于绝对。

34.【参考答案】A

【考查目标】理解文中的具体信息

【答案解析】此题考查引用例子的作用。文章第四段第三句提到了 Toyota Motor 的经历:在今年早些时候发生的召回危机中,丰田汽车公司采取了较快且较有序的社交媒体回应行动,从而挽回了部分损失。而在其前一句,作者提到,激动的消费者试图劝服其他人共同抵制两家公司的产品,如果企业的回应不够快或不够好,那么就可能酿成悲剧。由此可见,作者引用 Toyota Motor 的例子,正是为了说明公司反应迅速,处理及时的重要性,故选项[A]正确。

选项[B]、选项[C]和选项[D]选项内容,均与文中例子不相关,属于无中生有的信息。

35.【参考答案】A

【考查目标】理解主旨要义

【答案解析】本文主要介绍了除传统"付费"媒体之外的四种新媒体形式:"免费"媒体、"自有"媒体、"售出"媒体以及"劫持"媒体。文章首段第三句指出,虽然传统的"付费"媒体仍然起着重要作用,但如今企业还可利用许多其他形式的媒体。后文则主要介绍了其他媒体形式。选项[A]能够概括全文的主要内容,故为正确答案。

选项[B]、选项[C]和选项[D]三个选项,均为文中的具体信息,属于以偏概全。

Text 4

It's no surprise that Jennifer Senior's insightful, provocative magazine cover story, "I Love My Children, I Hate My Life," is arousing much chatter—nothing gets people talking like the suggestion that child rearing is anything less than a completely fulfilling, life-enriching experience. Rather than concluding that children make parents either happy or miserable, Senior suggests we need to redefine happiness: instead of thinking of it as something that can be measured by moment-to-moment joy, we should consider being happy as a past-tense condition. Even though the day-to-day experience of raising kids can be soul-crushingly hard, Senior writes that "the very things that in the moment dampen our moods can later be sources of intense gratification and delight."

The magazine cover showing an attractive mother holding a cute baby is hardly the only Madonna-and-child image on newsstands this week. There are also stories about newly adoptive—and newly single—mom Sandra Bullock, as well as the usual "Jennifer Aniston is pregnant" news. Practically every week features at least one celebrity mom, or mom-to-be, smiling on the newsstands.

In a society that so persistently celebrates procreation, is it any wonder that admitting you regret having children is equivalent to admitting you support kitten-killing? It doesn't seem quite fair, then, to compare the regrets of parents to the regrets of the childless. Unhappy parents rarely are provoked to wonder if they shouldn't have had kids, but unhappy childless folks are bothered with the message that children are the single most important thing in the world: obviously their misery must be a direct result of the gaping baby-size holes in their lives.

Of course, the image of parenthood that celebrity magazines like *Us Weekly* and *People* present is hugely unrealistic, especially when the parents are single mothers like Bullock. According to several studies concluding that parents are less happy than childless couples, single parents are the least happy of all. No shock there, considering how much work it is to raise a kid without a partner to lean on; yet to hear Sandra and Britney tell it, raising a kid on their "own" (read: with round-the-clock help) is a piece of cake.

It's hard to imagine that many people are dumb enough to want children just because Reese and Angelina make it look so glamorous: most adults understand that a baby is not a haircut. But it's interesting to wonder if the images we see every week of stress-free, happiness-enhancing parenthood aren't in some small, subconscious way contributing to our own dissatisfactions with the actual experience, in the same way that a small part of us hoped getting "the Rachel" might make us look just a little bit like Jennifer Aniston.

36. Jennifer Senior suggests in her article that raising a child can bring

[A] temporary delight. [B] enjoyment in progress.
[C] happiness in retrospect. [D] lasting reward.

37. We learn from Paragraph 2 that

[A] celebrity moms are a permanent source for gossip.
[B] single mothers with babies deserve greater attention.
[C] news about pregnant celebrities is entertaining.
[D] having children is highly valued by the public.

38. It is suggested in Paragraph 3 that childless folks

[A] are constantly exposed to criticism.
[B] are largely ignored by the media.
[C] fail to fulfill their social responsibilities.
[D] are less likely to be satisfied with their life.

39. According to Paragraph 4, the message conveyed by celebrity magazines is

[A] soothing. [B] ambiguous. [C] compensatory. [D] misleading.

40. Which of the following can be inferred from the last paragraph?

[A] Having children contributes little to the glamour of celebrity moms.

[B] Celebrity moms have influenced our attitude towards child rearing.

[C] Having children intensifies our dissatisfaction with life.

[D] We sometimes neglect the happiness from child rearing.

36.【参考答案】C

【考查目标】理解文中的具体信息

【答案解析】该题测试考生对第一段细节的理解。第一段第二句提到 Jennifer Sennior 的观点:我们应该把幸福看作是一种"过去时"的状态,而不应该把它看作是一种即时的快乐。最后一句补充道,那些一开始让我们情绪低落的事情,后来可能会是强烈的满足感和快乐感的来源。由此可知,选项[C]为正确答案。

选项[A]为反向干扰。选项[B]不符合原文现在(沮丧)与后来(幸福快乐)的对比。选项[D]属于无中生有。

37.【参考答案】D

【考查目标】理解文中的具体信息

【答案解析】该题测试考生推理能力。虽定位在第二段,但需要理解上下文的内容。第一段告诉我们"养育孩子能成为后来幸福快乐的源泉",认为生育孩子是好事。第二段承接这一看法,用名人妈妈的形象进一步举例说明。第三段首句承接了第二段,提到"In a society that so persistently celebrates procreation"(在一个如此崇尚生育的社会中)。这个承上启下的句子,包含对第二段的总结性信息,同时也符合第一段以及第二段对生育孩子这一问题的正面评价。可知选项[D]是对原文推崇生育孩子的正确表述,为正确答案。

选项[A]、选项[B]和选项[C]均偏离文章中心,故可以排除。

38.【参考答案】A

【考查目标】进行有关的判断、推理和引申

【答案解析】该题测试考生对细节的推断能力。第三段"but"转折句处提到,不幸福但育有儿女的父母很少会去思考他们当初是不是应该要孩子,但是那些不幸福且无儿女的夫妇却经常受到这样信息的困扰,即孩子是世界上唯一最重要的东西。后面又补充道,很明显,正是没有孩子这一人生空白直接导致了他们的痛苦。选项[A]中的"constantly"与文中"rarely"形成对照,故选项[A]符合此意,为答案。

选项[B]"在很大程度上为媒体所忽视",虽然媒体关注的对象的确不是无儿女的夫妇,但这不是第三段讨论的主要内容,故排除。选项[C]"未能履行他们的社会责任",文中未提到社会责任这一说,而且本文中心也非讨论无儿女夫妇的社会责任问题,故排除。选项[D]"更有可能对自己的生活不满",文中对不幸福但有儿女的父母和不幸福但无儿女的夫妇进行了对比,但没有明确说明哪类人更满意自己的生活,故排除。

39.【参考答案】D

【考查目标】理解文中的具体信息

【答案解析】该题测试考生对文章第四段细节的理解。从第四段第一句可知,像《美国周刊》、《人物》这样的名人杂志所呈现的父母的形象是非常不现实的、不切实际的。选项[D]是对原文"unrealistic"的同义替换,故为正确答案。

选项[A]、选项[B]和选项[C]均为无中生有。

40.【参考答案】B

【考查目标】进行有关的判断、推理和引申

【答案解析】该题测试考生推理判断的能力。定位到末段末句。这句话传达的信息是,我们每周看到的那些没有压力、幸福感十足的名人父母形象会无形中导致我们对现实经历的不满。由此可知,选项[B]是对这一信息的正确转述,为正确答案。

由以上分析可知选项[A]和选项[C],不符合文章中心。选项[D]属于无中生有,原文中没提到忽略这种幸福感。

Part B

Directions:

The following paragraphs are given in a wrong order. For questions 41-45, you are required to reorganize these paragraphs into a coherent text by choosing from the list A-G and filling them into the numbered boxes. **Paragraphs E and G** have been correctly placed. Mark your answers on ANSWER SHEET 1. (10 points)

[A] No disciplines have seized on professionalism with as much enthusiasm as the humanities. You can, Mr Menand points out, become a lawyer in three years and a medical doctor in four. But the regular time it takes to get a doctoral degree in the humanities is nine years. Not surprisingly, up to half of all doctoral students in English drop out before getting their degrees.

[B] His concern is mainly with the humanities: literature, languages, philosophy and so on. These are disciplines that are going out of style: 22% of American college graduates now major in business compared with only 2% in history and 4% in English. However, many leading American universities want their undergraduates to have a grounding in the basic canon of ideas that every educated person should possess. But most find it difficult to agree on what a "general education" should look like. At Harvard, Mr Menand notes, "the great books are read because they have been read"—they form a sort of social glue.

[C] Equally unsurprisingly, only about half end up with professorships for which they entered graduate school. There are simply too few posts. This is partly because universities continue to produce ever more PhDs. But fewer students want to study humanities subjects: English departments awarded more bachelor's degrees in 1970-71 than they did 20 years later. Fewer students require fewer teachers. So, at the end of a decade of thesis-writing, many humanities students leave the profession to do something for which they have not been trained.

[D] One reason why it is hard to design and teach such courses is that they cut across the insistence by top American universities that liberal-arts education and professional education should be kept separate, taught in different schools. Many students experience both varieties. Although more than half of Harvard undergraduates end up in law, medicine or business, future doctors and lawyers must study a non-specialist liberal-arts degree before embarking on a professional qualification.

[E] Besides professionalising the professions by this separation, top American universities have professionalised the professor. The growth in public money for academic research has speeded the process: federal research grants rose fourfold between 1960 and 1990, but faculty teaching hours fell by half as research took its toll. Professionalism has turned the acquisition of a doctoral degree into a prerequisite for a successful academic career: as late as 1969 a third of American professors did not possess one. But the key idea behind professionalisation, argues Mr Menand, is that "the knowledge and skills needed for a particular specialisation are transmissible but not transferable." So disciplines acquire a monopoly not just over the production of knowledge, but also over the production of the producers of knowledge.

[F] The key to reforming higher education, concludes Mr Menand, is to alter the way in which "the producers of knowledge are produced." Otherwise, academics will continue to think dangerously alike, increasingly detached from the societies which they study, investigate and criticise. "Academic inquiry, at least in some fields, may need to become less exclusionary and more holistic." Yet quite how that happens, Mr Menand does not say.

[G] The subtle and intelligent little book *The Marketplace of Ideas: Reform and Resistance in the American University* should be read by every student thinking of applying to take a doctoral degree. They may then decide to go elsewhere. For something curious has been happening in American universities, and Louis Menand, a professor of English at Harvard University, captured it skillfully.

G → 41. → 42. → E → 43. → 44. → 45.

41.【参考答案】B

【考查目标】文章结构

【答案解析】由于首段[G]是确定的,本段内容便可根据上文顺藤摸瓜。第一段末句提出:美国大学正在发生着一个不寻常的现象,这被 Louis Menand 敏锐地捕捉到了。句中"it"指代"something curious",但该段并没有具体说明问题所在。根据结构法,提出问题—分析问题—解决问题,初步推断接下一段会具体说明问题。浏览选项,发现在[B]选项中,首句出现了"His concern","concern"呼应[G]段中的代词"it",这正是说明具体问题所在。[B]选项中心句为第一句和第二句,指出:Louis Menand 教授担忧的主要是人文方面,这些学科不再是热门学科。这是对问题的具体说明,[B]选项内容与前文构成合理的衔接。另外,"His"与[G]段中"Louis Menand"构成代词指代关联。故[B]选项为正确答案。

42.【参考答案】D

【考查目标】段落的连贯性

【答案解析】可依据结构法、词义关联及逻辑关联确定本题的答案。从结构上来看,[B]选项提出问题,指出人文学科,如文学、语言、哲学等学科,不再是热门学科。[D]选项首句中出现"One reason"一词,说明该段用来解释原因,这正好呼应了"提出问题—解释原因"的结构模式。同时,[D]选项中"such courses"指代[B]选项中的"literature, languages, philosophy and so on",从而构成代词指代关联。这样来看,[D]选项放在[B]选项之后是合理的。

此外,[D]选项中首句出现了"separate"一词,与已给出的[E]选项中"this separation"正好构成代词指代关联以及原词复现关联。同时,[E]选项中逻辑关联词"Besides",承接前文,使上下文构成合理的逻辑关联。选项[D]应该排在已给选项[E]之前。故42题正确答案为[D]选项。

43.【参考答案】A

【考查目标】段落的一致性

【答案解析】本题要在剩下的[A]、[C]和[F]三个选项中选择。在通读各选项的过程中,可以发现,[A]选项末句出现"Not surprisingly, up to half of all doctoral students",与[C]选项首句中的"Equally unsurprisingly, only about half"构成原词复现与句式结构关联。由此可见,[A]和[C]选项内容相关且结构衔接,[A]选项应放在[C]选项之前。而[F]选项显然是提出解决办法,应放在[A]、[C]选项之后。这样从[A]、[C]、[F]三个选项排序来看,应填[A]选项。

从内容上来看,[E]选项指出,除了学科专业化外,美国顶尖大学对教授也实行了专业化,专业化已经使获得博士学位成为了学术生涯成功的前提。[A]选项具体到人文学科专业化,做进一步阐述,[A]选项能够合理地承接上文。此外,[A]选项中的"professionalism"与[E]选项中的"professionalising"及"professions"构成原词复现,同时,[A]选项中的"get a doctoral degree"以及"before getting their degrees"与[E]选项中的"the acquisition of a doctoral degree"均构成同义复现关联。故正确答案应该是[A]选项。

44.【参考答案】C

【考查目标】段落的一致性

【答案解析】[A]选项末句中的"Not surprisingly"及"up to half of all doctoral students",与[C]选项首句提到的"Equally unsurprisingly"以及"only about half"构成原词复现关联。从逻辑关联词"Equally"来看,[C]选项应是进一步解释说明[A]选项末句引出的内容,前后构成合理的逻辑关联。此外,从内容上来看,[A]选项末句指出"高达一半的英语博士在获得学位之前辍学"就毫不奇怪了。[C]选项首句指出,同样不足为怪的是,他们进入研究生院,但只有约一半的人获得教授职位。两段内容上衔接自然。故[C]选项应跟在[A]选项之后。

45.【参考答案】F

【考查目标】文章结构

【答案解析】可依据篇章结构来确定本题的答案。通观全文,前几段提出问题和分析问题,而[F]选项首句指出改革高等教育的关键在于改变过去培养知识分子的方式,属于问题解决段落。根据结构法,应该放在文章末尾。此外,该段首句中的"conclude"一词,往往用于总结说明,出现在文章末尾。故[F]选项应放在文章末段。

Part C

Directions:

Read the following text carefully and then translate the underlined segments into Chinese. Your translation should be written clearly on ANSWER SHEET 2. (10 points)

With its theme that "Mind is the master weaver," creating our inner character and outer circumstances, the book *As a Man Thinketh* by James Allen is an in-depth exploration of the central idea of self-help writing.

(46) Allen's contribution was to take an assumption we all share—that because we are not robots we therefore control our thoughts—and reveal its erroneous nature. Because most of us believe that mind is separate from matter, we think that thoughts can be hidden and made powerless; this allows us to think one way and act another. However, Allen believed that the unconscious mind generates as much action as the conscious mind, and (47) while we may be

able to sustain the illusion of control through the conscious mind alone, in reality we are continually faced with a question: "Why cannot I make myself do this or achieve that?"

Since desire and will are damaged by the presence of thoughts that do not accord with desire, Allen concluded: "We do not attract what we want, but what we are." Achievement happens because you as a person embody the external achievement; you don't "get" success but become it. There is no gap between mind and matter.

Part of the fame of Allen's book is its contention that "Circumstances do not make a person, they reveal him." (48) This seems a justification for neglect of those in need, and a rationalization of exploitation, of the superiority of those at the top and the inferiority of those at the bottom.

This, however, would be a knee-jerk reaction to a subtle argument. Each set of circumstances, however bad, offers a unique opportunity for growth. If circumstances always determined the life and prospects of people, then humanity would never have progressed. In fact, (49) circumstances seem to be designed to bring out the best in us, and if we feel that we have been "wronged" then we are unlikely to begin a conscious effort to escape from our situation. Nevertheless, as any biographer knows, a person's early life and its conditions are often the greatest gift to an individual.

The sobering aspect of Allen's book is that we have no one else to blame for our present condition except ourselves. (50) The upside is the possibilities contained in knowing that everything is up to us; where before we were experts in the array of limitations, now we become authorities of what is possible.

46. 【英文原句】Allen's contribution was to take an assumption we all share—that because we are not robots we therefore control our thoughts—and reveal its erroneous nature.

【考查目标】定语从句,同位语从句

【答案解析】复合句,句子的主干为"contribution was to take an assumption and reveal its nature",句子中的"and"用来连接并列成分,根据并列成分的一致性原则可判断"reveal"和"take"是并列关系,可还原为"was to take and to reveal"。定语从句"(that) we all share"修饰"assumption",因从属连词"that"在从句中作宾语,故可省略。破折号之间是插入成分,"that"引导同位语从句解释说明"assumption",其中嵌套"because"引导的原因状语从句。

【参考译文】艾伦的贡献在于,他拿出"我们并非机器人,因此能掌控自己的思想"这一公认的假设,并揭示了其谬误所在。

47. 【英文原句】While we may be able to sustain the illusion of control through the conscious mind alone, in reality we are continually faced with a question: "Why cannot I make myself do this or achieve that?"

【考查目标】让步状语从句,介词短语作状语

【答案解析】本句是一个复杂的复合句。句子主干为"we are ... faced with a question"。"While we may be able to sustain the illusion of control through the conscious mind alone"是"while"引导的让步状语从句,与主句构成对比关系,根据汉语习惯将其放在主句前面翻译,使译文更通顺。直接引语"Why cannot I make myself do this or achieve that?"意义上相当于"question"的内容,功能上相当于同位语从句,可翻译成独立的句子,由冒号引出。

【参考译文】尽管我们或许可以仅凭意识来维系"控制"这种错觉,现实中我们还是不断要面对一

个问题:“我为什么不能让自己做这个或实现那个?”

48.【英文原句】This seems a justification for neglect of those in need, and a rationalization of exploitation, of the superiority of those at the top and the inferiority of those at the bottom.

【考查目标】并列结构,介词短语作后置定语,代词指代

【答案解析】这是个简单句。句子主干为主系表结构“This seems a justification ... and a rationalization”,句子中的“and”用来连接并列成分,根据并列成分的一致性原则可判断“a justification”和“a rationalization”是并列关系,“the superiority of those at the top”和“the inferiority of those at the bottom”是并列关系。句子可还原成“This seems a justification for neglect of those in need, and (this seems) a rationalization of exploitation, (a rationalization) of the superiority of those at the top and (a rationalization of) the inferiority of those at the bottom”。介词短语“for neglect of those in need”作后置定语修饰“justification”;“of exploitation”、“of the superiority”和“(of) the inferiority”分别作后置定语修饰“rationalization”;“of those in need”作后置定语修饰“neglect”,“of those at the top”和“of those at the bottom”分别修饰“the superiority”和“the inferiority”。介词短语“in need”、“at the top”和“at the bottom”分别修饰其前面的“those”。“This”为指示代词,在此句中作主语,为了使本句语义表述清晰,可以把代词还原。回到原文不难发现,“This”指代上一句的“contention”,所以可以把代词还原为“这种说法/观点/看法”。

【参考译文】这似乎是在为忽视贫困者的行为作辩护,为剥削、为社会上层人群的优越及社会底层人群的卑微找理由。

49.【英文原句】circumstances seem to be designed to bring out the best in us, and if we feel that we have been “wronged” then we are unlikely to begin a conscious effort to escape from our situation.

【考查目标】并列结构,被动结构,条件状语从句,宾语从句

【答案解析】复合句。句子主干为“circumstances seem to be designed to ..., and we are unlikely to begin”。“if”引导条件状语从句,其中嵌套了“that”引导的宾语从句,做“feel”的宾语。

【参考译文】环境仿佛就是为了激发我们的最大潜能而设,如果我们觉得自己遭受了“不公”,就不太可能有意识地去努力摆脱自己的处境。

50.【英文原句】The upside is the possibilities contained in knowing that everything is up to us; where before we were experts in the array of limitations, now we become authorities of what is possible.

【考查目标】并列结构,状语从句,宾语从句,过去分词短语

【答案解析】本句包含由分号连接的两个并列主句。主句1主干为“The upside is the possibilities”;主句2主干为“we become authorities”。过去分词短语“contained in knowing that everything is up to us”做后置定语修饰“possibilities”,其中嵌套“that”从句做“knowing”的宾语。“where”引导让步状语从句,表示“虽然,尽管”。“what is possible”做介词“of”的宾语,该介宾结构修饰“authorities”。“where”引导的让步状语从句在翻译成汉语时,要体现出时间副词“before”和“now”的对比关系。

【参考译文】其正面意义在于,了解了一切都取决于我们自己,即有了诸多可能;此前我们是谙熟各种局限的专家,现在我们成了驾驭各种可能性的权威。

Section Ⅲ Writing

Part A

51. **Directions**:

Write a letter to a friend of yours to

1) recommend one of your favorite movies and

2) give reasons for your recommendation.

You should write about 100 words on ANSWER SHEET 2.

Do not sign your own name at the end of the letter. Use "Li Ming" instead.

Do not write the address. (10 points)

【考查分析】本次在考研应用文当中考到了信件。考生在写作的过程中,要注意信件的基本格式,不要遗漏写作指导部分提纲中的要点。

【审题谋篇】推荐信是一个人推荐另一个人做某事的信件。本次的推荐信是推荐给好友一部电影,并说明喜欢这部电影的原因。题目中给出的信息包括:写信的对象"a friend",写信的目的"recommend one of your favorite movies",信的主体内容"reasons for your recommendation"。需要注意的是,主体部分至少包括两方面的原因。

文章从布局上可以分为三段展开。第一段,直接点明主题,开门见山地说出写信意图,即向朋友推荐你喜欢的一部电影。第二段则要发挥想象力,从两三个方面阐述你推荐这部电影的原因。在写第二段时,一定要打开思路。可以从以下几个角度介绍,如可以介绍该电影语言优美,有助于英语学习,也可以介绍电影中隐含的文化要素能够丰富我们的日常生活。第三段,再次推荐,并盼望回复。

从语域角度讲,这是一篇给亲密朋友的推荐信,因此用词可较为口语化,但语气要真挚,以达到与朋友沟通和交流的作用。

【高分作文】

Dear Tom,

I am writing, without hesitation, to share one of my favorite movies, Forest Gump, with you, which is not only conducive to your study, but also beneficial to your life.

For one thing, the beautiful language in this original English movie may contribute to your study of English in listening, speaking, reading and writing. For another, the profound cultural elements implicit in the scene will equip you with foreign cultural background and, above all, enrich your daily life.

Would you like to see this movie after my recommendation? Remember to tell me your opinion about the movie. I am looking forward to your early reply.

Yours truly,

Li Ming

Part B

52. **Directions**:

Write an essay of 160-200 words based on the following drawing. In your essay, you should

1) describe the drawing briefly,

2) explain its intended meaning, and

3) give your comments.

You should write neatly on ANSWER SHEET 2.（20 points）

旅程之“余”

【考查分析】该写作部分考到的依旧是图画题，考生在写作过程中应该准确把握图画所反映的主旨，然后完成三段的写作任务。

【审题谋篇】该话题为大家一直比较关注的环保问题。环境话题在 1991 年、1999 年以及 2000 年都曾经考过，所以对各位考生来讲并不陌生。而且，2010 年考查的“文化”与 2002 年考查的话题一致，可见，话题复现是很自然的。这同时也说明考生熟悉往年话题的重要性。

文章采取总分总结构。第一段描述图画，描述的内容一定要与主题相关。与主题没有关系的内容尽量不要写，一方面有凑数的嫌疑，另一方面，容易造成语法错误。第一句可以总体描述图画，也可以开门见山的点明文章观点，因为这篇文章的主题很鲜明，一般不会出现跑题现象。接着，第二句和第三句具体描写图画内容，内容一定要围绕着第一句来进行，采取总分结构。最后一句应再次点题，也可以对第一句进行词义替换，起承上启下的作用。第二段揭示产生问题的原因，可以列举两三个原因。原因方面，可以是直接原因，也可以是间接原因，或者写此问题可能导致的结果。最后一段提出解决问题的方案或者措施。

【高分作文】

The terrible scene depicted in the cartoon shows that some people in our life still lack the awareness of environmental protection. The picture illustrates that two tourists are chatting and eating happily on a boat and casually throwing their rubbish into the lake which is full of litter and waste. The drawing sets us thinking too much due to its far-reaching influence.

Nowadays, though the awareness of protecting environment is being accepted by more and more people, we can still see many unpleasant scenes especially in scenic spots. Why does this phenomenon arise? Many factors are accounting for it. First and foremost, to some people, the consciousness of protecting environment is still not so strong. They may not think it is a big deal to throw rubbish everywhere. In addition, the environmental management system isn't so satisfying. For example, in some places there're few regulations, or the implementation is seldom performed actually.

From what has been discussed above, it is urgent to take some effective and relative measures. In the first place, we should continue to conduct more propagandas in communities and schools so as to let people realize the importance of protecting environment. In the second, more rules should be made and carried out by the government to restrain the conduction of destroying environment. People should work together to create clean and beautiful surroundings.

附　　录

附录1　常用的前缀和后缀

1. 常用前缀

aero-：concerning the air or aircraft
plane—aeroplane
space—aerospace

anti-：against；opposite of
nuclear—antinuclear
matter—antimatter
war —antiwar

auto-：of or by oneself
biography—autobiography
criticism—autocriticism

be-：to treat as the stated thing
friend—befriend
little—belittle

bi-：two；twice；double
lingual—bilingual
cycle—bicycle

bio-：concerning living things
chemistry—biochemistry
sphere—biosphere

by-，bye-：less important
product—by-product
way—byway

centi-：hundredth part of a unit
grade—centigrade
meter—centimeter

co-：together，with
author—coauthor
exist—coexist

col-：（used before *l*）together，with
location—collocation

com-：（used before *b*，*m*，*p*）together，with
passion—compassion

con-：together，with
centric—concentric
federation—confederation

contra-：opposite
diction—contradiction
natural—contranatural

cor-：（used before *r*）together，with
relate—correlate
respond—correspond

counter-：opposite
act—counteract
attack—counterattack

cross-：across；going between the stated things and joining them
country—cross-country
breed—crossbreed

de-：showing an opposite；to remove；

to reduce

code—decode

value—devalue

dis-: not; the opposite of

advantage—disadvantage

agree—disagree

honest—dishonest

em-: (used before *b*, *m*, *p*) to cause to become

body—embody

power—empower

en-: to cause to become; to make

danger—endanger

large—enlarge

ex-: former (and still living)

minister—ex-minister

wife—ex-wife

extra-: outside; beyond

curricular—extracurricular

ordinary—extraordinary

fore-: in advance, before; in or at the front

arm—forearm

warn—forewarn

il-: (used before *l*) not

legal—illegal

literate—illiterate

im-: (used before *b*, *m*, *p*) not

moral—immoral

possible—impossible

in-: not

direct—indirect

sensitive—insensitive

infra-: below in a range; beyond

red—infrared

structure—infrastructure

inter-: between; among

change—interchange

national—international

intra-: inside, within; into

city—intracity

department—intra-department

ir-: (used before *r*) not

regular—irregular

responsible—irresponsible

kilo-: thousand

gram—kilogram

meter—kilometer

macro-: large, esp. concerning a whole system rather than particular parts of

economics—macroeconomics

structure—macrostructure

mal-: bad or badly

function—malfunction

treat—maltreat

micro-: extremely small

computer—microcomputer

electronics—microelectronics

mid-: middle

day—midday

night—midnight

mini-: small; short

bus—minibus
skirt—miniskirt

mis-: bad or badly; wrong or wrongly
fortune—misfortune
understand—misunderstand

mono-: one; single
plane—monoplane
tone—monotone

multi-: more than one; many
purpose—multipurpose
national—multinational

non-: not
resident—non(-)resident
sense—nonsense

out-: outside; beyond
live—outlive
door—outdoor

over-: too much; above; additional
head—overhead
time—overtime

poly-: many
centric—polycentric
syllabic—polysyllabic

post-: later than; after
graduate—postgraduate
war—postwar

pre-: before; in advance
pay—prepay
war—prewar

pro-: in favor of, supporting
America—pro-America
abortion—pro-abortion

pseudo-: not real; false
name—pseudonym
science—pseudoscience

re-: again; back to the former state
unite—reunite
use—reuse

self-: by means of oneself or itself; of, to, with, for, or in oneself or itself
employed—self-employed
taught—self-taught

semi-: half; partly
circle—semicircle
final—semifinal

step-: not by birth but through a parent who has remarried
mother—stepmother
children—stepchildren

sub-: under, below; less important; part of the stated bigger whole
divide—subdivide
section—subsection

super-: more, larger, greater than usual
market—supermarket
natural—supernatural

tele-: at or over a long distance; by or for television
communication—telecommunication
screen—telescreen

therm(o)-: concerning heat
chemistry—thermochemistry
meter—thermometer

trans-：across，on or to the other side of；between

Atlantic—transatlantic

plant—transplant

tri-：three；three times

angular—triangular

cycle—tricycle

ultra-：beyond；very，extremely

modern—ultramodern

sound—ultrasound

un-：not

certain—uncertain

fortunate—unfortunate

under-：too little；below

develop—underdevelop

sea—undersea

uni-：one；single

form—uniform

directional—unidirectional

vice-：next in the rank；below

chairman—vice-chairman

president—vice-president

2. 常用后缀

（1）名词后缀

-ability，-ibility

able—ability

flexible—flexibility

-age

post—postage

short—shortage

-al

arrive—arrival

refuse—refusal

-an，-ian，-arian

library—librarian

music—musician

-ance，-ence

appear—appearance

refer—reference

-ancy，-ency

emerge—emergency

expect—expectancy

-ant，-ent

apply—applicant

correspond—correspondent

-cy

accurate—accuracy

private—privacy

-dom

king—kingdom

free—freedom

-ee

employ—employee

interview—interviewee

-er，-or，-ar

paint—painter

beg—beggar

-ery

brave—bravery

slave—slavery

-ese：

China—Chinese
Japan—Japanese

-ess
actor—actress
waiter—waitress

-ful
hand—handful
spoon—spoonful

-hood
child—childhood
man—manhood

-ics
electron—electronics
linguist—linguistics

-ion, -ition, -ation
collect—collection
observe—observation

-ism
Marx—Marxism
socialist—socialism

-ist
psychiatry—psychiatrist
violin—violinist

-ity, -ty
cruel—cruelty
pure—purity

-ment
move—movement
retire—retirement

-ness
dark—darkness
happy—happiness

-ology
climate—climatology
future—futurology

-ship
friend—friendship
scholar—scholarship

-sion, -ssion
decide—decision
expand—expansion

-th
grow—growth
wide—width

-ure
close—closure
expose—exposure

(2) 动词后缀

-en
deep—deepen
fast—fasten

-ify
class—classify
simple—simplify

-ize, -ise
modern—modernise / modernize
popular—popularise / popularize

(3) 形容词后缀

-able, -ible
suit—suitable
question—questionable

-al
nature—natural
structure—structural

-an, -arian, -ian
suburb—suburban
Canada—Canadian

-ant, -ent
differ—different
please—pleasant

-ary, -ory
advise—advisory
custom—customary

-ate
consider—considerate
fortune—fortunate

-en
gold—golden
wood—wooden

-ese
China—Chinese
Japan—Japanese

-free
care—carefree
duty—duty-free

-ful
care—careful
pain—painful

-ic, -ical
atom—atomic
psychology—psychological

-ish
girl—girlish
child—childish

-ive
create—creative
support—supportive

-less
hope—hopeless
pain—painless

-like
child—childlike
lady—ladylike

-ly
man—manly
month—monthly

-ous, -ious
danger—dangerous
poison—poisonous

-some
tire—tiresome
trouble—troublesome

-ward
down—downward
up—upward

-y
guilt—guilty
noise—noisy

（4）副词后缀
-ly
easy—easily
heavy—heavily

-ward, -wards
east—eastward(s)
north—northward(s)

-wise
clock—clockwise
other—otherwise

附录2 基础词汇列表

A
ability
able
about
above
abroad
absence
absent
accent
accept
accident
account
accuse
achieve
across
act
action
active
activist
actor
actress
actual
add
addition
address
administration
admire
admission
admit
adult
advance
advantage
adventure
advertise
advertisement
advise
aeroplane
affair
affect
afford
afraid
Africa
African
after
afterwards
again
against
age
agency
aggression
aggressive
ago
agree
agreement
agricultural
agriculture
ahead
aid
aim
air
aircraft
airline
airmail
airplane
airport
alarm
album
alcohol
alive
all
allow
ally
almost
alone
along
aloud
already
also
although
altogether
always
amaze
ambassador
ambulance
amend
ammunition
among
amount
amuse
amusement
anarchy
ancestor
ancient
and
anger
angry
animal
anniversary
announce
announcement
annoy
another
answer
Antarctic
Antarctica
antique
anxious
any
anyhow
anyway
anywhere
apartment
apologize
apology
appeal
appear
appearance
application
apply
appoint
appointment
appreciate
approve
April
Arab
Arabic
archeology
Arctic

area
argue
argument
arise
arithmetic
arms
army
around
arrange
arrangement
arrest
arrival
arrive
arrow
art
article
artillery
artist
as
ash
ashamed
Asia
Asian
aside
ask
asleep
assist
assistant
astonish
astronaut
astronomy
asylum
at
athlete
Atlantic
atmosphere
atom
attach
attack
attempt
attend
attention
attentively
attitude
attract
attractive
audience
August
aunt
Australia
Australian
author
automobile
autumn
avenue
average
avoid
awake
award
away

B

back
background
backward(s)
bacon
bacterium
bad
badly
badminton
baggage
bake
bakery
balance
balcony
ball
ballet
balloon
ballot
ballpoint
bamboo
ban
bandage
bang
bank
bar
barbecue
barber
barbershop
bargain
bark
barrier
base
baseball
basement
basic
basin
basketball
bat
bath
bathe
bathrobe
bathroom
bathtub
battery
battle
battleground
bay
be
beach
beam
bean
bear
beard
beast
beat
beauty
because
become
bed
bedclothes
bedroom
beef
beehive
beer
before
begin
beginning
behave
behaviour
behind
being
Belgium
belief
believe
bell
belly
belong
below
bench
bend
beneath
bent
beside
besides
best
betray
better
between
beyond
big
bill
billion
biology
bird
birdcage
birth
birthday
birthplace
biscuit
bite

bitter
black
blame
blank
blanket
bleed
blind
block
blood
blow
blue
board
boat
boating
body
boil
bomb
bone
book
bookcase
bookmark
bookshelf
bookshop
bookstore
border
boring
born
borrow
boss
botany
both
bottle
bottom
bound
bow
bowl
box
boxing
boy
boycott
brain
brake
branch
brave
bravery
break
breakfast
breath
breathe
brick
bride
bridegroom
bridge
brief
bright
bring
Britain
broadcast
broken
broom
brother
brotherhood
brown
brunch
brush
bucket
Buddhism
Buddhist
budget
build
building
bullet
burial
burn
burst
bury
bus
business
businessman
businesswoman
busy
but
butcher
butter
butterfly
button
buy
by
bye
C
cab
cabbage
cafe
cafeteria
cage
cake
call
calm
camel
camera
camp
campaign
can
Canada
Canadian
canal
cancel
cancer
candidate
candle
candy
canteen
cap
capital
capitalism
captain
capture
car
carbon
card
care
careful
carpet
carriage
carrier
carrot
carry
cartoon
carve
case
cash
cast
Castle
cat
catch
cathedral
cattle
cause
cave
cease
ceiling
celebrate
celebration
cell
cellar
cent
center
centigrade
centimetre
central
century
ceremony
certain
certainly
certificate
chain
chairman
chairwoman
challenge
challenging

champion
chance
change
changeable
channel
chapter
character
charge
chart
chase
chat
cheap
cheat
cheek
cheer
cheerful
cheers
cheese
chemical
chemist
chemistry
cheque
chess
chest
chew
chick
chicken
chief
childhood
children
chimney
China
Chinese
chips
choice
choke
choose
chopsticks
Christian
Christmas
Church
cigar
cigarette
cinema
circle
circus
citizen
city
civil
civilian
claim
clap
clash
class
classical
classmate
classroom
clean
clear
clearly
clergy
clerk
clever
click
climate
climb
clinic
clock
clone
close
cloth
clothes
clothing
cloud
cloudy
club
coach
coal
coast
coat
cocoa
coffee
coin
Coke
cold
collect
collection
college
colony
color
comb
combine
come
comedy
comfort
comfortable
comma
command
comment
committee
common
communicate
communism
communist
community
companion
company
compare
compete
competition
competitor
complete
complex
composition
compressed
compromise
computer
computer game
comrade
conceited
concern
concert
conclusion
condemn
condition
conduct
conductor
conference
confirm
conflict
congratulate
congratulation
Congress
connect
connection
conservation
conservative
consider
consideration
consist
constant
constitution
construct
construction
contain
container
continent
continue
contrary
contribution
control
convenience
convenient
convention
conversation
cook
cooker
cookie
cool
cooperate

cop
copy
coral
cordless
corn
corner
correct
correspond
cost
cottage
cotton
cough
could
count
counter
country
countryside
couple
courage
course
court
courtyard
cousin
cover
cow
cowboy
co-worker
crash
crayon
crazy
cream
create
creature
credit
crew
crime
criminal
crisis
criticize
crops

cross
crossing
crossroads
crowd
crowded
cruel
crush
cry
cube
cubic
culture
cup
cupboard
cure
curfew
curious
currency
current
curtain
cushion
custom
customer
customs
cut
cyclist

D

daily
dam
damage
damp
dance
danger
dangerous
dark
darkness
dash
data
database
date
daughter

day
daylight
dead
deadline
deaf
deal
dear
debate
debt
December
decide
decision
declare
decorate
decoration
decrease
deed
deep
deeply
defeat
defence
defend
deficit
define
degree
delay
delegate
delete
demand
democracy
demonstrate
denounce
dentist
deny
department
departure
depend
deplore
depression
depth

describe
description
desert
design
desire
dessert
destroy
detail
detective
determination
determine
develop
development
device
devotion
diagram
dial
dialogue
diamond
diary
dictation
dictator
dictionary
die
diet
difference
different
difficult
difficulty
dig
digest
digital
dine
dining room
dinner
dip
diploma
direct
direction
director

directory
dirt
dirty
disability
disabled
disadvantage
disagree
disappear
disappoint
disappointment
disaster
discount
discourage
discover
discrimination
discuss
discussion
disease
disk
dislike
dismiss
disobey
dispute
dissident
distance
district
disturb
dive
divide
division
dizzy
do
doctor
document
dog
doll
dollar
door
dormitory
dot
double
doubt
down
download
downstairs
downtown
downward
dozen
draw
drawer
drawing
dream
dream
dress
drier
drill
drink
drive
drop
drown
drug
drum
drunk
dry
dryer
duckling
due
dull
dumpling
during
dusk
dust
dustbin
dusty
duty

E

eagle
early
earn
earth
earthquake
ease
easily
east
Easter
eastern
eastwards
easy
easy going
eat
ecology
economy
edge
edition
editor
educate
education
educator
effect
effort
egg
eggplant
Egypt
Egyptian
eight
eighteen
eighth
either
elder
elect
electric
electrical
electricity
electronic
elephant
eleven
else
E-mail
embassy
emergency
emotion
employ
empty
end
ending
endless
enemy
energetic
energy
enforce
engine
engineer
English-speaking
enjoy
enlarge
enough
enter
entertainment
entrance
entry
envelope
environment
equal
equality
equip
equipment
eraser
escape
especially
essay
establish
estimate
ethnic
Europe
European
evaporate
even
evening
event
eventually

ever
every
evidence
evil
exact
examine
example
excellent
except
exchange
excite
excuse
execute
exercise
exhibition
exile
exist
existence
exit
expand
expect
expel
expense
experience
experiment
expert
explain
explanation
explode
explore
explorer
export
expose
express
expression
extend
extra
extraordinary
extreme
extremely
extremist
eye
eyesight
eyewitness
F
facial
fact
factory
fade
fail
failure
fair
fall
false
family
famous
fan
far
fare
farm
fast
fasten
fat
father
fault
fax
fear
feather
February
federal
fee
feed
feel
feeling
fell
fellow
female
fence
ferry
fertile
festival
fetch
fever
few
fibre
field
fierce
fifteen
fifth
fifty
fight
fighter
figure
file
fill
film
final
financial
find
fine
finger
fingernail
finish
fire
fireplace
fireworks
firm
firmly
first
fish
fist
fit
five
fix
flag
flaming
flash
flashlight
flat
flee
flesh
flight
float
flood
floor
flour
flower
flu
fluid
fly
fog
foggy
fold
folk
follow
following
fond
food
fool
foolish
foot
football
for
forbid
force
forecast
foreign
foreigner
forest
forget
forgetful
forgive
fork
form
fortnight
fortunate
forty
forward
found
founding

fourteen
fourth
franc
France
free
freedom
freeze
freezing
French
Frenchman
frequent
fresh
fridge = refrigerator
fried
friend
friendly
friendship
frighten
fright
frog
from
front
frontier
frost
fruit
fry
fuel
full
fun
funeral
fur
furnisher
furniture
future
G
gale
gallery
gallon
game
garage
garbage
garden
gardening
gas
gate
gather
gay
general
generation
gentle
gentleman
geography
geometry
German
Germany
get
gift
gifted
giraffe
girl
give
glance
glare
glass
glasshouse
glory
glove
glue
go
goal
goat
god
gold
golden
goldfish
golf
good
goodness
goods
goose
govern
government
gown
grade
gradually
graduate
grain
gram
grammar
grand
grandchild
granddaughter
grandfather
grandmother
grandpa
grandparents
grandson
granny
grape
grasp
grass
gray
great
Greece
Greek
green
greengrocer
greet
greeting
grill
grind
grocer
ground
group
grow
gruel
guarantee
guard
guidance
guide
guideline
guilty
guitar
gun
gymnastics
H
haircut
half
hall
halt
ham
hamburger
hammer
handkerchief
handsome
handwriting
handy
hang
hang
happen
happy
harbour
hard
hardship
harm
harmless
harvest
has
hat
hatch
hate
have
hawk
hay
he
head
headmaster
headmistress
headquarters
heal

health
heap
hear
hearing
heart
heat
heaven
heavy
heel
height
helicopter
hello
helmet
help
herb
here
hero
heroine
hers
herself
hibernate
hibernation
hide
high
hijack
hill
hillside
hilly
himself
hire
his
history
hit
hive
hobby
hold
hole
holiday
holy
home
homeland
hometown
honest
honor
hook
hooray
hope
horrible
horse
hospital
hostage
hostess
hostile
hot
hotel
hour
house
housework
how
howl
huge
human
humor
hundred
hunger
hunt
hurricane
hurry
hurt
husband
I
ice
idea
identify
idiom
if
ill
illegal
illness
imagine
immediate
import
important
impress
improve
in
incident
incite
include
income
incorrect
increase
indeed
independent
India
Indian
industry
infect
inflation
influence
inform
information
initial
inject
injure
ink
inland
inn
innocent
insane
insect
insert
inside
inspect
instant
instead
institute
institution
instruct
instruction
instrument
insult
insurance
intelligence
intelligent
intend
intense
interest
interfere
international
intervene
into
invade
invent
invest
investigate
invite
involve
Ireland
Irish
iron
island
issue
it
Italian
Italy
Its
J
jacket
jam
January
Japan
Japanese
jar
jaw
jazz
jeans
jeep
jet
jewel

job
jog
join
joint
joke
journalist
judge
judgement
juice
juicy
July
jump
June
jungle
junk
jury
just
justice

K

kangaroo
keep
keeper
kettle
key
keyboard
kick
kidnap
kill
kilo
kilogram
kilometre
kind
kindergarten
kindness
kingdom
kiss
kitchen
kite
knee
knife
know
knowledge

L

lab
laboratory
labour（美 labor）
lack
ladder
lake
lamb
lame
lamp
land
language
lantern
lap
large
laser
last
late
lately
latter
laugh
launch
laundry
lavatory
law
lawyer
lay
lazy
lead
leak
learn
leave
left
legal
legislation
lend
less
let
letter
level
liberal
lie
life
lift
light
lightning
like
limit
line
link
liquid
list
listen
literature
little
live
load
loan
local
lock
locust
London
lonely
long
look
loose
lorry
lose
loud
loudly
loudspeaker
lounge
love
lovely
low
loyal
luck
luggage
lunch
lung

M

machine
mad
madam
magazine
magic
maid
mail
mailbox
main
mainland
major
majority
make
male
man
manager
mankind
manufacture
many
map
maple
marathon
marble
march
mark
market
marry
mask
mass
mat
mate
material
mathematics
matter
maximum
May
may

mayor
meal
mean
means
measure
meat
medal
media
medicine
meet
meet
melon
melon seed
melt
member
memorial
memory
mental
mention
menu
merchant
merciful
mercy
merry
mess
message
messy
metal
method
metre（美 meter）
Mexican
Mexico
microcomputer
microscope
microwave
midday
middle
midnight
militant
military
milk
million
millionaire
mind
mine
mineral
miniskirt
minister
minority
minus
minute
mirror
miss
missile
missing
mist
mistake
misunderstand
mix
mob
model
moderate
modern
modest
Mom =Mum
moment
mommy
= mummy
Monday
money
monitor
month
monument
moon
mop
moral
more
morning
Moslem
Mosquito
most
motherland
mother
motion
motor
motorbike
motorcycle
motto
mountain
mountainous
mourn
mouse
moustache
mouthful
move
movement
movie
Ms.
much
mud
multiply
murder
mushroom
music
musician
must
mustard
mutton
my
mystery
N
nail
name
Narrow
Nation
nationality
native
natural
nature
navy
near
neat
necessary
neck
necktie
need
needle
negotiate
neighbourhood
（美 neighborhood）
neither
nephew
nervous
nest
net
network
neutral
never
new
news
newspaper
next
nice
niece
night
nine
nineteen
ninety
ninth
no
nobody
noise
nominate
non violent
none
nonstop
noodle
noon
nor
normal

north
northeast
northern
northwards
northwest
not
note
notebook
nothing
notice
novel
novelist
November
now
nowadays
nowhere
nuclear
number
nurse
nursery
nylon
O
object
observe
occupy
ocean
of
off
offensive
offer
office
officer
official
often
oil
old
on
once
only
open
operate
opinion
oppose
opposite
oppress
or
order
organize
other
our
oust
out
over
overthrow
owe
own
P
pace
Pacific
pack
package
packet
paddle
page
pain
paint
painter
painting
palace
pale
pan
pancake
paper
paperwork
parachute
parade
paragraph
parcel
pardon
pardon
park
parking
parliament
parrot
part
part-time
party
pass
passage
passenger
passer-by
passport
past
path
patience
patient
pattern
pause
pay
pea
peace
peach
pear
peasant
pedestrian
pen friend
penny
pension
people
pepper
percent
percentage
perfect
perfect
perform
performer
perhaps
period
permanent
permission
permit
person
personally
persuade
pest
pet
petrol
phone
photographer
phrase
physician
physicist
physics
physics
pianist
piano
pick
picnic
picture
pie
piece
pig
pill
pillow
pilot
pin
pine
pink
pint
pioneer
pipe
pity
place
plan
planet
plant
plastic
plate
platform
play

player
playground
playmate
playroom
please
plenty
plot
plug
plus
pocket
poem
poet
point
poison
poisonous
pole
police
policeman
policy
polite
political
politician
politics
pollute
pollution
pond
pool
poor
popcorn
popular
population
pork
porridge
port
porter
position
possess
possession
possibility
possible
possibly
post
postage
postbox
postcard
postcode
poster
postman
postpone
postpone
pot
potato
pound
pour
powder
power
powerful
practical
practice
prairie
praise
pray
pray
prayer
precious
prefer
preference
pregnant
preparation
prepare
prescription
present
present
presentation
president
president
press
press
pressure
pressure
pretend
pretty
prevent
preview
price
pride
print
printer
printing
prison
prison
prisoner
private
private
prize
probably
problem
process
produce
profession
professor
profit
program
progress
project
promise
pronounce
pronunciation
propaganda
properly
property
propose
protect
protection
protest
prove
provide
province
pub
public
publication
publish
pull
pulse
pump
punctual
punctuate
punctuation
punish
punishment
pupil
purchase
pure
purpose
push
put
puzzle
puzzled
pyramid

Q

quake
quality
quantity
quarrel
quarter
queen
question
queue
quick
quiet
quilt
quite
quiz

R

rabbit
race
radar
radiation
radio
radioactive

rag
raid
rail
railroad
railway
rain
rainbow
raincoat
rainy
raise
rank
rare
rat
rate
rather
raw
ray
razor
reach
react
read
reading
ready
real
realistic
reality
really
reason
reasonable
rebel
rebuild
receipt
receive
receiver
recent
reception
receptionist
recession
recite
recognize
recommend
record
recorder
recover
rectangle
recycle
red
redirect
reduce
refer
reform
refreshments
refrigerator
refugee
refusal
refuse
regard
register
regret
regulation
reject
relate
relation
relax
relay
release
religion
religious
remain
remains
remark
remember
remove
rent
repair
repeat
replace
report
reporter
represent
repress
republic
request
require
requirement
rescue
research
reservation
resign
resist
resource
respect
responsible
rest
restaurant
restrain
restrict
result
retell
retire
return
reuse
review
reviewer
revision
revolt
revolution
rewind
rewrite
rich
rid
riddle
ride
right
ring
riot
ripe
ripen
rise
risk
river
road
roast
rob
robot
rock
rocket
role
roll
roller
roof
room
root
rope
rose
rot
rough
round
roundabout
row
rub
rubber
rubbish
rude
rugby
ruin
rule
ruler
run
runner
running
rush
Russia
Russian
S
sacrifice
sad
sadness
safe
sail

sailing
sailor
salt
same
sand
satellite
satisfy
save
say
scholarship
school
schoolbag
schoolmate
science
scientific
scientist
scissors
scold
Scotland
Scottish
scream
screen
sculpture
sea
seagull
search
seashell
seaside
season
seat
seaweed
second
secondhand
secret
secretary
section
security
see
seed
seek
seem
seize
seldom
self
sell
semicircle
senate
send
sense
sentence
separate
separation
September
series
serious
servant
serve
service
set
settle
settlement
settler
seventeen
seventh
seventy
several
severe
sew
sex
shabby
shade
shadow
shake
shall
shame
shape
share
shark
sharp
sharpen
shave
she
sheep
sheet
shell
shelter
shine
ship
shirt
shock
shoe
shoot
shop
shopkeeper
shopping
shore
short
shortcoming
shorts
shot
should
shoulder
shout
show
shower
shrink
shut
shuttle
shy
sick
sickness
side
sidewalk
sideway
sideways
sightseeing
sign
signal
signature
silence
silent
silly
silver
similar
simple
since
sing
singer
single
sink
sister
sit
situation
sixteen
sixteenth
sixth
size
skate
skateboard
skeleton
ski
skill
skillfully
skin
skirt
sky
skyscraper
slave
slavery
sleep
sleepy
sleeve
slice
slide
slim
slip
slow
small
smash
smell

smile
smog
smoke
smoker
smoking
smooth
snack
snake
snatch
sneaker
sneeze
snow
snowball
snowman
so
soap
sob
soccer
social
socialism
socialist
society
sock
sofa
soft
softball
soil
soldier
solid
solve
some
somebody
someone
something
sometimes
somewhere
son
song
soon
sorry
sort
soul
sound
soup
south
southeast
southern
southwest
souvenirs
sow
space
spaceship
spade
spaghetti
Spain
Spanish
spare
sparrow
speak
speaker
spear
special
speech
speed
spell
spelling
spend
spill
spin
spirit
splendid
split
spoken
spoon
spoonful
sport
spot
spray
spread
spring
spy
square
squid
squirrel
stab
stage
stand
star
start
starve
state
station
statue
stay
steal
steam
steel
step
stick
stone
stop
stopwatch
store
storm
story
stove
straight
strange
street
stretch
strike
strong
structure
struggle
study
stupid
subject
submarine
substance
substitute
subversion
succeed
such
sudden
suffer
sugar
suggest
summer
sun
supervise
supper
supply
support
suppose
suppress
sure
surface
surgeon
surplus
surprise
surrender
surround
surrounding
survive
suspect
suspend
swallow
sweat
sweater
sweep
sweet
swim
swing
Swiss
Switzerland
sword
sympathy
system
T
tablet

tail
tailor
take
tale
talk
tall
tank
tanker
tap
tape
target
taste
tasteless
tasty
tax
taxi
tea
teach
teacher
team
teamwork
teapot
tear
technical
technology
teenager
telegram
telegraph
telephone
telescope
television
tell
temperature
temple
temporary
temptation
tennis
tense
tent
term
terrible
terrify
territory
terror
terrorist
test
text
textbook
than
thank
thankful
that
that
the
the Antarctic
the North (South)
theater
theft
their
theirs
them
theme
themselves
then
theoretical
theory
there
therefore
thermos
these
they
thick
thin
thing
think
thinking
third
thirst
thirsty
thirteen
thirty
this
though
thought
thousand
thread
threaten
three
throat
through
throw
thunder
thunderstorm
Thursday
tick
ticket
tidy
tie
tiger
tight
till
time
timetable
tin
tiny
tip
tire
tired
tiresome
title
to
tobacco
today
together
toilet
Tokyo
tomato
tomb
tomorrow
ton
tonight
too
tool
tooth
toothache
toothbrush
toothpaste
top
topic
tortoise
torture
total
touch
tough
tour
tourism
tourist
toward
towel
tower
town
toy
tractor
trade
tradition
traffic
tragic
train
transport
transportation
trap
travel
treason
treasure
treat
treatment
treaty
tree
trial
tribe

trick
trip
troops
trouble
truce
truck
true
trust
try
tube
turn
type
typist
U
ugly
umbrella
uncertain
under
underground
understand
understanding
underwear
undivided
undo
unemployment
unfair
unfit
unfold
unhappy
unhealthy
uniform
unimportant
union
unite
universe
university
unknown
unless
unlike
unmarried
unpleasant
unrest
unsafe
unsuccessful
until
untrue
unusual
up
upon
upper
upset
upstairs
upward
urge
urgent
us
use
used
useful
usual
usually
V
vain
valley
valuable
value
vanilla
variety
vase
vast
veal
vegetable
vehicle
version
very
vest
veto
vicious
victim
victory
video
videophone
view
viewer
village
villager
violate
violence
violin
violinist
virtue
virus
visa
visit
visitor
vocabulary
voice
volcano
volleyball
vote
voyage
W
wait
walk
wall
want
war
warm
warn
wash
waste
watch
water
wave
way
we
weak
wealth
weapon
wear
weather
week
weigh
welcome
well
west
wet
what
wheat
wheel
when
where
which
while
white
who
whole
why
wide
wife
wild
will
willing
win
wind
window
wire
wise
wish
with
withdraw
without
woman
wonder
wonderful
wood
word
work
world
worry

worse
worth
wound
wreck
wreckage
write
wrong

X
X-ray

Y
yard
year
yellow
yes
yesterday
yesterday
yet
you
young
yourself
yourselves
youth

Z
zebra
zebra crossing
zero
zip
zipper
zone
zoo

附录 3　核心词汇列表

A
abandon
abdomen
abide
aboard
abolish
abound
abrupt
absolute
absorb
abstract
absurd
abundance
abundant
abuse
academic
academy
accelerate
acceptance
access
accessory
accidental
acclaim
accommodate
accommodation
accompany
accomplish
accord
accordance
according
accordingly
accountant
accumulate
accuracy
accurate
accustomed
ache
acid
acknowledge
acquaint
acquaintance
acquire
acquisition
acre
acrobat
activate
activity
acute
adapt
addict
additional
adequate
adhere
adjacent
adjective
adjoin
adjust
administer
adolescent
adopt
adore
advent
adverb
adverse
advice
advisable
advocate
aerial
aesthetic
affection
affiliate
affirm
affluent
afternoon
agenda
agent
aggravate
agitate
agony
agreeable
air-conditioning
aisle
alert
alien
alike
allege
alleviate
alliance
allocate
allowance
alloy
alongside
alphabet
alter
alternate
alternative
altitude
aluminum
amateur
ambiguous
ambition
ambitious
amiable
amid
ample
amplifier
amplify
analogue
analogy
analyse
analysis
analytic

anchor
anecdote
angel
angle
anguish
ankle
annual
anonymous
ant
antenna
anticipate
anxiety
anybody
anyone
anything
apart
appeal
apparatus
apparent
appendix
appetite
applaud
applause
apple
appliance
applicable
appraisal
approach
appropriate
approval
approximate
apt
arbitrary
arch
architect
architecture
arouse
array
arrogant
artery
articulate
artificial
artistic
ascend
ascertain
ashore
aspect
aspire
assassinate
assault
assemble
assembly
assert
assess
asset
assign
assignment
assimilate
assistance
associate
association
assume
assumption
assurance
assure
attain
attendance
attendant
attorney
attribute
auction
audio
audit
auditorium
augment
aural
authentic
authority
automatic
automation
autonomy
auxiliary
avail
available
avert
aviation
await
aware
awe
awful
awkward
axe
axis

B

baby
bachelor
badge
bag
bait
bald
banana
band
bankrupt
banner
banquet
bare
barely
barn
barrel
barren
basis
basket
batch
bearing
beautiful
bee
beforehand
beg
behalf
beloved
belt
beneficial
benefit
benign
bet
beverage
beware
bewilder
bias
Bible
bibliography
bicycle
bid
bin
bind
biography
bit
bizarre
blackboard
blackmail
blade
blast
blaze
bleak
blend
bless
bloody
bloom
blossom
blouse
blueprint
blunder
blunt
blur
blush
boast
bold
bolt
bond
bonus

boom
boost
boot
booth
bore
bosom
bother
bounce
boundary
bowel
bowling
brace
bracket
brand
brandy
brass
breach
breadth
breakdown
breast
breed
breeze
bribe
briefcase
brilliant
brim
brisk
brittle
broad
brochure
bronze
brook
brow
browse
bruise
brutal
bubble
bud
buffet
bug
bulb
bulk
bull
bulletin
bully
bump
bunch
bundle
burden
bureau
bureaucracy
burglar
bush
bypass

C

cabin
cabinet
cable
calcium
calculate
calendar
calorie
campus
cannon
canoe
canvas
capable
capacity
cape
capsule
captive
carbohydrate
cardinal
career
caress
cargo
carpenter
cart
cashier
cassette
casual
casualty
catalog
catastrophe
category
cater
Catholic
caution
cautious
cease
celebrity
cement
cemetery
census
cereal
certainty
certify
chair
chalk
chamber
champagne
chancellor
chaos
chap
characteristic
characterize
charity
charm
charter
chef
cherish
cherry
chill
chin
chop
chorus
Christ
chronic
circuit
circular
circulate
circumference
cite
civilization
civilize
clarify
clarity
clasp
classic
classification
classify
clause
claw
clay
client
cliff
climax
cling
clip
cloak
clockwise
closet
clothe
clue
clumsy
cluster
clutch
coarse
cocaine
cock
code
cognitive
coherent
cohesive
coil
coincide
coincidence
collaborate
collapse
collar

colleague
collective
collide
collision
colonel
colonial
column
combat
combination
comic
commemorate
commence
commend
commerce
commercial
commission
commit
commodity
commonplace
commonwealth
communication
commute
compact
comparable
comparative
comparison
compartment
compass
compassion
compatible
compel
compensate
compensation
competent
competitive
compile
complain
complaint
complement
complicate
complicated
complication
compliment
comply
component
compose
composite
compound
comprehend
comprehension
comprehensive
comprise
compulsory
compute
conceal
concede
conceive
concentrate
concentration
concept
concerning
concession
concise
conclude
concrete
condense
confer
confess
confidence
confident
confidential
confine
conform
confront
confuse
confusion
conjunction
conquer
conquest
conscience
conscientious
conscious
consecutive
consensus
consent
consequence
consequently
considerable
considerate
consistent
console
consolidate
conspicuous
conspiracy
constituent
constitute
constrain
consult
consultant
consume
consumption
contact
contaminate
contemplate
contemporary
contempt
contend
content
contest
context
continual
continuous
contract
contradict
contradiction
contrast
contribute
contrive
controversial
controversy
conventional
conversely
conversion
convert
convey
convict
conviction
convince
cooperative
coordinate
cope
copper
copyright
cord
cordial
core
corporation
correlate
correspondence
correspondent
corresponding
corridor
corrode
corrupt
cosmic
costly
costume
cosy
couch
council
counsel
counterpart
county
coupon
courtesy
coward
crab
crack
cradle
craft

crane
crawl
creative
credential
creep
cricket
cripple
crisp
criterion
critic
critical
criticism
criticize
crow
crown
crucial
crude
cruise
crust
crystal
cucumber
cue
cultivate
cunning
curb
curiosity
curl
curriculum
curse
curve
customary
cyberspace
cycle
cylinder
D
dairy
damn
dare
darling
dawn
daytime
dazzle
dealer
dean
death
decade
decay
deceit
deceive
decent
decimal
decisive
deck
declaration
decline
dedicate
deduce
deduct
deem
deer
defect
deficiency
definite
definition
defy
degenerate
deliberate
delicate
delicious
delight
deliver
delivery
democratic
denial
denote
dense
density
dental
depart
dependent
depict
deposit
depress
deprive
deputy
derive
descend
descendant
descent
deserve
designate
desirable
desk
desolate
despair
desperate
despise
despite
destination
destiny
destruction
destructive
detach
detain
detect
detector
deteriorate
deviate
devil
devise
devote
dew
diagnose
dialect
diameter
dictate
differ
differentiate
diffuse
dignity
dilemma
diligent
dilute
dim
dimension
diminish
diplomatic
directly
disastrous
disc
discard
discern
discharge
discipline
disclose
discourse
discovery
discreet
discrepancy
discriminate
discuss
disgrace
disguise
disgust
dish
dismay
disorder
dispatch
disperse
displace
display
disposal
dispose
disposition
disregard
disrupt
dissipate
dissolve
distant
distill

distinct
distinction
distinguish
distort
distract
distress
distribute
disturbance
ditch
diverse
diversion
divert
dividend
divine
divorce
dock
doctorate
documentary
domain
dome
domestic
dominant
dominate
donate
donkey
doom
doorway
dose
dove
doze
draft
drag
dragon
drain
drama
dramatic
drastic
drawback
dread
drift
drip
driver
drought
dubious
duck
dumb
dump
duplicate
durable
duration
dwarf
dwell
dwelling
dye
dynamic
dynasty

E

each
eager
ear
earnest
ebb
eccentric
echo
eclipse
economic
economical
economics
edible
edit
editorial
effective
efficiency
efficient
ego
eighty
eject
elaborate
elapse
elastic
elbow
elderly
electrician
electron
elegant
element
elementary
elevate
elevator
eligible
eliminate
elite
eloquent
elsewhere
embark
embarrass
embed
embody
embrace
emerge
emigrate
eminent
emit
emperor
emphasis
emphasize
empire
empirical
employee
employer
employment
enable
enclose
enclosure
encounter
encourage
encyclopedia
endeavor
endow
endurance
endure
engage
engagement
engineering
enhance
enlighten
enormous
enquire
enrich
enroll
ensure
entail
enterprise
entertain
enthusiasm
enthusiastic
entire
entitle
entity
entrepreneur
envisage
envy
epidemic
episode
epoch
equation
equator
equivalent
era
erase
erect
erosion
erroneous
error
erupt
escalate
escort
essence
essential
establishment

estate
esteem
eternal
evacuate
evade
evaluate
eve
everybody
everyday
everyone
everything
everywhere
evident
evoke
evolution
evolve
exaggerate
exam
exceed
exceedingly
excel
exception
exceptional
excerpt
excess
excessive
excitement
exciting
exclaim
exclude
exclusive
excursion
executive
exemplify
exempt
exert
exhaust
exhibit
exit
exotic
expansion
expectation
expedition
expend
expenditure
expensive
experimental
expertise
expire
explicit
exploit
explosion
explosive
exposure
exquisite
extension
extensive
extent
exterior
external
extinct
extinguish
extract
extravagant
eyebrow

F

fable
fabric
fabricate
fabulous
face
facilitate
facility
factor
faculty
faint
fairly
fairy
faith
faithful
fake
fame
familiar
famine
fancy
farewell
farmer
farther
fascinate
fashion
fashionable
fatal
fate
fatigue
faulty
favor
favorable
favorite
fearful
feasible
feast
feat
feature
federation
feeble
feedback
fellowship
feminine
fertilizer
feudal
fiction
filter
finally
finance
finding
finite
fireman
fisherman
fixture
flame
flap
flare
flatter
flavor
flaw
fleet
flexible
fling
flock
flourish
fluctuate
fluent
flush
foam
focus
footstep
fore
forehead
foremost
foresee
forever
forge
formal
format
formation
former
formidable
formula
formulate
forth
forthcoming
fortune
forum
fossil
foster
foul
foundation
fountain
four
fox

fraction
fracture
fragile
fragment
fragrant
frame
framework
frank
fraud
freight
frequency
friction
Friday
fringe
frown
fruitful
frustrate
fulfill
fume
function
fund
fundamental
funny
furious
furnace
furnish
further
furthermore
fuse
fuss
futile
G
gain
galaxy
gallop
gamble
gang
gaol
gap
garlic
garment
gasoline
gasp
gauge
gaze
gear
gender
gene
generalize
generate
generator
generous
genetic
genius
gently
genuine
geology
germ
gesture
ghost
giant
gigantic
giggle
glad
glide
glimpse
glitter
global
globe
gloomy
glorious
glow
goodby
gorgeous
gossip
governor
grab
grace
graceful
gracious
gradual
grant
graph
graphic
grasp
grateful
gratitude
grave
gravity
graze
grease
greedy
greenhouse
grey
grief
grieve
grim
grin
grip
groan
grope
gross
grown-up
growth
guarantee
guess
guest
guideline
guilt
gulf
gum
gut
guy
gymnasium
H
habit
habitat
hail
hair
hamper
hand
handbook
handful
handicap
handle
harassment
harden
hardly
hardware
harmony
harness
harsh
haste
hasty
hatred
haul
hazard
headache
heading
headline
healthy
heave
hedge
heighten
heir
hell
helpful
hemisphere
hen
hence
henceforth
her
herd
heritage
heroic
heroin
hesitate
hi
hierarchy
highland

highlight
highly
highway
hike
him
hinder
hinge
hint
hip
historian
historic
historical
hitherto
hoist
holder
hollow
homework
homogeneous
honey
honorable
hop
hopeful
horizon
horizontal
horn
horror
horsepower
hose
hospitality
host
hound
household
housewife
housing
hover
however
huddle
hug
hum
humanity
humble
humid
humidity
humiliate
humorous
hungry
hurl
hut
hydrogen
hypocrisy
hypothesis
hysterical
I
ice-cream
ideal
identical
identification
identity
ideology
idiot
idle
ignite
ignorance
ignorant
ignore
illiterate
illuminate
illusion
illustrate
illustration
image
imaginary
imagination
imaginative
imitate
imitation
immense
immerse
immigrant
immune
impact
impair
impart
impatient
imperative
imperial
impetus
implement
implication
implicit
imply
importance
impose
impossible
impression
impressive
improvement
impulse
incentive
inch
incidence
incidentally
incline
inclusive
incorporate
increasingly
incredible
incur
independence
index
indicate
indication
indicative
indifferent
indignant
indignation
indispensable
indoor
induce
indulge
industrial
industrialize
inertia
inevitable
infant
infectious
infer
inference
inferior
infinite
influential
infrared
infrastructure
ingenious
ingredient
inhabit
inhabitant
inhale
inherent
inherit
inhibit
initiate
initiative
injury
inlet
inner
innovation
innumerable
input
inquiry
insight
insist
inspiration
inspire
install
installation
installment
instance
instantaneous
instinct

instrumental
insulate
insure
intact
integral
integrate
integrity
intellectual
intelligible
intensity
intensive
intention
interact
intercourse
interesting
interface
interference
interim
interior
intermediate
intermittent
internal
internet
interpret
interrupt
intersection
interval
interview
intimate
intimidate
intricate
intrigue
intrinsic
introduce
introduction
intrude
intuition
invalid
invaluable
invariably
invasion
invention
inventory
inverse
invert
investment
invisible
invitation
inward
irony
irrespective
irrigate
irritate
isle
isolate
item

J

jargon
jealous
jolly
journal
journey
joy
judicial
jug
junction
junior
justify
juvenile

K

keen
kid
kidney
kin
king
kit
kneel
knit
knob
knock
knot

L

label
labor
lace
lad
lady
lag
landlady
landlord
lane
lapse
laptop
largely
lash
latent
later
lateral
Latin
latitude
laughter
lawn
layer
layman
layoff
layout
leadership
leading
leaflet
lean
leap
learned
learning
lease
least
lecture
leg
legacy
legend
legislation
legitimate
leisure
lens
lest
lever
levy
liability
liable
liberty
librarian
lick
likelihood
likely
likewise
limb
limitation
limited
limp
linear
linen
liner
linger
linguistic
literacy
literally
literary
lively
liver
living
living room
lobby
locality
locate
location
locker
locomotive
lodge
lofty
log
logic

logical
longitude
loom
loop
loosen
lord
loss
lot
lottery
lover
lower
loyalty
lubricate
lucky
lumber
lump
lunar
lure
luxury
M
machinery
magistrate
magnet
magnetic
magnificent
magnify
magnitude
maiden
maintain
maintenance
majesty
malignant
mammal
manage
management
maneuver
manifest
manipulate
manner
manual
manuscript
March
margin
marginal
marine
marital
marriage
married
marvelous
Marxist
masculine
massacre
massive
master
masterpiece
match
mathematical
mature
maybe
me
meadow
meaning
meantime
meanwhile
mechanic
mechanical
mechanism
medical
medieval
meditate
meditation
meeting
melody
membership
memo
menace
mend
merchandise
mercury
mere
merely
merge
merit
messenger
metaphor
metric
metropolitan
microphone
midst
might
migrate
mild
mile
mill
millimeter
mingle
miniature
minimize
minimum
ministry
minor
miracle
mischief
miserable
misery
misfortune
mislead
mission
missionary
mistress
mixture
moan
mobile
mobilize
mock
mode
modernization
modify
module
moist
moisture
molecule
momentum
monarch
monetary
monkey
monopoly
monotonous
monster
monthly
mood
morality
moreover
mortal
mortgage
mosaic
moss
mostly
motel
motivate
motive
mould
mount
mouth
mug
multiple
multitude
municipal
murmur
muscle
muscular
museum
musical
mute
mutter
mutual
mysterious
myth
N
naked

namely
nap
napkin
narrative
nasty
national
native
naughty
naval
navigation
nearby
nearly
necessitate
necessity
necklace
negative
neglect
negligible
Negro
neighbor
nerve
nevertheless
nickel
nickname
nightmare
nitrogen
nod
noisy
nominal
nonetheless
nonsense
norm
normalization
nose
notable
noticeable
notify
notion
notorious
notwithstanding
noun
nourish
novelty
nucleus
nuisance
numb
numerical
numerous
nurture
nut
nutrition

O

oak
oar
oath
obedience
obedient
obey
objection
objective
obligation
oblige
obscure
observation
obsession
obsolete
obstacle
obstruct
obstruction
obtain
obvious
occasion
occasional
occupation
occur
occurrence
o'clock
October
odd
odds
odor
offend
offset
offspring
okay
omit
one
oneself
onion
onto
opaque
opening
opera
operation
operational
operator
opponent
opportunity
opt
optical
optimistic
optimum
option
optional
oral
orange
orchard
orchestra
orderly
ordinary
ore
organ
organic
organism
organization
orient
oriental
orientation
origin
original
originate
ornament
orphan
orthodox
otherwise
ought
ounce
ours
ourselves
outbreak
outcome
outdoor
outer
outfit
outing
outlet
outline
outlook
output
outrage
outset
outside
outskirts
outstanding
outward
oval
oven
overall
overcoat
overcome
overflow
overhead
overhear
overlap
overlook
overnight
overpass
overseas
overtake
overtime

overturn
overwhelm
overwhelming
owing
owl
owner
ownership
ox
oxide
oxygen
ozone
P
pact
pad
pail
painful
pair
palm
pamphlet
panda
panel
panic
panorama
pant
pants
paperback
paradigm
paradox
parallel
paralyze
parameter
parasite
partial
participant
participate
particle
particular
partly
partner
passer-by
passion
passive
paste
pastime
pasture
pat
patch
patent
pathetic
patriotic
patrol
patron
pave
pavement
paw
payment
peaceful
peak
peanut
pearl
pebble
peculiar
pedal
peel
peep
peer
pen
penalty
pencil
pendulum
penetrate
peninsula
per
perceive
perfection
performance
perfume
periodical
perish
permeate
perpetual
perplex
persecute
persevere
persist
personal
personality
personnel
perspective
persuasion
pessimistic
petition
petroleum
petty
pharmacy
phase
phenomenon
philosopher
philosophy
physiological
pickup
pierce
pigeon
pile
pilgrim
pillar
pinch
pirate
pistol
piston
pit
pitch
plague
plain
plane
plantation
plaster
plateau
plausible
plea
plead
pleasant
pleasure
pledge
plentiful
plight
plough
plumber
plunge
plural
pneumonia
poetry
poke
polar
polish
poll
ponder
pope
porcelain
porch
portable
portion
portrait
portray
pose
positive
posture
potential
poultry
poverty
practically
practitioner
preach
precaution
precede
precedent
preceding
precise
precision
preclude

predecessor
predict
predominant
preface
preferable
prejudice
preliminary
premier
premise
premium
preposition
prescribe
presence
presently
preserve
preside
prestige
presumably
presume
pretext
prevail
prevalent
previous
prey
prick
priest
prime
primitive
prince
princess
principal
principle
prior
priority
privacy
privilege
probability
probable
probe
procedure
proceed
proceeding
procession
proclaim
product
production
productive
productivity
professional
proficiency
profile
profitable
profound
progressive
prohibit
projector
prolong
prominent
promising
promote
prompt
prone
pronoun
proof
propel
proper
prophet
proportion
proposal
proposition
prose
prosecute
prospect
prospective
prosper
prosperity
prosperous
protein
prototype
proud
provided
provision
provoke
prudent
psychiatry
psychology
pub
publicity
puff
punch
puppet
purify
purple
purse
pursue
pursuit

Q

qualification
qualitative
quantify
quantitative
quart
quarterly
quartz
queer
quench
quest
questionnaire
quit
quiver
quota
quote

R

racial
rack
racket
radiant
radiate
radical
radius
rage
rake
rally
random
range
rap
rape
rapid
rarely
rash
ratio
rational
reader
readily
realize
realm
reap
rear
reassure
rebellion
recall
recede
recipe
recipient
reciprocal
reckless
reckon
reclaim
recognition
recollect
reconcile
recovery
recreation
recruit
rectify
recur
reduction
redundant
reed
reel

reference
refine
reflect
reflection
refrain
refresh
refuge
refund
refute
regarding
regardless
regime
region
regular
regulate
rehearsal
reign
rein
reinforce
rejoice
relationship
relative
relativity
relevant
reliable
reliance
relief
relieve
relish
reluctant
rely
remainder
remarkable
remedy
remind
remnant
remote
removal
renaissance
render
renew
renovate
repay
repeatedly
repel
repertoire
repetition
replacement
reply
representative
repression
reproach
reproduce
reptile
republican
reputation
resemblance
resemble
resent
reserve
reservoir
residence
resident
resistance
resistant
resolute
resolve
resort
respective
respond
response
responsibility
restless
restore
restraint
resultant
resume
retail
retain
retention
retort
retreat
retrieve
retrospect
reveal
revelation
revenge
revenue
reverse
revise
revive
revolutionary
revolve
reward
rhythm
rib
ribbon
ridge
ridiculous
rifle
rigid
rigorous
rim
rip
ritual
rival
roar
robe
robust
rod
romance
romantic
rotary
rotate
rotten
rouse
route
routine
royal
royalty
ruby
rug
rumor
rural
rust
ruthless

S

sack
sacred
saddle
safeguard
safety
saint
sake
salvation
sample
sanction
sane
sarcastic
satire
satisfactory
saturate
saving
saw
scale
scan
scandal
scar
scarce
scarcely
scare
scatter
scene
scenery
scent
schedule
scheme
scope
score
scorn

scout
scramble
scrap
scrape
scratch
screw
script
scrutiny
seal
seam
secondary
sector
secure
seemingly
segment
segregate
select
selection
selfish
semester
semiconductor
seminar
senator
senior
sensation
sensible
sensitive
sentiment
sequence
serial
session
setback
setting
seven
shady
shaft
shallow
sham
shampoo
shatter
shear
shed
sheer
shelf
shepherd
shield
shift
shilling
shipment
shiver
shortage
shorthand
shortly
shove
shrewd
shrug
shutter
siege
sight
sign
significance
significant
signify
silicon
silk
simplicity
simplify
simply
simulate
simultaneous
sin
sincere
singular
sip
sir
siren
site
situated
six
skeptical
sketch
skilled
skillful
skim
skip
skull
slack
slam
slap
slaughter
slender
slight
slipper
slippery
slit
slogan
slope
slot
slum
sly
smart
smuggle
snap
sneak
sniff
snowstorm
soak
soar
sober
so-called
sociable
sociology
soda
software
solar
sole
solemn
solidarity
solitary
solo
soluble
solution
somehow
sometime
somewhat
sophisticated
sophomore
sore
sorrow
sour
source
sovereign
spacecraft
spacious
span
spark
sparkle
specialist
speciality
specialize
species
specific
specification
specify
specimen
spectacle
spectacular
spectator
spectrum
speculate
sphere
spicy
spider
spine
spiral
spiritual
spite
splash
spoil
spokesman

sponge
sponsor
spontaneous
sportsman
spouse
sprinkle
sprout
spur
squeeze
stability
stable
stack
stadium
staff
stagger
stain
staircase
stake
stale
stalk
stall
standard
standpoint
staple
startle
statement
statesman
static
stationary
stationery
statistical
statue
status
steamer
steer
stem
stereo
stereotype
stern
sticky
stiff
stimulate
sting
stir
stitch
stock
stocking
stomach
stool
stoop
storey
straightforward
strain
strap
strategy
straw
stream
streamline
strength
strengthen
strenuous
stress
stride
strife
striking
strip
stripe
strive
stroke
stroll
stubborn
stuff
stumble
stun
sturdy
style
subjective
submerge
submit
subordinate
subscribe
subsequent
subsidy
substantial
subtle
subtract
suburb
subway
success
successful
succession
successive
successor
sue
suffice
sufficient
suicide
sulfur
sum
summarize
summary
summit
summon
Sunday
sunshine
super
superb
superficial
superfluous
superior
superiority
supersonic
superstition
supplement
supreme
surge
surgery
surname
surpass
survey
survival
susceptible
suspicion
suspicious
sustain
swamp
swan
swarm
sway
swell
swift
switch
symbol
symmetry
sympathetic
sympathize
symphony
symposium
symptom
syndrome
synthesis
synthetic
systematic
T
table
tackle
tactic
tag
talent
tame
tan
tangle
tar
tariff
task
tease
technician
technique
tedious
temper

temperament
tempo
tempt
ten
tenant
tend
tendency
tender
tension
tentative
terminal
terminate
terrific
testify
testimony
textile
texture
Thanksgiving
therapy
thereafter
thereby
thermal
thermometer
thesis
thigh
thorn
thorough
those
thoughtful
threat
threshold
thrift
thrill
thrive
throne
throughout
thrust
thumb
thus
tide
tile
tilt
timber
timely
timid
tissue
toast
toe
token
tolerance
tolerant
tolerate
toll
tone
tongue
torch
torment
torrent
toss
tow
toxic
trace
track
trademark
tragedy
trail
trait
traitor
tramp
transaction
transcend
transfer
transform
transient
transistor
transition
translation
transmission
transmit
transparent
transplant
trash
tray
tremendous
trench
trend
tribute
trifle
trigger
trim
triple
triumph
trivial
tropic
tropical
trumpet
truth
tub
tuck
tug
tuition
tumble
tumour
tune
tunnel
turbine
turbulent
turnover
tutor
TV
twice
twinkle
twist
typical
U
ultimate
ultraviolet
unanimous
uncle
uncover
underestimate
undergo
undergraduate
underlie
underline
underlying
undermine
underneath
undertake
undoubtedly
uneasy
unexpected
unfortunately
unify
unique
unit
unity
universal
unlikely
unload
update
upgrade
uphold
upright
uproar
up-to-date
urban
usage
utilize
utmost
utter
V
vacant
vacation
vacuum
vague
valid
valve
van
vanish

vanity
vapour
variable
variation
various
vary
vegetarian
vegetation
veil
vein
velocity
velvet
ventilate
venture
verb
verbal
verdict
verge
verify
versatile
verse
versus
vertical
vessel
veteran
via
vibrate
vice
vicinity
viewpoint
vigorous
violent
violet
virgin
virtual
visible
vision
visual
vital
vitamin
vivid
vocal
vocation
void
volt
voltage
volume
voluntary
volunteer
vowel
vulgar
vulnerable

W

wage
wagon
waist
waiter
waitress
wake
waken
wallet
wander
ward
wardrobe
warehouse
warfare
warmth
warrant
waterfall
waterproof
watt
wax
wealthy
weary
weave
web
wedding
wedge
Wednesday
weed
weekday
weekend
weekly
weep
weight
weird
weld
welfare
well-known
western
whale
whatever
whatsoever
whenever
whereas
wherever
whether
whichever
whip
whirl
whisky
whisper
whistle
whoever
wholesome
wholly
whom
whose
wicked
widespread
widow
width
wine
wing
wink
winter
wipe
wisdom
wit
witch
withhold
within
withstand
witness
wolf
wooden
wool
worker
workshop
worldwide
worm
worship
worst
worthwhile
worthy
wound
wrap
wreath
wrench
wretched
wrinkle
wrist
writer
writing

Y

yawn
yearly
yell
yield
youngster
your
yours

Z

zeal
zigzag
zinc
zoom

附录4 常备词组列表

1. 常用动词固定搭配

abide by	遵守(法律、诺言、决定等),坚持(意见)
abound in	富于
abstain from	戒绝,避免
accuse sb of	指责
account for	占,说明,解释
act for	代表
act on	实行,起作用
adapt to	适应
adhere to	坚持
admit to	承认
agree on / with	同意(某事)/(某人)
allow for	考虑到
answer to	符合,适合
approve of	赞成
arrive at / in	到达(某地)
associate with	联合,联系
assure sb. of	使放心
attend to	专心,留意
back up	支持,倒退
back down	放弃,退却
benefit from	得益于
blame sb. for sth.	因某事而责备某人
belong to	属于
break away (from)	脱离,逃脱
break down	损坏,瓦解,崩溃
break in (on)	强行进入,打断,插嘴
break into	闯入
break off	中止,中断
break out	逃出,爆发
break through	突围,突破
break up	中止,结束,打碎,拆散
bring about	带来,引起
bring around	改变主意
bring back	归还,带回
bring down	击落,打倒,降低
bring forth	产生,提出

bring forward	提议
bring out	出版,使显出
bring to	使恢复知觉
bring up	培养,抚养
call at	访问,拜访(某处)
call for	邀请,要求,需要
call forth	唤起,引起,振作起,鼓起
call off	放弃,取消
call on / upon	访问,拜访(某人),号召,呼吁
call up	召集,动员,打电话,使人想起
carry away	激动(常用被动)
carry back	唤起回忆
carry off	致死,获得
carry on	继续
carry out	实现,完成
carry through	实现,完成,帮助某人渡过难关
come across	偶然碰到,偶然发现
come away	断裂,脱落
come by	获得
come down	传给,降价
come in	进来,流行
come off	发生,举行,脱落,停止表演
come on	快点,出现,出场,开始,进展
come out	出版,出现,结果是
come round	苏醒,复原
come through	经历,脱险
come to	总计,苏醒
come up	走进,上来,发生
come up to	符合,达到
come up with	提出,提供
cut across	抄近路,走捷径
cut back	消减,减少
cut down (on)	消减,降低
cut in	打断,插话
cut off	切断,阻碍
cut out	删除,停止
drop by / in	顺便拜访
drop off	减弱,减少
drop out	退出
fall back to	求助,转而依靠

fall behind	拖欠,落后
fall in with	与……一致
fall out	争吵,解散
fall through	落空,失败
fall off	从……上落下
get across	解释清楚,使人明白
get along / on with	进展,过得
get at	够得着,理解
get away	逃脱,离开
get by	通过,经过
get down	写下
get down to	开始,着手
get in	进入,收获,收回
get into	进入,陷入
get off	从……下来,动身,起身
get out of	逃避,改掉
get over	克服,痊愈
get rid of	除掉,摆脱
get through	结束,完成,接通电话,度过(时间)
get together	集合,聚集
give away	泄漏,分送
give back	送还,恢复
give in	交上,投降,屈服
give off	放出(蒸汽,光),释放
give out	分发,放出(气味、热)
give rise to	引起,使发生
give up	停止,使放弃
give way to	给……让路,被……代替
go after	追求
go ahead	开始,前进
go along with	陪同前往
go around	足够分配,流传
go back on	违背
go by	(时间)过去,遵循,凭……判断
go down	下降,被载入
go for	追求,喜爱,适用于
go in for	从事,致力于,沉湎于
go into	进入,研究,调查
go off	爆炸,进行,动身,离开
go out	熄灭,外出,过时

go over	复习,检查
go through	遭受,经历,仔细检查
go with	伴随,与……协调
go without	没有……而将就对付
hand down	流传下来,往下传
hand in	上交,递交
hand on	传下来,依次传递
hand out	分发,分给
hand over	移交,让与
hold back	抑制,阻止
hold on	继续,握住不放
hold out	维持,坚持,支持
hold on to	紧紧抓住,坚持
hold up	举起,阻挡,延迟,抢劫
keep back	阻止,隐瞒,保留
keep down	压制,镇压,压低(声音)
keep off	不接近,避开
keep on	继续,保持
keep to	坚持,遵守
keep up	保持,维持,继续进行
keep up with	跟上,向……看齐
lay aside	放一边,储蓄
lay down	放下,制定
lay off	(临时)解雇,停止工作(休息)
lay out	摆开,布置,设计,制定
let alone	更不用说
let down	放下,降低,使失望
let go (of)	放开,松手
let off	宽恕,免除
let out	放掉,发出
live by	靠……生活
live on	以……为主食
live through	度过,经受住
live up to	做到,不辜负
look after	照料,照看,关心
look at	看,看待
look back	回头看,回顾
look down on	请示,看不起
look for	寻找,寻求
look forward to	盼望,期望

look in	顺便拜访
look into	调查,窥视
look on	旁观,观看
look out	留神,注意,提防
look over	察看
look up	查阅,查考
make for	走向,有利于
make out	写出,辨出,理解
make up	组成,构成,编造,化妆,补充,和好
make up for	弥补,偿还
pay back	偿还,回报
pay for	支付,付出代价
pay off	还清(债务),取得成功
pick out	挑选,辨认
pick up	拾起,搭车,学会
pull down	拆毁,拉倒,拉下,降低
pull in	(车)停下,进站,(船)靠岸
pull out	拔出,取出,(车)驶出
pull up	(使)停下
put across / over	解释清楚,说明
put aside	储存,保留
put down	放下,记下,镇压,平定
put forward	提出
put in	驶进
put off	推迟
put on	穿上,上演,增加(体重)
put up	建造,搭起,张贴,提供食宿,提价
put up with	容忍,忍受
run across	跑着穿过,偶然碰见
run away	失去控制
run away with	带(某人)私奔,轻易接受(意见)
run down	跑下,人精疲力竭,撞倒,贬低
run into	跑进,使撞,偶然碰见,使陷入
run out	用完,伸向,流出
run over	碾过,浏览
run through	跑着穿过,贯穿,浏览
run up to	跑到,(物价)高涨到……
see off	给……送行
see through	看穿,识破,干完
see to	负责,照料

set about	开始,着手
set aside	留出,把……搁置在一边,驳回
set at	袭击
set back	把(钟表)往回拨,延缓,阻碍
set down	卸下,使着陆,记下
set in	到来,开始,缝上
set off	出发,动身,引起,使发生
set out	出发,陈列,陈述,企图
set up	建立,树立
show in	领入
show off	炫耀,卖弄
show up	揭穿,露出,(口)出席,到场
stand by	支持,站在一边,袖手旁观
stand for	代表,意味着
stand out	清晰地显示,醒目
stand up for	维护,支持
take after	(外貌)相像
take back	收回,使回想起……
take for	以为,误认为
take from	减少,减损,降低
take in	接待,吸收,领会,欺骗,包含,改小(尺寸)
take off	把……带往,起飞,脱下,取笑(通过模仿)
take on	雇佣,承担,呈现
take over	接管,接受,接任
take to	开始从事于,养成……的习惯,沉湎于
take up	拿起,着手处理,吸收(水分),占据(时间)
turn aside	避开,偏离,使转变方向
turn away	离开,转过脸去,解雇,防止(灾祸)
turn (away) from	对……感到厌恶
turn back	停止前进,折回
turn in	拐入,上缴,上床睡觉
turn into	进入,变成,使成为
turn off	关,避开(问题),解雇,生产
turn on	开,把……指向,对……发怒
turn out	结果是,证明是,制造,生产
turn over	使打翻,交给,反复考虑
turn up	出现,被找到,翘起,来到

2. 常用动词固定搭配

care for / about	关心,担心,计较(用于否定或疑问句)
check upon / up	检查,检验

ut	办理付账及退房后手续
up	整理,收拾,天气变清
ide with	冲突,碰撞
onform to	遵守(规则等)
cope with	处理,应付
cover up	掩盖(错误、非法自之事)
cross out	取消,删去
cut across / along / through	穿过(某地)
destined to do sth. / for sth.	命定,注定做某事
die down	逐渐消失,平息
die out	(习俗等)渐渐消失
direct at	针对
dispose of	处置,处理,舍弃
double sb. up	使躬身,使弯腰
dwell on / upon	细想,详述
dwell at / in	住,留居
excuse from	使免除责任
feed into	提供原料
fill in (for sb.)	临时替换,补缺
flare up	突然发怒,突然烧起来
give sb. sth. away	出卖,泄漏
give oneself up (to sb.)	投案,自首
go along with	相处得……,赞同,同意
go for	适用,喜欢,支持
go under	下沉,失败
hang back (from sth.)	踌躇,犹豫
head for	向……前进
impose on	将……强加于某人
knock out	击倒,击晕
let loose	释放,放开
participate in	参加
pass off	(药效,疼痛等)停止
preside over	主持,长官
prey on	捕获,捕食
result in	导致,结果
run for	竞选
run out	用完,耗尽
see about sth. / doing sth.	办完,办理
set out to do sth.	开始做某事
smooth over	使(问题)缓解

snap at	厉声斥责
stand up to	经得起考验
step in	介入,干预
stick sth. out	坚持到底,忍受
subject sth./sb. to	使服从,使遭受
switch on	接通(电流),开(电器)
talk into	说服
talk over	商量,商讨
touch up	修改,改进

3. 常用名词固定搭配

absence from	缺席
accent on	着重
admission to	许可,准许
application for	申请
application to	应用到
arouse sb.'s curiosity about sth.	激起某人的兴趣
approach to	接近,来临
attach importance to	重视
be in (out of) contact with	与……接触(失去联系)
be out of balance	不平衡
be friend(s) with	与……保持友好
be in (out of) harmony with	与……一致(不一致)
bear responsibility for	对……负责
break a promise	违背诺言
bring / put into operation	实施,使生效
bring shame on oneself	给某人带来羞辱
bring sth. to sb.'s notice	使某人注意……
bring/call to mind	想起
bring to a halt	使停止
bring into action	采取行动
catch one's breath	喘息
call down / lay a curse upon sb.	诅咒某人
cast a shadow over	蒙上阴影
catch at shadows	捕风捉影
catch sb.'s eye	引人注目
catch fire	着火,烧着
catch / get a glimpse of	对……瞥一眼
catch sight of	看见
come to sb's knowledge	被某人知道
come to sb.'s notice	引起某人的注意

come to a point	到紧要关头
come / go into effect	实施,生效
come into a fortune	继承一笔财产
come into fashion	开始流行
come to a halt	停止
combination with	与……结合
commander in chief	总司令
communication with	与……交流,与……通信
commit a crime	犯罪
commit / make an error	犯错误
come into possession of sth.	占有某物
come / go into operation	实行,生效
come to one's senses	恢复理性,苏醒过来
come to / arrive at a decision	做出决定
come to / arrive at an agreement with	与……达成一致
reach / make an agreement with	与……达成一致
come to sb.'s assistance	帮助某人
complaint about/of	对……抱怨
competition with / against sb.	与某人竞争
do a threat to	对……有威胁
do damage to	损害……
do/try one's best	尽力,努力
do sb. harm	伤害某人
do one's share for sth.	为……贡献自己的力量
draw a clear distinction between	区分,分清
draw/reach/come to/arrive at a conclusion	得出结论
drive sb. to despair	使某人绝望
entrance to	……的入口,进入
enjoy privileges	享有特权
express one's satisfaction at / with	对……表示满意
express sympathy for/ with sb.	对某人表示慰问
express one's gratitude to sb. for sth.	为某事尔感谢某人
fall in love with	爱上
fall into temptation	受诱惑
farewell to	与……永别,不会再
feel sympathy for sb.	同情某人
find fault (with)	找碴,抱怨
follow the fashion	赶时髦
follow / tread in sb.'s steps	踏着某人的足迹
gain / have an advantage over	优于,胜过

get command of	控制
get hold of	抓住
get into trouble	陷入困境
get / go / fly into a temper	发脾气
give / extend assistance to sb.	给某人帮助
give a description of	描述
give (accept) a challenge	挑(应)战
give / show evidence (s) of	有……的迹象
give no evidence of	没有……的迹象
give one's regards to sb.	向某人致敬
give way to	让步,让路
go out of fashion	过时,不再流行
go shares	分享,分担
grant sb. the privilege of doing sth.	赋予某人做某事的特权
have access to	有权使用,有权利用
have a talk with sb.	与某人交谈
have an influence on/upon	对……有影响
have a preference for	偏爱……
have a preference of sth. to/over	喜爱某物胜过……
have a prejudice against sb.	对某人有偏见
have / run a temperature	发烧
have authority over	对……有权利
have a terror of sth.	惧怕某事
have a nodding acquaintance with	与某人有点头之交
have confidence in sb.	信任某人
have / make contact with	和……接触
have control over/of	控制……
have / hold a conversation with	与……谈话
have the determination to do sth.	决心干某事
have / find difficulty/trouble (in) doing sth.	做某事有困难
have faith in	信任……
have sth. in mind	记的,想到
have mercy on/upon	同情……,怜悯……
hunger for / after	渴望
have resort to sb.	求助于某人
have no reference to	与……无关
have trouble with	与……闹纠纷
hold the position of (as)	担任……的职务
keep an eye on	照看,留意
keep / control one's temper	忍住不发脾气

keep one's balance	保持平衡
keep (break) one's appointment	守(违)约
keep company with	与……结交,与……亲热
keep sb. company	陪伴某人
keep competition between	在……之间进行竞争
keep(break) faith	忠于(背弃)信仰
keep one's mind on	专注于
keep/bear in mind	记住
keep one's head	保持镇定
keep pace with	与……并驾齐驱
keep (carry out) a promise	遵守(履行)诺言
keep in touch with sb.	与某人保持联络
keep track of	记录,保持与……联系
keep one's word	守信用
keep to the point	紧扣主题
lay a claim to	主张,要求,自以为是
lay / put / place emphasis on / upon	着重于,强调
lead the way	领路,带路
learn by heart	记住,背过
leave sth. out of consideration	不考虑某事
lose control of	失去对……的控制
lose one's balance	失去平衡
lose one's head	慌乱,惊慌失措
lose heart	失去信心
lose contact with	与……失去联系
lose sight of	看不见
lose one's temper	发脾气
lose faith in	失去对……的信任
lose track of	失去……的线索
make an appeal to sb. (for sth.)	向某人呼吁某事
make an appointment with sb.	与某人约会
make an attempt to do sth.	企图做某事
make the acquaintance of sb.	结识某人
(make) comments on/upon sth.	评论
make a comparison between	把……进行比较
make a complaint against	控告
make / offer an apology to sb.	向某人道歉
make the best of	充分利用
make a decision	决定
make a difference between	区别对待

make a difference to	使……产生变化
make an exception of	把……作为例外
make no exception(s)	不容许有例外
make one's farewell (s)	告别,道别
make fashion	做做样子
make a fortune	发财
make friends	交朋友
make inquiries of sb. about sth.	向某人询问某事
make preparations against	为防止……做准备
make preparations for	为……做准备
make mention of	提及,谈到
make up one's mind	下决心
make a point	立论,证明论点
make a promise	许诺
make a reduction	减少
make references to	提到
make a response to	对……做出答复
make satisfaction for	补偿
make /offer resistance to	抵御,抵抗
make sense	讲得通,言之有理
make talk	聊天,闲谈
make way	让路,腾出地方
make trouble	找麻烦,闹事
make use of	利用
obstacle to	是……的障碍
pay regard to	重视
pay attention to	注意
place an order for sth. with	向……订购某物
present a striking contrast between	使两者形成鲜明的对比
put / bring / carry into effect	实行,起作用
play a joke on sb.	开某人的玩笑
play a role in	在……中扮演角色,起作用
play a trick on sb.	作弄某人
play a part (in)	扮演……的角色
put in / into practice	实施,实行
put sb. to shame	羞辱某人
put / place / lay stress on/upon	把重点放在……
put to use	使用
reaction to	对……的反应
recovery from	从……中恢复

resist temptation	抵制诱惑
run / take a risk	冒险
set up (remove) a barrier between	在……中设置(拆除)障碍
set up a claim to sth.	对……提出要求
set / give a good example to sb.	给某人树立榜样
set the fashion	创立新式样
set fire to	点燃
set a trap	设陷阱
substitute for sth.	代替物
take into account	考虑
take (no) account of	(不)考虑
take advantage of	利用,趁……之机
take care	注意,当心
take care of	照料,照顾
take a chance	冒险,投机
take charge of	接管,管理
take (seek) comfort in	在……中得到(寻求)安慰
take command of	指挥
take into consideration	考虑
take (a) delight in	以……为乐
take one's departure	动身,出发
take effect	生效,起作用
take one's farewell of sb.	向某人道别
take / give a glance at	对……粗略地看一下
throw / cast light on/upon	使人了解某事
take notice of	注意到
take /make an objection to	反对……
take pains	努力,尽力
take part in	参加
take place	发生,进行
take the place of	取代,代替
take possession of	占有,占领
take pride in	以……自豪
take the resolution to do sth.	决心做某事
take the responsibility for (of)	负起做某事的责任
take / bear one's share of	承担自己的一份
take the firm stand	坚定立场
take a stand for (against) sth.	赞成(反对)某事
take one's temperature	量体温
take one's time	不着急

take turns	依次,轮流
thanks to	由于
throw a scare into sb.	吓坏某人
throw / cast / put into the shade	使逊色,使相形见绌
try one's fortune	碰运气
yield / give way to temptation	经不起诱惑

4. 常用形容词固定搭配

be absent from	缺席,不在
be accustomed to	习惯于
be applicable to	适应于,应用于
be ashamed of	对……感到羞愧
be aware of	意识到,知道
be beneficial to	对……有利
be blind to	对……视而不见
be bound for/to	准备到……去,一定
be capable of	有……能力的,可……的
be characteristic of	特有的,表示……特性的
be common to	共同的,共有的
be compatible with	适合的,一致的
be confident of	确信,相信
be conscious of	意识到
be consistent with	与……一致,与……相符
be content with	对……感到满意
be contrary to	与……相反
be convenient to / for	对……方便
be crazy about/on	对……着迷,热衷于
be crazy for	渴望
be critical of	对……表示谴责,对……感到不满
be dependent on / upon	依赖,依靠
be distinct form	与……不同,有区别
be diverse from	和……不一样
be doubtful about/of	怀疑
be due to	由于,应归于,(按计划)将做……
be eager for/about/after	渴求……
be economical of	节俭,节约
be equivalent to	等于,相当于
be essential to/for	必不可少的,基本的
be familiar to	为……所熟悉
be familiar with	熟悉
be fit for	胜任……,适合……

be fond of	喜欢
be foreign to	陌生的,与……无关的
be good at	擅长于
be generous with / in (doing)	慷慨,大方
be grateful to sb. for	对……表示感谢
be guilty of	对……感到内疚,犯……的罪
be helpful to	对……有帮助
be identical to/with	与……相同
be ignorant of	不知道,无知
be independent of	不依靠
be indispensable for / to	必需的
be inferior to	劣于,(地位等)低于……
be innocent of	清白的,无辜的
be jealous of	妒忌……,注意提防的
be keen on	喜爱,着迷于……
be liable to	易于……的,应受(处罚)的
be liable for	有责任
be loyal to	对……忠诚的
be married to	和某人结婚
be new to	陌生的,不熟悉
be opposite to	对立的,相反的
be preferable to	更好的,更可取得
be prior to	在……之前
be proportional to	与……成比例
be proud of	对……感到骄傲
be qualified for	胜任,具有……的资格
be qualified in	胜任,适合
be ready for	为……做好准备
be relative to	和……有关系的
be relevant to	与……有关
be representative of	代表
be resistant to	对……有抵抗力的
be responsible to sb. for sth	对……负责
be ripe for	准备好的,时机成熟的
be secure from / against	安全的
be sensitive to	对……敏感的
be shy of	对……迟疑,畏缩
be similar to	和……相似
be skillful at / in	善于,精于
be strict with	对……严格要求

be subject to	易受……的,受……的支配
be sufficient for	充足的,满足……
be suitable for / to	适合……的
be superior to	优于,比……好
be suspicious of	怀疑,猜疑
be thirsty for	渴望……
be tired of	厌烦,厌倦
be typical of	典型的,具有代表性的
be uncertain of/about/as to	对……不确定
be worthy of	值得……

5. 常用介词固定搭配

above all	尤其是,最重要的是
after all	毕竟,终究
ahead of	在……之前
ahead of time	提前
all at once	突然,同时,一起
all but	除了……都,几乎
all of a sudden	突然
all over	到处,遍及
all over again	重新,再一次
all right	行,好,安然无恙
all the same	依然,照样
all the time	一直,始终
and so on / forth	等等,诸如此类
anything but	根本不
apart from	除……以外(别无)
as a matter of fact	事实上
as a result	结果,因此
as a result of	由于,作为……的结果
as a rule	照例,通常
as for / to	关于,至于
as regards	关于,有关
as usual	像往常一样,照例
as well	叶,又,同样
aside from	除……以外(尚无)
at a loss	困惑,不知所措,亏本地
at a time	一次,每次
at all costs	不惜一切代价,无论如何
at all times	无论何时,一直
at any rate	无论如何,至少

at best	充其量,最多
at first	起先,最初
at first sight	乍一看,第一次看到
at hand	在手边,在附近,即将到来
at heart	在内心里,本质上
at home	在家,在国内,自在
at intervals	不时,(在时间、距离上)以……的间隔
at large	详尽的,普遍的
at last	最后,终于
at least	至少,无论如何
at length	最后,终于,详细地
at most	最多,不超过
at no time	决不,从不
at once	立刻,马上
at one time	曾经,一度,同时
at present	目前,现在
at sb. 's disposal	由某人支配,供某人使用
at the cost of	以……为代价
at the same time	同时,然而,不过
at this rate	照此速度
at times	有时,间或
back and forth	来回,反复
because of	由于,因为
before long	不久(以后)
beside the point	离题,不相干
beyond question	毫无疑问
by accident	偶然
by air	通过航空途径
by all means	务必,尽一切办法
by chance	意外地,碰巧
by far	(修饰比较级、最高级,表示数量、程度等)……得多,最……
by hand	用手,手工的
by itself	独自的,单独的
by means of	依靠,借助于
by mistake	错误地,无意中做了错事
by no means	决不,并没有
by oneself	独自的,单独的
by reason of	由于,因为
by the way	顺便地

by way of 经过，以……方式
for good 永久地
for the better 好转，向好的方向发展
for the sake of 为了……，为了……的利益
for the time being 暂时，眼下
from time to time 有时，不时
in a hurry 匆忙，急于
in a moment 立刻，马上
in a sense 从某种意义上说
in a / one way 在某种程度上
in a / one word 总之，简而言之
in accordance with 依据，与……一致
in addition 此外
in addition to 除……以外
in advance 预先，提前
in any case 在任何情况下，无论如何
in brief 以简洁的方式，简言之
in case of 如果发生，以防
in charge of 负责，主管
in common 共有的，共同的
in consequence 结果，因此
in consequence of 由于……的缘故
in debt 欠债
in detail 详细地
in difficulty 陷入困境
in effect 实际上，事实上
in fact 实际上，其实
in favor of 赞同，支持，有利于
in front of 在……前面
in future = from now on 今后，从今以后
in general 总的来说，大体上
in half 分成两半
in hand （工作）在进行中，待办理
in honor of 为纪念，为庆祝
in itself 本质上，就本身而言
in line 成一排，成一直线，有持续
in line with 符合，与……一致
in memory of 为了纪念……
in no case/way 决不，无论如何不
in no time 立刻，马上

in order to	为了,以……为目的
in other words	换言之
in part	在某种程度上,部分地
in particular	特别,尤其
in person	亲自,本人
in place	在合适的位置,适当地
in place of	代替,取代
in practice	在实践中,实际上
in proportion to	与……成比例
in public	公开地,当众
in quantity = in large quantities	大量
in question	正在被谈论,被争论
in / with relation to	涉及,关于 ,
in return	作为回报或报答
in return for	作为……的交换
in short	总之,简言之
in / within sight of	看得见,在视野范围内
in spite of	不管,不顾
in step	合拍,步调一致
in step with	与……合步调,与……一致
in tears	流着泪,哭泣
in the course of	在……过程中,在……期间
in the end	最后,终于
in the event of	万一,如果发生
in (the) face of	面对,在……前面
in the first place	首先,本来
in the future	将来
in (the) least	丝毫,一点儿
in the light of	鉴于,根据,由于
in the way	挡道,妨碍人的
in time	及时,最后
in / within touch	联系,在……附近
in touch with	与……有联系
in turn	依次,轮流,反过来
in vain	徒劳地
instead of	代替,而不是
more or less	或多或少
no doubt	无疑
no longer	不再
no more	不再,不再存在

now and then	不时,偶尔
off and on / on and off	有时,断断续续地
on a large scale	大规模地
on a small scale	小规模地
on account of	由于,因为
on (an / the) average	平均,通常
on behalf of	代表
on board	在(船、飞机)上
on business	因公,因事
on condition that	在……条件下,如果
on duty	值班
on earth	究竟,到底
on fire	着火,起火
on foot	徒步,步行
on guard	值班,站岗
on hand	在手头,现有,在场
on occasion(s)	有时,间或
on one's guard	警惕,提防
on one's own	独自地,独立地
on purpose	有意,故意地
on sale	出售,廉价出售
on schedule	按时间表,准时
on second thoughts	继而一想,进一步考虑后
on the contrary	相反
on the ground (s) of	根据,以……为理由
on (the) one hand	一方面
on the other hand	另一方面
on the point of	即将……之时,正要……的时候
on the road	在途中
on the spot	在现场,当场
on the whole	总的来看,大体上
on time	准时,按时
once again	再一次
once (and) for all	一劳永逸,永远地
once in a while	偶尔,间或
once more / again	再一次
out of breath	上气不接下气
out of control	失去控制
out of date	过时的,废弃的
out of doors	户外的

out of order	不整齐,出故障的
out of place	不在合适的位置,不恰当的
out of practice	久不练习,荒疏
out of sight	看不见,在视野之外
out of the question	不可能,办不到的
out of touch (with)	与……无联系
over and over (again)	反复,再三
so as to	为的是,以至于
so... as to	如此……以至于
so far	迄今为止
so/as far as... be concerned	就……而言
sooner or later	迟早
to the point	切题,切中要害
under control	被控制住
under / in the circumstances	在这种情况下
under way	在进行中
up to date	时新的,现代化的
with / in regard to	关于,至于
with respect to	关于,至于
with the exception of	除……以外
without question	毫无疑问
word for word	逐字地,一字不变地

附录5 超纲词汇列表

accessible
adaptive
affinity
allegation
anecdote
anthropology
antigravity
arbiter
aspirin
astronomer
autonomous
availability
backbone
beneficence
biomedical
blueprint
blunt
capability
cataract
citizenry
clone
cocaine
collectivism
compassionate
competitive
complementary
connotation
cosmology
counteract
courteous
creationism
creationist
depletion
detrimental
disintegrate
disparage
dispassion
disproportionate
distortion
diversity
divert
dormant
downsize
druid
editorship
elimination
ember
embryo
emotional
emulation
encompass
enthrone
entrench
epithet
equate
espionage
expectancy
extremist
far-fetched
formulation

forsake
futurologist
gizmo
harmonious
harsh
holodeck
homicide
hospice
hum
husbandry
hyperactive
hypocritical
immunization
imperative
incomplete
indecisive
inedible
inevitably
infection
infirm
info
infrastructure
ingenuity
injection
insatiable
insecurity
insider
integration
intranet
inventiveness
ironically
irony
lawsuit
legislation
lifestyle
liken
lockout
logo
manipulation
marathon
maturity
maximize
mediocrity
merger
microbiologist
millennium
misguided
misinformation
mobility
morphine
multinational
municipality
mutability
neuroscientist
newsletter
objectionable
oncogene
optimism
paraphrase
parliamentary
partisan
patriarchal
perceptual
persuasive
pervasive
praisable
preconception
prediction
premium
prescientific
presumptuous
promotional
psychedelic
psychoactive
purist
quadruple
radiation
radically
rap
recitation
referee
refinement
revival
scapegoat
scary
schism
shipper
signpost
silt
smallpox
sovereignty
spacious
spatial
speculative
spymaster
stakeholder
stamp
standstill
stockpile
strategic
subconsciously
subtly
supersystem
surgical
teens
tighten
timidity
trigonometry
trustworthy
unabomber
unaware
underpriviledged
unenlightened
unparalleled
unsustainable
urbanization
Utopia
vaccination
validate
volcanic
vulgar
ware
wastage

郑重声明

高等教育出版社依法对本书享有专有出版权。任何未经许可的复制、销售行为均违反《中华人民共和国著作权法》,其行为人将承担相应的民事责任和行政责任,构成犯罪的,将被依法追究刑事责任。为了维护市场秩序,保护读者的合法权益,避免读者误用盗版书造成不良后果,我社将配合行政执法部门和司法机关对违法犯罪的单位和个人给予严厉打击。社会各界人士如发现上述侵权行为,希望及时举报,本社将奖励举报有功人员。

反盗版举报电话:(010)58581897/58581896/58581879

传　　真:(010)82086060

E - mail:dd@hep.com.cn

通信地址:北京市西城区德外大街4号

高等教育出版社打击盗版办公室

邮　　编:100120

购书请拨打读者服务部电话:(010)58581114/5/6/7/8

特别提醒:"中国教育考试在线"http://www.eduexam.com.cn 是高教版考试用书专用网站。网站本着真诚服务广大考生的宗旨,为考生提供名师导航、下载中心、在线练习、在线考试、图书浏览等多项增值服务。高教版考试用书配有本网站的增值服务卡,该卡为高教版考试用书正版书的专用标志,广大读者可凭此卡上的卡号和密码登录网站获取增值信息,并以此辨别图书真伪。